Review

Stefan Vučak's passion for writing science fiction truly comes natural to him as he has written numerous intriguing novels involving extraterrestrials and space travel, and he also hits on the hot topics of politics and religion versus science. Stefan creates magic when the pen hits paper and he does not disappoint in *Shadow Masters*. His imagination and creativity amaze me because his novels are like no others out there that I have read before; they are completely genuine and unique. I love the use of Stefan's descriptive words and the depth of his characters. I could feel the suspense and terror all around me and could hardly set this book down.

Readers' Favorite

I0592742

Books by Stefan Vučak

General Fiction:
Cry of Eagles
All the Evils
Towers of Darkness
Strike for Honor
Proportional Response
Legitimate Power
Autumn Leaves
All My Sunsets
F/X-26
28th Amendment
Night Sirens
Broken Rose

Shadow Gods Saga:
In the Shadow of Death
Against the Gods of Shadow
A Whisper from Shadow
Shadow Masters
Immortal in Shadow
With Shadow and Thunder
Through the Valley of Shadow
Guardians of Shadow

Science Fiction:
Fulfillment
Lifeliners

Non-Fiction:
Writing Tips for Authors

Contact at:
www.stefanvucak.com

SHADOW MASTERS

By

Stefan Vučak

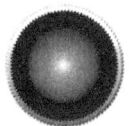

Stefan Vučak ©2009
ISBN-10: 0648473155
ISBN-13: 9780648473152

Dedication

To Roman ... when reaching for faith

Acknowledgments

Mystic Mountain Nebula – Credit: NASA, ESA, and M. Livio and the Hubble 20th Anniversary Team.

Cover art by Laura Shinn.
http://laurashinn.yolasite.com

Map of the Serrll Combine

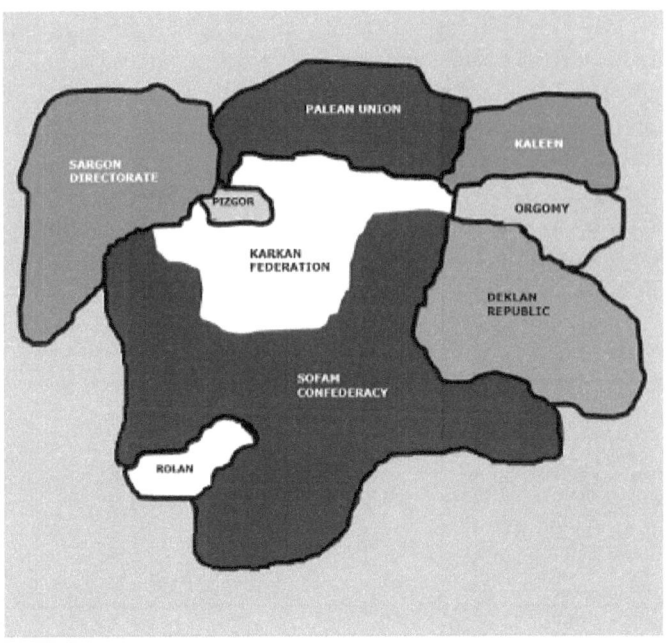

Composition of the Serrll Combine

The 247 star systems that make up the Serrll Combine is an association of six interstellar power blocks, split between two rival camps—the Servatory Party and the Revisionists. Each star system has a single representative in Captal's General Assembly from which members are elected to the ruling ten-seat Executive Council. Seats are based on a percentage of systems occupied by each power block in relation to the total number of systems in the Serrll Combine.

Name	No of Star Systems	Percentage of Total	Executive Council Seats
Sofam Confederacy	83	34	4
Deklan Republic	19	8	1
Palean Union	28	11	1
Karkan Federation	46	19	2
Sargon Directorate	32	12	1
Independents:		15	1
- Kaleen	8		
- Rolan	5		
- Orgomy	6		
- Pizgor	3		
- Other systems	17		
General Assembly	**247**	**100**	**10**
Outposts	40		
Protectorates	34		

Principal political blocks:

Revisionist Party:	Palean Union
	Deklan Republic
	Sofam Confederacy
Servatory Party:	Karkan Federation
	Sargon Directorate
	Nonaligned Independents

Composition of the Executive Council:

Security Council	Bureau of Colonial and Protectorate Affairs
	Bureau of Defense
	Bureau of Cultural Affairs
Administrative Council	Bureau of Administrative Affairs
	Bureau of Justice
Economics Council	Bureau of Economic Affairs
	Bureau of Technology and Development
Central Planning Council	Bureau of Central Planning and Development

Chapter One

Sheeva broke through the dark cloud layer and buttery sunlight streamed into the nav bubble, bathing the command deck with a diffuse golden glow. Below them, bunched white cloudbanks cleaved the horizon beneath a brilliant blue sky. Sensing freedom, the M-1 surged up, ripping the thin atmosphere blanket in its wake. No one heard the rolling boom of its passage. A tinge of violet colored the planet's curve before darkness descended and stars glared back with cold indifference. Earth rolled beneath them as the scoutship shifted course and accelerated toward a gray crescent moon.

Terr lounged back in his seat and let out a satisfied sigh. Everything felt right with the world, almost. He'd dodged the chop over the C-32 and his two unwelcome charges were safely back where they belonged. Admittedly, armed with knowledge of the Serrll, unavoidable under the circumstances, but all in all, not too shabby. Still, the Bureau of Colonial and Protectorate Affairs desk drivers might not view his actions in the same glowing light, but right now, he would not allow the prospect of possible future bureaucratic entanglements spoil his day. Besides, Anabb had forgiven him his little trespasses, however grudgingly. Right now, the only thing that mattered.

Okay, nosing around the American carrier group might not have been the wisest thing to do, seeing how it got him shot down, but if Sariman had bothered to warn him of Earth's bistatic laser radar capability, it would have avoided the ensuing complications. Anyway, the canal worm got his butt in the crack properly when he violated the agreed comms protocols, which inevitably led to all the subsequent unpleasantness. Did

1

Sariman expect Dhar to leave Lauren behind to die at Co-malcalco with their primitive medical facilities to care for her? Because she would have died had he not taken her. What his brother did was not merely correct, but honorable.

At any rate, Sariman should have known better than kow-tow to someone like Laraiana with her caustic behavior and vindictive personality. Serves him right what that got him. Foremost a Scout Fleet officer, he should not have crawled to her, only to get stomped on. The woman was an opportunistic user and didn't care who got trampled along the way to her version of success, whatever that might be.

Hindsight is such a wonderful tool.

As Earth shrank behind him, Terr swiveled his seat and grinned broadly at Dhar. "I never thought I would say it, Nightwings, but I'm glad to be away from that nutty place."

Dharaklin checked the status displays with a quick sweep and leaned back onto the couch, pleased to see Sankri happy, given the things that had gone wrong. He did not know which was worse, downed by that Aegis cruiser's point defense system, or recovered by the Russians. Both were grim items at many levels whose repercussions, he figured, were still to be fully resolved by everyone involved, including Earth. Territorial rivalries colored and absorbed so much of that planet's energy. When he thought about it, were Serrll's rivalries any different? Despite some difficulties, the mission completed successfully and they were homeward-bound. The future now for them to write.

"I must confess to a level of relief myself, my brother," he said comfortably, his voice deep and resonant. "Although—"

Terr raised a hand and winced. "I know. You don't have to remind me. As jobs go, not my finest moment ever, but post-mortems can wait."

Dhar suppressed a smile. "Far be it for me to criticize my superior officer."

"Your unflagging support shall not go unrewarded," Terr

said dryly.

"Comforting, but what I wanted to say, my brother, when I brought Lauren and Bill to the Moon Base, I violated a number of standing regulations."

"You did the only possible thing," Terr said promptly, giving Dhar a hard look. "Never doubt it. I would be extremely disappointed had you done otherwise."

"It might have been the correct thing to do and I thank you for your words, but it caused you a major problem with Anabb."

"I wouldn't fret it. He'll get over it."

"I cannot put it out of my mind. Despite his assurances, there could still be trouble over this with the BCPA."

"Maybe, but I don't believe it," Terr said with more assurance than he felt. The BCPA took its protectorate responsibilities seriously, and Anabb's Diplomatic Branch umbrella might not be wide enough to shield him should they decide to get unpleasant. Ah, to the pits with all of them. "Look at it this way. After capturing Tanard, we're heroes, remember? It wouldn't look good for the government to mess with us right now."

Dhar raised a questioning eyebrow. "It might not look good, but it does not mean they would not do it. Besides, those Captal busybodies have long memories," he added darkly. "They will find a way to even the score."

"You worry too much. We'll handle it, if and when," Terr growled and stretched his arms. "What can they do? Drum me out of the Fleet? Somehow, I don't think so. Right now, all I want is to pack our stuff and get back to Taltair. On the other hand, should those chair experts decide to give us trouble, I can always sweet-talk my uncle to drop the matter."

"Unless he is after your hide himself," Dhar commented candidly, but a twinkle of amusement lit his eyes.

Terr sighed and shrugged. "There is always that."

Dhar stared at his brother for a speculative moment, curious how Sankri could brush off the problem so easily, then turned to check their approach. At one-fifth boost, the Moon got visibly larger. They were in no danger of auguring in, and SC&C would override if that were the case. He just did not want to appear sloppy.

Although Sankri appeared unruffled regarding the conduct of their mission, he suspected his brother secretly feared Anabb would see it as a shoddy operation; certainly more so than worry about any Bureau of Colonial and Protectorate Affairs repercussions. Dhar knew how important it was for Sankri to create a favorable impression with their boss. Regardless of any mitigating circumstances and Anabb's forgiving manner, as a first field test, the job left something to be desired.

"We did get the C-32," he said gently, reminding his brother that despite everything, they *have* completed their mission. That had to account for something.

Terr gave him a wry smile. "So we did. Things can't be all bad, even if we did leave a trail of confusion in our wake."

"And we learned something more of Earth's detection capabilities. That should be good for a footnote somewhere," Dhar said gravely and Terr grinned at him.

"There you are! They'll pin a medal on us. Still, if Anabb is going to have us doing more of these hair-curling crazy stunts, I can see this undercover crap will take some time getting used to."

"You are not regretting joining the Diplomatic Branch, are you?"

"Tah, the gods will tell," Terr said gravely. "It's somewhat wrenching to realize we're no longer Scout Fleet, where the only thing I had to worry about is missing report schedules and bending *Ramora*. Although we did bend it pretty badly in the end, didn't we? I do miss her, a sweet ship. One thing, though, working for Anabb certainly beats the hell out of routine patrol duty." He cocked an eyebrow at his brother. "And you?"

"So far, it has not been dull, I must give him that."

"A strange first assignment, all right," Terr agreed moodily.

"Second, if you count *Zavian* and bagging Tanard. He is some piece of work. You know, I almost feel sorry for him."

"He took out his M-3 and wiped out innocent merchant ships, my brother," Dhar reminded him sternly.

Terr nodded. "Yes, he did. What's more, I can understand why he did it."

"There is a world of difference between understanding and condoning. That's what the Paleans were doing, condoning open piracy."

"Well, he'll have plenty of time to reflect on Cantor. Talking of reflection, we left Earth with a lot to reflect over as well."

"The C-32's data? Hard to imagine that somehow we left the ship behind," Dhar mused and shook his head.

Terr grinned. "Yeah, and there's no one left to blame now. I wonder what Earth will make of their download? They've got so much potential, yet still so tribal and territorial."

"Not like us at all, are they?" Dhar added softly, pointing out the illogic of Sankri's argument.

Terr could not say anything, afraid if he started picking at it, examining the rivalries between the Servatory Party and the Revisionists, the looming Sargon/Palean merger, Deklan's religious fundamentalism, raiders plaguing shipping corridors, he wouldn't like the inevitable conclusion. Technology always magnifies a society's moral and ethical shortcomings.

Surface Command and Control guided them in and the little scout glided over jagged peaks that hid the Serrll Moon Base in perpetual northern polar darkness. With the base installations spread across the crater floor like a toy erector set, the ship hovered for a moment, then settled on the softly glowing landing ring beside a brooding M-3. An access tube immediately slid from a gray wall and connected with a muffled clang when the clamps engaged.

Terr slapped his thighs and stood up. "Might as well get this over with. We could get lucky and leave without getting noticed."

Stefan Vučak

"I like your optimism," Dhar said, doubting they'd be able to simply slink away, but the prospect of leaving the Moon Base and its internal byplays felt good. He looked forward to an assignment where they would not need to use the hand of Death, provided Anabb kept them together. It would be unsettling working without his brother at his side, although he knew a day would come when that might be necessary. He thought about it, but never quite got around to deciding how he would react. It won't be pleasant, he knew that much.

Tah, whatever the gods decided.

They took the cable-tube down to the main deck and proceeded to the access tube hatch, then a short walk through the brightly lit tunnel to the other end. Terr stood at the entrance and tapped a brown sensor pad. It pulsed and the hatch opened at the SMB's launch level. Sweet, acid, rancid smells assaulted him as he strode into the base and his face wrinkled with distaste. He still found it hard to ignore the ambient odors. A familiar figure waited for them in the corridor.

"Sir!" the young Deklan officer barked and stood to.

Terr smiled affably at the boy's stiff features. The kid had gone through a lot and probably enjoyed little of it.

"Doing penance, Mister?"

Dreading this meeting, Third Scout Tembel allowed himself a small grin. "No, sir. The executive officer has requested that you see him at your convenience."

"First Scout Patrlin?"

"Yes, sir." Tembel tried to cover his embarrassment and his face colored. "With Master Scout Sariman under close arrest, Mr. Patrlin is in temporary command."

"I see. Very well. This is a convenient time as any. Lead the way."

Tembel's blush deepened and he cleared his throat, wishing he were someplace else. If only the deck would open and swallow him.

"Sir...I want to extend my personal apology to you and Mr.

6

Dharaklin for everything." The image of two humans sauntering into the chamber that housed the C-32 and Sariman suddenly standing behind him, quietly ordering him not to report it, still haunted him. He knew it to be wrong, but Sariman was his superior officer and he only a lowly Third Scout. He carried out orders! It didn't help him sleep better.

Terr patted the boy's shoulder. "Don't worry about it. Not your fault."

"That's the point, sir. I think it was," Tembel said miserably, his large wide-set eyes tragic and lost. Mr. Terrllss-rr ended up gravely wounded as a direct result of what he did and the Earth woman almost died. He shuddered to think of the political consequences set into motion by his seemingly innocuous act.

"It took courage to say what you did, Mr. Tembel," Terr said softly, sympathizing with the boy's dilemma. "If you're ever placed in a similar position again, you'll know how to refuse an illegal order."

"Yes, sir," Tembel squeaked, turned and marched stiffly toward the nearest cable-tube. Disobey an order? Not so easy when you were on the bottom rung of a career ladder. Still, he felt relieved the Diplomatic Branch Head of Mission didn't seem to hold the incident against him. A negative report from him would have been an effective career gasper.

Terr stared after the boy, shook his head and walked after him. He hoped the experience hadn't scarred him too much. Well, the kid would just have to learn to deal with it. In adversity the spirit grows. Sometimes, though, there was too damn much adversity.

The ride up taken in uncomfortable silence. When the cable-tube hatch opened, Tembel hurried toward the base commander's door. The two translucent panels parted with a hiss and he stood to.

"Diplomatic Branch Mission, sir!" he snapped, glanced at Terr and hurried off.

Terr gave him a passing nod of encouragement and walked into the office. Still hot and humid as he remembered. Patrlin stood behind the matte black desk, waiting for them. Behind him, a floor-to-ceiling window screen provided a dark Moonscape backdrop. The Karkan hissed and extended his arm at the formchairs before the desk.

"Please be seated, and thank you for seeing me."

"No problem. I planned on doing so anyway before departing," Terr said formally and settled himself into a chair. The Karkan's demeanor cold, his body language hostile, and Terr wondered what soured his milk today.

"Quite." Patrlin's tongue flickered.

The green scales shimmered when he tilted his head. With Sariman under arrest, he expected to take over the SMB permanently, a natural reaction given his seniority and experience with Earth. Not to mention a year on this barren rock. Not getting the coveted promotion was a source of intense personal irritation, and what he considered a blight on his record. Didn't Sector TACOPSCOM trust him to do the job? It was a First Scout billet anyway. He wondered if this young pup sitting before him had anything to do with it. Probably not, he decided grudgingly. The boy didn't appear to be the type to involve himself in service politics, at least not yet. Besides, they'd hardly seen each other. Terr had no reason to sabotage his career. Ah, Laraiana? She represented a much more realistic possibility and something to be looked into. He had rubbed her the wrong way. Stupid female! Did she expect him to fall at her feet because of her powerful Captal connections?

"With destruction of the C-32, I take it your mission here is now officially concluded?" Patrlin grated with forced politeness.

Terr suspected that more lay hidden behind those seemingly innocent words, but right now, he couldn't be bothered figuring it out. There would be enough explaining of his own once he got to Taltair, to worry about the Karkan and his problems.

"It is. I am recalled and I intend to lift immediately we clear our quarters."

"And the Diplomatic Branch does not anticipate any adverse fallout from its unorthodox disposal?"

The temporary SMB commander might be concerned that Earth was now contaminated by information gleaned from the C-32's computer, but Terr didn't think so. The Karkan probably wanted to cover his own position, worried what effect Earth's heightened security posture might have on future Serrll overflights.

"I cannot say, First Scout. The BCPA will undoubtedly carry out an evaluation to make that determination."

"Of course." Patrlin curled his lips and gave a slow hiss. "An awkward situation with Master Scout Sariman, Agent Terr. Awkward and embarrassing. For a senior officer to have done what he did…" he trailed off and shrugged. "Due to your imminent departure, TACOPSCOM considered that you carry Sariman back to Salina. Fortunately, and I agree with them, COMROLOPS vetoed the idea. Besides sparing you any personal discomfort at having him on board, this is an internal Fleet matter and of no concern to the Diplomatic Branch."

"I wouldn't have consented to the plan regardless of any suggestion coming from TACOPSCOM. Not without orders to that effect from Taltair," Terr said stiffly, annoyed at the very idea. The thought of having Sariman underfoot for two or three days was, how would he put it, distasteful.

"Yes, certainly. This is somewhat awkward, but I have a request from Scholar Laraiana."

"Oh?" Terr's face fell at the thought of confronting the woman again. He'd hoped he had seen the last of her. A blanket of darkness hung over her like a menacing thundercloud, ready to stab forth lightning at everyone around her. What brought him within her range, he couldn't tell. Surely the GS-4 shuttle's loss couldn't be the cause of her evident deep-seated enmity. Because he refused to click his heels before her? "What's *her* problem?"

Clearly uncomfortable, Patrlin winced. "I am not insensitive to the fact she casts a frosty pallor over everything near her, but in this case, it would be better if you heard it from her," he said by way of sidestepping an imminent explosion and tapped a pad on the inlaid console in his desk. "Mr. Tembel, please ask Scholar Laraiana to come in."

"Yes, sir."

Terr exchanged a questioning glance with Dhar, who shrugged. Well, at least she made it a request, he conceded, not a demand. Coming from her, it might be hard to tell between the two, he decided somewhat uncharitably. He could not shake off the fact the woman irritated him unbearably. Like having sand in his underwear.

"Did she tread on *your* toes?" he asked and Patrlin hissed, clearly not relishing having the acerbic scientist around.

"When you decided to return the Earthman and his woman without first consulting her, she came raging to me, insisting I hold them, ignoring the fact I had no jurisdiction."

"I regret any inconvenience—"

"Not your concern, Agent Terr," Patrlin said heavily. "I told her if she had a problem with the Diplomatic Branch Head of Mission, she can file a complaint to the Branch Director, which I suspect she already did, and received scant support for her trouble."

The door panels slid into the walls and Laraiana strode through, surrounded by a cloud of coldness, a shield against the world. She carried herself with her usual haughty bearing and imperious authority, impatient of underlings, expecting to get her own way. Her pale blue eyes scanned the office occupants like mapping sensors. Of medium height, her one-piece dark blue coverall hid a curvy figure. It could be a block of ice for all the warmth it held, Terr reflected. His defenses came up with an audible clang, an instinctive reaction.

Laraiana glared at Patrlin. The man had thwarted her once. Would he do it again?

"You told him?"

"Given I have no authority over Agent Terrllss-rr, I thought it advisable that you made the request yourself, Scholar," Patrlin said stiffly, not at all awed or intimidated by her presence. While he sat in this seat, he made the rules here and she can make a complaint to the BCPA if she didn't like it. Even if she *had* already complained, he would not repeat Sariman's mistake by deferring to her.

Laraiana bit her lip in frustration and filed away the insult. Clearly, the Karkan would not be manipulated, at least not directly. However, another word or two in the right ear at COMROLOPS, certain that Patrlin's uncooperative attitude would change smartly—if he valued his career. She would not be interfered with, least of all by the bovine military or male underlings. Expect deference and you will get it.

"Very well." She turned to Terr, annoyed the boy sat in her presence. Another score to settle later, but right now, she needed to remain focused. She swallowed her resentment and took a deep breath. "First Scout, after your thoughtless destruction of my GS-4 shuttle, Salina Tactical Operations Command grudgingly sought fit to provide me with a replacement. This is great news as it means I'll be able to resume my research program with a minimum of delay caused by your, ah, clandestine operation. Fortunately, it won't be dispatched for another five days."

"Fortunately?" Looking at her, Terr suppressed a smile. The woman cannot help herself. Push and grind until something gives way. Still, he was intrigued enough to listen. It could be amusing watching her crawl to him cap in hand, so to speak.

"Yes. You see, this gives me a perfect opportunity to check out the shuttle's systems and have Salina make the necessary modifications that would otherwise have to be done here, which would further delay my research program. To do that—"

"You must get to Salina," Terr finished for her, knowing what was coming and not bothering to hide the irony in his voice.

"Precisely. Since you're going—"

"Scholar Laraiana, I hate to spoil your day, but I'm not going to Salina," Terr said, relishing prolonging her discomfort. She was too easy a target and he really should not be baiting her.

She waved her hand with an impatient gesture. "I understand. It would be a minor detour on your way to Taltair to take me there." She swallowed her chagrin, hating having to beg, especially before this boy. She would rather eat glass, but then, she had a mission to consider, for now. "I am asking that you please transport me to Salina."

Terr nearly laughed at her expression, a mixture of loathing and pleading, knowing full well what it cost her to ask. Grudgingly, he admitted it was a reasonable request. For a pleasant moment, he savored the temptation to hide behind a façade of officialdom and tell her to go through channels, a fleeting indulgence. Although it would give him momentary satisfaction to see her rage at him, he did not have a valid reason to refuse her. Besides, when the dust of acrimony settled, he could be in for a reprimand from the BCPA *and* Anabb. Personal satisfaction or not, she simply wasn't worth it. BCPA's rancor he can handle, but he didn't want to give Anabb another reason to be upset with him. Not right now, at least.

"It will be a pleasure, Scholar," he said at length. "Please be ready to depart within the hour."

"Why…thank you," Laraiana forced herself to say after overcoming her surprise. She fully expected him to be obstinate and was ready to threaten him, but wasn't prepared for this quick acceptance. Perhaps the boy had more sense than he showed. Nevertheless, this in no way deflected her determination to ruin his career. He had it coming to him. "I shall be ready," she said stiffly and walked out without a backward glance.

"A hard personality to warm up to," Patrlin muttered with a rueful shake of his head as the door panels clicked shut. "You were wise to accede to her request, Agent Terr."

Terr's smile was grim. "It'll give me a chance to throw her out the lock."

Patrlin stared, then hissed with amusement, his tongue flickering. "Perhaps a better outcome. As for the GS-4, I must inform you that a formal inquiry will be held into its loss and both of you will be required to provide affidavits, supplementing the SMB's SC&C sensor logs."

"I understand," Terr said, a standard procedure and to be expected. He gathered Dhar with his eyes and stood up. "If there is nothing else, First Scout, we shall be on our way."

Patrlin rose and glared at Terr with obvious dislike. "There is one more thing, Mister. What Master Scout Sariman did to frustrate your mission cannot be condoned, but if the Diplomatic Branch intends to conduct another one of its operations around Earth while I am base commander here, don't you be part of it. Is that clear?"

Terr's mouth twitched, but without humor. "I shall keep it in mind."

Karkans!

Rit!

Chapter Two

A soft chime shattered the silent stillness of his quarters, drawing him away from images of strangely shaped text displayed by the Virtual Interface. He'd been studying Kran writing for some time now and still found it unfathomable. He did not expect to crack the enigmatic writing, he had linguistic specialists, but over time it became one of his hobby drivers. After what he and his crew went through since transiting the Karina Shield Nebula, he wanted to learn what motivated the machine creatures' drive to annihilate all intelligent organic life. He hoped cracking the text would provide a window into their thinking. It also gave him something to distract himself with.

On his right, four softly contoured beige couches surrounded a low oval table. A shallow blue-veined purple crystal bowl, filled with sparkling mineral shards, stood reflected against the table's polished surface. Soft pile covered the deck and kept darkness at bay with its indirect amber glow.

"Karhide Zor-Ell?" the housekeeping computer prompted diffidently, the smooth masculine voice floating before him. A voice he came to know intimately. In a world where he could not unburden himself to anyone and still expect to command, Cent Comp remained the only faithful confidant. A delicious irony of fates that he could be closer to a machine than another living person. It wasn't merely a machine, but that was semantics. Enclosed in a bubble of duty and responsibility, surrounded by his officers and crew, he lived alone. Yet, for all its demands, isolation and emotional toll command exacted, the self-questioning, doubts and sacrifices, he could not imagine himself anywhere else. He had found his destiny.

For the right to command, he accepted and paid the price willingly a long time ago. The yearning to reach beyond himself and grasp the stars brought with it a measure of personal fulfillment surely worth the price. Had he known its true cost when he could still choose to turn away from it all, would he have been as eager? A question without meaning, an exercise in imponderables, for that other version of himself who first trod on his path of destiny where he now stood was but a pale shadow of what he had become. A gulf of experience and knowledge separated him from his younger self, deep as the chasm between the stars.

"What is it?" he asked and mentally suspended the VI image of Kran text.

"No deviation in the emission trace from a subspace distortion field consistent with a small vessel, Karhide. Range is now one point-six light-years. Speed, point-two-two standard boost. Course analysis confirms heading toward nebula NB-9, fifty-eight light-years in our rear port quadrant. No divergence since initial detection."

A tight smile of grim humor tugged at the corner of his powerful mouth. There it came again, another anomaly. The entire damn system ahead of him one teasing, murky irregularity, and reason why he wasn't heading home right now. Analog, frequency modulated, and digital carrier wave comms signals were intercepted coming from the third planet, but nothing to indicate subspace capability. Moreover, all energy signatures were consistent with a pre-spaceflight culture. Not a single profile indicator suggested a technology able to support a craft now tracked. Yet such a ship was out there and clearly subspace capable. So where did the diabolical thing come from?

Energy leakage from the planet's moon hinted at another potentially far more troublesome and exciting possibility. The system must be occupied by aliens, keeping watch on an emerging culture? It gave him one more tantalizing reason for wanting to take a closer look, delaying his departure.

He had duty and there was home. Zaron, deep in the Orieli Cluster with the entire White Cloud galaxy a magical swirl of stars wheeling seemingly within reach. From here it seemed an unimaginable distance to the steep hills, tumbling waterfalls, thick forests, and gentle valley of the family estate. His parents would be there, always glad to see him, and no one else. An older brother lived in Skaro, a prominent member of the Klanina Caucus administration. They were cordial, but never close. Their differing interests, desires, and goals kept them too far apart. He didn't know the whereabouts of his sister's ship, patrolling somewhere in the White Cloud. He smiled, remembering his little mischievous Tilla, an officer now. Slowly, the smile faded.

Once, someone did wait for him.

He could see it vividly, the platform tumbling out of control to slam into a wooded hillside. Its screen down, nothing protected the two occupants. Before they hit, she threw herself at him as he wrestled with the controls, shielding him with her body. It took a long time for the hurt to fade. Only a memory now and he'd moved on—had to move on—leaving her behind.

There were no lasting relationships afterward. For a while, he hadn't wanted one, and later, his duties left him with few opportunities. Oh, one or two women he knew would not mind drawing him out of his shell, but he did not have to hurry. With a life expectancy of one hundred and sixty, at forty-six, he figured he still had enough time for love. That's what he told himself.

"Project plot," he ordered harshly, not expecting to see anything new. He studied the initial emission trace thoroughly. Immediately, his lounge dissolved and he found himself in naked space. Ahead and to his left, painted against the tactical plot overlay, pulsed a blue dot of the unknown ship. A faint red line extended from it toward a distant nebula.

"Confirm point of origin and display," Zor-Ell asked,

knowing the answer, but going through the motions anyway. A red line backtracked from the blue dot toward the third planet and the image expanded. At extreme resolution, he could make out the whorls of white girthing the pretty blue world. The quarter moon hung back pearly and aloof, brooding in the planet's protective shadow, hiding whatever secrets it held.

"Opturkarh Karth has altered course to intercept the craft as per orders and raised preparedness status to condition two," Cent Comp advised, showing *Valon's* green track veering gently to port toward a pulsing red square along the alien's course where the two ships would eventually meet. "The intercept triangle will close in seventy-six minutes under current flight parameters."

"Very well." Although he did not expect a confrontation with the alien vessel and did not look for one, he fully approved Karth's caution. Besides, it was standard operating procedure. He found that size can be deceptive and cannot be relied upon as a guide to capability. This far from home and the information they carried, overconfidence could be potentially disastrous.

By not deviating from its course the unknown ship indicated that *Valon* hadn't been detected or it wasn't bothered by his presence. Zor-Ell considered the former far more plausible and wondered how long it would take before the alien ship became aware of him and what it would then do. Though, with his ship running stealthy, he didn't consider it likely the alien would detect him at all until *Valon* exited relational normal. A nagging thought bubbled and surfaced. All very well trying to establish contact with the strange vessel, but if he inadvertently trespassed, a growing possibility, what if other ships appeared; heavier, more powerful ships? And if they resented his presence?

Well, he was out here to make contact, be it friendly or otherwise. Considering what they endured on this survey, he would prefer not having to bare his teeth, and very few species were openly hostile. Some causal factor always triggered a response.

"Detach VI coupling and inform Opturkarh Karth I'm on my way to PFC."

The neural link with the ship's central computer severed at once. He blinked hard as reality crashed into his senses and the lounge materialized around him. Breaking the link with Cent Comp always left him with a sense of loss and inadequacy. Through the VI, *Valon's* entire sensory array and ship capabilities, plugged directly into his cortex, lay available at his disposal. Without the VI coupling, operating the powerful cruiser would be unmanageable.

For all its undoubted advantages and benefits, in a broader sense, that same technology also exacted its levy of social misery, perhaps an inevitable byproduct. Who would want to face the travails and uncertainty of life's burdensome reality when the nearest VI coupling delivered at a whim tailored and infinitely varied perfect and safe alternatives. Faced with the limitations of his senses, he fully appreciated the dark attractiveness of those alternatives. Unfortunately for some, the only sane substitute when life became intolerable. Clearly, where such abuse was practiced, it could be argued that the Orieli collective social structure had failed somewhere in support of its citizens. He could and did maintain that freedom of choice, and free will meant freedom to escape from personal responsibility. Not everyone could realize their dreams, and he did not judge those who faltered along the way.

"Opturkarh Karth has acknowledged," Cent Comp said softly.

With determined strides, Zor-Ell walked toward a glowing concave alcove set into the wall, stepped in and turned to face the lounge.

"Initiate personal transport to PFC."

In a moment of unbearable pressure and cold, he hurtled through the trans-dimensional threshold. Materializing, he waited for the transceiver's after-effect tingle to subside, and then mumbled an improbable suggestion to the device. Every time he used the thing, it felt like his body was sliced and squeezed to a point at the same time, although only a psycho-somatic reaction.

He stepped out of the PT alcove and automatically swept his eyes around the ellipsoid of Primary Flight Control, taking in information from ceiling-high full-dimensional holoview status displays running the length of Command level, a protruding platform that curved along the long axis halfway up the chamber wall. Swivel-couches faced the holoview repeater readouts from the main operations stations below, projected along the platform's edge. Using voice commands or touch-recognition backup pads, provided authorized access to all ship's functions when not hooked through the VI coupling.

Operations stationed three kanampirs below the command level, a giant bowl, its inner surface mounted one continuous backup console, above which were displayed three-kanampir-high holoview images. One showed a schematic of a yellow star with a family of ten planets and a vast outer ring of scattered debris and planetesimals.

On his left, three watchkeeping officers looked up from their repeaters and nodded. On his right, two wide swivel-couches were set against the curved command platform. Simple color-coded pads covered the broad armrests. He turned to Karth's imposing form sprawled on the far couch and sauntered toward him.

"Karhide," Karth said with a friendly nod.

Zor-Ell grasped the armrests and eased himself down. The couch contoured itself around his body and he relaxed into its soothing embrace.

"All right, Opturkarh. What do we have?"

"Interesting case, but nothing much I can add to what we already know," Karth said briskly and his pale pink tongue ran quickly around black, fleshy lips. "No matter which way I look at it, the drive emission signature suggests a small craft. Something like our RV/4 dart. Probably a scoutship or courier of some sort."

"Mmm." Chewing his lower lip, Zor-Ell extended a finger at the repeater plot. "That ship has no right being there," he complained belligerently.

"It certainly isn't from around here," Karth agreed. "Whoever they are, they haven't occupied the system. Apart from emission leakage coming off the third planet's moon, we have nothing."

"But what we do have is suggestive enough," Zor-Ell noted and exhaled loudly. "I'm afraid we're facing a quarantine scenario. Well, that's why we came out here, to meet aliens."

"First contact protocols are now in effect, I presume, Da?" Karth asked formally, understanding perfectly what the alien ship represented.

"You assume correctly, Opturkarh."

"I just had a horrible thought," Karth ventured. "It's a long way from Karina, but whoever is looking after this system, do they know of the Celi-Kran?"

Zor-Ell smiled somewhat grimly. "More importantly, do the Krans know about *them*!"

"That's one nightmare I don't want to even consider," Karth reflected and licked his lips. "If that abandoned station on System 4-Three did transmit a beacon pulse and the Krans come visiting, there could be trouble...for everybody."

They surveyed three systems after emerging from the Karina Shield and came across planets that once held budding and thriving civilizations. What they found were obliterated worlds and desolation. Where systematic destruction was avoided, the population remnants had reverted to near savagery, struggling to reclaim a lost heritage. What triggered that indiscriminate cycle of extermination some two thousand years ago could only be guessed at. The clues left by the Krans, including deactivated worker and command units, were both tantalizing and chilling.

Of equal importance, and something to be assiduously studied, what stopped them from working their way farther into this part of space? Of course, the nanometric constructs were not around to offer an explanation. Their very name and evidence of their existence retrieved from historical remnants on cindered worlds.

Karth saw no reason to complain. He'd had his chance to pass up this assignment. On the prospective commander short list, before this mission started, OSCOM, Orieli Space Command, Bureau of Personnel, offered him a coveted command billet. Admittedly, it would not be a cruiser, but nevertheless a command; an officer's dream to be master under no one, and a vital career prerequisite toward future advancement. The offer turned out to be BuePer's version of satirical humor, which everyone knew it had, for nearly immediately news broke that six ships would be sent through a newly found corridor in the Karina Shield Nebula, and *Valon* was one of the designated ships. Karth could only chuckle at the delicious irony of it all. In fairness, Zor-Ell urged him to accept the appointment, knowing full well the disruption it would cause to his command structure, but clearly relieved when Karth refused, as much from self-interest as anything else. Karth knew that breaking in a new first officer during a key mission would be a major inconvenience.

A mug's choice anyway. Ambitious, good at his job, Karth aspired to command, but to miss out on being part of a survey that came around once in forever? A serving officer could spend several lifetimes seeing nothing more than the same old Orieli Cluster stars or push the settled White Cloud extremities, herding merchants, muscle flexing in some wayward system or chasing down an enterprising marauder. In that one rare moment when he could reach out for the first time into a truly unknown part of the galaxy, to see for himself what lay beyond the Karina, there was nothing to decide.

The Orieli had studied the staggeringly huge gas cloud and

its baffling properties for centuries, but it wasn't the same thing as being there and looking around for himself. That *Valon* could be lost in the attempt, he faced with equanimity. Ships were lost before in that murky expanse, swallowed without trace in the nebula's deeps. They even knew why. The possibility that this time it could happen to him did not sway him at all. To his vast relief, BuePer did not raise even a token protest when he declined the command posting and agreed to keep the slot open until his return. All officers knew that such billets didn't come up every day, and he feared his resolve to stay with *Valon* would send him to the bottom of the selection list. Career management a capricious mistress at the best of times.

It hadn't been easy climbing to his current position. A native of Ceti II—the original world destroyed in catastrophic orbital bombardment by the old Zaron Concordiat three-and-a-half thousand years ago, the survivors creating a new beginning under another star; he wanted to space as far back as he could remember. Building and flying model spaceships was one thing, but to actually serve in one meant rigorous schooling and competitive selection examinations. He overcame those obstacles and eventually obtained an appointment to the sector's Space Arm Academy. Trapped for four years in an intensely challenging environment when young blood ran hot, was a testing experience, and inevitably, some failed to meet the challenge. Karth survived the trials, academic and personal, and in his final year, they sent him to the famed Zaron Academy where a young officer's remaining rough edges were further polished. After graduation, he served a year in a training ship. At twenty-three, a commissioned officer, he received a posting to an operational Space Arm vessel. Eighteen long years later, promoted to opturkarh, he received a posting as *Valon's* executive officer and a slot on the prospective commander list. Now, three years on, he stood on the edge of another life's milestones.

Zor-Ell also shared concern about the signal from 4-Three, but not necessarily on behalf of aliens represented by the small ship out there. After two thousand years the Krans would have evolved, no doubting that. If they somehow forced the Karina breach, he was confident Perilian Sector Command could contain them. What if they came and stumbled across Orieli worlds like Setlan Eleven from deeper within the galactic arm without an impenetrable gas cloud to hide them? That sector was at the limits of settled space with no major Space Arm facility. Providing military infrastructure always seen as an afterthought. After all, the Orieli were peaceful and embraced new species. Whatever their physical differences, underneath it all, weren't they brothers? Not to the Krans apparently.

He had nothing to consider. OSCOM must be prepared to meet the new threat and meet them with real warships. Cruisers like *Valon* were armed and powerful, but they were not dedicated weapons platforms. Primarily exploration and survey ships, their hulls were well armored, but once breached, the internal bulkheads were comparatively fragile and vulnerable. To flush out the Krans meant executing more expeditions along the Karina and inward along the galactic arm to find the limits of their expansion and technological advancement. A tactical increase in Space Arm presence on this side of the Karina would demand a secure passage through the nebula, and that meant establishing a transport portal on this side linked to the PERCOM portal. The effort could be all for nothing if the Krans turned out to be dust, which he doubted. Those things were intelligent constructs, not an organic species subject to evolutionary vagaries. They were still out there somewhere, he felt it. Why destroy everything in their path? Finding the answer could be crucial to everyone's survival.

There was, of course, a perilous corollary to seeking them out. Once found, what if they couldn't be stopped? OSCOM would have to face that possibility, and some in the Klanina could undoubtedly urge isolationism and containment; collapse the Karina breach, they would say. Whatever option they took, the Orieli needed to protect its thirteen hundred systems spread through the White Cloud galaxy.

At the moment, there were simply too many unknowns to identify available courses of action. One cannot direct disposition of forces, exercise logistics and command, and apply doctrine without understanding the enemy. The ticklish problem everybody faced, no one knew the Celi-Kran, their motivation, goals and intentions. Zor-Ell had two-thousand-year-old archaeological data, but hardly sufficient to formulate a coherent military strategy in line with political objectives still to be defined. Lack of information could lead the Klanina into inaction, leaving the Orieli dangerously vulnerable. After thousands of years of relative peace and security, would the association of worlds have the moral resolve to accept the consequences of potentially unrestrained and absolute expression of force against an alien species—and themselves? They might not unless the Krans were perceived a threat to their very existence. Unfortunately, right now, he couldn't say they were a threat, regardless of what might have happened two millennia ago.

They waited in silence for *Valon* to close the triangle.

"Caution. Five minutes to initial point," Cent Comp advised.

"At forty million ampirs, depolarize defense net, match speed with contact and parallel its course," Zor-Ell ordered quietly, attuned to the ship's whispers around him.

"Acknowledged."

Karth grinned. "This is bound to raise an eyebrow or two in that ship."

Perhaps on both sides, Zor-Ell reflected silently.

* * *

Blackness stared at him from the deeps, thick and impenetrable. Terr sensed an almost sinister quality emanating from that desolate nothingness, as though something invaded and devoured his soul. Even as a child, reaching with tiny hands for the flimsy whorls of light that lit the shadows of his nights, the immense band did not inspire fear, only insatiable curiosity and a desire to grasp the pretty, shiny thing. Right now, he feared this exposed night stretching into forever and where his ship now took him. To tread into this chasm meant stepping into darkness deeper than any nightmare.

Stars were few and far apart out here at the edge of this vast nothing. They glowed dull white, hard and unsentimental, loners—leftovers in the dustbin of creation. He was wrong to imagine that stars were pinpricks of light in the tapestry of night. As he stood alone in his cabin, hands clasped lightly behind his back, the ship whispering around him, he slowly realized that galaxies were in fact pinpricks of light, and the curtain of night but a shroud of eternity. And the naked face of eternity could be hard to look upon without getting scarred by that pitiless gaze.

A shiver of unease ran through his body.

Being moody and morbid, indulging in introspection, catered to his antipathies, merely avoided reality and his responsibilities. Still, couldn't he have even a moment of indulgence? He came far to touch the bare face of night, perhaps too far. Earth had left an indelible imprint of wonder, bemusement and perplexity on his mind that would haunt his days for some time, and he welcomed the prospect of familiar stars ahead that were home.

Pale brown gravity waves twisted and shimmered, roiling with turbulence in the ship's wake.

He knew what bothered him, of course. Partly, reaction to the mildly tumultuous events of his mission, whose consequences were still to be played out. Mostly, though, he still grappled with the realization that joining the Diplomatic Branch, an important phase of his life had ended, perhaps forever. No longer shrouded by the cloak of comforting familiarity and security that belonging to the Fleet engendered, he needed to find its replacement in the unknown future of his newly chosen

Stefan Vučak

path.

But was he true to himself? Did he genuinely miss his old ship that much, and his future so jarring? Uncertain yes, but daunting and insurmountable? Hardly, and he relished the challenges that were to come. He would be challenges, Anabb would see to that. Did this nostalgia stem from a desire for the predictable orderliness of ship command?

Still moody, but somewhat mollified, he turned away from the transparent bulkhead and climbed into bed. He adjusted the blanket just right, wriggled his toes and squirmed with contentment. Yesterday was a closed doorway. The bed soft and warm, he allowed himself to drift, flushing away distractions and nagging uncertainties.

Getting pleasantly drowsy, the comms alert beeped, the sound stabbing rudely through his mind. He muttered a curse at the unfairness of it all, then rolled over and reached for the comms pad.

"Just a few hours of sleep, Nightwings, that's all I want," he complained petulantly.

"I am detecting a subspace distortion field consistent with a large vessel, Sankri," Dhar said apologetically, hating having to wake his brother. If he didn't do it now, he knew that Sankri the commander would be more than petulant later.

"And what am I supposed to do about it?" Terr was grumpy and knew it, but Dhar spoiled it all by forcing him out of his cozy cocoon when the demons had finally fled.

"It is paralleling us. Range, forty-nine million talans. The computer estimates a mass of sixty-four thousand mikans. The contact is exhibiting a non-standard power emission signature and shield grid configuration. Course analysis suggests it's probably heading toward Sol. No divergence since first detection. I have gone to initial alert."

Terr's brow creased and he sat up, the blanket bunched around his waist. Sixty-four thousand mikans? That made it nearly twice as heavy as an M-4. The ship could be a Sofam

26

Industries experimental design. They liked to conduct live trials of new configurations in secluded places where no one watched, and here was secluded as one could get. To carry that mass…

"How big is the thing?"

"Approximately eight hundred katalans at the longest axis."

Phew! Big hauler.

"How come we only detected it now?" *Sheeva's* sensor suite should have clamored when the thing broke through the two-light-year detection limit.

"I cannot account for it, my brother. The contact just suddenly appeared," Dhar said regretfully. Terr suspected he knew why and his skin prickled at the prospect.

"Raise them."

"Already tried."

"Okay. Let's check their intentions. Slow to one-third boost and send a single ranging ping. Don't shoot 'em up until I get there."

Rit!

Eyes still heavy, he worked his mouth to get the stale taste out and stared vacantly at the opposite wall. He only wanted a few hours of sleep. A narrow green safety strip hugged the bottom of the cabin walls, giving the shadows an eerie glow. With a resigned grunt, he swung out his legs.

The tube hatch hissed open and he swept the command deck with a quick look. He blinked at the harsh brightness, unlike the subdued lighting he preferred, and glanced at the opaque nav bubble displaying the tactical plot, noting the position of the contact. Dhar climbed out of the central command couch and took the right seat. Terr glanced at the main plate and sat down. The unknown ship slowed and paced them, still at forty-nine million talans.

"Slow to one-fifth boost. We want to tell them they're noticed. In two minutes, drop normal and come to a full stop. We'll see if our strange friend out there is curious enough to give us a closer sniff."

"Slowing to one-fifth boost." Dhar tapped commands, then swiveled his seat. His eyes were searching. "Sankri—"

"I know," Terr said gently.

If the unknown ship was not one of theirs, he mulled over the sobering alternative. Inviting closure could be inviting an encounter, but his instincts told him no. If the alien's intentions were less than friendly, it could have forced action before *Sheeva* became aware of it. The thing already demonstrated it could creep about virtually undetected, something that would make CAPFLTCOM go pale. If this was indeed an alien contact, was he showing arrogance by appointing himself Serrll's ambassador? He didn't really have much of a choice, and he did not see anybody else around to do the job, and he could not simply ignore the contact. Call Anabb? That would only be passing the buck and he cringed at what his boss would say about that. Of course, Anabb could view either decision with disfavor, as could Captal. Call the BCPA? Same argument.

Well, since fates appointed him man on the spot…

The unidentified ship slowed with them. Two minutes later, *Sheeva's* distortion field flickered and depolarized. The ship dropped into normal space and waited. Nine seconds later the alien vessel materialized above the M-1, dwarfing it; an astonishing demonstration of precision piloting and chilling in its implication. Terr saw a huge black mass hanging above him that obscured the stars, dispelling any last-minute suspicions this was a new Sofam Industries design. Looking at the enormous thing, he wondered what he'd gotten himself into. He remembered reading somewhere that despite the honor, first contacts too many times ended being last for the heroic unfortunate. A historical footnote was not exactly the obituary he cared to leave behind. Not at this stage of his career anyway. Nevertheless, his eyes glowed at the prospect of a closer encounter.

The tube hatch opened and Laraiana walked in, her imperious eyes cold, trying hard to avoid looking at the object of her displeasure. Not trying *too* hard. She meant to make Terr's life miserable and saw no reason to stop because of an exciting development, or the fact that he did her a favor by taking her to Salina. Besides, in her view, it was his obligation. The military served *her*, not the other way around. They were an anachronism, an outmoded tool that should have been scrapped long ago; too dangerous a toy to be left in the hands of impulsive males playing their juvenile games of dominance.

Terr barely glanced at her and his shoulders drooped in resignation, not in the mood right now to deal with her peppery tirades. He regretted not leaving the vinegarish scientist on the Moon with Sariman, repercussions notwithstanding. They made a perfect pair. But no, he allowed himself to be persuaded by her apparent contrition for past sins. Bar her from the command deck? No, that wouldn't do either. Damn the woman anyhow, wishing she had slept through this.

"Whatever it is, Scholar, it will have to wait."

Suppressing a flash of annoyance, she bit her lip. The boy was doing his job; she could hardly fault him there. "I was working when I saw the strange ship in my repeater plate."

"And it's here now, we know." He turned to Dhar. "What do you read?" he asked, his voice soft, calm, hiding the slow winding up of all his senses.

"They are holding approximately two talans above us and we appear to be within what I read is a shield grid envelope. It isn't anything like what we have. And our own nav screen is down," Dhar added as an afterthought, aware of Laraiana and the current of tension that now enveloped the command deck in a cloak of doom. What grudge did she hold against Sankri? To his knowledge, his brother had done nothing to the woman to make her so openly hostile. Denying her use of the SMB's GS-4 shuttle, thereby delaying her research program? Was that it? His brother was simply carrying out his mission. She must realize that. It must be something else.

"Down?" Terr queried with a raised eyebrow, wondering how the alien managed that trick.

"More accurately, it was neutralized."

"Mmm."

Terr nibbled at a fingernail. Alien and powerful and curious, and a first for the Serrll Combine in three-and-a-half thousand years. The Bureau of Colonial and Protectorate Affairs will be in little knots over this, perhaps distracted long enough to forget their pique at his handling of the C-32. Don't worry about it.

The tactical plot showed a rectangular shape with downward-sloping flowing sides. A dark, menacing black slab, which wasn't really strange. Why weaken hull integrity with transparent ports when there were more effective ways to see out. Besides, nothing out there to see from a window. At any rate, with hull material whose crystalline structure allowed it to become transparent, windows were irrelevant. The plot rotated the alien's profile through various views. It didn't give him any new answers.

Attuned to the keen tension generated by her presence, which she didn't mind at all, Laraiana stood behind the empty left couch and arched her neck. She surveyed the plot with critical scrutiny, not really understanding the columns of data flowing across it, and gave a low hiss. She didn't have to understand the data to recognize the possibilities. If this was an alien ship, she had an opportunity to salvage something of her mission after the loss of her GS-4 shuttle at the hands of Earth's forces in such spectacular fashion. Seeing the shuttle shot down, she watched two years of planning and wrangling with intransigent BCPA and Fleet officials sink beneath the waves. To have success snatched from her lips like that was infuriating. She urged Sariman to relieve Terr on the spot for gross negligence, only to see the spineless worm himself under arrest for sabotaging the Diplomatic Branch mission. What a bungle!

In her view, all Fleet officers were a useless luxury and a drain on real work and resources, like her research. Dashing about in warships was so…dated! Macho male childishness. What set her teeth on edge, she simply could not understand why Terr hadn't been relieved for obvious incompetence, given her evidence and protests to the Diplomatic Branch and the BCPA. Was the boy's uncle holding a protective hand over him? And what a shock when he told her that Enllss-rr was a relative, and a powerful one. In one swoop, her thoughts of delicious retaliation were dashed from her grasp. She refused to believe the Commissioner would compromise his integrity by stooping to nepotism. Still, he wouldn't be the first if he did, she admitted candidly. Power existed to be used, something her father ceaselessly drilled into her. Father…

If going through Enllss-rr was no longer an option, there were other ways to exact retribution, and she had a powerful relative of her own.

"What do you intend doing, First Scout?" she demanded haughtily, not able to get the image of M-9s holding station over Hakran, to the impotent fury and everlasting humiliation of the Dumas Conclave and all of Sargon. Such impudence! Her father, a senior Pro-Consul, took it particularly badly. Schooled in the old ways and observance of the Code, the Pizgor scandal and the unmasking of Lemos had hit him hard. That this young officer was responsible, however indirectly, for Sargon's embarrassment and her father's suffering was simply intolerable. This strange ship may offer an opportunity to erase some of that dishonor, if she could bend the situation to her advantage.

About to tell her what he intended doing, Terr refrained. He really didn't mind antagonizing her, but she simply wasn't worth his time. Her obvious animosity made her an easy target. Why did she have to keep pushing? She did a great job saving Lauren and he took pains to tell her that her efforts were appreciated, but she brushed aside his peace overtures and simply kept on remonstrating. Clashing chemistry? Frankly, he

31

couldn't be bothered any longer. Two more days and he'll dump her and her emotional baggage on Salina. They were welcome to her.

"I intend to establish contact, Scholar," he said patiently, eyes fixed on the plot.

"And then?"

"And then we see what happens."

"You're not going to request instructions from the Bureau of Colonial and Protectorate Affairs?"

"I know what has to be done, Scholar. Now if you'll excuse me...Dhar, power down nav deflector grid and stand down."

"Standing down."

Laraiana grabbed his arm. "You're leaving us defenseless! If they—"

Terr cut her off with a chilling glare. "Scholar, you have my permission to observe, not to interfere in the tactical operation of this ship. Is that clear?"

"As the senior representative—"

"Is that *clear*?" Terr repeated with a bit more snap this time, his gray eyes boring into hers.

Bright red spots appeared on her cheeks and her mouth firmed into a tight line. Her eyes blazed with fury. To be treated like some minor functionary by this...this military *moron*! The young man's cold eyes glittered dangerously, seemingly indifferent to her indignation. This wasn't the time. She must keep focused on the broader aspects of this contact.

She gave a single jerking nod. *I will not forget this, First Scout. Count on it.*

Turning to face the main display plot, Terr wished he'd spaced the woman.

"Dhar, give them a comms interrogative."

A second later Dhar looked at him. "Interrogative sent back."

"Hah! At least they understand subspace comms. Not that I'm surprised. Tell the computer to transmit the interlingua data pack."

"First Scout, this situation is far too important for you to proceed alone," Laraiana protested in a last-ditch effort to regain some control. "I insist that you contact Salina for instructions."

Terr swiveled his seat and stared hard at her. "Scholar, to be clear, you're not in a position to insist on anything. Secondly, there isn't time to seek instructions from Salina or Captal, even if I were predisposed to do so. Which I am not."

"And I—"

"Our interrogative has been sent back," Dhar interrupted her. "This time with a file attachment, tagged with a request for a visual."

Terr turned and looked at the comms plate. "So they want to chat, eh? Very well. Download the file and let's see what's there."

"First Scout! I—"

"Not now, Scholar!" Intolerable woman! He really should have dumped her out the lock.

Staring at the display plate, Terr broke into an amused grin. He hardly knew what to expect, but the flickering images and scrolling text left him bemused and enthralled. It would take time to go over the material properly, but at least the aliens did leave them with something to go on with. When the download completed, Dhar raised an eyebrow.

"A primer?"

"Fair is fair. We told them who *we* were." Terr wiped his palms against his thighs and took a deep breath. A lot depended on how he handled himself in the next few minutes. "Here we go. Open the channel."

The main plate cleared and he looked at two aliens. The hair on the back of his neck prickled. He could only see them from chest up, but they exuded a confidence and a dominance that was overwhelmingly compelling. One of them had skin a beautiful shade of blue-green, growing black around the eyes and powerful mouth. Large brown eyes shone with intense intelligence. His hair short, black and thick.

Nothing subtle about the other alien who gave an impression of towering height and solid muscle. His straight red hair spilled to his shoulders. Dark brown skin covered a reasonable solid, angular human shape. His red eyes were cold and impersonal, eyes that had seen and experienced everything. Their garments were dark indigo one-piece uniforms, unadorned by extraneous gold braid. They wore a yellow circle emblem on the left side of their chest filled with a cluster of little white stars.

They intimidated by their very presence.

The blue-skinned alien touched his forehead with the tips of his long fingers and gave a small, but graceful bow.

"Scout Fleet vessel, the Orieli Technic Union extends cordial greetings to the worlds of the Serrll Combine," the alien said in a rich masculine voice that vibrated with assurance and power. A computer translation, but there was no mistaking his self-assured bearing. He carried himself with authority, and given the size of his ship, probably with justification, Terr thought. Well, this didn't seem to be an invasion, yet.

"On behalf of the Serrll Combine, I bid you welcome, sir," Terr said cautiously. It seemed a safe thing to say. The alien bared his sharp teeth into a smile, but it served to make Terr's skin prickle. He felt like a child standing before a schoolmaster waiting to be lectured.

"Da, if I may introduce myself…I am Karhide Zor-Ell, commanding the survey vessel *Valon*. With me is my first officer, Opturkarh Karth."

"Sir, I am Agent Terrllss-rr," he said and nodded to Dhar. "My associate, Mr. Dharaklin."

Laraiana gave a sharp hiss of annoyance when he failed to mention her, but realized this was hardly the time to make an issue of it. She could not help noting the aliens were *men*! Even with them, it appeared that women were subordinate. Perhaps they were not so advanced after all.

Terr noted with interest the brief exchange of looks between Dhar and Karth sizing each other up. They were two of a kind, but did he interpret the alien's facial expressions correctly? He needed to be careful here. After all, they were aliens and he couldn't afford to assume anything.

"Da Terrllss-rr...Terr, if I may...If your mission is not a pressing one, I would welcome an opportunity to extend my hospitality to you and Da Dharaklin aboard my ship."

Terr blinked. Was the alien kidding? Right now, he had nothing more urgent than finding out everything he could about the Orieli, which he suspected Zor-Ell knew. This would blow the Bureau of Colonial and Protectorate Affairs right out of its Captal complacency. He pictured Enllss rampaging in tight little circles when his data pack arrived, and suppressed a smile, wishing he could be there to see it. Knowledge of the Orieli would no doubt pour a considerable amount of sand into the Serrll's ingrained social matrix. Perhaps everyone required a reminder that space was big and they were not alone. Would that reflection act as a uniting catalyst or serve to polarize existing political divides? Glad to leave that problem to Captal.

"It would be a genuine pleasure, sir," Terr said warmly.

"Splendid! If you don't have a means to transfer—"

"I can extend an access tube."

"Excellent. I await your convenience, Da." The alien bowed and the display plate faded.

The Orieli ship immediately rotated in place and stopped to reveal the lighted maw of a huge opening in the sloping edge. Terr felt certain it was large enough to take the whole M-1 without scraping the sides. Did they expect him to drive his ship inside? No, Zor-Ell appeared satisfied when Terr mentioned an access tube. If the alien wanted him inside, Terr figured he would have said so. He realized he needed to watch himself with these guys, and wondered if he could do this.

"Dhar, bring us into position. Hold at five katalans separation and extend the tube."

"You're going to extend an access tube into open space?" Laraiana snapped, unable to contain herself any longer. What the boy proposed was reckless and foolhardy in the extreme. He *had* to see that.

"Hardly," Terr said, annoyed that she hadn't thought it through. Zor-Ell would not invite him to dock without taking precautions. He felt fairly sure a force field protected that enormous entrance. Of course, there was always room for doubt. Well, he figured he would find out quickly enough. Anyway, he had sensors to back up his judgment.

"Moving into position," Dhar said quietly.

As *Sheeva* closed, the alien ship managed to look even more forbidding, impossible to discern detail in the smooth hull. The brightly lit maw opened before them into a hangar bay. Figures stood watching *Sheeva's* approach, demonstrably protected by a force field. The M-1 stopped and the access tube slid out. The docking end slowed near the entrance barrier. With a barely discernable ripple of shifting distortion the tube pushed past the force field and held position several tetalans above the alien deck.

Terr slapped the armrests and lifted himself up. "Dhar, you're with me."

Alarmed the situation had slipped away from her, Laraiana interposed herself between him and the cable-tube hatch, hands on hips.

"I must be included, First Scout! As an accredited BCPA Mission Leader, I effectively represent the Serrll government and I am heading this contact."

Terr grinned. He couldn't help it. The woman was insufferable, just when he was prepared to forgive her foolishness.

"Scholar Laraiana, I acknowledge your BCPA accreditation, but unless you hold plenipotentiary endorsement or expertise in alien protocols among your qualifications…"

She snorted and tossed back her head. "You know I don't. I'm, ah, a geneticist—"

"In that case, I hate to spoil your fun, but I can't use you."

"This is an outrage! I rank you! I demand that you contact the BCPA offices on Salina!"

"Scholar, you can demand whatever you want, but I have no time for your remonstrations. Now if you'll excuse me? It won't do to keep our visitors waiting."

"I'll have you broken for this! Captal shall hear of your insolence, First Scout!" Laraiana raged, galled at getting thwarted again, and stamped her foot in frustration. Whenever she wanted to exert her authority, some *man* sought to peg her down.

"Be my guest," Terr said mildly, glanced at the comms station and pushed past her.

Swallowing her resentment and chagrin, she reached for his arm. It might not be too late. "Please, First Scout. This could make my career. At least let me join you."

Terr stopped and looked at her. Gone was the arrogance and loathing, but she still had a gleam of cunning in her eyes. She schemed something. He didn't doubt this contact could make her career; it won't do anything bad for his either if he didn't stuff things up, but could he risk offending the Orieli if she flew into one of her overbearing exhibitions? No one would thank him for the ensuing mess because technically, she ranked him. As *Sheeva's* commander, he could not relinquish the responsibility.

"I'm sorry, Scholar. That isn't possible."

She paled. Her lips tightened and she swung at him with the fury of loathing and disgust of all men. Before the slap could connect, Terr grabbed her wrist and stared into her eyes.

"You can see why," he said softly and dropped her arm. Leaving her gaping at him, he turned around and pressed the request pad beside the hatch. It opened with a hiss and he strode in. Dhar followed, his face expressionless, but the vertical red slits in his eyes were wide with amusement.

"Main deck," Terr ordered and shook his head. The hatch

slid shut.

"That is one imperious lady, Sankri."

"And a monumental pain. I cannot work her out."

"She bears a hate for you that is beyond understanding."

"Yeah. I guess she's naturally mean. Gods, can you imagine what would happen if she started throwing her weight around with Karhide Zor-Ell? Talk about seven years of bad luck! I'll take Tanard and his raiders any day." He frowned and cast a speculative eye at Dhar. "You know what this could mean for the Serrll if *I* should mess up?"

"With exalted rank comes greater responsibility," Dhar rumbled with a straight face, but his eyes twinkled.

"Asshole!"

They walked quickly to the access tube hatch, cycled the lock and made their way along the tube. At the other end, Dhar hesitated.

"Bio contamination?"

"I am sure our alien friends have considered that little detail," Terr said tiredly. "At least I hope so, or this could be the end of two very promising careers."

Dhar raised an eyebrow and touched the release pad. Despite his levity, Sankri was concerned, but some things must simply be faced. In reality the risk not too great. Diverging evolutionary paths ensured that Orieli viruses or bacteria would not immediately find Terr's, or his, for that matter, bodily environments compatible, but could do so if brought to a Serrll world. Bio contamination is never to be taken lightly. The hatch cycled.

The hangar space large, but not overwhelmingly intimidating, and from a functional point of view, instantly familiar. On their left three saucer-shaped craft some thirty katalans in diameter, hovered above blue-glowing circles set into the deck. A maintenance gang clustered around open access panels of the first craft. Holoview displays hung in the air, tracing intricate circuit patterns. Along the wall, workbenches were littered with tools, parts and what could be diagnostic equipment. Against the opposite far wall a row of small rectangular slabs lay parked on the deck, their sides smoothly sloping down, vaguely resembling the drooping shape of the Orieli ship. They reminded Terr of sled-pads.

Zor-Ell and Karth waited for them to alight. Although different and alien, Terr recognized the affinity and closeness between them that transcended mere rank. If he read them correctly, these two knew each other intimately and worked as one. Maybe the Serrll and the Orieli were not so dissimilar after all. When he stepped on the deck, Zor-Ell gave a small bow.

"Welcome aboard my ship, gentlemen," he said amiably and held out his hand. Two small brown spheres rested in his palm. Terr noticed faint interference distortion and realized that he, Dhar, and the tube were isolated from the Orieli ship.

"Thank you, Karhide. It's a unique privilege to be here."

"Da Terr…Dharaklin, please take a sphere. It generates a personal protective field. I regret the necessity…"

"I understand completely, sir." Strange to see Zor-Ell talk in an alien language and hear the computer's translation above his head. He reached for the sphere and recoiled momentarily when the force field touched Zor-Ell's hand. The sphere slipped through the field and Terr stared, nonplussed. Some force field! The sphere felt warm and surprisingly heavy. He pocketed the object.

"Da Terr—"

"Sir, I gather you're using a formal mode of address. Just Terr will do fine, if that's acceptable."

Zor-Ell smiled and nodded. Terr was shorter, much shorter, than his imposing companion, but carried himself with a relaxed poise borne of command and total confidence. His features were firm and strong without appearing rough or angular. A small cleft in his chin added character. A lock of brown-black hair hid a broad forehead. Clear gray eyes looked back at him without guile above an aquiline nose. A small scar

Stefan Vučak

on his temple above the left eyebrow showed someone who wasn't afraid to put his body in the way of danger. Of course, he could have gotten that by falling out of bed, Zor-Ell mused, but he didn't believe it. Somehow it didn't fit the profile. Terr announced himself an agent, which implied either a policing or intelligence service. Given his obvious military bearing, Zor-Ell figured it could be either.

Where Terr appeared open and engaging, Dhar held his drawn frame with reserve and restrained power, ready to be unleashed if called for. The vertical red slits of his large orange eyes hinted at something that stirred a faint racial memory, which Zor-Ell couldn't quite place. Dhar's yellow skin dry, pulled tight over the ridges of his long face, framed by reddish-bronze hair that spilled to his shoulders. His nose, broad and flat, gave him a haunted lost look, like he belonged somewhere else, certainly not in uniform or aboard a ship.

Zor-Ell's scrutiny took an instant as he swept his eyes over the two figures. They made an unlikely pair and he suspected to the lament of their superiors. Unaccountably, he was relieved and his initial misgivings at having to nurse two frightened junior officers evaporated instantly. He sensed that Terr would tell it like he saw it, which Zor-Ell preferred to the stilted formality had he encountered a stuffy senior commander interested in protocol and word fencing. Would the boy be sophisticated enough to understand and appreciate the impact of this encounter, on both of them? Only the crucible of experience would reveal that.

"Thank you. While Cent Comp makes an excellent language bridge, if I can suggest, the Virtual Interface will be more convenient."

Terr felt fine with whatever the alien proposed—short of drilling into his head. He was prepared to put up with hearing an indirect translation, but if the alien had a shortcut, he was agreeable. Merely being here, absorbing the sights and sounds of this incredible ship more than enough for him.

"Direct exchange through the computer? What does it involve?"

"You consent, Terr…Dhar?"

"Of course, sir."

"Excellent!" Zor-Ell said and Terr gasped at the simultaneous sound of the alien's voice in his head. He heard Zor-Ell's words directly when they were spoken. What a translator!

Ultimately tactful, Zor-Ell ignored Terr's transitory distraction. "If you wish, we can retire somewhere more amiable and accommodating."

And relaxing, Terr thought ruefully. Gracious of the alien not to subject the local primitives to an overload of shocks. It was also a remarkable application of psychology. He didn't mind. He'd glimpsed enough of Orieli technology—like the personal shield he wore—to appreciate the web of complexity and sophistication underpinning the ship's deceptively simple exterior design. Incredibly, he wasn't even aware of the shield. It did not disrupt his vision, sound, breathing or anything—a useful thing to have. He wondered if he could talk Zor-Ell into giving him the thing, in the interest of fostering mutual relations, of course. In his new line of work, he figured he could use it.

Zor-Ell's approach hinted that although alien, their thinking processes were sufficiently alike for them to understand each other. They could do business. In the excitement, it would be prudent not to lose perspective. After all, the Orieli *were* alien. He did not fear their ability to understand one another, but getting into trouble by breaching unstated customs and behavioral mores, which could happen through a seemingly innocent gesture or word.

"We're at your disposal, sir."

Zor-Ell extended his hand and they walked toward the far right wall. Dhar and Karth followed silently. Seeing Karth and the crew standing idly, watching the procession with interest, told Terr much. The Orieli were an integrated culture encompassing many races and systems. The ship large, evidently meant to cover considerable distances. An exploration vessel as Zor-Ell indicated, or something much more? Probably both. No one would be so foolish to send an unarmed ship into unknown space, and he didn't consider the Orieli foolish. One thing nagged at him. They could not be from anywhere close or the Serrll would have run into them long before. Powerful indeed.

Where *did* the Orieli come from? He knew the BCPA had sent exploratory ships all around the Serrll Combine, some farther then ten thousand lights. Some talked of sending ships to the galaxy core. What they found so far, mostly classified, but they certainly hadn't met anyone like the Orieli.

Zor-Ell stopped beside one of four elliptical alcoves set into the bulkhead. "Our Personal Transport system."

"A matter transfer device?" Dhar queried, his eyes alive with interest.

Karth grinned and shook his head. "Nothing so ambitious, I'm afraid," he said in a sonorous voice. "It's been tried, but with the exception of pure elements, complex molecules, especially organics, don't do too well in the process."

Terr could appreciate that. The Serrll had experimented with matter transfer technologies in one form or another for a long time without able to achieve that vital engineering breakthrough necessary to make the process viable and safe. The theory behind the idea was sound enough, but its application unwieldy in the extreme. Part of the enormous problem was the staggering computing power needed to process the matrix of an object to be transferred. Decomposition worked well enough; destroying something always came easy. The reconstitution cycle had so far defeated them, involving as it did spontaneous creation of ordered molecular groups. Anything more complex than simple multi-celled organisms came out the other end as blobs of greasy goo. Quantum uncertainty ruled.

He looked inquiringly at Karth.

"We sidestepped the classical problems by using one of the available dimensions that underpin the multi-string matrix theorems."

Terr stared, trying not to gape. A dimensional doorway? The idea was…absurd! What he knew of it, string theorems postulate curled point dimensions. On reflection, it wasn't as crazy as it sounded. Forgetting the technical jargon, what everybody commonly referred to as subspace was, after all, a simple inter-dimensional interface. Well, not *that* simple. Point-to-point transfer *could* be viewed as two linked nodes through subspace.

When this hits them, the Bureau of Technology and Development would be tearing their hair out while opening a fresh avenue of research. After all, the Orieli had already proved the concept. Many scientists throughout the Serrll would be extremely unhappy at this development. No one liked having his life's work, career and wedded ideas trashed.

"Gentlemen," Zor-Ell interrupted gently. "Please step inside. I took the liberty of informing Cent Comp of our destination." To assure his guests the process actually worked, he stepped into the nearest alcove, turned two-dimensional and simply vanished. There wasn't even a stir of displaced air.

Terr looked at Dhar, grinned and stepped into the alcove. A scimitar of cutting darkness, infinite and cold, swept through his body, accompanied by an instant of unbearable pressure. He wanted to cry out, but his moment of irrational panic passed when he crossed the trans-dimensional threshold. Materializing, he waited for the transceiver's after-effect tingle to subside. Zor-Ell stood before him wearing a teasing smile.

"Rit! We must get ourselves one of these," he said in awe and Zor-Ell laughed, a pleasant normal sound.

Dhar and Karth appeared in quick succession.

"I trust the Observation Deck will be less distracting," Zor-

Ell said and indicated at one group of several low couches clustered in semicircles.

Terr followed him and looked around. The bulkheads were transparent, showing the expanse of the ship's sloping black hull. Around them the stars were bright and harsh. It felt like being in open space with only the deck and ceiling to give him an anchor to reality. An impressive view, but this was technology he understood, although the application might be on an altogether different level.

He settled himself onto the couch. It yielded beneath his weight and contoured to support him in the right places. He told himself he must introduce the Orieli to formchairs.

When they were all settled, Zor-Ell crossed his legs and folded his hands in his lap. What he had seen of his visitors, he liked. Both aliens were unpretentious, clearly curious and sophisticated enough not to ask redundant questions. He wondered if they were typical representatives of the Serrll. Probably not, which didn't come as an overwhelming revelation. Being what they were, made them naturally superior. He realized wryly the corollary applied to him as well. Would the aliens pick that up? Gazing at them, he did not doubt whatsoever.

"A somewhat unexpected, but pleasant encounter," he said warmly.

Terr looked for hidden meanings, but the alien appeared genuinely friendly. He needed to remember there were many ways to stalk prey. More likely, he was acting like a paranoid fool. So far the aliens had done nothing to suggest they held hostile intentions. Why would he automatically assume that every encounter must have a military component? A product of his training or a species pattern set against the Serrll's social matrix? Was Dhar's observation that they were not so different from Earth true after all? Definitely something for the BCPA's second guessers to think about.

"And an eventful one for the Serrll Combine, sir. A first for us in some time." Terr wanted to hint gently that the Serrll had been around for a while and thoroughly explored this section of space. The Orieli might be powerful, but they were now playing in his sandpit.

Zor-Ell noted the inference and took it in his stride. "I have already surmised that we might be trespassing when we detected your ship. A somewhat smaller craft, alone and subspace capable, meant a complex social and technological infrastructure able to produce and support it. The fact that you *were* alone, far from advanced energy sources, suggested immediately that this part of space belonged to a sizeable interstellar union."

Terr grinned. They understood each other.

"If you're harboring concerns that you will inadvertently offend us in some way, please don't be alarmed," Zor-Ell added. "I can hardly expect you to be familiar with our behavioral customs and hope you'll reciprocate in the same way."

A wave of relief swept through Terr and he relaxed fully for the first time, at least as far as these extraordinary circumstances permitted. He should have expected that the Orieli would be sophisticated enough to understand potential difficulties that can arise from a seemingly innocent remark or gesture, and make appropriate allowances.

"I appreciate that very much, Karhide. I would feel real bad if I blew this contact by committing an impropriety."

Zor-Ell grinned. "I am pleased to relieve you of that anxiety."

"Sir, your course is taking you toward a nearby yellow G star. The Serrll maintains a base on the third planet's moon…" Terr paused, suddenly suspicious. "You were attracted to this system by energy leakage from our installation?"

"I was ready to head home after a lengthy mission when Sol presented me with an intriguing irregularity. We intercepted carrier wave signals coming from the third planet, but nothing to indicate subspace capability. I could not account for your ship. When we detected energy leakage from the Moon, the rest became clear," Zor-Ell said simply and Terr nodded.

"Earth is an emerging nuclear civilization that has recently ventured into space—"

"And is presumably under some form of, ah, care by the Serrll?"

"It is a protectorate."

That simple statement told Zor-Ell much. The Serrll may be territorial, divided by political factions, but despite internal rivalries, they had risen above parochial interests sufficiently to nurture emerging societies. It demonstrated an unexpected level of ethical maturity and behavior.

"Of course. Don't be alarmed. I have no intention of compromising Serrll's trust by revealing my presence to them. I merely request permission to carry out a brief analysis scan."

Nicely put, Terr admitted. He could do damn little do to stop the Orieli should they wish to do more than that, and both of them knew it. Rolan TACOPSCOM maintained a triad of M-4s in the area, but he had no idea of their current movements schedule, and the situation did not call for a force multiplier here. He knew the alien's request had little to do with Earth. Any meaningful and productive future relationship between them rested on what happened here and now. He looked into Zor-Ell's large brown eyes and knew the alien had grasped it all.

This aspect of the Orieli psyche chilled him. Zor-Ell's raw intelligence seemed to comprehend things at a dizzying speed. As if reading his mind the alien smiled.

"Your caution is a credit to your duty, Da Terr, but unwarranted," he said gently, pleased that his expectations were not mistaken. It would be interesting to visit their worlds, but under first-contact protocols, clearly not possible.

Terr's mouth twitched. At how many levels was Zor-Ell playing? Formidable indeed. "Are you able to tell me something of your survey?"

"Simple curiosity. Orieli space lies beyond what you call the Moanar Nebula—"

"The Moanar!" Terr let out a silent whistle and glanced at Dhar. No wonder the Serrll hadn't encountered them before.

The nebula was one of nine super gas filaments that girthed the inner and outer galactic cores—a 6,800 light-year-long barrier to anyone rash enough to venture into its deeps. A stellar nursery of staggering proportions and furious star formation, but also forbidding and deadly; full of ices, organics and metals, highly charged and extremely reactive plasma flows churned by raging magnetic fields. There were regions of intensely hot and dense gas, some up to eleven million degrees. Normally the gas mass too thin to cause gravitational instability, but given the nebula's average cross-sectional thickness of four hundred light-years the mass profile invariably begins to affect a ship's field precursor when transiting through it. Penetrating deeper, the general mass density eventually causes the field to decay and collapse. Once a ship is forced to drop normal the surrounding mass potential prevents transition into faster than light speed, effectively stranding anybody unlucky enough to be caught inside the nebula, doomed to try limping out at sublight speed. The Serrll lost ships trying to bore through and Terr suspected the Orieli hadn't fared any better.

"You went around it?"

"No, the nebula is simply too enormous a barrier, and we never had a compelling inclination to come this way before. Its complex gravitational and energy fields defeat even our technology. We located a temporary breach, a tear if you like, allowing us passage through it. Given its fortuitous discovery, OSCOM decided to explore the other side. The breach could close and we might not have another opportunity to visit this side for some time."

From Sol, the Moanar was some three thousand lights away. The Orieli have traveled a long way indeed. Terr wanted to ask whether more than one ship came through, when he realized the obvious and chuckled. For such a major undertaking, of course, more than one ship would be sent.

"When you emerged, had you shifted your course a mere ten degrees to port, you would have encountered our worlds."

Zor-Ell became momentarily distracted and the seemingly innocent remark set off faint alarms. *Okama* had the adjacent portside survey cone. Why hadn't they come across the Serrll? He lacked information to form an opinion and worrying about it solved nothing.

"Perhaps this is a better outcome?" he suggested meaningfully.

Terr appreciated the inference. Landing on a Palean or Sargon world would have caused a sensation. This contact would be sensational enough once the news broke. Besides, everyone needed time to step back and digest the implications.

"As to your next question, Terr, Orieli space extends along the local arm of The Arch, as you call the galaxy. We occupy some thirteen hundred systems. Our real home is a globular cluster twelve thousand light-years above the galactic plane. The Orieli Cluster holds nineteen hundred inhabited, unified systems."

Terr tried not to gawk. With those innocent words, Zor-Ell had quickly sketched the relative dimensions of their respective cultures, economies, social structure and military potential. Three thousand two hundred systems? The Serrll's 247 systems, not counting seventy-four protectorates and outposts, paled into insignificance beside such numbers. The Executive Council will deliver breach kittens. Perhaps a good thing the Moanar stood between them.

"How do you traverse the distance to the cluster, sir?" Dhar asked and Zor-Ell looked at Karth.

"We maintain several transport portal nodes throughout The Arch. Each portal is powered by an artificial quantum point instability anchored to a local star," Karth explained and licked his lips

"A singularity?"

Karth grinned. "Not exactly, as the locus is not a collapsed mass. It is more akin to a leakage, a rip in the fabric of the multi-dimensional space-time continuum that is allowed to momentarily fluctuate in place. The resulting energy discharge is harvested and channeled to the portal interface conventionally."

Terr was sure there was nothing conventional about it, at least not to him.

"Most of our ships are powered by such an energy source," Karth added dryly, enjoying the reaction from the aliens.

Terr cleared his throat. He sat on top of an artificial black hole? Zor-Ell smiled at his expression.

"It's safe, I assure you. Any failure in the support system and the rip would instantly evaporate."

"And if it didn't?"

"The physical laws underpinning the process forbid any other result. Theoretically, it's possible that under certain circumstances the fissure could momentarily jump into normal four-dimensional space. Massless, there is no gravitational flux or event horizon and the fissure would instantly collapse."

"I'm relieved to hear it," Terr remarked dryly, allowing himself a sardonic grin. He wanted to ask something, but refrained. If the quantum point drew its energy from a multi-dimensional rip, why anchor it to a star? That presented another problem for him. How did they overcome frame dragging of the local space-time induced by the star's gravity well? Of course, the portal's entry/exit aperture did not have to be near the quantum point rip. However the Orieli did it, the system certainly beat antimatter reactors. He figured that BueTech would have a lot to mull over.

Zor-Ell studied his down-to-earth visitor, then leaned forward. "Terr, your interlingua data pack has given us a small, but tantalizing glimpse into the Serrll Combine and its culture. The information is welcomed and we'll examine it thoroughly. For reasons I am sure you'll appreciate, apart from sending you a brief primer, I regret that I'm not able to reciprocate more fully. At least not now."

Normal first-contact procedure forbade further interaction, but Zor-Ell had more pressing concerns. Discovery of the Celi-Kran presented a genuine strategic threat to the Serrll, which OSCOM would need to consider carefully before engaging them further.

"I take it you won't be visiting our worlds?"

"Future contact between us needs to be evaluated at many levels, by both of us. You must understand the need for that."

Terr understood, all right. He might not be up on the latest first-contact protocols, but he knew enough to guess the disruption and possible hysteria that could ensue at the appearance of the Orieli ship on Captal. Appropriate public conditioning, by everybody, had to be done before formal contact could be considered. Terr figured it would probably require more conditioning on the Serrll's part than the Orieli's.

He looked curiously at the alien. Were the Serrll too primitive to warrant attention by the Orieli? Perhaps not primitive, but certainly insular. After more than five thousand years of comfortable expansion, Orieli superiority would come as a rude shock, and certainly a threat to some.

Definitely more conditioning.

Sympathetic to his dilemma, Zor-Ell continued. "My invitation to you and Da Dharaklin is not intended to demonstrate our social or technical superiority, or alarm Captal with the fact of our presence in your space, but as a genuine gesture of friendliness with an expectation of peaceful future cultural exchange. I anticipate that both of us will benefit from such a relationship."

Terr didn't need to have the argument elaborated. "You're right, of course, Karhide. Premature contact without adequate preparation would cause unwarranted alarm. I can only trust that your primer will go some way toward ameliorating that. Speaking personally, and I hate to say it, but right now the Serrll may not be ready to embrace a new, and what I would like to consider, powerful friend."

Zor-Ell smiled with genuine pleasure. If this alien was an authentic example of Serrll's culture, the Orieli could look forward to a profitable exchange. However, Terr's attitude may not reflect that of the Serrll government or its general population. Nothing to be done until time came to instigate the next contact protocol phase.

"I wouldn't hesitate for a moment to visit your worlds, Terr, if the genuine acceptance you showed us was reflected within the entire Serrll Combine."

"But since I don't represent the Serrll..."

"I regret that our exchange at this time has to be out of necessity brief."

"Satisfying my curiosity will have to be deferred. I understand," Terr said and rose. "Karhide Zor-Ell, the Serrll awaits formal contact with the Orieli Technic Union with anticipation."

They exchanged small pleasantries and Karth escorted them back to the hangar deck. He didn't allow them to keep the spheres, which Terr thought was too bad. The access tube retracted and the Orieli ship immediately moved off, a black shadow that momentarily cut a hole through the stars and it vanished. On the main deck, Terr waited for the tube hatch to cycle and clasped his hands behind his back.

"Imagine it. They came through the Moanar."

"It could become somewhat uncomfortable for them should that breach close while they are still on this side," Dhar commented ironically and Terr chuckled.

"I dare say. Still, they can always go over it if things fall apart. Might take them some time to get home, but better than stuck inside the nebula." He shot Dhar a sidewise glance. "In the long run, you know what I'd do?"

Dhar grinned, used to Sankri's mind-probing outrageous scenarios. "I would set up a transport portal at each end. It wouldn't matter then if the breach collapsed."

"You got it. Not our problem, though. Prepare an initial

data pack brief for Anabb. He'll want to alert the Bureau of Colonial and Protectorate Affairs."

"The worthy Scholar may have already done that for us in our absence, my brother."

Terr looked pained. "Don't spoil what has otherwise been a great day, okay?"

"We should also warn Serrll Moon Base," Dhar plowed on, walking into the cable-tube.

"You're spoiling my day…"

Pleased to see his brother in such high spirits, Dhar felt unconcerned by the wave of political and personal consterna-tion bearing down on Captal and Fleet command. Sankri seemed to relish the prospect of witnessing the ensuing chaos. Dhar suspected that his brother harbored a sardonic streak of mischievous cruelty. Cruelty or not, he realized the impact of this simple innocent meeting would be profound, and whose effects were likely to alter the Serrll forever. He glanced at Sankri wearing a satisfied smirk and nodded. Let chaos begin, it said.

On the command deck, they saw no sign of the overbear-ing Laraiana, for which Terr was extremely grateful, his patience exhausted through constant placating of her petty pouting. He slid heavily onto the central couch, gave a long sigh and looked through the nav bubble. The Orieli ship gone, the stars stared at him with cold indifference. Maybe now, he could get some sleep!

"Resume our base course and get SMB, will you?" he or-dered and rubbed his eyes.

First Scout Patrlin looked wary, regarding Terr through the comms plate. His thin tongue flickered from his mouth in a low hiss.

"Is it true what Scholar Laraiana reported?" Patrlin de-manded without any preliminaries.

Terr bridled, too weary to play the game. "I don't know what Scholar Laraiana reported—"

"If you're insolent, Agent Terr—"

"First Scout, I called you as a courtesy to advise you that I encountered an alien vessel and I wanted to let you know that they're heading your way. Scholar Laraiana had no business contacting you, and whatever she might have said is irrelevant."

Patrlin gave a slow hiss. "You're right, of course, and I apologize, but the way she put it—"

"I can imagine how she put it. Forget it."

"The aliens, they're coming to Sol?"

"That's right. They detected an emission trace from SMB's power core and wanted to check it out. Since Earth—"

"I understand. Do they intend to make contact with me?"

"I don't know that, but it doesn't seem likely."

"Why not? As the Serrll representative—"

"They're not interested in us, First Scout, at least not at this time. Their immediate interest is Earth."

"Earth? The place is nothing but a backward outpost."

"On which we've been keeping an eye on for over three thousand years," Terr reminded him. "The Orieli are on a survey mission and Earth is a curiosity. They'll be getting around to us in due course, you can count on it, but not right now."

Patrlin's tongue flicked out. "Allow us to assimilate the idea of a superior civilization, is that it? Very well, Agent Terr. We shall see what happens when they get here. You wouldn't know when I should expect them, do you?"

"This is only a guess, but I would say within four to six hours."

"Oh?"

"I would be surprised if they weren't capable of at least an M-4's boost."

"Mmm. You will send me a data pack, just in case?"

"Within the hour."

"Very well," Patrlin hissed and cut contact.

Terr glared at the main plate and bit his lip. "Rit! What's with the Karkans anyway?"

Dhar grinned and shrugged. "Just antisocial, I suppose."

"Yeah. I'm going below. Call me when you've got that data pack brief done. No more aliens, all right?"

Chapter Three

"Thunderation! I send him on a simple assignment to dispose of a piece of museum trash, and what does he do? He drags in aliens!" Anabb complained bitterly and Enllss laughed, enjoying the intelligence director's earthy version of humor.

"Come on, Anabb, you're consumed at the prospect of getting your hands on the Orieli."

"Like hell I'm consumed."

"Like hell you're not," Enllss shot back, vastly amused as he watched his protégé fulminate, although he found little amusement in the situation. It was also the reason why they were having this conference. The ripples were still to be felt, but as they expanded to touch the various government bureaus and the Serrll Combine at large, he suspected his days would not be dull, and he did have other things to do. His Bureau not directly impacted by the Orieli's appearance, apart from the fact they surfaced at a Serrll protectorate, but he couldn't wash his hands off the contact. Every Bureau within the Executive Council was interlinked, and he didn't want miss anything that might affect his portfolio. Well, that's why he had a staff to do his worrying for him.

Anabb squirmed in his seat, torn between two conflicting interests. As head of the Diplomatic Branch, he should maintain focus on his area of responsibility and not be distracted by side issues, regardless of how tantalizing they might be. Rationalizing would not remove the fact that he *was* consumed by appearance of the Orieli, intensely so. Thunderation, who wouldn't be? And the flow-on effect on his Branch? Probably none; not immediately anyway, and not unless the Orieli decided to set up camp somewhere within the Serrll, which he didn't consider likely. Even then it would properly be a matter for the Bureau of Defense and CAPFLTCOM, Captal Fleet Command, to handle. Not discounting reverberations on a personal level, macro effects on the Serrll social fabric must be considered, intertwined as they were with the economic and political fallout. The difficulty, apart from the Orieli primer and the preliminary analysis data pack young Terr transmitted, they knew precious little about their visitors. What they did know was disturbing enough. Disturbing or not, Anabb felt glad it wasn't his problem, but the development wasn't going to stop him from enjoying the ensuing furor.

Observing the byplay between Enllss and his irascible Branch director, Sill-Anais less sanguine about the impact the Orieli would have on Captal. When the nuances played themselves out, and that shouldn't take too long, the strategic implications could be unsettling. Would it be business as usual or would this contact serve to trigger events not in Captal's best interest, or those of the Revisionist Party coalition? When he thought of Captal's interest, he meant the Serrll as a whole, of course. He maintained a holistic approach, a mandatory requirement of his position. Lamentably, it did not mean everyone shared his outlook. Given the current fallout over Lemos, he had more than a passing concern how Sargon and the Paleans would react to the news; in particular, Ed-Kani Takao and Ti Inai, the movers behind the Sargon/Palean merger. Another dimension that someone in his department should look into.

Eventually the Path would sustain them, he thought comfortably.

At the moment, his problem had little to do with the Orieli or the impact the contact would have on Serrll's political factions. He missed his partner. Living alone in his spacious Captal apartment, although luxurious and more than adequate for their needs, didn't make up for the empty side of the bed or still the echoes of silence that followed him from room to room. She was on a pilgrimage to Deklan, attending the Kall-oon festival. A priest of the Path, he should have been with her, and he burned with silent guilt at having been remiss in this most crucial religious observance. Six long years since he last stood in the shadow of the ancient shrine seeking absolution, for his sins were many. Unfortunately, the unremitting demands of his job kept him chained to Captal. An excuse, he knew, and the realization did nothing to salve his conscience.

He also missed his sons, his digits. Not to have them underfoot, for both were grown men now, but an opportunity to engage in sober talk. Like sands flowing between outstretched fingers, he suspected he'd allowed that moment to pass as well. One a Third Scout grade two, and Sill didn't even know where he was. The eldest still on Deklan, a Junior Councilor in Anall-Marr's administration after having graduated from the Ecumenical Seminary, majoring in strategic studies. He felt a moment of sinful pride that at least one of his offspring was wise enough to walk in his father's footsteps and joined the Diplomatic Corps. He did not begrudge the choice his other son made. He understood well that the young were impetuous and sought to explore the marvels of creation, away from well-meaning, but stifling parental control. It did not mean he liked it. Truncated and out of sync, that's what he was, as Enllss once said.

He muttered the fourth litany of subservience and prayed for guidance.

"At least this development will take the focus off Lemos and the Paleans for a time, Anabb. Ach!" Sill added with a wintry smile, absently running stiff fingers through his hair. The twin bands of gray glittered like silver before they settled back into place. His face, pinched and dry beneath an olive complexion, bore creases of responsibility. He shifted his two-katalan-tall wiry frame and sighed. "It should help to screen some of your ongoing clandestine operations against Palean raiders."

Anabb frowned and adjusted his bulk more comfortably. The formchair squirmed beneath him in sympathy. Looking at them, Enllss and Sill could be sitting side by side behind the same desk. The full-dimensional Wall image nearly seamless. What betrayed the fact they were in different rooms were their backgrounds. Behind Enllss the sprawl of Captal's skyline glittered in evening dusk while some of the gloom surrounding Celean Park hung heavy in Sill's window screen.

"I'd be happy if I only had raiders to contend with, but chasing down links to the Alikan Union Party cells has muddied the waters."

"But necessary, ach! Somebody must be providing them with financial and logistical support."

"Stands to reason, but if we simply clamped down on them, any political dimension would disappear."

"Let's not lose our focus, Anabb," Sill reminded him sternly. "Ach! Use of raiders as an expression of political policy cannot be tolerated. If AUP cells or this Provisional Committee are using raiders to affect targeted planetary economies, I want them doing it on Cantor, not against innocent carriers."

Anabb grunted and shifted in his seat. He couldn't argue the point because essentially, Sill was correct. Raiders were vermin and freebooters to be exterminated like any other household pest. When a political organ started using them as a tactical tool to influence a system's course of action, that definitely stepped over the line. Just because Lemos and Italan were exposed did not necessarily mean the machinery that created them was dismantled, confident this Provisional Committee would strike again. One operation he recently started appeared tailor-made as another test for Terr and his shadow Dhar. He derived momentary pleasure as he imagined Terr's caustic reaction to the assignment and the challenges he would face.

"Since we're talking of focus, I received a complaint from Scholar Laraiana," Enllss said with an amused glint in his gray eyes, and Anabb raised a bushy eyebrow. "Several complaints to be exact. She wasn't very happy when Terr canceled all flights to Earth and commandeered her GS-4 shuttle."

"She was breaking my heart," Anabb growled, his chiseled face stamped in a prominent scowl of disapproval. "I put her in place when she came sniveling to me. Besides, it wasn't her shuttle. Assigned to her program perhaps, but the boy had a job to do."

"And bungled it!"

"A matter of perspective, Enllss." Anabb glared and amber flecks glittered their warning in the brown pools of his eyes. A ragged blue-veined burn from a phase rifle creased his left cheek. He knew he should remove it, but it served as a useful intimidation tool. In his position, every advantage counted. "What I meant to say before you interrupted, Laraiana had no business throwing her weight around. If he has bitten her head off, she probably deserved it."

Enllss shook his head in exasperation. "Terr's job, Anabb, has disrupted Scholar Laraiana's critical review program and caused a stir in the Assembly. His high-handed tactics and her complaints could set into motion several long-term repercussions not altogether desirable, and I'm not talking only about Earth. The incident has shaken dust off some old skeletons best left buried."

"Too many skeletons in Captal already. Getting rid of some will clear the air. Anyway, we only have her word that he was high-handed. Besides, it only delayed her work, and eliminating the C-32 had priority. As far as I am concerned, the genetic engineering program is a dead issue. The damage, if I can put it that way, was already done by the meddling we finished some three thousand years ago."

Enllss grinned; he couldn't help himself. Anabb's outspoken take-no-prisoners approach was refreshing, but also dangerous. Anabb had still to learn that Captal could not be manipulated along planned military lines. Or perhaps he refused to embrace the obfuscating protocol relished by so many that not only served to take up time, but actually designed to avoid confronting issues? Something to ponder on. Perhaps it *had* been a good idea to shift his Branch to Taltair. Anabb rampaging through Captal's corridors of power caused more than one bureaucrat to go pale.

"I don't want to debate history, Anabb," he said and thrust out his square jaw to emphasize the statement. His aquiline nose protruded sharply above a firm mouth. He might be tending toward getting a bit on the heavy side lately, time to visit the gym more, but he still carried himself with authority. "Scholar Laraiana may be an officious pain, but her review is an integral component in ongoing monitoring of Earth's progress. What you need to keep in mind is that we maintain other protectorates, and her work supports broader objectives."

Anabb raised an inquiring eyebrow. "You're telling me we're still meddling—"

"I'm not telling you anything," Enllss countered smoothly. "Remember, this is still a delicate subject for the government. Some Deklan and Palean religious orders hold radical views on what they regard as interference in the natural order of things…sorry, Sill."

"Ach! No need to apologize. The Ecumenical Order officially frowns on such extreme interpretation of dogma—"

"But not enough to stop the raiding of ecoforming worlds," Anabb said to his boss, and Sill frowned.

A touchy and complex issue, which he found troubling, especially when he was still to clearly define his personal position. Habitable, ready to occupy worlds were scarce, and ecoforming provided an invaluable tool that supported Serrll's expansion and colonization program. Intellectually, he understood and supported the policy, but many Ecumenical Order hardliners viewed the practice as nothing less than blasphemous, and extremists actually attacked ecoforming stations. Although following a different ideology, many Paleans shared in condemning what they saw as disrupting the divine order and carried out raids brutal in the extreme.

"Some things cannot be solved overnight, Anabb. Ach! As a government the Deklan Ecumenical Synod does not specifically prohibit ecoforming. We have always advocated a singular policy against direct intervention in a planet's or species' normal development. On Earth, we're witnessing the fruit of our intrusion. The Path—"

"Without getting into a prolonged philosophical debate," Enllss interrupted calmly, aware of the rising temperature, "we must keep in mind that whatever their motive, in the past the Serrll government has taken certain liberties which have now returned to touch a raw social nerve. Regardless of our respective individual persuasions, I must deal with the aftermath of that legacy. We all do."

"Scholar Laraiana and her team, they were taking a holiday, eh?" Anabb prompted with a wicked smile, relishing stirring the issue. He did not consider ecoforming a problem. The current generation of hardliners would die out and their more pragmatic descendants either don't have the stomach to continue raiding or recognized the outdated futility behind it.

"It wouldn't do to underestimate her, Anabb." Enllss glared at him. "She wields some powerful Captal connections. Nothing that could hurt you directly, but her efforts could disrupt some BueCult programs. While we're talking of complaints, she was even less happy when you refused to countermand Terr's order denying her the shuttle."

"I've seen her comms. She simply wanted to push a personal agenda, is all."

"And she's put in another complaint about you when Terr brushed her aside after she requested joint access to the Orieli."

"Thunderation! I'm guilty and you can put me away."

"Take it easy, Anabb. Terr and you were both right. She had no business interfering in a Diplomatic Branch matter. Nevertheless, both of you may have made a serious enemy."

"I'll live with it."

Enllss chuckled. "I am sure you will. Ordinarily, I wouldn't be bothered with such trivia, but as my Bureau initiated her project and you were involved, I got to hear about it."

"So?"

"So, a dash of diplomacy will go a long way when greasing the wheels of Captal machinery."

"The pits you say!"

Anabb didn't have time for Captal's machinery, greasy or not. Although the Orieli contact was Enllss' problem, he had a responsibility to evaluate all possible threats against the Serrll, from *any* quarter. Right now, he dismissed Laraiana from his concerns list. She simply confirmed his image of a meddling, self-important, power-seeking busybody building her little empire over people she happened to trample on. He'd dealt with the type before and had no problem if Terr stepped on one.

"Just a friendly warning, Anabb," Enllss said, amused. "But don't be alarmed if she rears her head some time on your tactical plot. One other thing. Don't forget the upcoming General Assembly session. There is a backlog of legislation to be approved, and as a member, you need to be there."

"I haven't forgotten," Anabb growled, acknowledging the downside of having his Branch on Taltair. Still, he had little to moan about. As a representative of his system, he had a duty to make regular appearances on Captal, however personally inconvenient. Most of his Assembly responsibilities he managed to discharge through a Wall holoview hookup, but sometimes one just needed to be there.

The comms alert beeped and he tapped a pad on the desk console.

"What?"

"It's Agent Terrllss-rr, sir," Ariane announced calmly, unfazed by Anabb's blunt manner. She had grown to accept it, better than fawning politeness or coping with veiled seduction gambits. At least she knew where she stood with him. Nothing personal. He was equally mean to everybody. Although he would never admit it, she knew her boss genuinely cared for his people, not that one could tell, though.

"Hah! About time! Goofing off while we're sitting on our hands," Anabb muttered sourly. "He needs a special invitation? Patch him in."

Enllss rolled his eyes and shook his head. With Anabb's acerbic approach, it surprised him that none of his agents had him assassinated yet. By all accounts, his team were fiercely loyal, even fanatical. The way he ticked people off, it couldn't be due to hero worship. Well, Enllss figured a person had to have a special bend to be in such a job to begin with. He put it down as one of life's enigmatic phenomena, beyond unraveling. In the end it did not matter how Anabb treated his staff as long as the Diplomatic Branch continued to produce results. So far, he was satisfied. Well, almost satisfied.

A full-dimensional window opened at the bottom right corner of the Wall. Seeing them side-by-side, Anabb noted the family resemblance with Enllss. It wasn't immediately striking, but it clearly there. In the backdrop were the small sounds of an M-1 under way.

Terr felt alert and his gray eyes sparkled, but they couldn't mask his fatigue and lack of sleep. Even though Dhar did the work preparing full data packs, he had to ensure it was all properly formatted and sanitized. This would be one of those historical reports where the chair experts would debate his every word for centuries to come. He needed to be not only factually, but politically correct, and there were far too many ways to screw *that* up.

"Reporting as ordered, sir," he said crisply and Anabb snorted.

"I am glad that you managed to join us."

"Don't worry about Anabb, my boy," Enllss cut in before Terr could reply. "It's his sore-at-the-world day."

"It might not be without cause, sir," Terr said cautiously,

pleased to see his uncle. Enllss may be a powerful figure in Capital, but no one could accuse him of nepotism—even if Terr consented to such maneuvering. He'd seen it done and didn't like it. Still, nice to know he had someone with influence on call if things got particularly precarious. If he was going to be handling more of Anabb's peculiar assignments, he might be forced to use that gambit sooner rather than later. Influence was something not to be dismissed lightly. His aspect? Something altogether different. He made a bargain with the god of Death and only time would tell how that would work out.

Enllss leaned back and tilted his head, regarding his nephew with a speculative twinkle. The boy was confident, unabashed at the possible consequences of his actions, and ready to take them all on. A byproduct of his Wanderer personality? Consciously or unconsciously, the boy wielded power and it showed.

"You've been in trouble again, my boy, if I am to believe the stories."

"This time it's all true, I'm afraid," Terr said with a straight face, but could not hide the genuine affection in his voice. He reminded himself to drop in on Enllss next time he was on Capital, assignments permitting. It's been a while since he last saw his Aunty, and he wouldn't mind catching up on the latest family gossip, scandal, and floating innuendos. He also wanted to find out if his mother still denied him for joining the Fleet, instead of following in his uncle's footsteps, to her a much more acceptable career path. They hadn't spoken for, oh, years, and Aunty would know. Enllss certainly knew how things stood, but it wasn't something Terr could ask. The Llss-rr clan were a peculiar lot.

"By damn! I knew it. Anabb had you psyched."

"Don't tempt me! Entertaining as this family chitchat is, can we get on with the matter at hand?"

"Quite right. To business." Enllss nodded and cleared his throat. "You managed to keep yourself busy, son. Trouble or not, Lemos was a haul, bigger than you realize. Prime Director Kernami Asai Tainam is still gushing with praise and Ambassador Rayon Tantour had only good things to say about your efforts. Your actions have thwarted a major Sargon/Palean maneuver and placed Pizgor in Captal's debt, which we won't be shy collecting. Then you went and topped it off by capturing Tanard and exposing Italan. Controller Marrakan was very impressed."

"A fortuitous sequence of events, sir," Terr said gravely. Although pleased at the attention and subsequent promotion it got him, he knew how easily it could have all come unstuck. Success hadn't come cheap, paid with full toll: Mati and young Osinara dead, and others. Bodies and souls bruised, perhaps forever. Ships battered and scarred, also crying out their silent agony. He could see it now; Razzo throwing himself in the path of a needler bolt meant for him, still in hospital. No, it hadn't come cheap.

Looking at his uncle, Enllss evidently cared little for the human cost, busy weighing up political advantages that could be wrested from an opponent's misfortune. Terr didn't hold it against him. They simply played in different arenas and for different stakes.

"Perhaps, but the results are not."

"Can I ask what happened to Tanard?"

"The Anar'on government has taken jurisdiction, ach!" Sill snapped, clearly frustrated at having such a prize snatched from his grasp, with Tanard's wealth of intelligence now in the Unified Independent Front's hands. Although sympathetic to Sill's request for extradition, Controller Marrakan remained unmoved. When Tanard attacked *Zavian*, he made a direct assault against UIF delegates, and by extension, Anar'on itself. Sill could have him once they were through with him. Or what was left of him, he amended bitterly. With more than a passing familiarity with the Wanderer Discipline, he could count on them extracting every possible scrap of information from their hapless captives. The damned stumbling thing, legally, Captal could do nothing. Any interference in Anar'on's internal affairs would not only be futile, but would serve to raise the ire of all nonaligned independents in the Assembly. Ungodly blasphemers, all of them.

"He is hospitalized and unlikely to get his arm back. Genotherapy doesn't always work. We didn't walk away entirely empty-handed. Anar'on has thrown us one piece of vital intelligence, though. Ach! Existence of the Alikan Union Party Provisional Committee running him."

Terr raised an eyebrow. A secret cabal behind the Sargon/Palean merger? In Serrll's intermeshed political environment, it didn't seem possible that a lone group could manage and execute such a massive operation outside the authority of Sargon's Dumas and the Palean Congress. The movement simply too complex, too well financed and organized to be an underground conspiracy. Both governments *had* to be involved, or at least supported by enough key legislators on both sides to make the taking of Pizgor worth the risks. The fact that Tanard operated using Fleet assets tended to lend some credence to that hypothesis. Of course, Sill would be aware of all that.

Enllss waved his hand. "Tanard is no longer your concern, my boy, and we're not here to give you a pat on the back, no matter how well deserved it might be, or spoil the proceedings by your less than spectacular disposal of the C-32. We'll dissect that botch later."

"How about we dissect it now!" Anabb thundered, his voice ringing with authority. "If the Bureau of Colonial and Protectorate Affairs has a complaint about one of my operations, you can make it through the usual channels. Terr was doing his job. Any displeasure at his performance comes from me, and not from you or some desk-driving Captal snot polishing regulations. If you have a problem with that, take it up with Sill."

Sill cleared his throat and Enllss raised a hand to silence him, appraising Anabb with interest. Determination and self-assurance stood stamped in his prominent features, earned through years of command and inevitable service infighting. Anabb clearly would not stand for any interference in his Branch, even from a commissioner, and damn the consequences. Despite an occasional clash of wills, Enllss did not regret sponsoring Anabb into the General Assembly. Once the rough edges were filed down, his protégé would one day make a formidable Captal mover. When he did glance at Sill, he found little support in his friend's disapproving glare. A vivid reminder to Enllss that he no longer ran the Bureau of Cultural Affairs.

"No need to be touchy, Anabb, by damn!"

"Thunderation! If touchy—"

"Enough! Ach!" Sill interrupted and glowered at Enllss. "You and I will handle this later. Right now, we have more important things to discuss."

Enllss frowned, then turned to Terr, ignoring the coloring burn on Anabb's cheek. Terr may be his nephew, but what happened on Earth could not be swept under a rug. Only the fact that the Russian government chose not to publicize Terr's capture saved him from some very unpleasant proceedings, which could have resulted in the loss of his commission and worse.

"For the moment at least, your contact with the Orieli overshadows any issues I may have with your handling of the C-32. Not to mention a new headache its unorthodox disposal has given my Bureau. Your report, my boy, better be complete in every respect, but Sill is right. We have a more pressing item to deal with. Until you reach Taltair, I want you to liaise with a team from the Bureau of Central Planning and Development on everything you learned about the Orieli."

"Full analysis packs are getting prepared, sir," Terr said cautiously, embarrassed at witnessing a family fight and not wanting to be splattered by any shrapnel from Captal. Enllss noticeably sore at him over the C-32, he appreciated Anabb's support. Perhaps the evil old fart had a heart after all. Could Enllss be feeling pressure from the Executive Council over Laraiana's mission? It didn't seem likely. Her work couldn't be that important. Whatever the reason, it might be a good idea to lie low for a while and not attract attention to himself.

"Useful enough," Enllss agreed, "but the material must be interpreted, and you and Agent Dharaklin are our experts at hand, unless you have some pressing business to attend to before you hit Taltair?"

Terr noted the warning and shook his head. Promotion or not, to Enllss, he was still very much a junior agent. There were many traps lying in wait to snare the unwary innocent officer, which could see him herding an oiler on the Cantor run.

"No, sir."

"Glad to hear it," Enllss said and stared at Anabb, letting him know that his outburst would not be forgotten. "Anything from the Serrll Moon Base?"

"The Orieli hardly paused as they overflew the Moon," Anabb replied gruffly, annoyed that Enllss had pulled such a stunt. Most of the time, Enllss chose to hang a congenial look on his face, but it would not pay to underestimate the Commissioner. The way he heard it, if you made Enllss an enemy, better get out of town.

Ah, to perdition with him! He had his own problems.

"When they approached Earth, their ship simply vanished. The SMB lost track and could not reacquire. At least they kept their promise about not revealing themselves to Earth's prying eyes."

"And ours as well. Ach! Nasty business, that. As a military expert, can you account for it, Anabb?"

"Must be their funny defense grid. It must somehow absorb all sensor pings, and it must mask the ship's power emission signature as well."

"Nothing funny about it. Ach! And to have the M-1's

screen neutralized? I wonder how they did it, and how far they can project the effect?" Sill speculated and shook his head. "I can tell you this. When the Bureau of Defense hears of it, they'll howl. The Orieli may appear friendly enough now, but should that position change, it would place the Serrll Combine in a most invidious position."

"If I can venture an observation?" Terr said diffidently, knowing he risked a reprimand sticking his nose into commissioner-level discussions.

"Spill it," Anabb ordered.

"During my stay aboard their ship, nothing suggested the Orieli harbor any covert intentions. I admit it could have been an elaborate ploy on their part to deceive me, but frankly, I don't see it. Karhide Zor-Ell—"

"Karhide?" Enllss prompted.

"Equivalent to a Master Scout," Anabb snapped. "You should read his report."

Enllss glared at him. "One day, Anabb…"

"Thunderation! Go on, boy."

"Zor-Ell and Opturkarh Karth were genuinely friendly and intensely interested in us. I might have missed some subtleties in their body language, but neither showed anything I could construe as deliberate misdirection."

Enllss chewed his lower lip. "Maybe they're so powerful they didn't need to be subtle. With thirteen hundred systems on the other side of the Moanar, why should they be interested in occupying us? But that's something else for BueDef to agonize over, and I don't envy them the dilemma. Too bad you didn't have a first-contact specialist on board, my boy. Tell me. Will the Orieli be heading for Captal?"

"They will not, sir."

Enllss raised an eyebrow. "They discover a major spacefaring civilization and promptly decide to ignore us? That doesn't make any sense!" He gave Terr a speculative stare, then grinned slowly. "You wouldn't happen to be keeping something from us, are you?"

Terr chuckled, amused at the workings of a bureaucratic mind. Did Enllss think he sought another promotion? He was still getting over the last one.

"I wouldn't do that to you, Uncle, even if the thought had occurred to me."

"By damn!"

"What does occur to me, despite appearing friendly the Orieli are still alien," Terr said, letting them work it out.

"Thunderation! He's right. We're not in a position to understand their methods or the psychology behind them."

Sill looked thoughtful, ran a hand through his hair and leaned forward. "Ach! What *are* the Orieli's intentions, Agent Terr?"

"As far as I can gather, sir, despite Zor-Ell's interest in us and their desire to establish formal relations, it will be at some unspecified time in the future. He didn't elaborate, expecting us to understand."

"Understand what?" Sill demanded.

Terr suppressed a flash of annoyance. Everyone seems to have forgotten everything they knew about first-contact procedures and were expecting him to bail them out. Reluctantly, he realized he was being uncharitable. It wasn't like the Serrll were making contact with a new civilization every day. Still…But if he made a mistake in his analysis, he knew who would wear the blame. Highly unlikely that Enllss would rely on his amateurish conclusions. Enllss had experts of his own to make amateurish conclusions.

Rit!

Enllss pulled at his chin and nodded slowly. "Of course. Time for both of us to evaluate the impact of our contact and adjust to any political and social dislocation it might cause."

"There is something else to consider, if I may," Terr added. "Zor-Ell is intelligent in the extreme."

Enllss snorted. "And we might not be in their league, is that it? A good point, my boy, very good. Well, bound to happen sooner or later. I'm only surprised it hasn't happened already. With this Pizgor and Lemos business going on right now, it would have been more convenient if they'd picked another time. I guess we take our lumps as they come. Your casual remarks were very useful, my boy. Now you see why I want you on the Central Planning team?"

Terr sighed in resignation. "Yes, sir, I'm afraid I do, but I don't know what more I can add that will not be already in my briefing data pack."

"I wouldn't worry too much. Central Planning will know what questions to ask and you'll be surprised at how much you know. This has priority. If necessary, you and Dhar will be recalled to Captal. Am I clear?"

Anabb bridled, but kept his peace. He might not like Enllss' interference, and he didn't, but he was shrewd enough to realize that for a multitude of reasons, some of them even valid, evaluation of the Orieli contact too important to play bureaucratic games. Judging by Sill's sour look, the Commissioner for the Bureau of Cultural Affairs understood it as well.

"Aye, sir," Terr said with a marked lack of enthusiasm. He'd had run-ins with Central Planning's excitable, darting little men before and did not look forward to another dose of brain peeling. At least Nightwings would be with him to share the pain if it came to that and the realization made him feel better.

Enllss regarded his nephew with scant sympathy and gave him an evil smile. "Look at it this way, my boy. It will keep you out Scholar Laraiana's way."

Terr groaned. "Great! That'll make up for everything."

Chapter Four

Valon broke out of subspace high above the ecliptic with barely a ripple in the background gravitational flux streaming from Sol like a gale. The star shone brilliant yellow, a sink that distorted space itself, which could trap anyone venturing too close. Clad in swirling snowy clouds, Earth blazed like a suspended blue jewel, cutting a sharp crescent against the black deeps. In quarter phase the gray Moon looked inordinately large tucked behind its parent's shadow. At half standard boost the ship slanted down into the system.

Hooked through the VI coupling, Zor-Ell studied the characteristic antimatter energy bloom that hugged the Moon's northern pole and slowly nodded. The Serrll really should shield their power grid. If he could detect it from nine light-years off, the Celi-Kran certainly would. The power emission a dead 'I am here' beacon. Then again, so was Earth's incessant outpouring of carrier wave streams. The bottom line? There was simply no effective way to shield an emerging civilization from the Krans, or anybody else, for that matter, who happened to be looking. Should those animated constructs venture into this part of the galaxy, he feared the Serrll wouldn't be able to stop them. Well, he couldn't do anything, and it was unlikely the Krans would come boiling out of subspace anytime soon.

In the mainframe plot, purple rings of energy rippled in pulses from the alien base, speeding through subspace, waiting to strike resistance from gravitational distortion left by an object, moving or still. Fainter green cones of radiated signals surrounded Earth in expanding spikes—active high-frequency carrier wave emissions—searchlights probing the skies. The planet awash with them.

"At IP, two million ampirs, Karhide," Cent Comp announced quietly. "Tactical caution. Detecting nav scans from the Serrll Moon Base. No belligerency indicated. Navigational net now polarized. Status. Primary interceptor net down. Condition one on passive standby. Maintaining course for Earth orbital insertion."

"Very well," Zor-Ell acknowledged the mental transmission without showing any external reaction. The computer didn't bother reporting Earth's primitive radar sweeps, but he had nothing to worry about there.

With the nav screen polarized, *Valon* effectively disappeared from the SMB's tracking sensors, their pings absorbed by the complex frequency modulation of the net. The effect no doubt, causing the alien operators to scratch their heads and Captal's CAPFLTCOM would definitely be doing far more than that. *Valon* didn't go stealthy to confound the Serrll, but to ensure it remained undetected by Earth's ground observatories and military satellites. Zor-Ell had a promise to keep. He wondered how diligent the Serrll were at keeping theirs, but it was unlikely Earth had the necessary technology to detect subspace transmissions. If he believed the information in Terr's data pack, that deficiency might be remedied relatively soon. Then again there were all those visual sightings of Serrll ships to consider. Joyriding in violation of quarantine directives? It wouldn't be anything new and the Orieli labored under similar problems with its protectorates. Too bad that procedures prevented him visiting Captal, but young Terr was correct. Everyone should sit back and consider the implications.

When the ship closed to half a million ampirs, Earth started showing discernible topographical features. On the night side, sprawling clusters of light lit the northern hemisphere. Clearly, someone was home.

"Cent Comp, show orbital tracks," Karth ordered and immediately the VI image of Earth became surrounded by hundreds of points in elliptical orbits crisscrossing each other in a numbing profusion of lines. The image replicated in holoview repeater displays and Operations below him.

Karth glanced at his commander and grinned. "If we're not careful going in, one of those things is bound to run us over. It's been a while since I've seen such clutter."

"Mmm. Looks like a ball of yarn all right," Zor-Ell agreed. Staggering volumes of data streamed out from spaceborne and surface transmitters, but were nonetheless diligently recorded by Cent Comp for later analysis by specialists back on Zaron. Data storage would never be a problem where quantum mediums held bit states at photon levels. He allowed sensor images pouring through the VI coupling to wash over him: cities, power grids, road infrastructure, ships, and aircraft. It was a thriving world.

"Entering low polar orbit. Holding at three hundred ampirs," Cent Comp advised.

The ship slowed and slid smoothly into position, getting an ongoing assist from the planet's rotation that required using minimal power to maintain station. By taking a polar rather than equatorial orbit, the planet would slowly rotate beneath them, allowing for detailed mapping and sensor scans of the entire surface.

"Launching Burlig scanners…data interfaces enabled and functional." On the forty-degree north and twenty-degree south latitude lines, the ship commenced dropping sensor probes at thirty-degree intervals, blanketing the globe.

Earth hung above them, huge and brilliant.

Zor-Ell waited until the ship crossed the terminator into its dark embrace, rubbed his chin and looked at Karth.

"From data we've already gathered, what does this place tell you?"

Still hooked into the VI, Karth raised an eyebrow, not

minding playing the game. "The most significant? I'd say captured carrier transmissions in multiple languages. Although not conclusive, it's indicative of territorial rivalry and lack of an integrated central governing body. They achieved nuclear capability and probably applied it to military systems. With all that baggage, I can understand why the Serrll have not established formal contact. It might be a truism, but regional suspicions generally preclude trust and cooperation. Appearance of alien ships would have only highlighted those suspicions. Despite evident technological progress, to me, Earth is still likely to be tribal."

"Probably, and as a consequence, aggressively territorial," Zor-Ell added pensively. "Which also means, it's unlikely to follow a cohesive, ethically structured standard of behavior." A fascinating step into history, and he felt a stirring of interest that brought back a rush of memories, memories of his first career.

"Likely, but not necessarily true," Karth countered. "A martial culture can have a highly developed philosophy and ethics. Our own history is replete with such examples."

"Although true, you forgot something. Most of those examples also show that while ethical behavior is expected from the population at large and generally adhered to, but when threatened, ethics is the first casualty of expediency. When you add sophisticated weaponry, that society risks self-annihilation. Our history has one or two such examples as well."

"Agreed, but that scenario cannot be automatically applied to Earth," Karth remarked, pushing the argument.

"Perhaps not, but I fear you'd be disappointed. Trust me. Every classic indicator is there." Zor-Ell turned to fully face his first officer. "This place is intriguing. It's like looking into Zaron's distant past. We were also ethically aware, materially prosperous, but still driven by a species identity, personal power and domination through application of military and economic force."

"If I remember, that philosophy served Zaron well. You

used it to conquer the Orieli Cluster," Karth added dryly and his tongue whipped around his lips.

Zor-Ell cocked an eyebrow. "Was there a veiled hint of criticism in that remark?"

"Far be it for me to infer unethical behavior by the old Zaron Concordiat."

"Mmm. It wasn't exactly our finest period in history."

"And you see parallels with Earth?"

"Some. They cannot simply blow each other up; too disruptive for business. Especially as they appear to have reached a point where previously military objectives are now subordinated to global economic drivers, but the extremist elements in their society makes them vulnerable."

"You could say the same thing about the Serrll."

"To a degree, but the Serrll were already integrated interstellar blocks when they came across each other. Their road to unity has been mostly paved, although not necessarily smoothly. They have their territorial, economic, and religious rivalries, but they learned to control their excesses. With Earth, on the other hand, they're probably aware of the terminal consequences inherent in tribal behavior, and despite their intellect, their ethics may not be ingrained enough to stop them from using destructive technology in pursuit of those instincts. Sometimes mutual annihilation is an acceptable price if it delivers total defeat to an enemy."

"A dangerous combination, Karhide."

"That it is, especially if you have the weapons to do it with. Frankly, Earth fascinates me. I keep going over Terr's data pack. Think of it. In two hundred and fifty years, they progressed from an agricultural society into a global economy. And they also ventured into space. We could learn much by giving them a closer look. What this place needs is an Observer."

To follow through on his idea entailed a level of risk, to himself and the Orieli. Discovering the Celi-Kran, he was duty-bound to alert OSCOM. He also needed to consider crew morale. *Valon* had ventured far from the stars of home and he would be on his way back were it not for the Serrll. Can he legitimately delay for twenty days to indulge a personal curiosity? It wouldn't be altogether personal. The Orieli *could* learn a lot from Earth.

Karth blanched in alarm. "I know that look, Da! This was supposed to be a flyby scan only, not a full-blown survey. Besides, we're out of Observers."

"Not quite," Zor-Ell replied softly and Karth's face twisted in consternation.

"You? The last time you were an active Observer was when, fifteen years ago?"

"Something like that, but I still know how."

"A long time to be out of action. There have been a slew of new procedures, protocols, and updates since then."

"We owe them a closer look, Karth. Isn't that why we're out here?"

"That gambit won't work, Karhide. You cannot abandon your command."

"I won't be abandoning anything. It's only a TDY."

"Temporary duty? That's what OSCOM will consider your command when we get back."

"You worry too much. Plot a least-time course to pick up our Observers. By the time you get back, I'll be done," Zor-Ell said, brooking no interference.

"Is that an order, Da?" Karth asked carefully.

"It is."

* * *

Fully shielded and immune from radar detection, the dart glided over the rolling Australian landscape, another silent ghost in a silent autumn night. A partial Moon glowed bright in the northern sky. Hiding somewhere below the eastern horizon, Melbourne betrayed its presence with buttery light reflected off drifting clouds. Overhead, stars shone clear and sharp, a thick band of creation that humbled the pretentious efforts of mere mortals.

Taroptur Coni lifted his head from the bioscan display and glanced at the crewman sitting beside him.

"All right! We have a body, male and alone. Appears to be camping out. Take us down slow."

"Down slow, aye, Da."

For what Coni wanted, any warm body would do. He hadn't deliberately chosen Australia as his target. The dart's orbital insertion and descent happened to take him in that direction. Come in, grab someone hot, and get out without creating a fuss. That was the objective. A lone camper, isolated from any settlement and prying eyes…perfect. He'd carried out retrievals before and the procedure now routine. What was not routine, the Old Man himself would be doing this mission. Coni knew, everybody did, the karhide had once been an active Observer and an expert in symbiotic social structures before transferring to line command, but to actually go out again? Earth must really be tickling his curiosity. After anticipating a quick return home, the ship would now be delayed while the karhide indulged in a bit of nostalgia. Well, it definitely gave everyone a discussion topic. The survey had given him his share of excitement and wonder, and he wasn't hankering for more. It was a while since he'd seen his family.

Still, orders were orders and there was no counting on what senior officers were liable to do.

Nestled against the forest with a winding creek cutting through two low hills, the campsite looked normal enough: a dark tent, gray smoke curling above glowing red embers, and a wheeled ground vehicle parked under three trees. Out on a hunting trip or soaking in some nature? After sitting cramped aboard *Valon* for one hundred and fifty days, Coni wouldn't have minded a bit of nature himself. Besides, as tactical officer, he'd had an easy time of it. *Valon* didn't end shooting anybody. There were two scary shit episodes with Kran remnants, but nothing terminal.

Hovering three kanampirs above the still meadow, he touched a glowing yellow pad on the instrument console. An invisible beam lanced at the tent. The body inside didn't move. Coni would have been surprised if it had.

"Okay, that was easy enough. Got your shield on?" he asked, his brown eyes, sunk deep in their sockets. The crewman nodded. "Down and extend the landing ramp," Coni ordered.

The dart settled and the hatch slid into the hull, revealing an opening of a square sunk on one of its corners. The landing ramp extended and angled down. Coni swiveled his seat, rose and headed for the lift-well, the crewman trailing after him. Down on the main deck, he walked to the hatch, peered out and stood on the ramp. It quickly bore him down. He felt a momentary resistance when his personal shield interacted with the dart's nav screen, then he went through. Stepping into ankle-high grass, he paused and looked around, his short stocky body alert. Nothing stirred, and thick stillness enveloped him in a dark blanket. The air felt crisp, mixed with the smell of smoke and oily redolence from the forest. He thought he could hear a faint gurgle of water, but probably only his imagination. Not a bad place to camp at all.

Getting back to business, he strode to the tent, saw the open flap and leaned in, only to strike an invisible mesh. Startled, he pulled back. Reaching into his pocket, he pulled out his energy sphere and issued a mental command. The sphere immediately glowed dull white, enough to see by, and he put it down. With both hands outstretched, he gingerly felt the mesh contours and smiled at his moment of fright. A simple insect screen, but how to get the thing open without ripping it? He couldn't see or feel anything around the edges. His powerful fingers traced the centerline down, feeling along the bottom until he found a little metal tag. He gave it an upward tug and the mesh parted with a faint rasp. He moved the tag easily all the way to the top, but that solved only part of his problem. The mesh was open in the middle, but still tied together along the bottom and top. *Space! How complicated can this get?* With more fumbling, he found two more tags on the bottom centerline that opened sidewise. Pushing aside the loose mesh, he stepped into the tent.

Slipping his hand into a side pocket, he dragged out a second sphere, shoved it into the sleeping form's shirt pocket and issued another command. Although he couldn't see it, he knew the body was now enclosed in a hugging shield and would be safe against possible contamination from *Valon's* environment or its crew—and vice versa. It was unlikely that Earth's microorganisms would find the aliens palatable, but still a risk to be studiously avoided.

Behind him, the crewman crouched and stepped into the tent. A thick blue covering draped the unconscious form of their subject. Coni reached down and pulled it to one side. With barely a glance at the young man lying on a crude mat, he looked at the crewman, who reached for the legs while Coni grabbed the figure under the arms. The limp body not heavy, but awkward maneuvering it out of the tent. Coni paused, retrieved his sphere and they shuffled toward the dart. Reaching the ramp, the crewman stopped and hissed.

"Da! On your right!"

Coni froze and slowly turned his head, expecting to see another native. All kinds of bad thoughts flashed through his mind at the prospect of such an encounter. At the edge of a shaft of light lancing from the hatch, stood a bulky four-legged beast. It had a thick, elongated head crowned by two sharp-looking horns. It shook its head, looking at them with large eyes and gave a snort. He couldn't tell if the animal was dangerous and didn't relish the prospect of finding out the hard way. He glared at the crewman and tugged.

"Quick!" he whispered fiercely and hurried up the ramp.

Once inside, they carried their subject into a cabin and laid him on a bunk. The crewman straightened and leaned against the bulkhead.

"What in stars *was* that thing?"

Coni shook his head. "I've got no idea. You want to go out and ask?"

"Me? No thanks! I'm happy for it to stay where it is."

"In that case, let's get out of here," Coni said and led the way to the lift-well.

With the landing ramp retracted, the dart slowly rose, angled west and surged toward the welcoming stars. Still below the terminator, *Valon* met the little ship and Cent Comp brought it directly into Hangar Bay Two. Coni shut down, pushed back a lock of black hair, then glanced at the crewman and made his way out. Two blue-garbed medical technicians were hovering outside the hatch and climbed past him when he stepped out, dragging a gravplate bunk in their wake.

Coni saw the first officer and walked toward him.

"Any problems, Taroptur?" Karth queried, his eyes following the technicians.

"No, Da, unless you count almost getting gored by a horned beast," Coni said casually, watching the medics emerge, their patient lying on the bunk. Ignoring everybody, they hurried toward the large cargo PT alcoves.

The first officer grinned at Coni's understated report, which reflected his casual and irreverent attitude toward all authority. Irreverent attitude or not, Karth knew that Coni's unperturbed approach to command was but a veneer of cynicism that hid a dedicated and consummate professional. His men liked him and Coni drove them unmercifully in search of perfection in the execution of their duties. The taroptur's informal treatment of his responsibilities something Karth bemoaned. All things considered, he could have done worse in a tactical officer.

"Good. Turnaround in twenty minutes. Don't go wandering off," he said and made for the smaller individual PT alcoves. He didn't like what the karhide was doing, but nobody sought his opinion. Then again, the karhide could be right. They were here to gather information on alien civilizations.

Coni shrugged and went back into the dart, figuring he might as well prep and be ready to go down.

In Medical Bay, Karth strode quickly to the Transfer Lab. Two translucent milky panels retracted into the bulkheads as he approached. Walking in, he stepped into a twisted reality. The room itself not large, having sufficient space for two hard beds separated by a console interface. The striking part were full-dimensional holoview displays beside each bed, which created windows into an infinity of multicolored information icons and data flows, making it appear he was in a much larger space. Two technicians were studying the overlay displays, occasionally exchanging comments and quick nods.

The Earthman supine on the left bed, features slack, eyes closed. Karth turned to the second bed and locked his hands behind his back. Zor-Ell lifted his head and smiled.

"Don't look so worried, Karth. I've done this once or twice before, you know."

"This is highly irregular, Karhide. For the last time, any chance that I can talk you out of it?"

"It's my decision," Zor-Ell said with finality and glanced at the other bed. "And it's a bit late for second thoughts."

The technician beside the Earthman looked up. "Malfe, we're ready to proceed."

"Very well." The senior technician glanced at Zor-Ell. "We are go, Da."

"Right. Let's do it."

Karth licked his lips, still not liking it, but a bit late for second thoughts. "In twenty days then."

Zor-Ell nodded and closed his eyes. Next time he opened them, he would be looking at a new world.

Malfe immediately touched several pads on a touch console between the two beds and a faint blue aura sprang above both subjects.

"Cent Comp?"

"Cent Comp ready."

"Enable transfer link and conduct status check."

"Transfer link enabled…Status check complete…All systems within acceptable parameters. Ready to commence memory trace."

"Commence trace," Malfe ordered. Copy of the subject's memories was a last resort backup in case something went horribly wrong.

"Memory trace completed. Ready to commence transfer buffering."

"Commence transfer."

"Transfer sequence enabled."

A furious flicker of data hashed both holoview displays. Karth could not make anything of seemingly jumbled color-coded streams, but the two technicians kept a vigilant eye on the proceedings, clearly aware of what was happening. At a basic level, Karth understood the procedure, of course. The central computer scanned Zor-Ell's memories, converted them into a data stream, and sent it into the Earthman's brain where neurons were tagged to recognize the input as permanent memories. Given that a brain can hold a lifetime of information, there was little danger of overloading the neural capacity, provided the subject was young. On transfer completion, Zor-Ell's body would remain in stasis. On mission completion the Earthman would be retrieved and Zor-Ell's accumulated memories transferred back and reintegrated into his brain, leaving the Earthman with nothing but shadows of a strange dream.

From what Karth could see, everything appeared to be proceeding normally. At least Cent Comp hadn't raised a warning, although Malfe did make a slight adjustment to the transfer rate of several data streams when the permissible bandwidth started to drift toward the amber zone. Malfe shrugged when asked why he did that. An ingrained feeling, he explained briskly, something that transcended technology.

Watching Zor-Ell surrounded by the blue aura, the karhide looked tranquil and strangely vulnerable. Karth wondered what it would be like to see through another's eyes, think with someone else's brain, always having to refrain from exerting volition over the body or intrude into the other's conscious thoughts. From what he understood, should the subject become even partially aware of another personality, it could spell disaster. Crude drugs could easily break the Observer's memory matrix and the personality would be lost. The Observer himself in no physical danger. Safely held in stasis, he could be wakened at any time, personality intact, but the mission would have failed.

A while back, Karth had puzzled about something. If they had the subject's captured memories, why go through the additional problem of imprinting and subsequent retrieval of an Observer's personality? The answer, of course, obvious. There was information and there was understanding of that information, something that could only be accomplished through active integration by an Observer. They found that one out the hard way.

Despite elaborate procedures developed over centuries of fieldwork, problems did sometimes occur. Procedures simply cannot cover every possible contingency. Life was too startling for that, as some surveys discovered. Early in its history, Observers were lost, left with a mindless body, but that ended once they fully understood how to transfer a copy of the Observer's matrix rather than stripping the brain clean.

"Operational caution," Cent Comp announced suddenly. "Data channel streams thirteen, fourteen, and twenty-three approaching transfer tolerance limit. Transfer rate reduced by eight percent. No physiological dysfunction indicated with either subject."

Malfe leaned closer to Zor-Ell's holoview display and

frowned. After a moment, seemingly satisfied, he turned to the technician monitoring the Earthman.

"Anything?"

"Data streams nominal," the technician replied.

"How is the subject's absorption rate?"

"Within the bandwidth, but I had to compensate for drift."

"So did I," Malfe mused and pulled at his chin.

"Do we have a problem?" Karth demanded and Malfe looked up.

"I don't think so, Opturkarh. The data streams feeding the primary cognition matrix layers show the subject not accepting input at the initially indicated rate and it started to affect his memory mapping. I cannot account for it. From the initial diagnostic scan the subject should be absorbing data at a faster rate. We're still within acceptable limits, and there'll be a postmortem analysis of everything as a matter of procedure, Da, but there is no immediate cause for concern. However, a matrix density test should have been done."

"So why wasn't it?" Karth said and Malfe shrugged.

"Karhide Zor-Ell didn't think it necessary. Don't worry about it."

Karth knew he should return to PFC, but there was nothing for him to do there, simple watchkeeping. In the end, he waited. After thirty-four minutes and another warning, Cent Comp announced the transfer completed. It took a further six minutes for the computer to run a post-transfer scan before it was satisfied. Only one thing remained to be done.

"Transfer sequence completed," Cent Comp advised finally. "Tracer injected."

Malfe glanced at the first officer. "If after twenty days the subject has not returned to the designated retrieval point induced by an imperative subliminal command, the nanocell tracer can be triggered to emit a command that will compel the subject to return to the retrieval point."

The blue glow faded around the Earthman, but intensified

over Zor-Ell. A flat pad emerged from an aperture in the bulk-head and slid into a slot in the bed. With a barely discernable hiss the pad bearing the body retracted into the aperture and a panel closed over the spot. The karhide now safely stored in stasis with other Observers until retrieval.

The technicians had already moved the Earthman to the gravplate bunk. With a glance at Karth, they pushed it from the facility.

Karth watched them go and allowed himself a tight grin. Unless the taroptur encountered the horned animal again, he should have no trouble returning the subject. He walked out, the weight of command a comfortable load on his shoulders.

Twenty days…it didn't sound like much, but Karth knew a lot could happen in twenty days.

Chapter Five

Surface Command and Control guided *Sheeva* through the afternoon's dying glow toward the brilliantly lit sprawl of Tal Field's terminus buildings, run-up ramps, parking aprons and landing rings. Civilian liners crowded the docking spokes, tied to the terminus by access tubes, their polarized nav bubbles glowing white like bulging eyes of some prehistoric monster. A tubby Deklan liner, clad in an orange shimmer of its nav screen, slowly rose above its landing ring and picked up speed as it slanted into a purple sky.

The Field Administration building's color-reactive sides glowed in blue and white strips, using the sun's stored energy to power the SC&C complex. The tower was an imposing landmark against Barden's glittering sprawl stretching into a hazy skyline. Supported by a flared base the structure a giant mushroom with two enormous platforms jutting a third of the way down. The lower and larger platform acted as a landing ramp for civilian and commercial traffic. The smaller upper level restricted for official and military use.

As a major base, Tal Field housed support hangars, refurbishment facilities and Scout Fleet vessels. Two M-4s lay parked side by side at the eastern end of the Field, black shapes of death, their dark blue inverted triangle emblems flashing in the fading light. One hangar loomed open with an M-6 squatting inside, its portside hull torn down to the skeletal frame.

Sheeva angled toward the military terminus, paused, then sank onto a landing ring. Utility umbilicals rose from the apron and connected to hardpoints in the ship's belly. An access tube slid from the sheer terminus wall and mated to the hatch with a dull thump.

Dhar powered down and sat back on the right command couch. "Ship on ground power and secured, Sankri."

"I hope this isn't going to be a debriefing session," Terr reflected and stood up. He stretched his arms until the joints creaked and gave a satisfying grunt. Right now, he wanted a luxurious bath, a long massage, quiet dinner of raklish lamb in a subdued, refined atmosphere, accompanied by a glass or two of dark rumboli vintage, followed by a soft bed. That would be a real homecoming.

"Anabb must have a reason for wanting to see us," Dhar's voice rumbled from deep within his chest.

"Yeah. He wants to ruin our evening."

"I am sure he is worried about ruining our evening," Dhar said dryly and made for the cable-tube.

Terr grinned and strode after him, curious to know what was so burning urgent that Anabb couldn't wait until morning to jump them. Did the Old Man change his mind and wanted to take a chunk out of his hide for the C-32 drama after all? Although possible, he believed that ruining their evening still his best bet.

"Talking about ruining our evening, when we're done, do you feel like going out for dinner somewhere? I've got a craving for raklish lamb."

Dhar looked down at his brother. "Raklish lamb or distracting female company?"

"Hey! Why not both? But seriously, do you want to go out?"

"It might not be a bad idea, but I'll leave the lamb to you." Dhar naturally a vegetarian, meat a rare delicacy for the Wanderers at the best of times.

"Each to his own. It's settled then."

On the lower deck, they entered the access tube and made their way into the terminal. A stocky MP guarding the entrance, phase rifle at his side, stood to when they emerged. Terr walked past him and made for the glidewalk that went to the lower level exits. There were enough uniforms scattered in the hall that their footfalls didn't create a lonely echo. Like everybody else, he disregarded the usual announcements of arrivals and departures. Giant Wall display stations showed the Field's layout, ship berths, the Center and Barden's various attractions.

He saw a young Second Scout emerge from another tube and was immediately swarmed by two little chirping girls. His partner smiled broadly and gave him a hug. Terr shrugged. He wasn't ready to make that kind of commitment, and besides, agents shouldn't get into a stable relationship. It could be distracting, and also something Anabb had said. Still, it would be nice to come home to someone after a mission instead of a lonely bed.

Dhar followed Terr's glance. The couple, hand in hand, oblivious to everyone around them, slowly moved toward the exit. The children danced around their parents, chattering incessantly. He saw his brother's wistful expression and understood something of what must be going through Sankri's mind. He loved once and knew the tug of heartstrings and the fire that burned without flame, but just as dangerous. External scars can heal, not necessarily true with internal ones.

They cleared security on the lower level and were free to exit. The place nearly empty, but Terr longed for the peace and silence of the Saffal. His brush with Tanard during the attack on *Zavian* had left him deeply marked. Afterward, the clumsy recruiting attempt by the Resident on Anar'on had done nothing to ease the mental anguish of being nearly a god. Anyway, he didn't like crowds.

Outside, darkness already embraced everything. A gentle breeze ruffled his hair and he paused to take a deep breath of warm scented air, ignoring the noises, footfalls, and voices. Gnarled old trees lined the Beltway's wide avenue, along which people strolled or traveled on broad glidewalks going both ways. Bars, restaurants, shopping complexes, and establishments of dubious reputation lined the ring road approach to the spaceport. Terr saw it all before around other spaceports, other planets. Beyond the trees, the city towers beckoned, linked with glowing tubeways above which streams of traffic moved in orderly flows: communals, sled-pads, personal combies and cargo carriers.

They walked quickly toward a row of waiting communals. The first driver in the queue scrambled out to hold the door open. Terr settled himself into the upholstery and the bubble canopy closed over them. A safety green strip ran along the bubble boundary. He thumbed the mike pad and the driver's face glowed in the plate.

"The Center. Diplomatic Branch Admin building."

"You got it." The driver bobbed his head and the plate cleared.

With a surge of power the communal rose, got into the control network and headed for the forest of lit spires. Terr didn't feel much like talking, watching the city move beneath him in a kaleidoscope of images. In a way, he was glad to be on the ground. Six days at standard boost from Salina to Taltair was long enough to be sandwiched within the austere comforts of an M-1, breathing the same canned air and eating the same shipboard fare. Good to see open skies again, feel the wind against his face and take in new sounds and smells—if for a little while. Like a drug, a city should be taken in small doses before the walls, sounds, and endless humanity began to press in, to stifle. At least he could escape into the empty void of space with its infinite deeps, its unfathomable silence and emptiness. Akin to the stillness of the deep desert. He pitied the people below, frozen in a matrix of their lives, unable to extricate themselves even if they wanted to, trapped souls searching for release that would not come. Perhaps that's why he fancied he could hear a cry of anguish emanating from every city he ever saw.

The towers loomed closer.

Still, the trip from Salina hadn't been all bad. He didn't have to cater to Laraiana's tirades and tiresome remonstrations. Leaving the Orieli and Sol far behind them, she had been relatively quiet, preferring to remain in her cabin, only occasionally venturing to the command deck. Terr didn't complain. There were no warm embraces when he dumped her at Cel Field. At least his duty done, he was happy to leave her to the unfortunates on Salina.

Nevertheless, the woman schemed something. He could feel it. She was not the type to overlook a slur and he hadn't exactly fawned over her. Somewhere, she would surface and they would clash. Forget her!

The communal drifted leisurely toward the Admin building's main landing ramp. It crossed the entrance marker and followed a glowing yellow ribbon into the interior. A security portal barred entry into the parking lot. Terr pressed his palm against the charge plate and the bubble lifted. A burly MP in parade grays, white gloves and boots, stared suspiciously as Terr and Dhar got out. He lowered his rifle and stood to.

Without looking at the MP, Terr stepped to the ID booth and swept his palm against the plate. After a pause the entrance portal slid open and Terr moved through. He waited for Dhar to clear himself and they strode toward a bank of cable-tubes.

At the executive level, Ariane flashed them a smile when they got out and Terr became captivated all over again. She had delicate high cheekbones, full lips, and a long neck. Her head narrow, oval, with no hair. Tall, one point-eight katalans, deliciously slim with narrow hips that melted into a set of long, graceful legs. Every male in the building drooled after her. Totally entranced, Terr ignored the crowded floor and the bustle of a busy office. The Diplomatic Branch an around-the-clock operation.

"Welcome back to Taltair, gentlemen," Anabb's executive aide gushed in a crisp voice, reminding Terr of tumbling water.

"May I add my congratulations to a successful mission on Earth. Your encounter with the Orieli sounds fascinating."

"Thank you, Ariane." This was high-level treatment indeed to be met at the front door. He liked that kind of efficiency. Or maybe Anabb simply wanted to make sure they didn't get lost on their way to his office. It didn't stop him from wearing a drooling smile. "The Orieli *were* fascinating and I would love to tell you all about them sometime."

She laughed and extended a slim arm. She left herself open to that one, but didn't mind Terr's advance, practiced at fielding gambits from fast talking field agents.

"The Director is waiting. If you would follow me, please."

Anywhere, Terr thought. Watching her walk, the movement made a series of contrasts, all pleasant to see, and he allowed himself a moment of harmless fantasy. A dinner with her could be interesting, but she probably had all the come-ons there were by now, but he would never know if he didn't ask.

She led them past several empty open plan workstations toward a walled-off area, greeting familiar staff. Without pausing, she sat behind a wide desk that held two display plates and an input console. Behind her, a floor-to-ceiling window screen showed Barden's lit avenues. She touched a pad and leaned forward.

"Agents Terrllss-rr and Dharaklin, sir."

"Hah! About time. Show them in."

Terr instantly recognized the heavy, rasping voice and winced. He would have preferred doing this in the morning, not in the mood to wrestle with a debriefing right now. What was the rush? Translucent panels seamed along the middle and slid into the walls.

Ariane looked up and smiled brightly at them.

Terr glanced at Dhar, shook his head in resignation and walked in. Another time, perhaps.

The office spacious, but functional, devoid of extraneous fittings. A window screen framed the entire corner wall and

Anabb's sprawling desk took the other. Directly before it a large full-dimensional Wall display station filled part of the opposite wall, pooling through a tumble of twisting colors. Three form-chairs surrounded a small entertaining table on Terr's right. Behind it stood open shelving covered with odd memorabilia, data cubes, a twisted mineral specimen and an empty beige rock vase shot through with spiraling red veins.

"Take a seat, you two," Anabb ordered, rose and stepped away from behind his desk. The ragged blue-veined burn on his left cheek twitched as he stamped his mouth into a scowl. Although the former Prima Scout was only one point-seven kata-lans tall, he carried his bulk with authority and steely determination. Terr considered himself fortunate never to be one of his ship commanders. There were easier ways to die.

He waited for the Director to sit down before following.

Anabb sat back and the formchair squirmed around him, accommodating his bulk. Studying his two brand-new agents, he approved of what he saw. Terr did not look at all intimidated and seemed ready to take on anything. Not unlike his father at all. Both were impertinent scamps! Terr's Wanderer brother, on the other hand, a study in inscrutability. The desert creature patiently sat, waiting. He fancied he could sense power radiating from him. They made a formidable pair, and right now, exactly what he wanted. Did he expect too much? They were capable, and despite the mishaps, Terr showed himself to be remarkably resourceful and resilient in handling Kai Tanard and the C-32 mission. Unfortunately, resourcefulness wasn't always enough. No matter, it would have to do. They were tools, meant to be used. If they broke, there were others. He couldn't afford to think any other way. Silently, he chided himself for a hypocrite.

Terr saw the amber flecks brighten in Anabb's close-set oval eyes and waited. The sharp narrow face tightened and the Director leaned forward.

"How was your trip? Any problems?"

"It got better once we dropped off Scholar Laraiana," Terr

mused and Anabb smiled.

"I don't doubt it, and we'll talk about her later. Your contact with the Orieli has raised a stinger's nest, but that's not your concern. Bound to happen sooner or later, and for some, it's an unwelcome development. In one respect, it was fortuitous as it deflected BCPA's attention from Earth and your C-32 mission." He shot Terr a penetrating look. "I read your report and it seems comprehensive, but I would stay out of their way for a while, if I were you, at least until your uncle gets over his pique."

Terr squirmed at the memory of shadowing the American naval vessels and shot down for his trouble. That was bad enough, but getting picked up by the Russian cruiser had torn it. It wasn't a mission to emulate.

"I must express my thanks for your support, sir," he said humbly. "I know I haven't handled some things too well."

"Thunderation! You're not kidding. That's how you gain experience. Despite BCPA's fulmination the damage is minor and Earth has weathered the storm. They're better off without that relic, even though contaminated from computer downloads they undoubtedly made. Their problem. The Orieli contact, on the other hand, you dealt well with it. Both of you. Commissioner Sill-Anais saw fit to place commendations in your records." His agents had limited usefulness before they were either burned or took up supervisory duties. A gesture of recognition didn't cost much and meant a lot to someone who could be dead tomorrow. Anyway, he can always take the medals back if they screwed up.

Terr blinked in surprise and glanced at Dhar. "That was kind of him, sir."

"A fine example it was of first-contact procedure, executed in the best tradition of the Service."

"Thank you, sir," Terr said cautiously. Okay, he was wrong. The old geezer had a heart after all, somewhere. More likely setting him up for something else more nasty. He learned to be suspicious when a superior offered fulsome praise. Not being suspicious had landed him in a crack with *Zavian*.

"Now, although the Orieli might be occupying your minds and the ramification of their existence will be far-reaching, the work you started with Kai Tanard and raiders in general didn't stop. Although most Palean marauders are religious zealots and simple opportunists, we have evidence of organized networks I suspect have political backing. A disturbing development that could seriously undermine Serrll's social integrity. Captal cannot allow Paleans, or anybody else, to use raiders as a political instrument in execution of their policies. With Lemos exposed, it uncovered a link to one such network Tanard used, probably without his knowledge, which we're pursuing. You can guess what I'm referring to."

"Askaran?" Terr ventured and Anabb nodded.

"The one that ran Re Nette, exactly. When you caught her, her fate was sealed and she is on her way to Cantor. Good riddance. As you know, the prison planet has no government and no laws except what the inmates might enforce on each other. It's a rough place and perhaps shooting them would have been a kinder thing, but I don't make Captal policy and I am not feeling too sorry for them. They're vermin and better off dead, but that's another picture. Re Nette and her crew were fully interrogated and we gained considerable intelligence. Not all of Cantor is a horror. In exchange for information, I promised she would be landed at one such place. You can imagine what they do to women in some settlements. Re Nette wouldn't last long."

"Knowing her, she would probably be running the place within a week," Terr offered with a grin, remembering his encounter with the proud Palean when he captured her. It took command presence to run a raider manned by cutthroats, but he shared Anabb's judgment of her. She was a raider and a killer, and deserved whatever Cantor dished out. He wouldn't be losing any sleep over her.

"Thunderation! You could be right. Anyway, she made a

deal. Your idea to track fuel cells was brilliant. That approach bagged us several raiders and opened links to other networks near Palean/Karkan space. When she attacked the bulk carrier *Rakish* and landed on Mitlan, she inadvertently exposed part of her operation. Although useful, it is her support base on Askaran, some eight lights off, and the identity of her two partners, that's particularly valuable. As far as they're concerned, her ship was destroyed with the loss of all hands. That's critical, as they feel secure to continue operating. I won't bore you with details and you'll have a full transcript of her interrogation, but Askaran has raised a salient line of inquiry. How were her partners able to finance her ship? Oh, I know that running costs were met from raiding proceeds, but it's not clear how they acquired an auxiliary hull in the first place, equip it with a Terrasec 14/E phased array projector and support her drive reactor overhauls. The operation simply didn't net that kind of cashflow. We checked accounts they hold with local finance brokers. On top of these problems, we have another puzzle. Re Nette's partners own and operate a freight disposal company acting as a raider clearinghouse. That took considerable backing. See what I'm getting at?"

Terr frowned, not liking the direction Anabb's line of reasoning took him. Right now, the last thing on his mind were raiders, and he needed to dredge up everything he'd learned while hunting Tanard. Getting further entangled in that murky business or its finances did not exactly fill him with gushing enthusiasm. The only way he wanted to confront a raider was with an M-3 strapped around him. Liking it or not, he couldn't help working the problem and it did have an insidious kind of fascination.

"Her partners could have obtained funds from other raider stakeholders, or…"

"It's the 'or' which is the telling item, my boy," Anabb agreed with satisfaction. "Raiders are lone scavengers and shun organized management when it means having to split profits.

Even the religious ones tend to operate alone. Besides, funding a competitor is not exactly a wise business decision. Given their nature, they don't trust each other. No, Re Nette's partners were funded by someone else."

"They could be part of a hypercorp seeking to put pressure on Pizgor commerce and they'd have the necessary capital to support a freight company," Terr pointed out. "After all, as far as we know, Tanard didn't reveal to raiders the political objective behind the Tai-Mari Line, although it wouldn't have been too difficult to figure out."

"That's true," Anabb agreed, waiting for the boy to make the obvious connection.

Terr peered closely at Anabb's smug expression. He could almost hear the mental gears grinding. If Re Nette's partners were simple freebooters, dismantling their network wouldn't require involvement by the Diplomatic Branch. A simple Fleet cleanup would have done just fine. Tanard may have used Re Nette, but as Anabb said, it didn't mean he knew who her backers were, or cared. The Old Man must be fishing for bigger game then, and there was only one of any interest right now.

"You don't believe her partners are ordinary raiders at all, do you, sir? If they're organized, you suspect a link with the local Alikan Union Party cell?"

"Or the controlling arm behind it," Anabb added with satisfaction. The boy was good, no getting around it, and he may have worked out what lay in store for him.

"The AUP Provisional Committee?" The idea not exactly novel, and the thought had already teased Terr's mind.

"Precisely! I'm not forgetting that cheap hulls can be got from lots of disposal yards, but arming one is a different story. Hypercorps have funded armed auxiliaries for defensive purposes, but for a raider to operate a business front, even if supported by an organized syndicate, I don't buy it. You see my problem?"

Terr gave a sour chuckle. He saw the problem, all right.

He'd trod this road before and didn't like it any better this time around. Getting tangled in a web of political maneuvering left too much room for getting caught in a sticky predicament. He only had to look back at what mixing it with the Pen Family on Elexi got him, and wasn't anxious for a repeat performance. He might not be as lucky.

"You want us to establish a connection between Re Nette's partners and the Provisional Committee." He made it a statement, resigning to the inevitable. As a resource, Anabb would use him as he saw fit. Grimly, he wondered at the mortality rate of Diplomatic Branch agents. Live hard and die fast, he figured. Opportunities or not, perhaps he'd been a tad hasty getting involved with the crusty old fart. Easy to be objective now. In a moment of hubris and self-importance, Anabb simply seized the moment to pounce and Terr swallowed the bait. If he got sanded on a job, he could only blame himself.

"Very good, my boy, and that's exactly what I want you to do. This is conjecture, but I smell a political motive behind that network. They must be operating with Alikan Union Party support, and Askaran is one of their strongholds. If they're connected, I want to know what they're up to. The Committee failed with Pizgor, but they might consider using the same tactic against someone else, and you can figure out who that could be. Captal doesn't want to see that happen." Anabb knew he asked much from these two, inexperienced as they were, but the challenge wouldn't mean much unless it stretched their capabilities. He could not imagine a better way for them to learn, provided of course, they survived the mission. He was realistic enough to acknowledge that.

Terr exchanged a glance with Dhar, knowing exactly what that target could be—Kaleen. If the Palean Union wanted to grab an odd system or two, Kaleen was the only one that had them. As nonaligned independents, nobody would get too upset if some of their border systems got into difficulties. The only other possibility was to peel off a Karkan fringe system, but he doubted the Provisional Committee would be so foolish as to mess with the Karkan Federation. After all, Sargon and the Karkans were the Servatory Party coalition, and you don't play hardball with your partner. Not openly anyway.

"Penetrating a raider organization is not like taking my M-3 and charging after Tanard, sir, especially if they're politically backed and have an official security screen. Any idea how I'm supposed to do this?"

"It's simple. We'll turn you into a rogue trader!"

"Ah, I always wanted to try that," Terr muttered and Anabb laughed.

"Deception and infiltration. You should brush up on your Kawisaku."

The inference wasn't lost on Terr. Kawisaku was one of the greatest Sofam strategists and tacticians in history, perhaps the greatest anywhere. Sofam had conquered the Deklan Republic and the Sargon Directorate using his strategies. Today, the Paravan Trading Association was the ultimate exponent in peacetime application of his philosophy. Everyone looked at it as Sofam's hidden military.

"I gather this will be a penetration in depth? One thing. While we're pursuing our political objective, raiders could be taking life and plundering innocent commerce."

"I understand that taking your M-3 and blasting them to dust would be more satisfying with immediate results, but sometimes we must stand back. Your mission is one such event. It might cost lives in the interim, but it will cost far more if we don't do this thoroughly." Anabb stared hard at his agent. "Keep in mind that this isn't an exercise in evidence gathering for civil prosecution. We're talking about Serrll security. Once we have what we want, we'll deal with them in our own way. And you can spare me a lecture on philosophy and morality," he said and stood. "We'll discuss operating details tomorrow. My office at eight." He leaned across the desk and tapped a pad in the inlaid console. "Ariane? They're ready."

Outside, Ariane ambushed them, holding passkeys. Accommodation in the visitors quarters, she explained. After what Anabb had laid on them, Terr lost all desire to have dinner with her, for now. In the tubeway, rushing toward the residential tower, he again shook his head with bemused wonderment.

"I can't believe we'll actually be doing this!"

Dhar allowed his brother's exasperation to wash over him, which only served to highlight his own concerns. He joined the Diplomatic Branch aware of possible moral conflicts working undercover. Equally aware of them, Sankri was venting his frustration and uncertainty. Everything they were asked to do violated the Discipline and his soul rebelled. The very quality of the realization told him this path was wrong. Yet, what choice did he have, either of them? This was not the open Saffal, or a simple village squabble where they could easily tell right from wrong and dispense immediate justice. He had no ready answer from the *Saftara* either. This time, he would have to formulate his own, and he felt uncomfortable at the prospect. A god may have touched him and he walked with power, but the god did not guide his footsteps or salve his conscience. He would have to do that himself and stand ready to receive the god's judgment next time they met. Would the god find him worthy?

"My brother, I am uneasy knowing we'll be dealing with ruthless men who have killed and may kill again, whether for political or personal objectives. More could die while we pursue Captal's schemes."

"The realization hasn't escaped me, Nightwings, or the fact that technically, we'll be operating outside the law."

Dhar did not like that taste either. "Perhaps Anabb is correct when he said we must keep focused on the broader objectives. When I think that Paleans would use raiders against Kaleen shipping, my level of sympathy for the due process has developed a very thin veneer, but they wouldn't dare."

"Why not? Abhorrent as the idea is, raiders are not a bad tactical tool. You don't have to know them, fund or support them. That's Anabb's problem and I'm happy for him to handle it."

"The notion that Kaleen could be ravaged fills me with foreboding."

"I'm not too excited by the prospect either, but I would hazard a guess the Rahtir Council has considered the possibility and taken steps."

Dhar remained silent for several seconds, hoping his brother was right. "I noted your uncertainty when Anabb disclosed the mission, Sankri. You doubt our ability to carry it out?"

Terr snorted and gave him a toothy grin. "I doubt the sanity of the whole concept. Expose links to the Provisional Committee? Anabb's dreaming. I don't expect Alikan Union Party cells to be amateurs. They would have covered their tracks."

"He clearly thinks otherwise."

"Yeah, but he's sitting in a nice air-conditioned office. It's our butts hanging out there. We could always get lucky, but I am suspending judgment until we hear the details."

Dhar crossed his legs and sighed. "Tah, the gods will tell."

"I did want to make a difference, didn't I? Well, my brother, we'll either make a difference or they'll be crating us back in a body box."

* * *

Grim, Ed-Kani Takao, Executive Director for the Bureau of Economic Affairs, senior Sargon member in the General Assembly and an AUP Provisional Committee powerbroker, faced the floor-to-ceiling window screen, hands clasped firmly behind his back. His body reflected underlying tension as he stood rigid, swept up in an emotional storm.

Dawn had broken sometime back in a splash of golden light, dispelling Captal's shadows, sucking the last strands of mist that hung above Celean Park and the city. The various

General Assembly administrative buildings—columns of reactive ceramic, composite fiber and crystal—climbed into a clear autumn sky. Beyond the park along Taiko Way, lost in pearly haze, were a tangle of spires from hotels circling the Center, over which swarmed stacked patterns of commercial traffic. Farther still lay the enclaves that made up Captal's sprawl. This high up, the Economics tower nearly within reach of the lower bands. Around him a cluster of black monoliths defined the Hiat District where the Executive Council and its Bureaus ruled.

And they did rule, after a fashion. The Sofam-dominated Revisionist Party coalition maintained peace, and with it brought a measure of material prosperity to the Serrll, but it lacked the orderly discipline and control that Sargon imposed on its own systems. The Dumas Conclave and the Pro-Consuls were not tyrants. Citizens enjoyed freedom and democratic rule, but that freedom was subservient to the Code and the greater good of Sargon. Ed-Kani wanted to bring the same discipline and focused social direction to the Serrll Combine as a whole and it frustrated him beyond patience that Sofam insisted on maintaining a policy of minimal interference in the internal workings of member systems. Without discipline, you have a rabble. With its majority in the Executive Council, everybody else had little choice but to toe the line, however unpalatable the taste for some. If Sargon succeeded in its merger with the Palean Union, the current looseness and waste would cease. There would be order!

Somewhere below along broad tree-lined avenues, people were making their way to work, hurrying on foot or taking a glidewalk. Confined in their small, narrow universes, each of them would face problems, challenges, successes and disappointments. The world revolved around them, or so they thought, blissfully unaware of larger forces that in reality shaped their destinies. Sometimes, he wondered if they even cared.

And what reality shaped *his* destiny?

His icy blue-white eyes were expressionless as he stared at Captal's expanse. Etched character lines were dug deep around his firm mouth. He learned painfully that in any game of ascendancy, emotion was a tool to be used sparingly, even in the confines of his office. For what he aspired, he only had room for brutal determination.

He would have liked to stroll through Celean Park, be part of the unencumbered open spaces around him and feel the ageless patience of the gnarled trees that had survived man's puny efforts. They were above it all. His security detail would never allow such indulgence. Even in the confines of his comfortable office, befitting his exalted status, the environment itself exerted an influence, which in turn helped, or possibly hindered, the pattern of his thoughts. Held captive in his office, indulging in a pleasurable stroll was out of the question. He bared his sharp teeth and gave a low hiss of frustration. Years of scheming, formulation of strategies, definition of tactics, evaluation of strengths and weaknesses, calculation of variables, it all came to nothing simply because of Lemos.

M-9s and M-6s over Hakran, to the eternal shame of the Pro-Consuls. Sargon's stock markets and trading houses savaged in punishment before the Executive Council, in reality the Revisionist Party slime, relented and lifted its hand. It was cold comfort that the Palean Union hadn't escaped the fallout.

Lemos should have been the Committee's masterstroke to bring Pizgor to heel, delivering its three primary systems and two outposts into the Alikan Union Party's hands, consummating the Sargon/Palean merger, entitling them to a third Executive Council seat. With that vital seat in hand, the Karkan-dominated Servatory Party would be annulled and Sargon could at last wage battle with Sofam for ascendancy over Captal's government as rulers of the Serrll Combine.

All that and a place in Sargon's history, dashed from his grasp by that fool Le Maran. Imagine ordering Tanard to strike at Fleet escorts! Such asinine stupidity. In the end, how easily it had all fallen. With it, two Committee members gone when they allowed themselves to be seduced by Ti Inai's ill-conceived venture to intercept Unified Independent Front delegates on their way to Anar'on. That piece of idiocy had cost them Italan. And Tanard captured! What a security disaster. All those carefully thought-out plans wasted, making the Committee look like fumbling amateurs instead of seasoned political tacticians they were supposed to be. If he had his way, it should have been Ti Inai's head on the block, but the canal worm fled to Palea when the operation melted and his two unfortunate accomplices were sacrificed instead. No matter. There would be opportunities to even the score later.

Sargon does not forget, *friend* Ti Inai.

Seven years to go before his last ten-year Assembly term ended and his career as a major political force in the Serrll with it. Not much time to change history, and he longed to leave behind something more than merely thirty years of unrelenting public service. Another debacle like Lemos and he would definitely leave a mark in history, but not necessarily an example to be followed.

The merger had suffered a setback, but he was far from done, and there were other tactics to pursue. He turned abruptly, strode to his desk and sat down. With an impatient gesture, he tapped a pad in the inlaid console.

"Keana? Would you come in, please?"

His fingers drummed against the gray matte surface and he gave a low hiss. The Wall in front of him pooled in swirls of tortured patterns, reflecting his mood. The translucent doors slid away and Keana walked in, sat down without an invitation and waited.

In all respects plain, dour and frigid, an invaluable administrator and confidant. Without her unflagging support, it would be impossible to manage his Executive Director duties and cope with growing demands on his time as a Provisional Committee member. He could only dread the damage she could wreak if she were ever turned. That, of course, was impossible. They had their differences and she wasn't shy in pointing them out, but in their devotion to the cause, they were one. Still, no one can predict a woman's mood or the whims of fate as Lemos so vividly demonstrated. Nevertheless, if he trusted anyone, he trusted his cheerless Keana.

"You wanted to see me?" she prompted when Ed-Kani continued to stare at her.

He pulled back his lips in a grim smile. She was the only one who saw right through him, beyond the facade of power. He didn't mind it at all. In fact, it was refreshing not having to posture always even if her occasional lack of respect did rankle sometimes. Well, she more than made up for it with her unfailing efficiency.

"I did want to see you, yes. Do we have anything new on the CAPFLTCOM tender for the new Fleet base?"

"The Palean Union has confirmed their bid, but my sources tell me the Fleet is seriously considering the Rolan proposal."

Her sources, he knew, were within Illeran's approval committee and the Fleet hierarchy itself. His position did accord him a measure of power and resources denied a simple Assemblyman, and he used every tool in the pursuit of his ends. After all, he wasn't betraying confidences. As the senior Sargon General Assembly representative, it was his obligation and duty to do everything possible to advance Sargon's interests. That's how they played the game.

"And our move to secure Rolan?"

Keana's suggestion that Sargon should throw its support behind the Rolan bid, absolutely masterful. In return for that support and continued autonomy, Rolan would cede its five systems. With those systems, there would be nothing standing in the way of a Sargon/Palean merger, the Committee's goal achieved in a single bold stroke. Of course, he was not so naive to imagine that Sofam wouldn't see through the tactic, but unless they were prepared to annex Rolan, they could do little if the secession was done voluntarily. Nonetheless, it would be extremely dangerous and foolish to underestimate them. He had plans of his own to ameliorate that threat; plans within plans.

"Things are moving well there. Trianon, Rolan's senior Assembly rep, is firmly in our pocket. We promised him a posting as Salina's Controller if we won the bid."

"Worth it," Ed-Kani said approvingly.

"Antarami, Rolan's Prime Director, is, ah, receptive," Keana announced dryly. The scrupulously honest politician took time to be convinced, but a promise of a Pro-Consul seat in the Dumas if Rolan ceded, brought him around. It was always that way. Men in positions of power would do almost anything to retain power. As far as she was concerned, Ed-Kani was no different. It was in the nature of the personality. One simply had to learn which strings to pull.

"Excellent! Things *are* going well. I've got old Mariawa turned, including his two principal backers," Ed-Kani added with evident relish. The First Pro-Consul initially baulked at the idea of supporting Rolan, but shrewd enough to see the strategic advantage for Sargon at relatively little personal cost. Not a member of the secretive Provisional Committee, and handling the wily representative taxed Ed-Kani's negotiating skills to the limit. In the end, he came on board. "As for Karshwin, he is amenable to persuasion and will support us," he added smoothly.

"What was his price?" Keana asked.

"Chair of the Arms Board."

Keana raised her thin eyebrows. "It's a prestigious posting, sure to ruffle some sensibilities."

"Not a problem. His will be a titular position. Like I said, all he craves is a munificent office and a grand title."

"Of course you know, emergence of the Orieli could be a decisive factor now. CAPFLTCOM may end up reviewing the terms of the entire tender, which could make Ti Inai's Palean bid suddenly far more attractive."

Ed-Kani hissed and snapped his jaws. "Damn the little shit! He's there to support Committee policy, not run a private agenda. You're dead right about the Orieli. Unfortunately, there is nothing we can do there. They are a random factor and only time will tell how that will play itself out."

"Has the Provisional Committee considered what impact the Orieli presence may have on the merger process?"

"You mean did I consider it?" Ed-Kani mused with a tight grin. "I've got some ideas, but the Orieli are still too much of an unknown quantity and we want input from the BCPA on first-contact details. However, our immediate problem is replacement of two vacant members. Until we get that sorted out the Committee is effectively paralyzed."

"Not if the Orieli are painted as a genuine threat," Keana said softly and waited.

Ed-Kani looked at her and nodded, thinking along exactly the same lines. The Moanar Nebula was on the Sargon/Palean side of the Serrll Combine, and that's where the Orieli came from. They'd be the first hit if the Orieli were to attack, although he didn't believe they ever would. Not a military expert, but even he knew that a three thousand light-year logistics support chain would be massively unwieldy. Why would the Orieli bother with the Serrll anyway? If they were after resources, they could probably find those much closer to the Moanar. As for territory, the same argument applied. No, the Serrll had little to fear from them—for now.

"The thought *did* cross my mind, you know, and I'm sure CAPFLTCOM will also review it in one of their risk assessment scenarios. It's a prudent measure, and as an Executive Director, is something I support. However benign their appearance now, the Orieli could turn into a problem for us later. I would be remiss in my duty if I didn't consider the possibility, but I understand where you're coming from. You're looking to turn this into a tactical advantage for the Committee now?"

Stefan Vučak

"That's what I thought," she said. "Some judicious conditioning inside Sargon and the Palean Union, added pressure on wavering Congressmen and the merger would be yours. Admittedly without the third Executive seat, but the Committee would have achieved a major strategic objective. Once the merger is secure, you can direct all your energies toward getting that seat, and Greater Sargon would rule."

"Mmm, it might be worth pursuing at that," Ed-Kani said thoughtfully and pulled at his chin. "There is a danger the tactic could backfire and cost us the Rolan bid. Still, it's worth testing the water. Prepare a publicity profile and run some polls to gauge civic reaction before I put it to the Committee, unless of course, the Bureau of Defense has a poll already running. In which case we'll use their data. It will look better coming from an official government organ anyway."

"What if the Orieli *do* turn hostile?"

"That's always possible, and the Fleet would have to deal with them. If things turn dire, there is always Anar'on."

"But on whose side would the Wanderers fight?" Keana asked softly.

Ed-Kani intended his remark to be flippant, but her reply definitely was not. Would the Wanderers necessarily fight against an invader? With the power of the Discipline in their hand, no one could stand before them. They would protect themselves and their systems, but would that protection extend to cover everybody else? The corollary obvious. Ignoring the variables, did the Scout Fleet have enough heavy assets inventory to defend the Serrll Combine? Perhaps a quiet chat with Commissioner Katan at BueDef might be in order. He studied his aide with interest.

"You know, it's a real pity you're not a Dumas official, my dear. You would make a perfect Committee member."

Keana's stern features remained expressionless.

* * *

Shadow Masters

When James Grant woke, Zor-Ell saw daylight on a strange new world. There was a moment of inner disorientation as Jim's memories flooded into his awareness. He was familiar with the sensation, having experienced transition numerous times during his period as an Observer. Like peeling an onion, the thought came to his consciousness. Onion? Images of onions stacked in the veggie section of a supermarket, overlaid with neat rows of green shoots in a garden, brought an inner smile.

While Jim yawned, threw back the sleeping bag flap and sat up to gaze vacantly through the tent's mosquito screen, Zor-Ell had accessed the alien's memory layers and established retrieval links. He knew everything Jim knew, but it would take some time to integrate that knowledge into an understandable whole. Yet, some things were immediately clear: who Jim was, why he camped out—a weekend in nature—his fears, ambitions and drives; all of it overlaid with a lifetime's accumulation of cultural background. The sheer volume of available data Zor-Ell needed to guard against, lest the torrent of memories overcame him and he would lose his anchor and personality perspective. Like turning on a tap, he had to be mindful of the pressure.

Sensory inputs bombarded his consciousness. For Jim, they were part of an understood environmental backdrop, but to Zor-Ell, the wealth of new sensations made him excited. He had forgotten the keen thrill being an Observer generated, to be able to eavesdrop on an individual and a culture, unfettered by protocol, behavioral nuances, and mores. Taking in the immediate sights and smells around him, the rudimentary camping equipment, the sounds coming from outside an experience to be savored. What would it be like to actually live with these people, be immersed in their lives, battered by cultural and racial nuances they took for granted, but which he had to assimilate and understand? To interact with new societies, comprehend how differing religions, political structures, economic, and military systems defined the social matrix, were the drivers that directed his initial career choice. Excited or not, he needed to apply a rigorous discipline and methodology to his data gathering if his analyses were to have any meaning.

He triggered a set of preset mnemonic procedures that would run the assimilation process more or less on automatic. That would leave him to concentrate on Jim's immediate actions and thoughts, careful to differentiate fact from Jim's personal prejudices, opinions, and assumptions. He also needed to be wary. Two things were drilled into him during three years of mind-numbing training, which he scrupulously obeyed: don't rush and don't judge. You are there to observe, his instructors constantly pounded into him. His job was to take in information and data, not be a moral arbiter. Of course, an Observer was much more than that, but everything else rested on the platform of those two basic directives.

Jim woke with a mild headache and felt like something nagged him, some voice, a memory below his direct awareness. He thought of taking a Panadol, the one with paracetamol, as the commercials emphasized. The explanation didn't bring any enlightenment. By the time he got out of the tent, stretched and took two deep breaths of crisp air laced with the scent of eucalyptus, he felt better.

Cockatoos were squawking somewhere over the small rise and he could see four gray wallabies grazing at the forest's edge. One of them looked up and stared at him before going back to feeding. Bright sunshine lanced between the branches of tall gums in yellow shafts. A faint film of white mist hung above the grassy meadow. The brook nearby gurgled as water tumbled over rocks.

For now at least, everything seemed right with the world.

It was good to get away for a day, away from domestic chores and the grind of daily routine. He longed to spend the day here and this was one of his favorite campsites, but he needed to go to work tomorrow. The bills would not get paid by themselves. He still had to clean the yard and do the washing before he headed back to Melbourne. He'd left that chore undone last time, and his organized, orderly mind baulked at the prospect of procrastinating for another week.

Raileen's birthday on Wednesday, she would kill her uncle if he dared show up emptyhanded. The six-year-old knew she could wind him around her little finger and Jim didn't mind it at all. Margie looked after her precocious daughter well and didn't spoil her. She left that one to her older brother. Sidetracked, he wondered again why she and Brian kept their two-bedroom apartment at the Docklands. Granted, they were right in the middle of the city with terrific bay views, but the convenience didn't make up for the fact that in his opinion, not a good place to raise a child. Kids wanted somewhere to run, open spaces, trees to climb. Melbourne had lots of sprawling parks, but it wasn't the same thing. They argued, but in the end, Jim let it go. It wasn't his family.

Packing quickly, not bothering with breakfast, he climbed into his dark gray Toyota Camry and drove slowly along a narrow gravel track that would take him through the Wombat Forest to Blackwood Road and Trentham. Twenty minutes and he would be home.

Once he hit the arterial, he accelerated, enjoying the cool shade of the forest, the gently rolling hills, open farms, and smoking chimneys from houses that clung to the roadside. Although the days were still sunny and warm, the nights were refreshingly crisp, heralding the autumn frosts and the bitter cold of winter. He did not particularly care for that part.

It always startled him how quickly he hit Trentham's small township. One minute, he was in deep forest, and the next, driving along a broad, tree-lined street. Slowing down to sixty kilometers, the cops around here had no sense of humor, he stopped at the High Street T-intersection and turned right. Everything quiet and a few pedestrians meandered along the footpaths. The restaurant near the hotel on his right doing slow business serving breakfast. At one time, not so long ago, it used to be a thriving hardware store.

Trentham always pleasant and picturesque, but in many respects a dying country town. When the Commonwealth Bank branch shut down some four years ago, a number of small businesses went with it. They said the ANZ Bank would be opening a branch soon, but the folks here said many things that turned out to be simply idle talk. Still, young city families were settling here again, having discovered the town's hidden charms, and the rumors could be true. He drove past St Mary Magdalene church, past parked cars and people making their way in for the eight-thirty mass. He exchanged waves with several familiar faces, crossed Forest Street and slowed when he reached the acre block, he still used the old measure, lined with a hedge of cypress trees. He pulled left into a gravel driveway and stopped in front of a two-meter wrought iron gate hung from brown brick pillars.

Hands on the steering wheel, engine murmuring to itself, Jim paused and studied the single-story brick veneer house. The place modest, but comfortable, and one acre gave him plenty of backyard room and maintenance work. That's why he hung onto the block, his little retreat from the high-pressure cooker of the city. Melbourne was convenient and he didn't need to commute to work, but Trentham replenished something the city took out.

He climbed out of the car, opened the gate and dogged the two halves down. He drove in and stopped in front of a large tin shed—a garage/workshop and his winter firewood store. He wouldn't be staying and didn't bother getting the car in.

The backyard an expanse of grass and fruit trees: apples, plums, and a scruffy chestnut, that yielded a couple of large buckets of useful nuts despite determined efforts by cockatoos to destroy everything. If the birds ate the nuts it wouldn't be so bad, but the pesky things seemed to take sardonic pleasure in mere destruction. The ride-on mower made cutting the grass a bearable chore, but he waged an ongoing war with dandelions and other weeds. Well, it gave him something to do. He made his way to the back of the house, opened the door into the enclosed veranda and walked through the open doorway into the kitchen/living room. When he came on Friday evening, he'd left the windows open to air the place. It never occurred to him that somebody would break in. Trentham not that kind of place, at least not yet. Even if someone did get in, there wasn't much they could take. If they wanted the TV or the DVD player, they were welcome to them.

He picked up the remote from the coffee table and switched on the TV. When the wide LCD screen lit, he selected channel seven's morning news and chat show for background noise, then opened the fridge to scrounge some breakfast.

He got into the car late afternoon and made his way to the Kyneton-Trentham Road that would take him to Woodend, then the freeway to the city. He planned to be in his apartment by seven, in time to catch dinner down one of many restaurants on Lygon Street. Tomorrow would be a big day for him, presenting a major strategic study for BHP Billiton. After all, KPMG had a reputation to maintain and he wasn't about to let his employer down.

* * *

Terr leaned forward and peered in disbelief at the lanky senior agent. The man's gaunt features would have looked comfortable on a medical skeleton. His white skin a piece of dry parchment covering a sharp face and a small bare head. The yellow eyes were two blobs that gave nothing away. Although tastefully dressed in a light brown suit the clothes hung loose on the bony frame.

"Let me see if I understand this. You will provide us with an unlimited drawing account—"

"Well, not exactly unlimited," Landau corrected softly and a small smile played at the corner of his severe mouth, knowing exactly what went through the young agent's mind; a feeling he'd been set up. From available information, he would have felt the same way. Despite Terr's misgivings, the operation had taken too much planning, investment in time and resources to be simply a setup. Besides, if Anabb wanted to get rid of his new agent, there were far simpler and less costly ways of going about it.

Terr waved a dismissive hand. "Whatever. I set myself up as a no-questions-asked cargo buyer, undercut my main competitor, drag in Re Nette's two partners into a joint venture and infiltrate their organization, which should hopefully lead me to their contact inside the Alikan Union Party cell who *might* be running him, or better still, the Provisional Committee who are running *them*! How I'm doing so far?"

"You forgot the local Diplomatic Branch Resident. Without Kandu Hall's support the local operators would eat you up. Apart from that, you've pretty much got it," Landau said comfortably and watched the play of emotions on the junior agent's face. A tall order to throw him into a complex and dangerous job first time out where lots of things could go wrong. He argued with Anabb to let him be the point man, but the Director didn't want to hear it. Only time would tell if the Director's confidence in the two agents was justified.

"That's what I thought." Terr looked sharply at Anabb. "You cannot expect only the two of us to pull off this stunt...sir?" he demanded, hooking a thumb at himself and Dhar sitting quietly beside him. When Landau initially outlined his plan, Terr thought he knew what was going on. The old man hadn't forgiven him the C-32 mess after all, and this was his way of getting even. Crafty, evil, dirty...

"There won't be just the two of you, my boy!" Anabb snapped. "You wouldn't last a day if you tried this alone. Despite what you might think, you'll be fully supported with every resource available to this Branch. You should credit Senior Agent Landau with the ability to do his job, which is far more than I can say for you!"

Terr let that one ride. Anabb being grouchy and a pain. Despite the assurances, he could not ignore the fact that those resources were on Taltair, not on Askaran where he would need them. He hoped this Kandu Hall guy had all his shit in one bag.

Landau took a small sip of tea. "Agent Terr," he said, replacing the cup on the saucer. "This is not a throwaway mission designed to get you captured or killed. The Executive Council wants raider networks in the Palean Union exposed and eliminated, but more desperately, they want to expose the Alikan Union Party Provisional Committee. If a Sargon/Palean merger is allowed to materialize, the Serrll Combine would face a dictatorial regime, serious social disruption and possible armed conflict with the Sofam Confederacy, and that's something the Executive cannot allow. I'm not telling you anything you don't already know, but exposing this Committee and its members would avert that. Obviously, your mission isn't the only avenue pursued to achieve this objective, but it's an important one.

"You and Mr. Dharaklin will be operating under impenetrable legends that no amount of investigation can compromise because they're real. We are running and constantly updating hundreds of fictional identities, civilian and military. You can expect Re Nette's partners and your competition to break you, but it won't be because of a blown cover. If you're harboring any misgivings that you could be compromised through your Scout Fleet records, put them aside. When you joined the Diplomatic Branch, apart from minimal profile entries, access to your files was restricted. No one will be able to pull out your face or biometric data. Any attempt to do so by anyone, even an Executive Council Director, will trigger a trace and the person will be up for some hard questioning. The Diplomatic Branch is not in the habit of losing operatives."

Intellectually, Terr understood the arguments underlining the mission and that Landau wouldn't send him out exposed, but the senior agent far too smooth for his liking. Either way, the job way out of his comfort zone, he could sense the sharp breeze of terminal exposure already whistling through his bones. This is what he signed up for: adventure, intrigue, back door deals. Wasn't it?

Dhar cleared his throat and pushed back a strand of loose hair over his shoulder. "You did take into account, sir, that Sankri and I know nothing about commerce, cargo handling, accounting or managing a disposal business?"

"Rest easy, Mr. Dharaklin," Landau said. "By the time you get to Askaran, both of you will be experts on the subject."

"Forced learning," Terr said and shook his head in disgust. That meant subliminal conditioning. The Internal Operations Division, responsible for tracking down criminal elements within the Fleet, used the technique to prime its undercover operatives. The process force-fed knowledge, but integrating the information was disorienting. He didn't look forward to it.

Landau locked the bony fingers of his hands and crossed his legs. "I can hear your unspoken questions, Agent Terr. Where is the detailed mission plan, risk profiles, exit strategy? *Sheeva's* computer is uploaded with the necessary instruction data packs. Assimilate them. It will take you eight days to reach Askaran, plenty of time to study them and for us to sort out any loose ends. Resident Hall is fully briefed and is expecting you." He reached into his jacket pocket and placed two silver cards on the table between them. "Your new ID data tags. No need to tell you that reaction to your assumed persona must be automatic."

"Presumably, there are data packs for them too?" Terr asked archly, fingering his card.

"There are."

Terr gathered Dhar with his eyes and his brother shrugged. A quantum leap in complexity over anything they had previously done and he lacked confidence he could hack it. A new sensation for him, as he always felt ready to take on anything. It was also disconcerting, this sudden fear that he might not be capable, that he could fail. Maybe once he got his head around the details, things would fall into place. Still, the breeze at the back of his pants already felt colder.

"There will be risks and you'll face danger," Anabb said gruffly. "And I am not underestimating the possible problems. The men we're after won't hesitate to kill you if they feel threatened. If all else fails, your special abilities will come in handy."

Scant comfort, and what was more, Terr felt sure everybody knew it. There were too many ways to slip up, and Death always hungered. Well, if this would be his last job, he might as well go out in style. Looking glum, he peered at Anabb.

"When do you want us off?"

"You have time enough for a last meal."

"I hope you didn't mean that literally, sir."

Impertinent scamp, Anabb thought and chuckled. "Just don't make it a banquet. I want you on your way without delay."

With the kiss-off, Terr stood and nodded to Landau. "I'll be in touch," he said offhandedly and strode to the translucent doors with Dhar trailing after him.

Outside, Ariane glanced from her workstation and beamed. "How was your briefing?"

"We just got our butts creamed," Terr told her, leaving her gaping after them.

In the cable-tube going up to the Admin lunchroom, he frowned at Dhar and shook his head.

"Did I say I wanted to make a difference?"

"In adversity the spirit grows, my brother."

"It won't grow if we don't survive the adversity!"

Rit!

Chapter Six

Even from orbit, Circa looked cold and forbidding. Patches of open water and greenery girthed the equatorial belt, keeping at bay the ice sheath covering most of the planet. A class three world, the atmosphere-warming generators still had over a century of work before the ice retreated sufficiently for most usable land to be reclaimed. Ecoforming projects took the long-term view.

For Terr, this minor world on the edge of Karkan space represented an ideal insertion point to Askaran without having to sweep up a convoluted trail after them. Any loose end a potential trap that could get them compromised. Landau did not disagree with him there. For anyone digging into their backgrounds, this sudden appearance on Circa would be odd, but without a lead to follow the people they were after could only scratch their heads and speculate.

Dhar brought the M-1 down at Petri Field with a request to SC&C for replacement of a suspect fuel cell—twitchy containment. SC&C did not even query the problem. It sometimes happened and he understood that a ship would want to get rid of the thing as quickly as possible. They dumped their data pack and the M-1 landed at the far end of the military apron, just in case. An antimatter explosion could level a substantial portion of the Field. Remote handling arms came up immediately and opened the fuel chamber access panel in the ship's underbelly. The suspect cell—tweaked that way—removed and a replacement installed. Seeking immediate clearance the M-1 filed a confirming flight plan for Kalakan and streaked into a leaden sky.

No one noticed two men, dressed in maintenance coveralls standing beside the closed hangar, holding undersized suitcases, watch the M-1 lift. When the small ship disappeared into low clouds, they started walking steadily through frozen slush toward the terminus building.

The facility might be primitive in comparison with more developed worlds, but efficient and comfortable enough. Terr and Dhar purchased shuttle tickets for Askaran at the flight desk using their new ID cards and were told boarding was delayed by twenty minutes; problems with cargo loading. Terr smiled at the attractive Osaku Lines attendant and headed for the departure lounge. Other passengers followed in his wake, carrying or dragging luggage. Reedy background music filled the empty spaces. He could not see any Immigration and Customs security portals and didn't bother asking. Their unorthodox entry had obviously missed them. At the back of his mind, he hoped the M-1 would make it to Kalakan okay, but didn't unduly worry about it. Computers were good at executing simple instructions.

He picked an empty comms booth and placed a call to Kandu Hall, advising him of their arrival schedule, and went in search of a snack. Frowning over the menu, he settled on a meaty broth and ambled over the hard, dark gray carpet to where Dhar sat in what looked like a comfortable couch. Terr sat beside his brother and crossed his legs. Facing three-katalan-high window screens showing the open Field, he sipped the steaming concoction, leaned back and sighed. So far so good. A breathless lush voice, announcing the arrival of a flight from Sarkeen, momentarily interrupted the background music. No one seemed excited by the news.

Dhar noted Sankri's relaxed poise and smiled. He knew exactly what his brother had gone through over the last few days, because he'd been in agony for exactly the same reason. His brother's memories and personality were too intertwined with his for him not to understand. Regardless of the outcome, the mission did start smoothly enough. Now, he only had to play out the potentially deadly game.

"Feeling mellow, Ser Kerill-aa?"

"Tolerably mellow, Ser Randakla, O fallen one."

Dhar's leathery features colored and his eyes turned dangerous. "Was that a slur on my character, Ser? I want to remind you that not every Wanderer is cut out to be a Discipline adept. Besides, I don't recall getting booted from the Fleet is something to be worn as a badge of honor."

"I wasn't booted out, I resigned," Terr said comfortably and both had a good chuckle.

And he *did* feel mellow.

After clearing Taltair, loaded with doubts and misgivings, he tucked himself away in his quarters and had *Sheeva's* computer feed him the memory data packs. Including one for the local Tashala dialect. Everyone on Askaran spoke standard Serrll interlingua, but knowing the local language would be a great business advantage. The procedure left him with a lingering headache for a day, but he'd developed a grudging respect for Landau's planning and organizational abilities. Everything he wanted neatly tabulated, the information concise and to the point, without extraneous clutter, see Appendix B. With the framework in hand, he had something solid to work with. When he broke things down into manageable pieces the mission lost some of its foreboding mystery. Of course, still only a plan, a do-it-yourself guide. He needed to put the meat on the bones himself. That's where the traps lurked, but he felt he could handle that part of the job.

Obviously, not everything could be clearly defined. Action would be taken as events unfolded and reality never conformed to plans. He also had a strategy and a series of tactics designed to manipulate events, which over time would limit his opposition's options until he achieved the objective. At least that's how the data packs made it out. Landau even provided guidelines for several alternate scenarios, something Terr appreciated and helped his preparations. Clearly, the senior agent had done this once or twice before, and that left Terr with a warm fuzzy.

He spent two days with Dhar picking over details without uncovering a major gotcha. The odd inconsistencies weren't troubling enough to rear themselves as problems. Terr told Landau the same thing when they started the Wall hookups. Cargo handling never high on his list of interests, he admitted the subject fascinated him. In its own way, running a business required a level of technical and management skill rivaling anything his Fleet training provided. He had one bright side to forced learning. If working for Anabb ever got dull, he could always scrounge a job as a stuffy warehousing executive.

Inevitably, he got himself into a minor jam when he used his new alias to query his Fleet records and got bounced by the humorless computers. That got him yelled at by Anabb for causing a security flap, but later, wearing a death's grin, Landau assured him the director didn't hold a grudge. It may have gotten him yelled at, but his effort wasn't a frivolous attempt at sardonic mischief. He wanted to establish the security of his real identity. After all, his ass hung on the line here, and Dhar's.

Having exhausted his broth, Terr eyed the departure lounge, studying his prospective fellow passengers with little enthusiasm. He counted twelve with two females among them, both Karkan. They all wore a stoic, patient expression of someone caught in events beyond their control. He knew how that felt. Waiting around, doing nothing, did not come easily to him. In his commander persona, he always moved with purpose. He could see this waiting crap would take some time getting used to. Job or not, it went against the grain.

When at last Osaku Lines announced departure of intersystem flight OL-319 for Askaran, and will all passengers please make their way to Gate four, Terr glanced at Dhar and gave a sigh of relief. His brother grinned as they picked up their lightweight suitcases and followed the others. Dressed in a conservative light blue jacket and pants, a peaked black cap on her head bearing a yellow badge, the attendant scanned their tickets and they were politely directed to the access tube.

A Karkan flight crewman met them at the hatch and pointed to the cable-tube; deck three, please. The business class cabin compact, with two sleeping compartments and a small lounge. Pooling colors made random patterns in the Wall. At standard commercial boost the flight would take eleven hours to cover the four-and-a-half lights to Askaran and Terr intended to make full use of the sleeping compartment.

No one waved bye-bye when the liner lifted.

Watching Askaran grow in the Wall as the shuttle approached orbital insertion, Terr was thankful it was a warm world. Some sixty percent of the surface was water, which accounted for the mild climate. An axial tilt of only nine degrees meant the planet did not undergo wrenching seasonal variations. Still, a vast southern polar ice sheath gave the adventurous at heart somewhere to indulge their wild spirits. Tourism provided fourteen percent of the planet's gross revenue, the rest made up from agricultural exports, hydrocarbon feedstocks, and general manufacturing.

SC&C brought the shuttle down smoothly at Kronas Field, nestled against a sickle-shaped range of craggy hills sheltering Karach's sprawl and the open sea beyond. Tauri II glared bright in the northern sky. It still lacked two hours to noon, which coincided fairly closely with Terr's internal clock, something he appreciated. Ordinarily, he didn't suffer from travel lag, but too many shifts to his time sense would invariably have exacted an unpleasant price.

Kandu Hall met them in the arrival lounge when they cleared Immigration and Customs. Although an Askaran citizen, his short heavy frame, thick arms and legs, betrayed his origin from a high gravity world. Glossy short-cropped black hair slicked back, covered a perfectly round head that rested on broad shoulders and hardly any neck. Brown eyes looked out of a pleasant face, a small flat nose and generous mouth. Despite the air-conditioning, his mahogany skin shone with a faint sheen of perspiration.

From his brief, Terr knew Hall had a thriving career within the local Bureau of Cultural Affairs office before getting approached by the Diplomatic Branch to serve as an analyst. Once snared within the intelligence business, he flourished, climbing quickly through the hierarchy. When the Resident position became vacant, Anabb did not hesitate appointing him to the post over several older and more seasoned heads. That initially caused friction, but Hall was a consummate professional, very good at his job, and took care of the personnel problem with several judicious transfers and retirements. From the brief, Anabb had no cause to regret making the appointment. At least that's what the official blurb said and Terr was keen to see if the man lived up to the promo.

Hall flashed them a short smile, revealing even white teeth, and hurried toward them, pushing his way around other arrivals dressed in a variety of colorful costumes and people waiting for relatives, friends or enemies. His small stature made him look conspicuous. He raised his right hand to shoulder level in greeting, palm open.

"Ser Kerill-aa…Ser Randakla, welcome to Askaran, gentlemen. I trust you had a pleasant flight?" A twinkle in the Resident's eyes betrayed his amusement, a senior government official meeting two underworld figures. The assignment promised an interesting diversion and he wondered whether Agent Terrllss-rr and his partner would match Anabb's character descriptions. A Kaplan and a Wanderer, it certainly made them noticeable.

"Pleasant enough, thank you, Ser Hall, but it's good to be on the ground again," Terr said solemnly in Tashala, maintaining the cover, and raised his hand. "Is everything arranged?"

"Yes. You have a suite at the Tillana Cove Apartments on a one-year revolving lease. We don't expect to use it for that long, of course. It's right on the waterfront and overlooks the harbor and the marina. You will find it comfortable," Hall added dryly.

Terr thought he could detect a touch of wistful envy, which he could understand. He and Dhar were meant to be high rollers and everything had to fit the image, including up-market accommodation. Life in the Diplomatic Branch was hell.

"I procured combies for you," Hall went on. "Also on a revolving lease. Now, if you would follow me, we'll be on our way."

With heavy footsteps, he led them from the terminus into mild humidity and bright sunshine. The air heavy and fragrant, typical of tropical seaside climates. Terr squinted at the glare and looked around like any other tourist, taking everything in at a single glance. A broad avenue, shimmering in the heat, ran along the spaceport boundary. The glidewalks were mostly empty, people preferring the walkways to gawk at storefronts and other attractions. The communal queue ran a brisk business, taking on arrivals or bringing in passengers. Hall walked past hopeful drivers and made his way toward the officially reserved spaces.

He stopped beside a brand-new black Lexia 1100 combie, swept his palm against a sensor plate and the bubble lifted. Terr eyed the luxurious interior, beige leather seats, tasteful paneling and nodded in appreciation.

"I didn't know the Resident business paid so well," he remarked wryly and Hall chuckled.

"Only since I met you, Ser Kerill-aa. You should find the units I procured for you and Ser Randakla equally satisfactory."

"I am sure they will be," Terr said seriously, tossed in his suitcase and got into the left front seat. The Resident clearly knew his business, and wasn't going to lower his guard for a moment. As head of the Diplomatic Branch intelligence network on Askaran, he would naturally be coming in for his share of surveillance from some less savory members of society.

Someone could be curious why Hall took the trouble to meet two arrivals and might be even now pointing a directional mike their way.

Dhar got into the back seat and the bubble closed over them. Hall gave the computer the nav coordinates and allowed himself to relax. The power plant spooled up and the combie lifted with a soft whine, then surged as it entered the control network. The city slowly glided beneath them.

"The combie is payoff for favors rendered, Agent Terr. I'm supposed to be on a take from you two, remember? You can speak freely now. The vehicle is swept each day and there is a suppression field that defeats any monitoring device that might be planted between the sweeps. Your combies are similarly equipped. That's not something usually available to the general public—"

"One of the, ah, favors a Resident on a take provides?" Terr ventured with a bland smile and Hall grinned. So far, Terr's behavior fitted Anabb's description. He was yet to make up his mind about the Wanderer.

"Yes. On this mission, gentlemen, you'll want all the favors you can get. I presume you know how to run your own sweeps and operate the field?"

"We've been through it," Terr said.

"Good. Right now, we'll get you checked into your suite. After lunch, I suggest you go and visit your new business. Introduce yourselves to the men and office staff. From the data packs, you know the company is called Karach Salvage and Disposal and is a going concern with eleven hauling trucks. The Diplomatic Branch wasted no time snapping it up when the government seized the company and put it on the market. That's not uncommon when shady operators run foul of the Central Revenue Office. In this case the previous owners were short-changing their squeeze payments, or what the local Alikan Union Party chapter calls a unification tax, on quarterly earnings and are now enjoying retirement at the less than salubrious Solon medium security facility on Farsi Island. You can expect a call from chapter officials about that tax. Don't play hardball with them, Agent Terr. The AUP owns the government here and we don't want trouble with them."

"Actually, I planned to increase KSD's contribution above the going five percent. After all, if I am to be a no-questions-asked disposal operator, I'll want the AUP in my pocket."

"Anabb is not going to like the cost overhead if KSD's cashflow can't cover it, you know," Hall warned.

"He can whine all he wants. I'm simply protecting one of my exposed flanks. Besides, it could give me a link to other raider networks."

Hall raised an eyebrow. "Not bad. I haven't thought of it that way and it could be an angle."

"There is something I don't understand," Terr said. "The Diplomatic Branch must have known for some time that the Askaran government is corrupt."

"And by implication, I must have known, yes?"

"Why wasn't a submission made to the Bureau of Administrative Affairs on Captal to throw them out?"

"Ah, if it were only that simple, Agent Terr. I gathered a lot of corroborative material linking questionable Alikan Union Party activities with a number of government ministers, but as is often the case in such situations, we lack sufficient proof for BueAdmin to act. We also face cultural differences and behavioral norms. Captal has considerable looseness when interpreting what is acceptable conduct by a planetary government and the Articles of Association sometimes bind our hands. None of it makes my job any easier."

Terr understood Hall's position and sympathized, even if he didn't like it, and he didn't. Still, some things had to transcend political expediency.

"Ser Resident, I understand that morality can be simply an

accepted code of behavior in a given social context, not a universal rule, but when a government openly supports raiders, you must be stepping over the line."

"Yes. I understand your dilemma and is something the Bureau of Justice on Captal has wrestled with for some time, but at the moment everything is channeled toward establishing a conduit to this Provisional Committee."

"My mission," Terr said and nodded. If that meant carriers destroyed and lives lost in the interim, Captal figured the Serrll Combine needed to pay that price to secure lasting stability. He wasn't entirely comfortable with that logic, if it was logic at all. Commanding an M-3, he found it easy to tell the good guys from the bad and dispensed rough justice on sight. Being a pawn in Serrll's political process and seeing how it played out was a revealing experience, if not exactly enjoyable. It certainly opened his eyes to some of the broader issues Anabb must be dealing with. He wondered how the old fart managed to sleep at night. Then again, how did his uncle? Were either of them concerned with the morality of their actions as long as those actions supported an outcome for the greater good of all? And who decided what was the greater good? In their grand schemes and counterplots did anyone care for the shattered lives of individuals left in their wake? Terr had no ready answer.

"Precisely," Hall said. "Raiders and governments like Askaran will always be with us. Right now, though, Captal's focus is on the more immediate threat. We haven't altogether forgotten local corruption. We'll get around to sweeping them up once your mission is done."

"How many personnel in Karach Salvage? It was in Landau's data pack, but—"

"Yes. Things could have changed. It's still the same. A warehouse boss, an accountant, office comptroller, a secretary, and nineteen floor grunts, which includes eleven hauler drivers. I wouldn't be surprised if all of them are robbing the company blind, but that's how business is done out here. There are also four security personnel provided by a fairly large hypercorp, Tal-Al-Jeer. Not many people for the size of the facility, but the place is almost completely automated. The two service rings can take a fully loaded million-mikan freighter and provide roll-on roll-off turnaround in nine hours.

"As you know, Re Nette's partners, Warat Pulman and Tan Segal, run a front company, Global Transport, which acts as a clearinghouse for raider cargo. Landau had a close look at their books and found several interesting entries that led us to accounts held with Morgian Holdings and Chase Investments. Both brokerage houses hide behind very sophisticated encryption and security protocols that protect their customer's interests, which we haven't been able to penetrate, yet. Local privacy laws make such inquiries extremely difficult here, despite the fact that the Diplomatic Branch sought the writ. Landau suspects the accounts are slush pipes for paying off raiders and the local Alikan Union Party chapter. I tend to agree with him."

"And he's got security experts trying to crack the protocols. I know," Terr said.

When Landau first brought this up, he was troubled, not entirely comfortable with the idea of a government agency breaking into corporate systems to spy on the activities of its citizens, no matter what the apparent justification. Once on that path, who decided what was in the public interest? What other freedoms could be targeted? Landau assured him that penetration of Morgian and Chase was confined to their mission and the unmasking of the Provisional Committee, but Terr still felt uneasy.

"Getting back to my history lesson," Hall said briskly, "before Karach Salvage was wound down, Global Transport made several bids to acquire them, but the owners kept holding out for a better price. Global couldn't buy up shares and make a hostile takeover as KSD was a family concern and not listed on the local stock exchange. Although no longer on the chapter's executive, Pulman still maintains powerful connections inside the AUP, but in this case, they couldn't or wouldn't help him. Maybe the AUP simply didn't care who owned KSD as long as they got their cut."

"And shortly afterward, Karach Salvage owners fell out of favor with the Central Revenue Office," Terr added with a grin, which Hall returned.

"This is a hard business, Agent Terr. Of course, Global Transport had nothing to do with their demise, but word somehow got out that they tipped off the Alikan Union Party about the squeeze."

"Your doing, I suppose?" Terr mused.

"Like I said, it's a tough business. It didn't harm Global's reputation, but they are still short a disposal arm. Fully operational interstellar cargo handling facilities are scarce on Askaran and you've got a choice one. The bottom line? Pulman and Segal still lust after KSD, which should give you the required entry into Global when they approach you, which I'm sure they will."

"Pulman is definitely fronting for the AUP?" Terr demanded.

"As far as I can tell, yes. Segal secured finance when he started off, but he couldn't have set up Global and got two ships operating without the AUP's money. I have an operative inside the cell, but there is only so much he can get his hands on. They've got things compartmented and security is tight."

"Figures. And Trans National Haulage?"

"They will be your main opposition," Hall confirmed. "Undercutting them is where most of the funds for this operation will go."

"I wonder why Trans National didn't put in a bid themselves when KSD folded?"

"They did, but it was a token gesture only. It took a while to sift through the federal Business Affairs data banks, but we established that Pulman and Segal own a controlling interest in

Trans National, which places them in a bind, as TNH is a legitimate business. Acting as a fence for raider cargo is a sideline TNH opened at Segal's insistence. Even with that outlet, with trade picking up, Global Transport is cramped for capacity. They hold a small operation in Otilando, but that's only a support facility for their remaining vessel, *Pilla*, after having lost *Drakin*, and has minimal cargo handling capability. When the Central Revenue Office announced tenders for Karach Salvage, it presented a perfect opportunity for the Diplomatic Branch to launch its penetration, and Anabb made sure our bid would win."

"If Pulman and Segal are run by the local Alikan Union Party cell, I'm surprised they allowed KSD to slip through their fingers."

"Yes. Nothing simpler. Funding AUP operations is expensive and backing Global Transport's bid would have been a considerable financial drain on the local chapter's resources. Allowing an outside party to buy Karach Salvage netted the government a windfall and the AUP secured an ongoing cashflow through the unification tax payments. What's more the deal didn't cost them a Serrll fiver. Or perhaps the chapter president, Sarek Laral, blocked Pulman's bid. They've sunk hundreds of millions into commissioning a new vessel, *Paun*, and the AUP may not have wanted to extend its exposure. Then again, it could be personal. From what I know the two men don't exactly get along."

"Landau said the same thing." Fighting for the Sargon/Palean merger was one thing, but that clearly didn't interfere with the waging of internal power struggles. Some things never change. "The AUP got what they wanted, but I bet Pulman and Segal were somewhat sore."

Hall shrugged. "Like I said—"

"Yeah, I know. It's a tough business," Terr added, his expression grim. Not only tough, but dirty as well. So, what else was new? "The Alikan Union Party doesn't mind getting a revenue stream, but at the end of the day, Global Transport are nothing but raider scum to be exploited until expiry of their use-by date, even when it's run by one of their own."

"A hardened attitude, but realistic," Hall agreed matter-of-factly.

"This Pulman character sounds like a real piece of work."

"Yes. Don't be mistaken. He is utterly ruthless and so is his partner. You don't want to be on the receiving end from either of them. You should be safe, at least until they get their hands on Karach Salvage."

"That's comforting to know."

"There is one more thing you must keep in mind. Rakliva, General Manager of Trans National, is Segal's brother-in-law."

"Which accounts for Global's interest to make TNH handle raider cargo." Terr snorted and shook his head. "Everybody one nice, cozy family."

"Yes, and Rakliva worked hard to keep it that way. He already absorbed several small operators who got in his way."

"Your warning being, if I start pushing, he'll push back?"

"That's his operating pattern."

"I am warned."

"Excuse me, Ser Resident, with the loss of *Drakin*, do you know if they are attempting to secure another hull?" Dhar queried. "Landau didn't have anything on that."

"I don't have anything either, Agent Dharaklin," Hall said. "They've got *Paun* almost ready to go, but a replacement hull for *Drakin*? Any leads you might uncover would be useful."

"Presumably you secured its ident dump and emission signature?"

"Yes. You can rest easy. *Paun* won't be going anywhere without the Fleet knowing about it, and neither will *Pilla*."

About to ask the obvious question, Dhar realized the equally obvious answer. Kandu Hall hadn't seized the ships because they were integral to penetrating Global's operation.

"Talking of ships," Terr added. "Do you know if Pulman and Segal have a private vessel stashed somewhere?"

"For a quick getaway, you mean?" Hall said and grinned. "They don't, but they're free to borrow the AUP chapter's run-about, *Trava*. It's a Laikar hull, somewhat smaller than an M-1, but equally as fast. My office has kept an eye on its movements through Kronas' SC&C. Nothing suspicious there as far as we can determine. It's a business vessel and they use it as such."

"I must say, I am impressed with what you've done here," Terr commented with genuine admiration. "It's one thing to absorb information from a memory chip and another to actually pick over the real thing."

Hall's smile was grim. "Believe me, Agent Terr, although I know this place well, I still have headaches from my own forced learning sessions."

Terr laughed, liking the man. More importantly, he trusted Hall, and on this assignment that counted for a lot. "Your office. Does anyone know if you're compromised?"

"Yes. Some of my staff suspect I'm bought by an underworld syndicate, which makes going to work less enjoyable. If you two do your jobs, I hope to see my reputation restored."

"If we don't, you probably won't have to worry about your reputation," Terr told him seriously.

Hall gave both of them a searching look. "One last thing, gentlemen. Be careful how you handle yourselves. You'll be dealing with tough operators and they don't mess around."

"We'll try not to get in the way of a falling crate," Terr assured him with a crooked smile.

As the combie neared the seaside it slowed and dropped from the control network. Soaring condominiums crowded the broad beachfront avenue and the marina, with lesser buildings huddling in their shadow. Long smooth swells creamed against white sands. There were lots of people in the water and even more on the wide beach itself, in the open or hiding under broad, colored umbrellas. Rows of majestic palms lined the boulevard, sheltering stores, kiosks, and vendor stalls. There were no glidewalks and Terr understood why. Anyone coming here wouldn't be in any hurry to leave.

The combie swung around a white rectangular tower, its sides patterned in blue strips of color-reactive ceramic, and descended. The block probably forty stories high, but not the tallest. With the power plant spooling down, the combie settled on a circular landing pad in a crowded parking lot surrounded by broad-leafed trees and immaculate green lawns. Hall opened the bubble and waited for his passengers to collect their luggage. The air moist and warm, filled with the hiss of surf, laughter, and animated noises. Terr took a deep breath of salty scented air, wishing he could take a few days off to enjoy the attractions on offer. Giving a wistful sigh, he squared his shoulders and strode after the Resident.

The circular foyer well lit from real floor-to-ceiling windows and overhead chandeliers. From the humid atmosphere outside, the controlled climate inside nearly cold. A sprinkling of guests dressed from beach shorts and revealing swimsuits to formal wear filled the floor. Hall walked briskly to the front desk and waited. A starched individual in a wine-red uniform saw him and hurried over.

"Ah, Ser Hall! Welcome!"

"Ser Kerill-aa and Ser Randakla checking in," Hall announced crisply and the attendant's smile warmed noticeably.

"Of course, Ser Hall. We were expecting them. Gentlemen, welcome to Tillana Cove Apartments. Your slightest desire is our command."

Terr hoped so, given the cost of the fully serviced suite, but he didn't say anything as he stared at the man. Might as well start cultivating an image of a hard-nosed son of a bitch right away. The individual bit his lip and cleared his throat.

"If I can have your ID tag, Ser...to complete the check-in?" he said weakly and held out a manicured hand.

Terr dug out the tag and held it out. The attendant scanned

it and gave it back. "Everything in order…Ser?" He glanced at Dhar, who handed his over. Satisfied, he looked up. "Front!"

A little urchin appeared, also dressed in red, towing a brass luggage rack. He pushed back his little round cap, grabbed the two suitcases and piled them onto the trolley.

"Thirty, suite two," the attendant snapped.

Hall looked at his two charges and grinned. "Dinner at seven. I'll pick you up."

"I shall be expecting you, Ser Hall," Terr said sternly.

The Resident nodded to Dhar, turned and walked quickly toward wide entrance panels. They slid out of his way and he was gone.

Terr glared at the page. The urchin gave a fleeting grin and pushed the trolley to a bank of four cable-tubes. Inside, he issued an instruction to the housekeeping computer and the door closed. The tube walls turned transparent as it surged up, giving the impression they were going up the tower's side. Only a holoview image, but the illusion was perfect. When the tube stopped, the image faded and the interior once again showed the tasteful solid-wood veneer.

Terr stepped out and his feet sank into thick creamy pile. The wide corridor lit with light strips along the floor edges and ceiling. The uniqueness came from walls showing an open beachfront on one side and the city on the other. Pale blue hip-high railing provided a semblance of mental security.

The page stopped and pressed his palm against a black rectangle set into the virtual railing and a doorway appeared.

"You can cancel the views, Ser, or change them through the housekeeping computer," the boy said brightly.

Terr held his palm against the rectangle and the door opened, the biometrics stored in the housekeeping computer from his ID tag. The boy unloaded the suitcases and Dhar stepped into the room. Terr gave the boy a Serrll fiver.

"Thank you, Ser! If you want anything, and I mean anything, ask for Darren."

"I will be sure to do that," Terr said gruffly. The boy blanched, bobbed his head and fled with his trolley. Terr smiled after him, his thoughts wandering to Alasi and what the kid was up to these days. No longer a kid, he reminded himself, but a young man now. He walked in and the door hissed shut behind him.

The entire front wall was one long polarized window. On his right stood a formal dining table surrounded by stylish formchairs with an open plan kitchen beyond it. A Wall display station took up the left wall, in front of which were laid two soft couches, four seats and a low tea table. Fragrant, rainbow-colored orchids spilled out of a crystal vase. A door beside him opened and Dhar appeared.

"Some setup, my brother. The beds are enormous and the spa in the bathroom is already bubbling. I don't believe it's ever off."

Terr raised a finger to his lips and opened his suitcase. He rummaged among the contents and brought out a small rectangular flat panel. A touch on a contact pad and he swept the device around the room. He checked both bedrooms and bathrooms. Dhar was right about the spa and he looked forward to trying his out.

"Okay, the place is clean."

"I apologize, Sankri," Dhar growled, clearly annoyed at his lapse in security.

"Forget it, Nightwings, but we need to be careful. Pulman and Segal will undoubtedly try to penetrate us sooner or later, as will Trans National."

"Or someone acting on their behalf," Dhar added woodenly.

"Count on it. We might as well get into the habit." He stepped to the window and looked at the azure sea as it met the sharp divide with the dark blue of the sky. There was something compelling about the deeps that always fascinated him. Even as a kid on Kaplan, he felt a kinship with those who ventured onto the open waters, not unlike the silent vastness of the Saffal. Far below the beach looked like a sandpit and the figures were dolls.

Thinking of his home, his mother's tragic face swam before him, contorted with grief at the loss of her beloved, his father's bleached bones scattered somewhere in the Saffal deeps, a Diplomatic Branch mission gone sour. Strange how Anar'on now claimed Terr as well. His mother never the same afterward. As her only son, he knew she loved him desperately, but that love had turned to control his life and destiny. The family Llss-rr were wealthy and powerful, politicians and spacefarers all. Follow your uncle's example, she urged, and reach for power on Captal…and continue the Llss-rr dynasty. She never actually said it, but she didn't have to.

Unfortunately for her, his father had reached for the stars and passed the wanderlust to his son. Terr remembered grasping for the whorls of light ever since he first saw the band of stars through an open window and understood what they were. His destiny was among those pretty lights, not in some hallowed chamber of power with its intrigues, murky deals and political backstabbing. The realization had come much later. When he left for the Fleet Academy, his mother denied him and he had no shadow. In the following years, he'd spoken to her only twice.

Gazing into the naked face of the sea, he wondered whether it ever returned the things it washed away from the beach of time. In the end, he looked away, afraid to see what might lie on those sands. He set his lips and sighed. He could not afford to indulge in contemplation, not now.

When he turned, all he could see were the red slits of his brother's eyes. Something passed between them and words came to him, blazing from the *Saftara*. Death stole over him and he reveled in its power, its comforting hand and a promise they would always be one. He reached with an open palm and held up his hand.

"Nightwings, the shadow who walks at night and lights my

days."

Dharaklin saw the glow of power surround his brother in a cloak of blue radiance and he hesitated, understanding that Sankri had undergone a mystical experience. Whatever his brother may be feeling, he knew without hesitation that Sankri wanted to share it with him, for they were one.

He took a step separating them and raised his hand. Sankri touched his chest and blue fires slithered along his arm and slowly spread until both stood beneath Death's hand. Dhar returned the touch and was satisfied.

"My strange brother from the skies, I feel your power and I am comforted," he said softly, lest something loud shattered the magic. Standing there, apart, yet together, the moment was eternal because they had nowhere to go, nothing to do, but simply share, bound as they were in Death.

Terr pulled back his hand. "I miss the Saffal deeps," he whispered, struggling to form into words the complexity of feelings tugging at him. "I miss the silence and the solitude and its rolling openness. When I am there, I have no wants, no desires. I am complete and fulfilled. Here, Death calls to me. Why is that, my brother of the night?"

Dhar found himself experiencing emotions not natural to a Wanderer. Shaped by the desert and the unrelenting demands it made simply to survive left little room for sentimentality. Sankri had contaminated him, or enriched him, not certain which, when on that fateful day he chose to unite with his alien brother. For him, the Saffal was…the Keep of Death and the Wanderers were god's children. He left it at that. Clearly, for Sankri it was far more.

"The Saffal completes you because there, you are one with Death. It has no expectations and seeks nothing from you," Dhar said carefully. "My brother, the worlds of the Serrll are not Anar'on and its people are not Wanderers."

"But Death doesn't see it that way," Terr said after a time and something cold ran down Dhar's spine.

He remembered an old, old fable his master used to tell him. Sidhara told of Sarumajan, the destroyer of worlds. An alien adept who had transcended Death, standing suspended in space with two stars adorning his feet, lightnings devouring a world. If true, Sankri was Death manifest and untold billions could die before his thirst was slaked and the gods relented.

"Perhaps it is you who does not see it that way, my brother. Who are you to stand in judgment? Until you resolve that question, you will have no peace."

Terr slowly lifted his head. "I could have peace, Nightwings, if I simply let go. It's only the thought of Death marching unchecked across the Serrll that holds me back."

"Then you are still to resolve the question."

Terr peered at his brother. "Have you resolved it for yourself?"

"I live by the words of the *Saftara*."

Terr said nothing, staring into some part of himself where Dhar could not go.

When the glow gradually faded, Terr looked at his Wanderer brother, gave a wan smile of loss, and patted Dhar on the shoulder. "Tah, the gods will tell." The moment passed and reality again intruded, and he wished it were not so. He cleared his throat and took a deep breath. "Do you want lunch, a break?"

Dhar also felt the loss of passing, disturbed by the experience. He took comfort knowing that when his brother needed him, he would reach out and Dhar would be there for him. He was prepared to wait until then.

"No. I ate enough on the flight over, but I will take a shower. Afterward, we can go and check out our new business venture. I kind of like the idea of being an underworld muscle."

When they freshened up, valuables and the snoop scanner were left in the room safe, keyed to both of them. A door in the kitchen took them to their private landing ramp. A blue and a gray Lexia 1100 combie hovered side by side.

Terr extended a hand at the vehicles and grinned. "Pick one," he said brightly.

Dhar shook his head and made for the nearest, the blue one. He pressed his palm against the bubble's right side and it immediately opened. Terr climbed in and settled back into the upholstery. Dhar closed the bubble and spooled up the power plant. The ramp's wall slid down and they were looking at an open sea. With a surge of power the combie shot away from the building and the bubble automatically darkened.

Following the long coastline with its unbroken expanse of white beaches and a scattering of resorts, the city gave way to an open countryside of gently rolling grasslands and fields of swaying grain. The craggy buttresses gradually flattened as they clawed toward the coast. Some forty talans from Karach, nestled against forested hills, Hydra Industrial City opened into a pattern of small landing aprons, chemical and industrial feedstock plants, and manufacturing complexes. Fractionation towers, cooling stacks and chimneys stabbed into a humid sky, belching white steam and dark wastes. Two aprons held parked freighters, apparently deserted with no movement around them. There were ordered pockets of greenery and trees, which softened the harsh utilitarian image. Lots of heavy air traffic, mostly long cargo haulers, fluttered around the facility.

The combie tilted to port and sagged as it swung toward the largest landing field north of the industrial complex. A three-katalan-high fence surrounded the four square talans of apron seemingly stretching into the hills, protected by an orange shimmer of a screen. At least the perimeter looked secure, Terr mused. Two huge warehouses, each one 200 by 300 katalans, stretched across the vast field. He knew they could hold over four million mikans of cargo, seemingly a colossal amount. Compared to a Bulk Carrier, which could haul two million mikans, for a ground facility it wasn't much, but the idea was to sell cargo, not hold inventory.

An empty landing ring took up the four hundred katalans

of open apron on the left of each warehouse, capable of taking a freighter. Clusters of silos, bulk chemical storage tanks and rows of stacked containers crowded the far field perimeter. Across the gray roof of each warehouse, what must be ten-katalan-high letters, spelled out Karach Salvage and Disposal. Beneath each name were painted equally large designators—A and B. Eight long cargo trucks hovered in a neat row beside Warehouse A. Before them, dwarfed by the towering structure of Warehouse B, a small two-story building flanked a parking lot filled with combies and several sled-pads. The whole thing made for a fancy layout and Terr was impressed despite himself.

Dhar brought the combie down and Terr watched a sled-pad with two men emerge out Warehouse B and race toward them. The sled-pad settled some two katalans from them and the men, hands on holstered needlers, warily approached the combie. They were dressed in black one-piece coveralls bearing yellow two-ringed Tal-Al-Jeer badges on their upper arms. With the power plant spooling down, Dhar opened the bubble.

Barely glancing at the security guards, Terr got out, squinted against the sun's glare and waited for them. Both were locals, over two katalans tall, of medium build and dark skinned. They stopped and everybody eyed each other. Not bothering with a greeting, the smaller guard glanced at the posh Lexia, then fixed Terr with a hard stare.

"This is a private facility—"

Terr raised his hand before the guard could finish. "Why wasn't my combie interrogated as we made the approach?" he asked softly, but his eyes glinted with ice.

"And what's it to you, Mister?" the guard snapped in return.

"The place is like a tube station," Terr said in disgust. "It's wide open. And what's it to me?" He glanced at Dhar. "We own it."

The guard did not seem overawed at the news. "New owners, eh? We heard you guys were coming. I assume you can prove who you are?"

Terr handed over his ID tag. The guard took one look and straightened. "Seems in order. Thank you, Ser Kerill-aa."

Dhar offered his tag without a word. The guard barely glanced at it.

"Now that we all know who I am, who're you?" Terr asked.

"Naralima, Chief of security."

"If this is an example of how you run security, that might not be for much longer. From now on, I want our SC&C to challenge anything flying in our space, including birds. Nothing lands at this facility unless they're properly authenticated. If they fail to comply, you're authorized to use whatever non-lethal force is required to prevent landing, or if that's not possible, detain the occupants. Clear?"

"Ser!" Naralima snapped to and raised his right hand, palm out.

"Right. You can show us to the office."

Tight lipped the guard nodded. "If you will follow me, please."

As they made their way to the administration block the second guard mounted the sled-pad and sped toward Warehouse B, the letter painted in dark blue on either side of one enormous opening. This close the sheer wall loomed like a cliff and at least forty katalans high. Although painted light blue, constructed from energy-absorbing ceramic, heat radiated from its surface in palpable waves.

Inside the admin block cool air and polarized windows made the atmosphere much more comfortable. Plush violet carpet muffled their footsteps as the guard led them to a large curved workstation. Two staffers stared at them from the background. Le Kara lifted her head and her small mouth tightened in a frown. The petit Palean looked too young to be an executive secretary and general receptionist, but Terr wasn't fooled. Kara's record showed her to be an accomplished woman with a Scholar's degree in business administration. Everyone and everything here were not as they seemed.

The guard raised his hand in a salute and quickly strode out.

"May I help you, gentlemen?" Kara asked pleasantly, a standard smile fixed on her face that didn't touch her enormous black eyes. Her bearing poised and confident without projecting indifference. Terr wondered if he looked at another Re Nette perhaps.

"You can take us to Nei Than, Kara," he announced frigidly. "In case he asks, I am Kerill-aa, and my partner, Randakla."

Kara's starched smile vanished and she scrambled to her feet. "Oh, I didn't know you had landed, Ser! Had you notified the office, someone would have met you at Kronas," she piped, her long fingers twining in agitation.

"No need to apologize. We were met," Terr told her.

She didn't know what to make of that. In the end, she extended a slim arm toward the cable-tube. "Senior corporate staff are upstairs, Ser."

They piled in and the tube immediately ascended. The doors opened onto a wide foyer. In the middle, luxurious form-chairs surrounded a small table. Large potted plants lined the walls. A long floor-to-ceiling window showed the parked haulers and the warehouse beyond it, set against the backdrop of a looming industrial complex. Hugging the foyer walls were offices—three on the left and four on the right. The floor decor an elegant light blue without being flashy. It looked like blue was the corporate color. Kara made for the nearest office on their right and touched a waist-high access pad beside what looked like a solid-wood door. The panel slid into the wall and Terr walked in without waiting for an invitation.

The middle-aged Palean inside looked up from the Wall and glared at Terr. "What in the pits is this? Who are these men, Kara?"

"You really should be more polite toward your new owners, Nei Than," Terr said pleasantly and the Palean's jaw sagged.

Terr turned to Kara. "I want Bai Linn, Gender Rull, and yourself in the meeting room. Five minutes."

"Yes, Ser." She glanced at Dhar and hurried toward the next office. The door panel slid shut after her with a soft hiss.

Terr made himself comfortable in one of the formchairs facing the desk and Dhar took the other. Without waiting, he offered Nei Than his ID tag. Still somewhat miffed the Palean scanned the tag and did the same with Dhar's.

"I apologize for my behavior, friend Kerill-aa…Randakla. I knew you were coming—"

Terr waved his hand. "It's all right, and we didn't give you any warning."

"Do you have accommodation—"

"Everything is arranged," Terr assured him, studying Palean.

In the man's confident posture and a general air of competence, he recognized a subordinate who did his job and more. Nei Than was also a blatant thief. Two rather bulky investment accounts testified to a successful secondary sideline, which meant he was keen to keep his job. Terr had gone over everyone's record with meticulous care without learning anything not already suspected. They were not outright criminals, corporate crime having a looser interpretation on Askaran, but his employees were not scrupulously honest either. With their own dealings, the previous owners had merely overstepped the tacitly recognized boundary. Anyone trading with raiders must be contaminated. Here, business was business and Karach Salvage hadn't been too particular where that business came from. However, when Askaran's entire government apparently slept with raiders, it wasn't difficult to understand the prevailing corporate culture. Nei Than would do what was asked of him without too many complaints, and Terr wasn't here to judge or reform his staff.

"Before we talk to the others, what's our operating position?"

The Palean relaxed slightly and folded his arms on the desk. The sudden appearance of the new owners unsettled him, especially the sight of the taciturn Wanderer. He was also relieved. Managing Karach Salvage was one thing, setting policy and responsible for it was a duty he did not care to shoulder. It also distracted him from his, ah, other interests. Taking note of Kerill-aa's stern expression, he wondered how viable those interests now were.

"I am glad you're here, Ser. The last few days have been difficult to say the least. You probably scanned our books and it doesn't look good. The Central Revenue Office fines and payment of unification back taxes were a considerable drain on our liquidity. To make matters worse, we had to pay off on cargo already delivered, which caused an additional strain on our solvency position. I was forced to take out an overdraft against our operating account with Talbian Trust in order to cover running expenses."

Terr and Dhar *had* poured over KSD's books, and so far everything the Palean told him matched Terr's brief, but there had to be more. "What's our inventory holding?"

"Warehouse A holds almost 800,000 mikans of assorted machinery and electronics. B has a million in perishables and we have 150,000 mikans of heavy fuel oil in our tanks."

"Way too much," Terr commented and Nei Than looked apologetic.

"We don't normally carry this much inventory, friend Kerill-aa, but we couldn't trade out of our position as Business Affairs effectively froze our account until we were sold. It's only within the last nine days that we returned to a positive cashflow. Still, the scandal has hit us hard and many of our customers have fled."

"Gone to Trans National Haulage, you mean," Terr said dryly and the Palean bobbed his head.

"Or Global Transport. We lost two important off-planet accounts and I don't see them coming back."

"We'll talk about them later," Terr said and stood up. "Under the circumstances, you've done well. Let's meet the others."

Nei Than rose slowly and cleared his throat. "I might as well give it to you all in one hit, Ser. We also carry three-and-a-half million Serrlls in outstanding account receivables. I fear we may have to write those off as bad debts."

Terr wagged his index finger. "No way. You get Le Kara to issue notices. Anyone who fails to pay up within ten days will be prosecuted and their name posted on the debtors bulletin board. I won't have customers taking advantage of our past difficulties."

"As you wish." Nei Than cast a wary glance at Dhar's imposing two point-three katalan frame and hurried out, striding quickly toward the first door across the foyer.

The three occupants inside the meeting room quickly rose when Terr and Dhar walked in. The windows were tinted to cut glare and the ceiling glowed a pleasant shade of pale green. Bai Linn was thin and wore a concerned expression, hands fluttering in a characteristic mannerism. Terr recognized the accountant type right away. Beside him, Kara had regained most of her composure and looked cool and beautiful. Across the long oval conference table, a rough-looking local towered over everybody, his black two-katalan body heavy, but none of it fat. Terr figured Gender Rull knew how to take care of himself and how to handle warehouse roughnecks, and that was good. He wanted someone who could crunch bones.

Nei Than made the introductions and Rull scowled, his eyes measuring Terr with clear disdain.

"New owner, eh? You don't look like a starched shirt to me, Mister."

Terr measured Rull and gave the warehouse boss a cold smile. "I handle the business end. My partner here takes care of problems."

"Problems? What kind of problems?"

Terr's eyes flickered at Dhar. "Show him."

Before Rull knew what happened, Dhar stood in front of him. His powerful fist slammed against Rull's chest and the burly straw boss went sprawling across the carpet. Kara gave a little yelp and her hands flew to her mouth. Nei Than and Bai Linn turned even grayer, their fingers still.

Rull picked himself up and massaged his chest. Terr took one step toward him and lashed out with his left leg. The kick connected with a dull thump and the big man went down again.

"In case you thought I was a sissy," Terr hissed and waited for him to get up.

Rull took a bit more time to heave himself up. When he did, he straightened and forced a rueful smirk. "Like I said, you don't look like a starched shirt to me...Ser Kerill-aa," he murmured and pulled out a formchair. Without waiting, he lowered himself into it and massaged his chest. The chair creaked beneath his bulk.

Terr swept his eyes across the others and took the chair at the head of the table. Dhar sat down on his left.

"Now that we're all properly introduced, I want to announce a few policy changes. The previous owners ran Karach Salvage and Disposal like a hobby and your balance sheet reflects that. They milked incoming receipts for their personal use and reinvested only enough to keep the operation viable. That's history. As of right now, the new business plan calls for making Karach Salvage the largest cargo clearinghouse on Askaran. That means upgrading and expanding our handling facilities. Extra capacity means attracting more customers, any customer. If they got cargo, we don't ask where they got it. Given our current fiscal position, we cannot afford to be picky. Clear?"

There was an exchange of meaningful looks and some clearing of throats, but Terr wasn't fooled. This crowd knew exactly what went down, they weren't innocents. He looked directly at Bai Linn.

"What's our per mikan margin spread?" He knew from the data packs, but wanted to hear it for himself.

The little Palean licked his lips and his large black eyes flickered at Nei Than. "We average twenty-three Serrlls gross per mikan on all freighted cargo. After fixed and operating expenses, we may net one. We buy and sell to a set price list for an item of merchandise. Cargo resale generates our principal cashflow stream and the margin is never less than eleven percent."

Terr looked hard at everybody. "Four percent on freight and eleven on sales. That's not nearly good enough. My backers and I didn't sink close to three hundred million Serrlls into this place for a lousy eleven percent return. We'll meet outstanding contracts, but as of right now Karach Salvage and Disposal ceases to cart freight. It's a mug's game and I am more than happy for Trans National Haulage to carry the business. Nobody makes much from handling cargo point-to-point. Margins are thin and haulers rely on volume throughput to survive, and there is only so much volume to go around. We cut out haulage and we also cut the associated operating and administrative expenses.

"As our name says, we buy and resell cargo. We'll use our trucks to simply pick up or deliver for those who don't have sufficient capacity to do it themselves. That's the value add, and we'll charge dearly for the service: ten Serrlls flat per mikan hauled. Customers can howl, but we don't waste our time anymore on small throwaway jobs. The accounting and grunt work is the same as for big volume items without the compensating revenue. The people we're after are bulk operators who can pick up and deliver using their own trucks. I want the landing rings out there occupied around the clock. Another thing. When we purchase cargo, we pay on valuation, there and then. No more crap about paying when we get paid."

Nei Than looked alarmed. "Ser, that means holding inventory which we might not be able to clear. We could be bleeding cash on a dubious future account receivable. With respect, that's a good way to go broke. I don't know your background in business, but I've been comptroller of KSD for six years and I don't intend seeing it run into the ground." And see his profitable sideline dry up as well, he added to himself.

Tempted to tell him if the business hadn't been run into the ground, Terr wouldn't be here now. Instead, he nodded and leaned forward.

"Neither do I, and nobody said we must buy junk. We stick to readily convertible commodities. If a seller doesn't like it, he can take his stuff to Global Transport. To make my policy work, we'll manage our margins. Our cost structure is pretty lean already, but I'm sure there are things we can do to make it even leaner. If not, we'll look at streamlining procedures. We cannot manipulate the price lists because they reflect an agreed position among all haulers and I don't want to get into a price-cutting war to gain market share just yet. We must put the concern on a much healthier fiscal footing before I consider that option. What we can and will do is manipulate *our* position. We'll start off by paying five percentage points above the list for inventory, and resell at five points below the list. For perishables, we'll go down to eight points, but we shouldn't be carrying perishables anyway. Once word gets out that we're paying up-front and paying a premium, we'll be swamped with customers, and the increased throughput should more than offset our acquisition costs. Inventory turnover should also improve when buyers realize *their* acquisition cost structure will come down if they deal with us. Admittedly, our net book margin will be lower, but *effective* earnings will be higher due to increased volumes."

"What's to stop our competition from aping our practice?" Nei Than demanded, not looking convinced.

"Nothing, but consider this. They're mainly set up as point-to-point freight haulers. Apart from Global Transport, cargo disposal is a secondary business line, whereas for us, it will be our only line. I want a planet-wide advertising campaign running within two days on all commercial channels and intersystem trade bulletin boards announcing the new policy. Before we do anything, we must clear our current inventory. To do it, we'll run a fire sale, twenty percent off everything. I want our warehouses empty. We'll spread the word to other haulers that we'll lease warehouse space on a cash-up-front basis. Trans National and some others may have larger storage capacities, but few can match us with roll-on roll-off automation, and that's our competitive advantage, which we'll exploit to the full.

"One more thing. Everyone here and the grunts in the warehouses are now on a percentage bonus, payable quarterly. The bonus pool is two percent of quarterly net earnings and will be divided as a proportion of an individual's base salary—which is now increased by fifteen percent across the board. Bai Linn? Accounting is to get this implemented immediately. Each person at Karach Salvage is a valuable resource and we won't succeed unless everyone pulls their weight. I'm prepared to reward effort, but if someone lets us down, I'll simply bury him. You can spread that around, Rull."

The muscular man's craggy features split in a wide grin. "I think I'm gonna like it here," he announced comfortably.

Terr slowly looked around the table. "We hold a lot of inventory and we push through a lot of cargo. I don't know what our leakage rate is normally and I don't care. Bear this in mind. Any personal sidelines somebody has going erodes KSD's profitability and everyone else's bonus. If I find that someone is profiteering at my expense, that person will simply disappear, permanently. Don't tempt me to demonstrate." He stared directly at the warehouse boss. Others shifted uncomfortably in their seats trying to look inconspicuous. "Rull, that's also one for your boys, and make sure Chief Naralima understands."

The big man set his mouth and nodded. "I'll pass the word along," he said heavily, maintaining a look of newborn innocence and suspecting it wasn't working.

"There is something else you need to consider, Ser," Nei

Than piped, hands twining nervously. "Our expanded activities could attract unwanted attention from regulatory authorities and the Diplomatic Branch."

Terr's smile anything but warm. "We don't want to upset the Alikan Union Party, do we? Bai Linn? Our quarterly unification tax payment is now six-and-a-half points. As for the Diplomatic Branch, they won't be sticking their nose into our business. That part is taken care of."

By the exchange of looks, they knew what that meant; Kandu Hall was bought.

Bai Linn licked his lips and his fingers twined. "Ser, increasing our tax payment could set a bad precedent for other haulers. You must know we don't have the liquidity to pay the tax or implement your policies."

"Our business plan is to grind down our competition, not worry about wounded sensibilities. To cover our immediate liquidity needs, you'll find five million Serrlls in our Talbian Trust operating account. That should be enough to get things rolling until business picks up and we recover outstanding receivables," Terr said briskly and rose. Everybody immediately followed. "Tomorrow, we'll work on the specifics." He gathered Dhar with his eyes and they walked out, leaving the others staring after them.

Chapter Seven

After fourteen days, Zor-Ell had grown comfortable wearing James Grant's persona. The week's routine always the same. At seven-thirty in the morning, Jim would make his way to work from his fifth floor Queensberry Street apartment near the Museum and IMAX center, along Exhibition Street until he hit Collins Street, then a block down to KPMG.

Initially, Zor-Ell could not believe the rush hour traffic, the swarm of pedestrians crowding the sidewalks, the pungent smell of vehicle exhausts and the overwhelming noise, far removed from the park-like atmosphere of cities he was accustomed to. Traffic lights provided a semblance of order in an otherwise chaotic environment.

From Jim's memories, Melbournians were comparatively well behaved; poignant images of New York, Los Angeles and Delhi gave him a real glimpse of chaos. With the exception of Delhi, Jim had seen the other cities first-hand, but had no desire to visit India. Television documentaries were vivid enough. Even Jim wondered how that multitude managed to eke out an existence in the pervasive squalor, abject poverty, lack of sanitation and basic services. Yet, the majority of people on the planet shared that way of life in varying degree as the norm. In contrast, what they called the developed world enjoyed a standard of living that could only be dreamed off by most, and that lifestyle bought at the expense of profligate use of natural resources and obsolescent industrial consumer output. It seemed incredible that someone could actually live on this planet without ever having seen a plasma television, a camcorder, a rocket launch, or knew a cell phone. Still, for those who did enjoy a level of prosperity, comfort didn't come free. People worked for it and some missed out, as beggars and derelicts around the Melbourne Central rail station testified.

The vibrancy of the people, their energetic rushing about, always doing something, having a sense of purpose, almost overwhelmed his senses. Zor-Ell understood those motivations, springing from a desire to excel, to dominate and prove one's superiority, whether materially or intellectually. Most of it biologically programmed, directed at either attracting a mate or pursuit of personal power, which in turn translated into political and national power. The competitive spirit of the species was unbelievably strong and accounted for the success of their technology and material prosperity, although not enjoyed by all. Karth was entirely correct in his assessment. Despite having reached the Moon, Earth was still very much tribal and exhibited every marker trait of that tribalism.

Lunchtime would be spent strolling, window-shopping, or resting under a tree at Treasury Gardens. Zor-Ell found those outings pleasant, allowing him to observe first-hand the texture and density of people's lives around him. At five-thirty, sometimes earlier if the workload permitted, Jim would finish up, crowd into an available elevator with others who only wanted out of the damned place, and walk home. For most, home was a suburb that had to be reached by car, train or some other mode of transport, an hour or more away; more tension, pressure, crawling traffic, road rage, and nervous exhaustion. Having a downtown apartment within easy walking distance, Jim was spared the stress and took full advantage of that freedom.

Sometimes, he didn't go home right away. An avid reader, he would browse the many bookstores along Bourke and Elizabeth Streets. His current passion was research into comparative religions and early history of Christianity. With a book open before him, sipping a flat white at a roadside cafe, happy to lose himself in the machinations, treachery and scheming of early church founders, or simply watch the centered intensity of self-absorbed pedestrians. When he wasn't studying religion, he worked through analyses of current politics, garnished with forays into science fiction, techno thrillers and all manner of sciences, from string theory to cosmology. What a shock to find that Earth researched string theory this early in its development. What they would do with the knowledge once they realized the equations could only be brought into a dazzling coherent whole within a three-dimensional time matrix, Zor-Ell dared not contemplate.

Apart from his sister Marjorie, Jim had no other family, not in Melbourne. Their parents were retired and lived on the Gold Coast near Brisbane, having purchased land near the sea in the '80s before the building boom there swamped the landscape with condominiums and high-rise hotels. They never came down and he seldom went up. He exchanged birthday and Christmas cards, and sometimes a phone call. They lived their life and he had his. When he felt the walls of his apartment crowding him, he would see Margie. She was always ready with a plate of real home cooking, faintly sneering at his culinary prowess, and of course, Raileen always relished seeing her uncle, a reliable source of candy, pocket money, an occasional movie or, smiling with a conspiratorial grin, a sinful dessert at some restaurant.

When Jim got home, he would change into black jeans and a plain sweater when cool, have dinner using previous night's leftovers or cook something fresh. He enjoyed dining out, but didn't overdo it. A bachelor, in between relationships at the moment, he learned to take care of himself, ate well and watched his weight. When one of his gastronomic delights failed to pan out as the picture in the cookbook made it out, the consolation was, he often ended consuming the experiment himself. Most were edible enough. He liked to entertain, but Zor-Ell was yet to meet any of his close friends.

After dinner, he watched SBS six-thirty news—commercial

channels dishing out utterly mindless content—and an occasional documentary on SBS or the ABC. He had no time for arcane British humor or the slew of American crime shows that were the staple of available entertainment, which spoke volumes for the Western mindset. Stan and Netflix program streaming provided adequate entertainment. When all else failed, he fell back to a tumbler of Elijah Craig bourbon and an interesting book, accompanied by an engaging piece of classical music. Zor-Ell delighted listening to this product of Earth's genius. Weekends were for chores, shopping, wandering about or visiting. Jim had no shortage of things to do in the city, and wasn't shy at availing himself of the offered opportunities. When the city began to crowd him, he had his retreat in Trentham and camping. Zor-Ell looked forward to another outing and a breath of crisp, uncontaminated air.

All in all, Jim was well-adjusted and able to cope with mild eccentric tendencies, phobias and anxieties. Zor-Ell sensed an underlying satisfaction and contentment, coupled with a healthy dose of ambition, and was pleased. It would have been extremely uncomfortable had he been coupled with a neurotic personality. Highly educated, Jim provided a wealth of accumulated information; and having a roving mind, his constant research into new fields helped Zor-Ell's analysis program enormously.

From what he uncovered, in many respects, Earth fitted into a well-established pattern of development: primitive nation-states, an emerging industrial and scientific base, philosophical learning, ongoing religious conflict, and a capability for self-annihilation that clamored for a new code of behavior. Over millennia the Orieli had observed numerous emerging and established civilizations, which enabled them to evolve broad predictive principles. Zor-Ell easily fitted Earth into a recognized niche and now filled in the gaps. Those gaps glared for attention and denied him peace.

Even this early in his study, participatory assessment of

Earth's technology revealed second-order institutional reactions in the sociotechnological dynamics not necessarily intended when the technology emerged, such as proliferation of personal telecommunication, home electronic entertainment devices, and the Internet. Undeniably, those advances provided comfort, convenience and productivity, but they also engendered individual disengagement from social relations and the natural environment. Of course, that was also true in the Orieli social context. He only had to look at the unintended application of the Virtual Interface. It was simply impossible to predict the collective impact any advance in technology would generate.

His other concern dealt with human physiology. How could adaptive evolution on this planet produce a hairless species totally unsuited to its environment? Fossil records showed early man to be sturdy, muscular, and furry. Suddenly, 150,000 years ago, a jump to an erect, thin-skinned, light and temperature-sensitive finished product. It is as though they were transplanted to the planet. Then there was their brain mass, another anomaly. To have developed its current size within a handful of millennia beggared all evolutionary principles. Nature simply didn't work that quickly. Anthropologists created elaborate theories, which purportedly provided linking evidence, but these were merely tenuous snapshots in an otherwise blank movie.

Zor-Ell wondered how long exactly the Serrll Combine had watched Earth, and have they only watched? Or did someone else do the watching long, long ago? Evidence of two million-year-old figurines unearthed in a well at Nampa, Idaho, a metallic sphere with three parallel grooves around its circumference found in a Precambrian mineral deposit in South Africa dated at two point-eight million years, and numerous other anomalies from around the world, cast grave doubts on traditionally accepted human evolution. Formal academia denied this evidence, as acceptance would result in ruined reputations and abandonment of comfortable theories, but the evidence was nevertheless there, and at some stage would need to be confronted.

Having come home early today, Jim did some cleaning and cooked while watching the SBS news. On Mondays, he usually saw the ABC's Four Corners, but tonight's program didn't interest him, something to do with private security guards hired by Westerners living or working in Baghdad. Although relatively peaceful now after the American withdrawal in 2011, with power shared between the Sunni and Shi'ia factions, Al Qaida still kept stirring unrest from time to time with roadside shootings or a suicide blowing up his car. A troubled part of the world, but not the only one.

Dinner over, Jim poured himself a glass of vintage merlot and crawled into bed with a book, *The Bible Unearthed*; archaeological evidence discrediting most Old Testament stories, including the Exodus. Needless to say this particular work and others like it were controversial for some, as they flew in the face of accepted Jewish dogmatic origins, but accepted by most rabbinical scholars as fact. It was worth remembering that myths, legends and history were written by men, and not handed down from on-high on stone tablets. Despite readily available evidence the preparedness of most believers to accept a politically self-serving interpretation imposed by a church to keep itself in power was deeply disturbing. The West prided itself for shedding superstition, embracing reason and logic while still clinging to an even more insidious superstition. Although a believer, Jim had a healthy dose of skepticism in God's earthly representatives.

Zor-Ell had no problem understanding that, or understanding how millions died in the name of various religions, or how Earth's political and economic systems were still shaped by conflicting ideologies. He had seen it on many planets in various guises and always a tragedy, an inevitable byproduct of social development. Even the Serrll were not immune from its influence. He fully subscribed to Jim's philosophy that religion everywhere is a mind destroyer, created by a priestly hierarchy as a mechanism for subjugation of ignorant masses on a principle of blind obedience to dogma, rewarded with an afterlife in paradise, and hand over your donation. That system enabled the priestly caste to enjoy a level of social respect and material comfort while preaching to the masses self-denial, suffering and rejection of self-worth as though their time on Earth something sinful.

Invariably, as technology, education, knowledge, and social behavior matured, based on ethical conduct and moral principles, religions, but not belief, withered and its parasitic hierarchy with it. Where a living god manifested itself, and Zor-Ell had visited two planets where a seemingly omnipotent being existed who could be worshiped as a god; even there, people did not create a religion out of them, but offered reverence and respect. A religion cannot exist if there is no requirement for a priestly order to act as a conduit and interpreters of a god's wishes, their own really. Especially where a living god can express those wishes himself, or where a social structure had outgrown the gods they invented.

Earth had begun to enter a dawn of reason, its historical philosophers and thinkers merely preparing the necessary path toward logic and rational thought. Traditional religions like Christianity, Judaism, and to a lesser extent Islam, were already failing. People still believed in a single god and a heavenly afterlife, which was socially healthy. What people no longer believed was the necessity for a mediating church to get them there. Add an individual's willingness to question, supported by archaeological fact, evidence of doctored religious texts to maintain allegorical stories as real history—an impossible convolution—Zor-Ell not at all surprised to see the Christian churches floundering, or see a shift toward philosophies such as Buddhism and Taoism, even though they too were also heavily laced with arcane mysticism and needles religious overtones.

Islam, on the other hand, despite many admirable aspects

Stefan Vučak

of it moral code, represented everything that typified an oppressive priestly caste, demanding unquestioning obedience, total dominance over the populace, oppression of nonbelievers, and destruction of those who resisted. Where the extreme version of this religion was practiced, little in it remained to warm the soul. Even Islam showed signs of internal dissent as willingness to reflect and question began to assert itself among its younger followers. Science and knowledge is an anathema to any dogma, and religious authorities everywhere fought vigorously to suppress it.

But Zor-Ell did not judge or attempt to influence James Grant's system of beliefs and values, or Earth's. Jim had developed a workable balance between his personal beliefs and the outward demands of society within which he lived. To tamper with that balance would be extremely dangerous, compromising his ability to exist within the social matrix, something Zor-Ell had no intention of doing.

Earth's moral and philosophical structures were evolving, however slowly, but he wondered whether it would be given an opportunity to apply its growing ethical maturity as military technology clawed for the high ground of space. Advancement in weaponry clear proof that tendency toward waging war had in no way been changed or modified through the progress of technological civilization. After all, warriors ruled Earth, not philosophers. He appreciated the story of Damocles—very apt.

Ignoring the little voice in his head, Jim yawned, closed his book and turned off the light.

* * *

Nightwings sat back and watched Sankri clasp his hands behind his head and cross his legs on the desk, a smug expression creasing his face. His brother had cause to be satisfied. Much of the old inventory cleared, they managed to net a reasonable profit from the transaction, even though some perishables were sold at a loss. Having inventory sitting in warehouses was a loss anyway. The advertising campaign had worked better than expected and they were trading again. He was not displeased either, and much to his surprise, relished playing the businessman, even if for a raider front, and certainly a far cry from his role as first officer in an M-3. If he survived his trial in the Diplomatic Branch, the experience would expand his horizons enormously. Still, he could not help wonder how long this moment of hiatus would last before their competitors started active retaliation.

With advancement to Second Scout, he was in line for a command of his own. He served in an M-2 as a Base Scout and fondly recalled the experience. He would not mind driving an M-2, but it came as a fleeting thought. His promotion notwithstanding, he could not see himself parted from his brother. When Anabb offered them a posting to the Diplomatic Branch, he hadn't hesitated, knowing instinctively what his brother would choose. He understood the price Sankri had paid: loss of *Psandra* and the prestige of command. His brother may joke about it, but he felt that both of them had already made a difference. Anabb said they would be together, but Dhar knew that one day their assignments would draw them apart. He was not entirely sure how he would react when the moment came.

He glanced out the window and nodded with approval. Beneath a clear sky and streaming sunshine, a medium freighter lay parked on the first landing ring, its boxy shape looming above Warehouse B. Loaded with containers, automated cranes made a steady stream into the warehouse. From hatches beneath the hull, underground conveyors collected and transported most of the freight. According to the manifest, the freighter carried mining, drilling and ore processing components, including 300,000 mikans of baru grain, destined for a distillery on the other side of Askaran. He expected KSD to make a healthy margin from the consignment. Another carrier hung in orbit, waiting its turn to take on cargo, which had caused Bai Linn to crack a weak smile.

Hidden behind the freighter a smaller ship stood parked on the Warehouse A ring, offloading 140,000 mikans of frozen mallard beef. He saw it come down and although not immediately visible without close inspection, the double sliding hatches in its belly were a dead giveaway. They had one purpose, to mask a projector housing. Something about it that said it was not defensive armament. The freighter was an auxiliary, a raider. All his misgivings and unease at everything their mission represented forcefully reinforced in that ugly shape. Moving cargo around the warehouses relatively simple, but the ship signified a sharp reminder how that cargo was procured.

Studying the deadly thing with disgust, he wondered how many lives that beef cost. His encounter with the taciturn Palean pilot not enjoyable and he initially resented Sankri's insistence that he meet him. He understood later what his brother did and why. There was no disguising the fact they were trading in blood, and the quicker he swallowed his moral outrage the better. Nevertheless, it would not take much effort to blast the damned thing where it stood. Allow a small evil in order to prevent a greater evil? He found little solace in the thought.

Turning away from the window, he found Sankri's gray eyes looking at him and he suspected his brother was equally revolted. For now, both would play out the charade and count the gains and personal cost later.

"You seem satisfied with the world today, Ser Kerill-aa," Dhar said and Terr smiled.

"I am, Ser Randakla. I am, and enjoying it. The books are in the black again, admittedly by a wafer-thin margin, and things are shaping up. Even Nei Than seems better disposed toward us, despite having to curb his sideline activities. What gives me a warm glow is that we caused no small amount of consternation among our competition. You know, if I could forget why we're here, I could get to like this."

"You might feel differently if you were actually responsible for the funding."

"Ah, you're spoiling things again."

When his brother was happy, Nightwings was happy. Their thoughts and emotions were so closely intertwined, both were affected by any mood swings. He expected that over time, Sankri's memories and the effect of his personality would fade, but it did not happen at all. Although those memories were four years old, the bond linking them remained unshakeable. He could not imagine a life without Sankri at his side.

The display plate set into Terr's desk glowed into life and the comms alert beeped.

"Garet Singh from the Stormen and Packers Union to see you, Ser," Le Kara announced gravely.

"Bring him up," Terr said and brought his feet down with a crash. "An S&P rep. That's all we need, problems with local labor unions," Terr muttered with a weary scowl, his upbeat mood dampened. "Just when I started feeling good about things. Maybe the day won't be totally spoiled by his presence."

"It's probably about that thieving grunt in Warehouse B I booted out the other day," Dhar commented. Although wary of taking a life, he wanted to make the storeman disappear as Sankri threatened. An early example would have served as a demonstration of resolve to others.

"Probably, but I don't want unions here on principle; any union. We need to get rid of Singh fast. We can't have him around with Pulman coming. Global could get scared off if they thought they'd have to deal with somebody like the S&P." Terr closed the Wall display in which they were studying the latest shipping figures and folded his arms over the desk. The door opened and Kara gave a small nod.

"Ser Singh."

"Thank you, Kara…come in, Ser Singh." Terr said, not getting up to greet his visitor.

The man strutted in carrying himself with authority and

looked around the luxuriously appointed office with interest. A well-developed paunch sagged over full trousers. His dark gray suit hung rumpled and there were brown stains on the lapels. Terr recognized the type; muscle for a corrupt organization, and disliked him on sight.

"Thanks, I will," Singh said with a small smirk, waved his right hand in perfunctory greeting, and immediately strode toward a spare formchair.

"I did not invite you to sit down," Terr said softly.

Singh's head jerked in surprise and he glared. "What is this? Do you know who I am?"

"You claim to be an S&P Union rep."

"Claim nothing! I *am* an S&P rep." He reached into his jacket and held out a card. Dhar plucked it out of his hand and glanced at it.

"Can I sit down now?" Singh didn't bother hiding his insolence. S&P wielded power on Askaran and he wanted to make sure these new guys knew it. No one messed with the S&P and got away with it.

"No," Terr said coldly. "Karach Salvage and Disposal is not a union shop, Ser Singh, and isn't likely to become one. Please state your business here."

Singh pursed his lips and gave a slow smile. "You might want to change your mind about that, *Ser* Kerill-aa. Okay, we'll play it your way for now. Two days ago, your partner here assaulted an employee and kicked him off the premises. He came to us asking for help with a claim for damages: 50,000 Serrlls for wrongful dismissal, assault and back pay. S&P will add its own costs to that claim. Before we take this to Business Affairs, I thought we'd give you a chance to settle this peacefully."

Terr tapped a pad on the inlaid console. "Kara, please have Chief Naralima come to my office." Resting his arms on the desk, he placed the tips of his fingers in a pyramid. "For your information, we caught the man mislabeling freight, directing remote handling vehicles to Warehouse B, where we subsequently found valuable cargo similarly mislabeled. He clearly intended to dispose of that cargo illegally. In plain language, he was stealing from me. My partner threw him out on the spot."

"After assaulting him first!" Singh snarled, glaring at Dhar.

"If you mean being picked up by his neck and dropped, he was assaulted. He got off lightly, if you ask me. As for his claim for back pay, we paid him in full and I have records from Talbian Trust to that effect."

"Look, you can't prove he stole anything from you. The freight was still in the warehouse. Kicking him out without due notice or warning constitutes wrongful dismissal, but I tell you what. You pay S&P 40,000 and you won't hear anything more about it."

Terr's eyes flicked at Dhar and chuckled. "You're right. I won't hear any more about it and I won't be paying S&P or anyone else anything. You can tell whoever sent you, I don't care much for standover tactics."

Singh grinned and shook his head. "Okay, if that's the way you want it, but you can't say I didn't try to do this the nice way. You'll be hearing from us, Mister!"

"I doubt it," Terr said as the door opened. Chief Naralima stood outside. Terr hooked his thumb at Singh. "He was just leaving."

"You haven't heard the last of this!" Singh spat and stormed out.

"I wonder who else will call?" Dhar mused and handed his brother Singh's business card.

"It's for sure it won't be him. Some people have to learn the hard way." Studying the card, Terr tapped a secure combination into the console pad. Kandu Hall's features cleared as the Wall glowed into life.

"Ah, Ser Kerill-aa…Ser Randakla. I hear your trade is going well."

"Very well so far, Ser Hall. Under different circumstances,

I could actually get to like this business. Unfortunately, there are those who don't seem to approve of our methods and seek to ruin my day. A request, if I may."

"Yes. What can the Diplomatic Branch do to smooth the way, gentlemen?"

"We had a visit from a charming fellow representing the local Stormen and Packers."

Hall winced. "They are bad news, all right. Business Affairs gets complaints about them and their roughhouse tactics all the time, but legally there isn't very much they can do. I hope you didn't upset him?"

"Kind of. To fix my problem and some of those complaints, I would appreciate it if someone could make a visit to their headquarters at Riverview and leave a message. Something that will make an impression on their building."

Hall smiled, looking happy. "What you're considering is a criminal act, you know, but I like it, and nobody at Business Affairs will be shedding tears. Consider it done, and call me any time, Ser Kerill."

The Wall faded as Terr sat back and beamed. "That should take care of Ser Singh and company."

"A plasma charge?" Dhar ventured and Terr shrugged.

"Whatever. I don't think we'll be bothered by any more visits from the S&P."

"You have an evil streak in you, Ser Kerill-aa, did you know that?" Dhar said, smiling broadly.

"Like the man said, it's a tough business," Terr quipped as the comms alert beeped.

"Excuse me, Ser. Warat Pulman, Global Transport's Managing Director is here for your eleven o'clock appointment," Le Kara announced briskly.

"Very good. Show him to the meeting room."

Dhar cracked his knuckles. "Our would-be partner. I trust we'll be avoiding similar measures with him?"

Terr laughed. "It wouldn't do to upset Pulman. We need

him more than he suspects."

They got into the large room when the door panel slid aside and Le Tara leaned in with a local hovering behind her. He had chubby rounded features, a prominent nose and dark eyes sunk deep within their sockets. Tending a little toward bulk, gray hair around the temples, at first glance there was nothing to distinguish him from any other polished businessman. The polished appearance, though, hid something altogether far more sinister.

"Ser Pulman."

Terr forced a smile, struck by the cold aura that surrounded the local like a blanket of bad omens. This man wielded death and wasn't bothered by it at all. And he was *aware*. Terr recognized the confident stance and the minute bodily nuances of someone in total command of himself and his surrounds at all times. He'd seen such men before and did not relish the prospect of working with this one. His eyes flickered at Dhar and they understood. His brother also sensed the predator in their midst. Predator or not, it would be a blunder to apply his personal code of behavior and assume Pulman to be a simple raider fence, which he was not.

He needed to keep in mind that he played in an environment using a different rulebook. Pulman considered himself a patriot of sorts, furthering the cause of the Alikan Union Party and the merger with Sargon. If in the process, he employed what others would consider less than ethical tactics and made a little money on the side while doing it was payoff for making the sacrifice.

Terr didn't believe it. Pulman might not personally soil his hands by firing a projector at a helpless merchantman, but in his mind, the man little better than a raider himself. Some lines nobody crossed, for any reason. A noble cause must be pursued through noble means, or expediency merely becomes a paved road to social anarchy and authoritarian rule.

"Welcome to Karach Salvage and Disposal, Ser Pulman," Terr said warily, his right hand raised in formal greeting.

Pulman eyed his host and raised his hand. "Thank you, Ser Kerill-aa. I am glad to be here."

"May I offer you something cold? A beer?"

"I would relish a Brut Cooler if you got it," Pulman said cautiously, his voice pleasant and measured.

"Excellent. Kara?"

"Right away, Ser. Three?"

"Yes."

When the door closed, Terr extended his arm at Dhar. "And this is my partner—"

"Ser Randakla, I know." Pulman smiled woodenly, his eyes missing nothing, probing for angles that would allow him to assume the dominant position. Kerill-aa looked young and probably inexperienced in the roughhouse world of cargo handling and local politics. He didn't anticipate too many problems manipulating him. A powerful syndicate may be backing him, but the heavies were not here now. Randakla, though, looked guarded and alert and he didn't particularly enjoy the Wanderer's cutting stare. Like everybody, he'd heard the stories and looking at this desert creature, perhaps some of them could even be true.

Aware of the byplay going on, Terr pointed at seats around the table. "Please…" He waited for everyone to settle in, then leaned back, a faint smile playing at the corner of his mouth. "You seem well informed, Ser Pulman."

"No less than you, Ser Kerill-aa."

"Indeed. Since we're all so well informed, please tell me what I can do for Global Transport. Although I always appreciate a social visit from a major competitor."

The door opened and Le Kara walked in bearing a tray with three brown bottles of beer and tall glasses. Everybody waited until she finished pouring, leaving the bottles on the table. When the door closed behind her, Terr took a pull of the rich dark ale, licked his lips and studied his guest more closely.

Shadow Masters

Pulman's clear eyes were intelligent and had precise, measured mannerisms. The man obviously cultured and sophisticated, not an ordinary raider, but Terr knew that already. Despite the external polish, he faced a dangerous customer and needed to be extremely cautious. As the Alikan Union Party front, Pulman would not associate himself willingly with ordinary freebooter scum, even if Global *did* need KSD's facilities. Terr wondered how far he could afford to push. A mistake now and Anabb would be getting those two body boxes sooner than expected.

He watched Pulman take a sip, carefully place his glass beside the bottle and cross a leg over his knee. The gesture probably meant to relax everyone, to ease the undercurrent of tension, but Terr wasn't fooled. This character did nothing superfluous that did not contribute to achieving his objective. Landau's data pack gave him extensive information on Pulman, but it left an important segment unanswered. With his education and background, what drove a man like that into raiding? Could he be another Tanard, using raiders as a tool to further someone else's ends without having to spill blood with his own hand? The simplest explanation most likely to be true. The AUP wanted revenue and an arm with which to attack commercial carriers, and Pulman had taken on the job. Whose carriers were they attacking and why? He didn't believe they used *Pilla* for indiscriminate raiding, not entirely. Well, that's what his job was all about, to find out.

"Frankly, Ser Kerill-aa," Pulman started, "I was curious to see the new owners of Karach Salvage and Disposal. A Second Scout, logistics manager at the Talon support facility, forced to resign or face charges for gross insubordination, conduct unbecoming, and dereliction of duty. Not to mention vocally supporting the Sargon/Palean merger, something frowned on by CAPFLTCOM. Your record is blank for a year, then you surface here. I mustn't forget your silent partner.

"A native of Anar'on, a Wanderer, but not a Discipline

adept. Odd, but under the circumstances, perhaps not. Held a comptroller's position with a minor interstellar freight outfit and charged with embezzlement and fraud. Charges dropped in return for giving evidence against the owners. Hardly the resumes one would expect from two reputable executives. But as they said, this is not an easy business. Something else bothered me. Where would men like that, appearing out of nowhere on Circa, accumulate sufficient funds to bid for a multimillion-credit corporation such as KSD, unless they were connected. You can see why I was curious."

Terr admired professionalism and Pulman had done his homework. The man's dissection was clinical, without inflection, like reading a recipe. If that was the approach, he would do a bit of dissecting of his own.

"Since we're exchanging resumes and not bothering with idle chatting, you left a puzzling trail in your wake as well, Ser Pulman. A Scholar's degree in business administration from Karach Polytechnic and a master's in management. Three years ago, you and Sarek Laral faced off in a power struggle to secure the local AUP chapter's presidency. Despite waging a campaign on a platform of progressive reform, you lost to your younger opponent. Shortly afterward, you resigned from the cell's executive to form Global Transport, although you're still a powerful player within the AUP. Your partner, Tan Segal, has a more checkered career and is not so well accomplished, only a master's in administration accounting, but impressive and resourceful enough to partially finance the creation of Global. He must have done something nice in life to acquire that much capital.

"With all those imposing credentials between you, I couldn't help wonder why you two would want to get involved in a messy racket like raiding. Not directly perhaps, preferring to pull the strings, but involved nonetheless. I know about *Drakin*, Ser Pulman, lost in the Zeller system, and your problems getting *Paun* commissioned. As you can tell, my curiosity was also somewhat aroused."

Pulman allowed himself a lazy grin, but his eyes remained cold and calculating. Losing the election to Laral was a humiliating personal setback, certain he had the numbers. He understood why he lost the presidency. It was simple enough. Laral must have bought at least two of his supporters. Pulman had never forgiven or forgotten, and still tried to identify who sold him out. Once he finds out…

The loss of *Drakin* came as a body blow for Global and removed a badly needed source of cashflow. Regrettable as that was, at least the ship's total destruction preserved his security. He shuddered to think what could have happened had Re Nette been captured. Having to commission *Paun* turned out financially brutal, especially after the Alikan Union Party chapter refused to provide additional financing—at Sarek Laral's urging! He resented being treated like a raider when he considered himself a patriot. Weren't they all using whatever tools were available to achieve a common cause? In any struggle, blood needed to be spilled, and he knew whose blood he wanted to spill.

Taking a slow breath, he reminded himself to stay focused on the job at hand. Getting sidetracked and emotional would achieve nothing.

Across the table, his young opponent looked calm and confident, obviously well briefed; too well for someone who just landed on the scene. Their unusual entry on Circa obviously deliberate to muddy the trail. The new KSD owners clearly didn't wish to advertise their shadowy origins. How reliable then the information he *had* been able to source? In the scheme of things, it didn't actually matter who Kerill-aa and Randakla were. His objective? Secure Karach Salvage by whatever means. Afterward, there would be time enough to permanently dissolve the partnership. After all, cargo handling had always been a dangerous business. He tolerated competition only when conducted on his terms, and on Askaran, he intended for it to stay that way.

"Clearly, we have all fallen from grace. At least we don't

have to pretend to be something we're not. Who are your underwriters? The Marian Syndicate? They're the only heavy players around here capable of penetrating my security screen. And I have a very good security screen."

Terr smiled and gave a small shake of his head. "Now, now, you don't expect me to answer that, do you? Suffice to say, my backers gave me the means to turn Karach Salvage into a very profitable concern. So far, I'm not doing too badly. Without repeating myself, what can I do for Global Transport?"

Uncrossing his legs, Pulman leaned forward and his mouth tightened. Was the boy toying with him? He wondered what a broken kneecap would do for Kerill-aa's humor, and slipped the mask back into place. However pleasurable the idea, he could not afford to indulge himself like that, not now. Still, he could savor the thought, couldn't he?

"Very well, I shall speak plainly. You've been here three weeks, but in that time, KSD has already caused a small stir in the ordered, placid lives of your competitors, myself included. Judging from the traffic outside, your promotional campaign has certainly hit a responsive chord, something not viewed with enthusiasm by everybody."

"What can I say? I need to recoup my investment," Terr said with a disarming shrug, sensing the byplay was about done.

"Yes, an understandable position. Playing outside the rules has a way of creating, shall we say, difficulties?"

Terr weighed Pulman's words carefully, although the meaning clear enough. If the Alikan Union Party wanted Karach Salvage badly enough, they certainly had the power to squeeze him out. It would be costly, but they could do it. If Pulman stopped raiders from offloading cargo at KSD, Global's lack of handling capacity meant that raiders would have to go elsewhere anyway, taking their revenue with them. Even if Global redirected business to Trans National Haulage, it would be a marginal solution at best, as TNH wasn't set up that way. The way he saw it, Pulman was in a bind no matter which way he sliced it. Despite the thinly veiled gambit, he decided the man would rather deal than threaten.

"Interesting, those rules. Oh, I don't doubt your backers could hurt me, but you understand, that tactic cuts both ways. Action against me may give you momentary satisfaction, but it would do little to solve your lack of handling capacity and diminished cashflow. There is something else you should consider. I'm not so sure your contacts within the Alikan Union Party would be willing to start something. Not if it meant disrupting payment of that nice unification tax."

Pulman laughed outright and took a sip of beer. This wasn't going exactly as planned and he began to develop a grudging respect for his opponent.

"I must admit, increasing your margin was a clever move, but it gave the AUP executive unwelcome ideas."

Terr looked innocent, pleased to see the raider squirm. "They want the same percentage from Global?"

"And everybody else. A deliberate ploy, Ser Kerill-aa?"

"As a new player, I simply wanted to make a good impression," Terr said easily and Pulman grinned.

"Of course, and you did. I see you will not be intimidated, and I didn't come here to do so—exactly. My backers intend to expand Global's operations, which means increasing cargo throughput. Since we cannot handle current cargo volumes, and there is little point in denying it, I have a problem, but I also have a strategy to deal with it without having to build a new handling facility. Although I considered it, the option would be far too expensive and time-consuming. I'll speak plainly. I need a commander for *Paun*. In all respects the ship is otherwise ready to commence operations. Despite your difficulties in the Fleet, your service record tells me you would make a good commander. To sweeten the deal, you would keep fifty percent of net profits and Global would underwrite all maintenance and support expenses if you used our Otilando facility."

Terr smiled broadly and shook his head. A basic ploy, luring him with an offer of command. Tempting—to a genuinely disgraced Fleet officer with no hope of advancement. Command and wealth, a powerful combination.

"Without asking how that would solve your capacity problem, I've had my taste of scary shit, Ser Pulman. Right now, I am happy to have my feet firmly planted on the ground. As for your sweetener, fifty percent sounds attractive, but we both know that on a net basis it might not amount to much. Besides, I'm making money right now without risking having my ass blown away by an M-3, and I kind of like it that way."

Pulman didn't react to the rejection and simply nodded. The boy had seen through the tactic, but he had to dangle it anyway. "Perfectly understandable. That's why I have another option I would like you to consider, one I suspect you already know, and something far more tempting. When the Central Revenue Office put out a tender for KSD, my bid failed, a miscalculation. I want to offer another bid."

Terr kept his face impassive, but his stomach gave a flutter of excitement. Pulman and Segal must be desperate, and a door into Global and his backers may be opening sooner than expected.

"I cannot see how you can buy me out, even if I were willing to sell. You don't hold enough liquidity with Morgian Holdings or Chase Investments to do it."

"You *are* well informed," Pulman noted approvingly. Perhaps he should revise his assessment of Kerill. "I am impressed. You understand now why I need *Paun* raiding. While she's on the ground my backers are prepared to extend a line of credit to cover the transaction."

"Ah, your backers. The local Alikan Union Party chapter, or someone else, perhaps? Powerful enough to scare off my trade and rich enough to acquire KSD. If I may ask, why didn't those same backers support you the first time?"

"As I told you, a miscalculation," Pulman said smoothly,

but his fists clenched in a moment of irritation. Rejecting his bid to save a few million had been a shortsighted view by the AUP cell and a slap in his face. A stalwart Party member, but when he started Global Transport, they were happy to fund him, then looked at him with scorn while no better than opportunists themselves. They liked the money he brought in, but didn't want to soil their own hands, pretending to hold the high moral ground. Hypocrites, all of them, but dangerous nonetheless. Still, he needed to be careful. If he antagonized Sarek Laral too much, it would only take one call to the Diplomatic Branch Resident and he could expect a lengthy vacation on Cantor, although he didn't expect anything so amateurish. The information he held would be far too damaging to the chapter and several serving ministers were something unpleasant to befall him.

"I may be willing to consider your offer," Terr said, ignoring Pulman's moment of discomfort and the reason for it, "but it would take more than you might be willing to pay."

"Go on."

"My partner and I aren't interested in selling out, but we would entertain a joint venture deal. We have the capacity you want and you've got the market and political connections I need. We create a holding company with Global and KSD as subsidiaries. Both would remain legal operating entities, simpler all around. Your partner and the three of us would have equal voting shares and twenty-five percent of all net receipts. To ensure perfect trust among thieves, I would open my books to you and you would open yours to me. The deal would cost you 125 million Serrlls."

"Indeed? I understand your need, but I'm intrigued at how you arrived at that figure and why I should pay it."

"Global Transport's book worth is 160 million. My backers and I invested—"

"Some 285 million in KSD," Pulman said wearily. "I know. We checked with the Central Revenue Office."

"I'm sure you did," Terr said dryly. Access to KSD's books had formed part of the government tender. What Pulman didn't realize, Landau had also secured Global's books. Its lack of capacity became one of the decision drivers to execute the penetration. "Even at that price, Karach Salvage is undervalued, but we won't quibble over details."

"You're not forgetting *Paun* and *Pilla's* hull values?"

"*Paun* and *Pilla* are not on Global Transport's balance sheet, Ser Pulman. You're running them as a separate concern. As such, their operating costs would be met out of your share of net profits."

"Even when they would generate income for us?" Pulman looked incredulous and Terr shrugged.

"To me, they're merely another raider selling cargo. Whatever they bring in is not income, but a cost until I resell that cargo."

"Ah, your policy to pay up-front."

"It's how I run things and my backers like it. The 125 million is to offset some of my outlays when I acquired the company. After all, KSD is a much larger concern than Global, and it's a bargain compared to paying 285 million. I am sure your backers would appreciate that fact. Then there is the sweetener, to use your phrase. With your controlling interest in Trans National Haulage, our three concerns would hold an effective stranglehold over all freight business on Askaran. With a free hand to manipulate the price lists and without anti-trust laws to stop us, the minor outfits won't be able to do a thing. We'd have the market to ourselves. I'd like to think you'd get some traction with that argument."

Pulman looked thoughtful, his eyes measuring Terr with vernier precision. Perhaps they *could* do business. The boy certainly knew his. Would his backers in the AUP chapter be prepared to make the necessary investment? They would if he pitched the deal correctly, which should offset those who blocked his initial venture into Global Transport and who worked against him now. Like any organization, the Askaran AUP chapter was not one unified happy family.

"For someone so young, Ser Kerill-aa, you have an astonishing grasp of this business. It's possible I made a mistake in my initial evaluation of you."

"We're all prone to making a mistake or two along the way, Ser Pulman," Terr agreed comfortably. "That's why I cannot afford to make any."

* * *

Rain pelted down over the Center, blurring the city's outlines. Yet on the other side of Celean Park, pale sunshine streamed through broken clouds. Although Ed-Kani couldn't hear it, whipping branches testified to the wind's raging fury. Overhead, murky cloudbanks moved quickly, obscuring the higher traffic lanes. He turned and surveyed the solemn faces on both sides of the long table. Holoview projections only, but it wasn't possible to bring the Committee physically together for every meeting.

"Are we agreed, then?"

The rotating Chairman, a wizened Palean Congressman sitting at the far end, noted the grave nods from everyone—all except one.

"You dissent, friend Ti Inai?" he piped softly, knowing the meeting would not be closing anytime soon. Ti Inai *always* had something to moan about. Just for once, he wished the younger man would simply shut up and go with the flow. It might happen someday, but clearly not today.

Back in the fold and with two new members appointed, Ti Inai still felt Ed-Kani's keen animosity. He understood the reason for it well enough and objectively didn't truly hold the Sargon member's antipathy against him. They were all playing for high stakes and sometimes things don't work out as planned. No one could blame him that Kai Tanard had the bad taste to get himself captured. Had Tanard managed to destroy the Unified Independent Front delegates on their way to Anar'on, Ti Inai would now be hailed a hero and brilliant tactician instead of getting reviled.

Essentially the same criticism is leveled now at Le Maran. His protégé was misguided when he ordered Tanard to engage Fleet units protecting Pizgor shipping, but Ti Inai hadn't hesitated sanctioning the same tactic against the UIF delegates. Absurd to imagine that *Zavian* wouldn't be escorted. Le Maran was simply too good a strategist to be liquidated for following orders. Ti Inai faced another problem.

Le Maran commanded support from too many key Alikan Union Party cells to be dismissed summarily. The action would cause increased resentment against the Committee when many Palean cells were already questioning the wisdom and speed at which the merger was pursued. It went against every tenet of careful and methodical planning, weighing of options, seeing how events unfolded before proceeding with the next step. What was the rush?

Moreover, if Sargon members refused to be tractable, he wanted Le Maran's skill. He would also want Tanard, although extracting him from his current predicament did present a degree of difficulty. The AUP had invested too much in both men to simply discard them, however politically expedient the move.

His small pinched lips twitched and his long fingers coiled like writhing snakes as his eyes swept around the table.

"I would like to remind the Chairman and other members that Le Maran has served the cause with unwavering commitment and honor. In hindsight, some of his decisions can be argued as questionable, but when they were made, no one here objected. Should the Committee proceed with its decision, I submit we'd not only lose a valuable resource, but also set an alarming precedent. What about the next person faced with making a hard decision? Can we rely on him to do what is necessary, knowing he had our full support, or would he take an expedient option that guaranteed keeping his head? I want to remind everyone here, before our cause is realized, we shall all be called upon to make some hard decisions. If we winnow out those capable of making them, this Committee will be reduced to an impotent club of weekend teetotalers, not a nascent government in waiting."

There was an approving ripple of murmurs and nodding of heads. Ed-Kani admired the Palean's smooth performance. Ti Inai looked and acted like a sniveling stooge, nervous and twitchy, but that was merely a facade that hid an accomplished predator. It wouldn't be wise to underestimate him.

"Mr. Chairman?"

"The Sargon member has the floor."

"I agree with many of Ti Inai's sentiments," Ed-Kani said. "Under different circumstances the issue wouldn't be raised, but for two things. I bring to the Committee's attention the fact that we sanctioned Le Maran twice already for ordering Kai Tanard to attack Fleet units. Those decisions brought the Fleet on our heads and almost cost us Lemos. Ignoring the lesson and the Committee's wishes, he repeated his mistake. This time, as you all know, his action did cost us Lemos. He then heaped stupidity on poor judgment by ordering Tanard to attack the Unified Independent Front liner *Zavian*. Tanard captured, and we lost Italan. The damage done to our security has been horrific, severely setting back the cause. Making courageous decisions, hard decisions, is one thing. Incompetence, on the other hand, cannot be tolerated. Not when so much is at stake. I urge that we approve sanction."

The Chairman glared at Ti Inai and banged his gavel. "The motion is carried. The Palean member is tasked to secure Le Maran and have him liquidated. He is to report to the Committee when done. Any other items?"

Even though Ti Inai had anticipated the Committee's decision, protecting Le Maran would now become much more problematic. Not impossible, just awkward, and he wasn't without resources.

"Has the Committee considered rescuing Tanard and his key officers? I understand that Anar'on has handed him over to the Fleet and he's now interned on Kalakan."

An old Pro-Consul member stared sharply at Ti Inai. "To what end? He's been compromised, and rescuing him would serve no useful purpose. Moreover, the operation would entail considerable risk and possible exposure of our network on Kalakan."

Ti Inai nodded, apparently accepting yet another setback, but this time, he was making a point for the record. Still, he had to appear suitably indignant. "I am shocked at the Sargon member's casual dismissal of someone who has done far more to promote our cause than some around this very table!"

As expected the comment raised a furor of protest. The Chairman banged his gavel to restore order and stared angrily at Ti Inai. As a fellow Palean, he acknowledged every member's right to voice his views, but this was getting out of hand.

"This Committee recognizes the valuable contribution made by Kai Tanard, but you must acknowledge the validity of the Pro-Consul's argument, friend Ti Inai. Even if we could retrieve him from Kalakan, a major Palean base, his usefulness to the Committee would be limited. Were he to be recaptured, the painful reorganization of our security screen now underway would have to be repeated. Unless someone has a countervailing argument, the motion is declared out of order."

The Pro-Consul looked amiably at the Chairman.

"If I may? Although Lemos is lost, it doesn't necessarily mean that our bid for Pizgor is lost. I propose we pressure our respective carriers to avoid using Pizgor's orbital cargo receiving and handling facilities. In effect, starving Pizgor of a vital revenue source. This in itself will not cause them to succumb, but if we were to increase funding to opposition parties within the Triumvirate, Kernami Asai Tainam's administration could be sufficiently destabilized to eventually fall and Pizgor would be ours. I acknowledge the long timeframe for this option, but I submit we should consider it."

There was an immediate and general acceptance of the proposal. After all, it would only cost some money and judicious use of blackmail. Carried, the Chairman banged his gavel and asked if there were further points for discussion. Ed-Kani raised his hand.

"The member for Sargon."

"Getting Tanard off Kalakan might not be viable, but getting his interrogation transcripts, including those from Anar'on, could be useful. It would confirm the extent of damage done by his capture."

The Chairman looked around the table. "The member is authorized to make the attempt. Was there anything else?"

"A report, Mr. Chairman," Ed-Kani went on. "A poll conducted by the Bureau of Defense suggests that emergence of the Orieli Technic Union has raised sufficient disquiet in the Sargon Directorate and the Palean Union to make the fact work for the Committee. I propose we initiate a propaganda campaign to turn that disquiet into actual alarm. Our message should be simple. Alone, we're vulnerable. United, we're a force able to resist an invader. We must pitch the message at an emotional level, as the argument breaks down under rational analysis."

When the murmurings around the table died down, the Chairman banged his gavel again. "Thank you for that observation, friend Ed-Kani. I take it the suggestion is carried? Very well. I propose that we establish a working group to execute the campaign and report progress on a ten-day basis. Perhaps our new Palean and Sargon members would take charge? Excellent! Any more items?"

Ti Inai immediately rose. "There is no question that Lemos is a grave setback, Mr. Chairman, having cost us Pizgor's five

systems, and I acknowledge the Pro-Consul's proposal to retrieve the situation. Although tragic, the loss has taught us a
valuable lesson. Our operations cannot be vulnerable to exposure by outside participants. I'm referring to our use of raiders,
of course. That's where Lemos was singularly vulnerable. My
point to the Committee is this. With Pizgor lost, where do we
look for our five systems? Before someone states the obvious,
I am aware of Sargon's campaign to induce Rolan to cede its
systems in return for supporting its bid for the new Fleet base.
Should that initiative succeed, we would have overcome a major hurdle to the Sargon/Palean merger. What if it doesn't succeed?" Ti Inai paused to study the startled expressions on the
faces of some of his colleagues. Surely this wasn't news?

"I want to remind the Committee that endorsing a campaign against the Orieli will in effect support the Bureau of Defense findings, putting increased pressure on Illeran's approval
committee to accept the Palean bid for the Fleet base, even
though the premise for that bid was to quell growing militancy
among some Alikan Union Party cells." He glared at Ed-Kani
and sat down. *Take that, friend, and chew on it!*

Fists clenched under the table, Ed-Kani clamped his jaw
and hissed. The Palean slime! Galled, he realized Ti Inai had
identified the one vulnerability in his proposal and he faced another possible personal setback. Was that why Ti Inai remained
silent, waiting for the Committee to commit itself before pointing out the blunder? Okay, his campaign against the Orieli
might scuttle Rolan's bid, but if it brought the Paleans closer
into his grasp through other means, he could still see Greater
Sargon rule.

He hadn't been mistaken in his evaluation. They should
have eliminated the Palean worm, not his two cronies.

When the ripple of voices around the table died down, the
Chairman looked at Ti Inai. "The Committee recognizes the
duality of the problem, friend Ti Inai. Do you have a suggestion
to overcome it?"

"I do, Mr. Chairman. I submit that we embark on a parallel strategy to secure our systems by attacking Kaleen."

The Chairman raised his voice several times before order was restored. "Does the member care to elaborate on this fantastic scenario?"

Ti Inai relished the moment and allowed himself a small smile. "At first glance the idea may seem somewhat farfetched, but consider this. Why did we initiate raids on Pizgor commerce? Attacking Kaleen has the same objective: to destabilize their trading base to a point where the economy of its systems is sufficiently disrupted to induce some of them to cede to the Palean Union. My proposal has another potential windfall. It could disorder formation of the Unified Independent Front, a desirable objective in itself. No one here relishes the prospect of another Executive seat in the independents hands. Or worse still, in Sofam's hands if the UIF were to align itself with the Revisionist Party."

"And how does the member propose we prosecute this attack?"

"Simple, Mr. Chairman. We use raiders." He waited several moments for everyone to settle down. The Chairman glared at him.

"A moment ago, friend Ti Inai, you reminded us that using raiders contributed to losing Lemos. You appear to be contradicting yourself."

"Not at all, Mr. Chairman. This time, the Committee and the Alikan Union Party cells would not be involved. I propose that we post shipping information on secure trade bulletin boards, which raiders could use in planning their intercepts. After all, apart from a support facility, that's the service provided by Lemos. Because we failed with Pizgor does not invalidate the original concept. Of course, increase in raider activity would generate a corresponding Fleet response, but I submit there is no shortage of enterprising marauders willing to risk all for quick profit. The Fleet cannot guard all shipping corridors, as

Pizgor's experience has demonstrated. To make this work will take careful planning and weighing up of all factors that could affect a successful outcome. We must be cautious and apply only the necessary amount of pressure on Kaleen to wear down their resistance. We need to remember that Kaleen is the Unified Independent Front, and that means dealing with Anar'on. We don't want to provoke a response from the Wanderers."

Ed-Kani stared thoughtfully at the Palean, chagrined that Ti Inai had thought of the idea, while ruefully admitting the validity of the approach. Sneaky and indirect, typical of all Palean schemes, and an utterly pragmatic fallback position. Subtlety, something Illeran would appreciate. He might not like the source of the idea, but he was nevertheless prepared to support the project, especially when it could actually work. However, he wasn't done yet.

He glanced at the Chairman, who nodded. "It's a laudable plan, but it overlooks the fact that Sargon and the Palean Union already have programs in place to attract nonaligned independents and protectorates that lie within our spheres, due to be given sovereignty after the next electoral session, to cede themselves to us. Attacking Kaleen could inflame resistance and undo work done over decades."

"Mr. Chairman," Ti Inai interrupted. "I acknowledge the potential value of those programs, but the members should note that none of them have yet yielded us a single system. I'm not suggesting we abandon them, but I submit that my proposal has a far higher success probability factor and should be considered."

"Your argument is well taken, friend Ti Inai. The proposal is submitted for feasibility evaluation," the Chairman announced formally and looked around the table.

"Seconded," Ed-Kani hissed, hating to accept that Ti Inai was right in his assessment.

Bang!

"Carried! Friend Ti Inai, you will set up a working group to identify risks, threats and tactics. You'll provide an initial report of findings and an action plan in twenty days." He raised the gavel to close the proceedings when Ti Inai rose again, which caused him to roll his eyes in frustration.

"Do you wish to add something else?"

Pleased at regaining some credit with the members, Ti Inai wanted to seize the moment. "Mr. Chairman, my argument is with the Committee's current structure. Everyone here is utterly committed to seeing the Sargon/Palean merger consummated. The Chairman's casting vote to break a deadlock has proved to be ineffective because of Sargon's five-four majority. They have used this to force through policies and actions, which in my view have unduly favored them. This has caused unrest and resentment, not only from the Palean members, but the Congress as a whole. I want to—"

The Chairman banged his gavel. "The member's item is out of order! We argued this issue argued before and settled. I see no reason to reopen it."

Bang!

Ti Inai saw around him the stony faces of Sargon members, Ed-Kani's satisfied smirk, concern from the Paleans, and masked his acute disappointed. He didn't really blame the Chairman for blocking him, not when Sargon members held those five votes. If the Sargon Directorate and the Palean Union were to be equal partners, he wanted Sargon to be more receptive to the Palean arm of the Alikan Union Party and its wants. Very well. If Sargon won't accept a rational argument, they might be amenable to more vivid persuasion. He enjoyed considerable support within the AUP on this, including Le Maran's more militant cells. What he contemplated was dangerous. When playing for high stakes you must make the outcome worth the gamble.

He played for high stakes all his life and knew how to call the turn. From his first campaign to secure election into Congress and subsequent struggles to gain appointments to key appropriation and oversight committees, he learned well the skills of influence and sponsorship. Many considered him naive and idealistic, an opportunist, but wasn't all politics a game of opportunity? Congress may have voted him a seat to the General Assembly to get rid of him, but Ti Inai thrived in Captal's cutthroat environment with no quarter given and none expected. That he now held a seat in an organization that was in effect a government-in-waiting, should the Sargon/Palean merger eventuate, spoke volumes for his mastery of the body politic.

High stakes? He would teach the Committee and Sargon its meaning.

The meeting broke up and Ed-Kani walked from the antechamber into his office. Rain still fell outside. Although Ti Inai had failed to reopen discussion on the Chairman's use of a casting vote, he knew the Palean wouldn't forget it. He saw the burning look of resentment in Ti Inai's eyes and a glint of cunning. The slime was plotting something. He could feel it in every pore of his body. This meeting hadn't been substantially different from many others he endured. If he could cut through the proclivity of Palean members to procrastinate, debate and vacillate, the Committee would be far more effective. Look at the facts, decide and act. How hard can it get? But Paleans were always averse to making snap decisions.

Sitting down, he pushed Ti Inai and his annoying presence out of his mind. The Rolan bid wasn't scuttled yet.

The comms alert beeped and he tapped a pad. "What is it, Keana? I don't want to be disturbed right now."

"Scholar Laraiana is waiting to see you."

His lips twitched in a stillborn smile. Keana never called him sir, and even when they were not alone, she managed to make the appellation sound trivial. A minor irritation, and he had become used to it. His Laraiana, though, something else altogether. He didn't particularly care for what she had to say, not right now, but she was family after all.

"Show her in, will you?"

He found it hard to picture Laraiana a grown woman and a prominent scientist. With professional success, which contributed to the breakdown of her marriage, she was probably more overbearing than ever. They were never terribly close, but he'd always been fond of her. He still saw her as a little girl he bounced on his knees before he set off for Captal and things had faded. When he did come home, he made it a point to see her. Daughter of his father's first cousin, a prominent Pro-Consul in his own right, even as a child, Laraiana showed flashes of determination and drive that enabled her to rise in her chosen field. She always knew how to manipulate her powerful relatives to get what she wanted. From what he knew, age hadn't mellowed her and only served to sharpen her skills.

When she appeared in the doorway, stern and confident, he stood and grinned broadly. "Ah, my precious. How long has it been?"

Dressed in a dark blue one-piece coverall, Laraiana cracked a small smile, walked quickly to Ed-Kani and they embraced.

"Four long years, Uncle, and a while since anyone called me precious." Not really her uncle, but ever since she could talk, he was her playmate, confidant and trusted friend. There when she needed someone, simply to talk or be a source of influence, and he never failed her. She fervently hoped he wouldn't fail her now. She had cultivated his friendship far too long to be dismissed now.

"A regrettable omission, I am sure. How is your father these days?"

Her blue eyes flashed icy fire and her shoulders drooped. "Not too good. The sight of M-9s over Hakran has hit him hard. To see Sargon humiliated before the entire Serrll…"

He patted her hand and inclined his head at the formchairs. "I know. It's been hard on all of us. We shall survive to see the Sofam slime humbled yet. Enough of that. Sit down and tell me what I can do for you."

She made herself comfortable and crossed her legs. "I'm in Captal for two days making a report to the BCPA on Earth's genetic engineering program. A routine follow-up mission."

"Anything startling that you can tell me?"

"It's compartmented, but I can tell you. Physiologically, they're following the mapped development curve. It's their social and technological evolution which is unusual."

"In what way?"

"I am not a social anthropologist, but even I can see the progression rate is above the predicted norm. I managed to obtain tissue samples from an Earth woman brought to the Serrll Moon Base, which should enable me to make a detailed analysis of their genome. We mixed up their gene sequences pretty thoroughly with our meddling, you know, and some of those sequences may identify a causal factor for what is happening now."

Ed-Kani sat up and frowned, not interested in genetics. He searched for a political angle. "Someone brought an Earth subject to the SMB in violation of protectorate guidelines?" Hiss.

"Believe me, Uncle, it wasn't authorized by me. It was that bungled mission by the Diplomatic Branch to destroy some old scoutship Earth managed to dig up somewhere."

"Yes, I heard something about it."

"Not enough apparently," Laraiana said archly and tossed back her head. "The officer in charge made a complete hash of it. Despite my reports to the Diplomatic Branch and Commissioner Enllss-rr, the whole episode seems to have been quietly buried."

"A coverup? That's not how Enllss usually works. Who was Head of Mission?"

"Terrllss-rr, a former First Scout. The insolence I endured at his hands, Uncle! And that Wanderer partner of his just as useless. It was absolutely humiliating. If it were not for Terr, I would have made the first contact with the Orieli."

"You were there?" Ed-Kani stared at her in astonishment.

"You didn't know? That's terrible! I want him broken, Uncle, humiliated as he humiliated me." Hiss.

"Terrllss-rr, the name sounds familiar," he mused and the memory suddenly surfaced. Of course, the young man who exposed Lemos and captured Tanard! Then there was an episode four years ago on Elexi and the plot by Kapel Pen to cede the Four Suns to the Karkans. The boy had been busy. "I can understand your frustration, precious, but the Diplomatic Branch is part of the Bureau of Cultural Affairs. That's Commissioner Sill-Anais. I have no authority there."

Laraiana uncrossed her legs and stamped her foot in irritation. Would he thwart her as well? "But, Uncle! You're an Executive Director. Surely you can do *something*!"

Ed-Kani fought back a grin. No, his little Laraiana hadn't changed at all. "I'll look into it, but I cannot promise anything. If Terr took credit for the Orieli contact that should be rightfully yours, I'll take care of it. Now, do you have time to talk to an old relative? We can go to the Executive Lounge and grab some lunch."

Laraiana flashed him a smile and rose. It looked like she would have her revenge after all. "Sounds grand. I would like that."

"Excellent! And you can tell me more about your Orieli contact. I want to know everything."

Chapter Eight

Earth hovered a bare three million talans on Anatol's port quarter, a brilliant blue-white sphere shepherding its blotchy gray satellite. An attractive world, much kinder to its inhabitants than his harsh, windswept home. While on the Serrll Moon Base rotation—he thanked the gods he wasn't stuck in that dreadful place permanently, and pitied the unfortunate base commander his hard luck—more than once, he'd taken a GS-4 shuttle down to a secluded white beach and enjoyed Earth's warm scented airs, transparent azure waters and the endless deeps of its tropical blue skies. With gulls slowly circling above him, screeching in protest at this alien intrusion, he would lie beneath limp palms and listen to the whispering surf while a bright sun burned pleasantly against his black skin. Of course, it was strictly illegal landing on a protectorate. If caught, the starched Captal functionaries at the Bureau of Colonial and Protectorate Affairs would make a harsh example of the luckless offender, which made it that much sweeter. Besides, everybody did it. An occasional whiff of sweet-smelling, oxygen-rich air, and life in the utilitarian Moon Base confines or his M-4 at least tolerable. These wayward excursions did sometimes bring them into direct contact with civilian Earth aircraft and occasionally a military one. The one time it happened to him, he had thrown the GS-4 skittering across the sky while the frustrated fighter tried for a missile lock, but it was only play, most of the time. The problem, those Earth jockeys had no sense of humor.

Attuned to the ship by the ambient sounds it made, he blinked and tapped powerful fingers against the command couch armrest. His three M-4s had two more days to go in their assigned ten-day rotation, and Earth's blue skies notwithstanding, he relished the thought of getting back to Salina and some real recreation.

A step below him, three seats faced an inward-sloping curved bulkhead housing arrays of two katalan-wide display plates, sensor stations, color-sensitized reactive control panels, and manned operator consoles. An M-4 was a complex warship and although many of its functions were fully automated, the crew still much to do.

"Talk to me, Mr. Patil," Anatol growled at his executive officer, his small pinpoint red eyes compressed into slits.

The exec frowned at this unwarranted interruption, lifted his head from the repeater plates and paused before swiveling his seat. Anatol didn't have to plague him because he liked to micromanage everything. He could see every display Patil could and better. The inputs were the same on his armrest repeaters as they were in the main plot. The plain fact, and Patil had grown fatalistic about it, Anatol liked the impression of being in total command. Some things couldn't be changed, and his commander was one of them.

"Target now showing 90,200 talans indicated," he announced coldly, a sign of his displeasure. "No course deviations. No anomalous power emissions. Detecting what I read as primary screen configuration only. Scan matches previously recorded ident curve. Profile confirmed."

Anatol's mouth twitched as Patil swung his seat around again, but without amusement. He knew his exec was annoyed, a game they played and helped to break the tension. Besides, discipline would be served if he showed the deck watch he expected everyone to be on the bounce, even his executive officer. If that generated a bit of irritation with Mr. Patil, well, tough nuts.

In the main plot display, the Orieli cruiser's profile rotated through various multi-dimensional position schematics. Anatol studied the figures and images with professional detachment.

Stefan Vučak

The alien ship was big: 810 katalans long, twice the size and mass of an M-4, and he figured a match for any M-6. What was it doing here again after First Scout Terrllss-rr's contact? Anatol squirmed and the couch shifted to accommodate him. Young Terr had stolen the glory that rightfully belonged to him! Twenty days ago his normal cruise pattern took him near the Rolan group and he missed the Orieli by what he later learned was less than a day. It was galling. The promotion and attention heaped on Terr could have brought *him* that coveted step to flag rank and a posting to CAPFLTCOM. Having first toyed with him, the whimsical fates were seemingly repentant by giving him this chance now and he planned to make the most of it.

The darkened command deck was quiet. Muted status reports, inter-deck comms and computer readiness notices disturbed the silence. The transparent nav bubble allowed a sprinkling of stars to stare in. A full-dimensional holograph node glowed in the center of the deck. The tactical plot it now showed reflected the Orieli ship moving steadily toward Anatol's force.

His thick stubby fingers tapped the armrest in a characteristic staccato. Unconsciously, he pressed his bloated purple-red lips into a tight line. Sitting back, he crossed his legs and his thin nostrils flared in concentration. He felt the prickling of an oily sheen on his perfectly round head in warning. Staring at the Orieli ship, he weighed his options. Whatever the reason for their return, simply standing back and allowing the alien unrestricted access to Earth would be servile subservience. It wasn't the impression he wanted to leave with the Orieli or Captal. He didn't plan on busting them up or anything, just aggressively show them who ran things around here. After all, they were the trespassers and he held all the tactical advantages: mass of force, unity of command, simplicity, maneuverability and offensive power. Security of his force and surprise did not apply here. Young Terr in his little gnat M-1 couldn't have done anything, but with three M-4s around him, Anatol figured he should have no trouble making his point. At two point-two katalans, heavyset, he knew how to intimidate opponents, whether by his sheer physical size or with a triad of ships. That approach had served him well enough in the past and he saw no reason why it shouldn't work now. Powerful as they might be, the Orieli needed to learn respect.

"The other two M-4s maintaining relativity?" he demanded, his voice deep and throaty. He could see in the nav plot that they were, but it did no harm to ask. He needed the watch sharp and frosty.

"In position," Patil confirmed without taking his eyes off the tactical plot. "Tandem fire control link in standby mode. All systems read nominal for active hookup on your command."

Anatol nodded. Time for business. "Indicate full stop," he ordered. "Set initial alert."

"Set initial alert, aye, sir." Patil had expected the order and immediately relayed instructions. The watchstanders instantly perked up and a ripple of speculative whispers raced around the deck. Under increased readiness, some displays changed from their soft yellow to steady amber. Previously inactive action contact pads rippled into life in arrays of colored strips and squares. Along the back bulkhead a cable-tube hatch slid open and two more watchstanders took their combat stations.

In the engineering spaces, directly above the huge projector dome, technicians monitored active displays as the computer initiated the first stage of a full energy management powerup. The primary fusion chamber for the twin Koyami 3/C generators brought to its ignition temperature and stripped helium nuclei plasma ignited into twisting blue-white coils. Power then bled into another chamber that fed the artificial antimatter convergence point. The energy surge from particle annihilation carefully controlled and allowed to bleed through the containment field directly into the primary shield grid, extending it twelve talans beyond the ship along spherical lines of force, enclosing the M-4 in a pulsing cocoon of impenetrable energy.

The ship slid to a stop. The other two M-4s of the triad kept station and stopped. At half a million talans separation the sensors could barely resolve the flowing rectangular shape as the Orieli ship became visible in the main plot. Its edges curved down, tapered like sagging wings. The metallic black mass did not show any lights. Nothing about the alien suggested menace, but its power nonetheless nearly palpable. Anatol studied the deceptive simplicity of its design and frowned. The exec raised a quizzical eyebrow and indicated at a repeater plate beside him.

"They're at rest. No weapons status indicated and their secondaries are down. What I read as their primary interceptor net is extended to twenty-four talans."

Anatol grinned. "Not very trusting, are they? Still, I guess I'd be doing the same thing if I had three ships in my way."

Patil turned to face Anatol, his features grave. "If our return ping from their interceptor net is correct, our 128 TeV bursts won't even touch her."

"I gathered that, Mr. Patil. If we were to fire in tandem with the other M-4s, 384 TeV is bound to be more persuasive. However, this is a peaceful contact. I am not considering firing at anybody."

Patil wasn't so sure as he turned his seat. He saw the gleam of anticipation in Anatol's eyes and wondered why the commander sought a confrontation. To make an impression with CAPFLTCOM? He knew Anatol saw himself more a strategist than a line commander, but he wasn't on Captal now. An experiment in ego-tripping could prove disastrously costly for everybody, not counting the impact on future Serrll/Orieli relations.

The comms officer looked up. "Sir, we have an incoming."

"Hah! Open channel," Anatol said and rubbed his hands. "Here we go."

The main plot cleared and Anatol studied the alien with

interest. He viewed extracts from Terr's data pack and recognized the Cetan immediately. The plain one-piece indigo uniform could not disguise the sheer size and tactile power the alien exuded. Dark brown, Karth's skin drawn tight over a long angular face. He had black, fleshy lips, and Anatol was startled when a pale tongue licked quickly around them. Deep red, his eyes were hard and uncompromising. Regarding those eyes, Anatol saw resolve and unwavering duty. Whatever the Orieli wanted, this individual seemed determined that nothing would get in his way of achieving it. Well, Anatol had three M-4s and was happy to be in the way.

"Serrll Scout Fleet vessel, I am Opturkarh Karth, commanding the Orieli Technic Union survey vessel *Valon*. I extend affable greetings, Da," the computer translated into perfect Serrll interlingua, the alien's voice deep and softly modulated. His tongue swept the lips.

Anatol took a steadying breath. "I am Master Scout Anatol Keller, commanding the SSF attachment. On behalf of the Serrll Combine, I am pleased to welcome you into our space."

Karth gave a graceful bow, but when he looked up, his eyes were still hard. "You're gracious, Da. I regret this intrusion into your territory and I trust you will accommodate me while I complete my mission here."

"Opturkarh, I understood Karhide Zor-Ell commanded your ship."

"He does, Da," Karth said, refusing to elaborate.

"Mmm. The Sol system is a protectorate, as no doubt Agent Terrllss-rr explained. You understand my concern, sir."

"Perfectly, Da Keller. It is not my intention to reveal myself or interfere with Earth in any way which might compromise Serrll's position."

"What exactly is your intention?"

"An orbital overflight to retrieve data packages left from our initial contact."

Anatol frowned. A perfectly plausible explanation. If he

conducted a survey, it was exactly something he would have done.

"Can these probes be detected?"

Karth raised an eyebrow. "By Earth's technology? No."

"I must consult with my government before allowing you to proceed," Anatol said evenly, watching for any reaction. If the alien was concerned, he hid it well.

"May I ask how long before you expect to receive a response?" Karth said at length. "My time here is rather limited."

"That's hard to say, Opturkarh. A day or so at least."

Karth's long face became even longer. Clearly, he wasn't happy, but managed to contain his disappointment. "Master Scout, please convey to your Bureau of Colonial and Protectorate Affairs greetings from the Orieli Technic Union. I would appreciate if you could advise them that due to aspects of my mission, which I am not at liberty to disclose, compel me to begin my retrieval sequence within twelve hours. In the meantime, I shall await their reply with anticipation."

Anatol's mouth twitched. The alien had a sense of humor after all, forcing the issue, and he thought Karth was as dour as he looked. Alone in a single ship, facing three M-4s, a joke worth retelling.

"Sir, if you're making a veiled threat—"

Karth's expression didn't change. "Please accept my unreserved apology for a poor choice of words, Da, but making a threat was the farthest thing from my mind. I simply attempted to explain an operational constraint beyond my control."

"I will convey your message to Captal, sir. It would help me a great deal if I could provide some clarification regarding the nature of your urgency. It could serve to expedite the matter."

"The data packages must be retrieved within a predetermined timeframe or they automatically self-destruct to avoid technology contamination in an unlikely case of possible recovery."

"By Earth?"

"No, Da. By the Serrll, now that you're alerted to their presence."

Studying the alien's impassive features, Keller didn't believe him. Karth had to know the Serrll didn't have the necessary technology to detect the probes, or the SMB would have already done so. His initial scan when the Orieli first departed revealed nothing. The aliens were up to something, but if that were the case, it was unlikely he would find out from Karth.

"Then you left it rather late, sir."

"As you say, Da Keller."

"You shall hear from me, Opturkarh," Anatol said and glanced at the comms officer. The main display plate reverted to its tactical status.

Brows knitted, Patil got up and stepped to the command couch. "Sir, we don't have to contact anyone. Why are we doing this?"

Anatol leaned back, looking pleased with himself. "Now that we're staring at each other and no one is going anywhere, I want to take a closer look at our alien friends. Send two Type F probes and have them go over their ship. There is no telling what useful things we might dig up."

"You may be throwing sand at a canal worm...sir."

Anatol grasped the armrests and glared at him. "Pits! Whose space is this anyway? We could learn much from this encounter, which could be invaluable in any future dealings with them. CAPFLTCOM won't be thanking us if we miss this singular opportunity."

"We could also get our asses smeared if we make a mistake. CAPFLTCOM will not be thanking us for that either."

Anatol sighed and shook his head in disappointment. He expected better from Patil. The man was a plodder with no vision.

"You're a pain, did you know? If any ass gets smeared here, it'll be mine. Just send the damned probes, okay?"

Patil resumed his station, ignoring the questioning glances from the other officers. The watchstanders kept their eyes rigidly on their consoles. Patil knew that once off watch the exchange would spread through the ship in a wave of wild speculation; the commander and the exec were at it again. Anatol should not have dressed him down in front of everybody.

He turned to his engineering watchstander. "Launch two Type F probes."

The flattened katalan-long pebble shapes slipped from the launch bay beneath the M-4 and accelerated toward a point in space where their sensors told them was a stationary anomalous energy source. With their small drives it took them twenty minutes to reach the Orieli ship. At two hundred talans, passive sensors recorded energy levels and force line contours of the alien's primary grid. The Orieli gave no indication they have noticed the probes, even when they began a pattern of active scans.

On the command deck, Anatol didn't overly concern himself with Patil's wounded mood or the flow of data coming from the probes. He had specialists to do that for him. A tactician and planner, the technical side of command was beneath him. Sector Tactical Operations Command were simply too dense to see it. He yearned for a posting to Fleet command on Captal, not run a ship. With the precision of a well-planned campaign, he guided his career through the chrysalis years until promotion to First Scout brought command, independence and opportunities to display his full potential. His actions and political correctness earned him several commendations and a fast track to Master Scout rank. Satisfying as that was, he knew he wouldn't make Prima Scout without cultivating Captal's powerbrokers. It took time to develop several carefully chosen Servatory Party luminaries, but his future now seemed assured and the Orieli have given him a unique opportunity to make those Captal desk drivers sit up and take notice. He wanted to provoke a reaction from the aliens. Nothing drastic, something that revealed how they behaved under pressure, and show CAPFLTCOM how *he* behaved under pressure.

After seven hours, they were still at a standoff. He climbed out of his couch and stepped beside his exec checking probe data in the holoview node.

"Anything interesting?" he remarked mildly and Patil looked up, his resentment forgotten.

"Very, and not only from what we can see."

"Such as, or are you going to make me beg?"

Patil grinned. "I should. Their interceptor net, for one. I suspect when they fire, it's not pulse sequenced. Another thing. The probes weren't able to detect anything like a projector housing."

To fire its projector an M-4 had to synchronize its pulses with the shield grid frequency, otherwise it would be firing into its own energy screen. If the Orieli didn't use a projector...

Anatol's eyebrows arched and he stared hard at his exec as the implication sank in. "You're telling me they discharge bursts directly from their interceptor net envelope?"

"Looks very much like it," Patil agreed. If Anatol showed concern, this piece of intelligence would make CAPFLTCOM go pale.

"Anything else?"

"Isn't that enough?"

Anatol's smile was grim. "You're right. It's more than enough. You still doubt the wisdom of my stand?"

"What we found is valuable, but as your executive officer, I must inform you that I am still concerned about our current course of action," Patil said softly, unable to hide his unease. "How long are we going to keep this up? We have our data and baiting the Orieli further could have unforeseen consequences. Should they lodge a protest with the BCPA, we could be in for some unpleasant questioning."

"No one is baiting anybody, Mister. This is simply a small exercise in protocol, and we have twelve hours to see how things develop. As for the BCPA, I wouldn't worry too much." Anatol saw Patil's eyes go expressionless. "I know what you're thinking, that I'm risking a confrontation and jeopardizing Serrll's future relationship with the Orieli. Well, let me tell you something else. That ship can be an M-9 for all I care. While they're in our space, I am the site commander and keeper of Serrll's territorial integrity. You have a problem with that?"

"It's my duty to warn you of all possible scenarios, sir," the exec said woodenly.

"And you do it well," Anatol grated with a sneer of contempt and stomped back to his seat. He glared around the deck, daring anyone to say anything. "Hah!" He sat down and frowned, his fingers automatically resuming an absent beat against the armrest. The exec was a nervous woman and lacked the vision to recognize an exceptional opportunity when thrust in his face.

After another hour of remote surveillance, he recalled the probes and waited. Exactly on the twelve-hour mark the comms officer looked up.

"We have an incoming."

Anatol nodded in appreciation. "Right on time. Precision, I like that. It tells me they're perfectionists. Interesting. Very well. Let's hear what they have to say."

The display cleared and Karth regarded Anatol without expression. "Master Scout, please excuse what could be interpreted as impatience—"

"Understandable, sir."

"May I inquire if you received a response from your government?"

"It's only been twelve hours, Opturkarh," Anatol said easily and shrugged. "Despite the priority of my message the wheels of bureaucratic machinery sometimes don't turn as quickly as we would like them to."

Karth's mouth twitched, digesting the news. "An unavoidable byproduct of governments everywhere, Da. This places me in a most awkward position, one which I trust will not create an incident, but my hand is forced. I am compelled to proceed toward Earth."

"Opturkarh Karth, you don't have permission to enter Serrll space."

"Da Keller, I am open to suggestions how to resolve this impasse."

"Wait."

"Under any other circumstance, Da, I would be most happy to comply. Regretfully, in this case, it's the one thing I cannot do for reasons already stated."

Anatol bridled at this impudence and his features hardened. "I caution you, sir. I'm prepared to defend Serrll's territorial integrity."

Karth looked genuinely surprised. "Da Keller, I don't represent a threat to Serrll security."

"That's not the way I see it, or how Captal may see it, sir."

"I keenly regret you view my request as an incursion, Da, but I also recognize you're simply carrying out your duty. In the same way, I hope your government will appreciate that likewise, I must do mine. Again, my respectful greetings."

The plate cleared before Anatol could reply and the tactical display showed the blue ring around the Orieli ship shrink. Patil turned to look at him.

"Sir, he has withdrawn his primary interceptor net to eighteen talans and the ship is moving. No anomalous power emissions or indication he's charging his net."

Pits! Anatol wasn't looking for a confrontation, but if the Orieli wanted to create one, he would happily accommodate them. Withdrawing, thereby defusing the situation, didn't even occur to him.

"Go to primary alert! Synchronize and ready projector for minimal bursts. Advise the supporting M-4s to assume a standard triangle formation."

"Enable tandem fire control?" Patil asked.

"Negative! I want to show them we mean business."

Patil wondered if the Orieli would be as understanding.

The M-4 extended its secondary shield grid by five talans. When the Orieli ship approached the 140,000-talan acquisition envelope the projector dome beneath the M-4's belly glowed a sullen orange in readiness.

"Initial firing point?" Anatol snapped.

"Six seconds."

"L-band lock established on target one. Optimum firing solution," the computer announced coldly.

"Comms? Order the other two M-4s to fire independently. Fifty percent bursts across the Orieli's line of advance. Any sign they're powering up?"

"No change in detected power emissions," Patil stated.

"Very well. Weapons? You can engage."

Energy surged from the two Koyami generators and flooded into focusing coils within the projector dome. The fire control computer synchronized the pulse sequence with the shield grid and a pale yellow 64 TeV beam flashed from the projector dome and lanced toward the Orieli ship, slashing past it in warning. *Valon* maintained its advance.

Anatol expected his half strength bursts would demonstrate his resolve and induced Karth to stop. Accordingly, he did not see fit to tandem his fire control with the other M-4s, drastically reducing the tactical effectiveness of his force. By ignoring him the Orieli have now placed him in a real bind. If he failed to fully prosecute now, he was effectively telling them his posture merely empty rhetoric. If he engaged actively, the situation could deteriorate to a point where he could be in a battle scenario, something he knew CAPFLTCOM would not view with favor, no matter what the apparent technical provocation. Unless the Orieli were prepared to withdraw, something he doubted they would do.

He set his mouth, accepting that events have now taken on

a life of their own. "Mr. Patil, you can fire for effect. Fifty percent. Advise the M-4s."

After a quick glance at Anatol, Patil also recognized the inevitability of the situation, and its stupidity.

"Firing for effect, aye, sir."

The M-4 fire struck the Orieli's outer net and bled along force lines without causing any apparent damage. Anatol fired again. The two supporting M-4s joined and three beams splashed harmlessly against *Valon's* shields.

The M-4 6/A Sofam-built main battle cruiser formed the mainstay of the Serrll Scout Fleet. It had a better part of nine tetalans grade C composite armor on top of four-tetalan-thick polymer hull construct. Even without secondary shields, it could withstand several bursts of up to 128 TeV at close range. Its twin Koyami 3/C phased array generators, channeled through a single projector dome, could deliver twenty-four-millisecond bursts to 140,000 talans almost indefinitely. Formed into a triad with two other ships, their fire control systems slaved to the command ship, the M-4 made a formidable offensive platform.

"They're still moving," Patil warned and cast a worried glance at Anatol. "Sir, given the deteriorating tactical situation, I recommend we stand down."

"To the pits with you, Mister! Engage tandem fire control link and prepare for full bursts."

Patil gaped, then started issuing orders, but too late. Still moving slowly a ripple of blue-white lightnings writhed along force lines of the Orieli ship's primary interceptor net and coalesced at a single locus. A pale blue lance of decaying ionization flicked delicately at Anatol's M-4 and tore through the two shield grids in a spectacular display of orange-white discharges. Massive backsurges arced from torn shields and played along the hull and projector dome. In a cascade of arcing lights, both shield grids collapsed. Without pausing the Orieli fired twice more and the M-4s of Anatol's force wallowed helplessly under the onslaught, their offensive capability neutralized.

Anatol paled when the ship shuddered violently beneath him. His knuckles hurt as he gripped the armrests. He could hear the exec bellowing orders and saw panels flicker from operational brown to pulsing green and white of total failure. In the nav bubble the Orieli ship moved silently into view, looking huge even at thirty talans. Anatol waited for *Valon* to fire, to end it all, but it only glided by. Then it vanished, swallowed in blackness.

The Orieli should have fired for effect, he mused bitterly. At least it would have been an honorable end. His actions may be theoretically correct, but he suspected the politically minded flag officers at CAPFLTCOM would probably not see it the same way. Had he managed to hold off *Valon*, his action would be hailed as decisive. Now, with his force stranded in full view of Serrll Moon Base the knives would be drawn and he knew full well who would carry the blame. Damn the Orieli anyway!

Regaining some of his composure, he got to his feet, albeit somewhat unsteadily, and looked around the command deck. He saw faces slick with sweat and there was a rank smell of fear in the air. He was appalled to see open relief on the faces, relief that they were still alive. This was a front-line crew meant to defend Serrll's integrity? Glowering at them, no one cared to return his stare.

The exec stood and leaned toward him. "Shall I warn the SMB?"

Anatol stared through him and snorted. "And tell them what?"

Patil didn't say anything. There was nothing to say. The SMB's sensors would have shown them everything. He nodded and started his inspection round. For an instant, he felt sorry for his commander. Anatol wanted a closer look at the Orieli cruiser and he had certainly gotten one.

* * *

Shadow Masters

Buffeted by swirling wind the dart shuddered and Coni muttered sullenly under his breath. Only a fool would be flying in this soup and he didn't consider himself foolish. Nevertheless, he *was* flying in this soup. If the Earthman he was supposed to pick up had any brains, the guy would be in a soft, warm bed somewhere, not camping out; subliminal imperative notwithstanding.

After monitoring the site all day, he saw the ground vehicle emerge from the forest late in the afternoon. A composite sensor image taken through the cloud layer, but Cent Comp didn't require ordinary light to see. The mainframe plot showed the Earthman pitching his tent and not wasting time getting inside. Coni would not be surprised if the guy hadn't questioned his sanity for being out in that weather.

The dart broke through the cloudbank a mere nine kanampirs above the valley floor, the ship's computer squawking a proximity warning. Heavy dusk and driving rain cut visibility to nearly nothing. Unless someone actually stood below them, there was little risk of anyone seeing the dart settle. Lit from within, the tent glowed a buttery yellow. Coni could see the Earthman's shadow outlined against the translucent walls. He glanced at the crewman and a disabling beam slashed through the tent.

Not wanting to linger, Coni activated his shield and they went down to the main deck. Outside, he frowned at the wind's mournful howl and the hiss of swaying branches. Even though enclosed within the shield's protective environment, he sensed the cold. This time, he didn't fumble with the damned tent fasteners and quickly unzipped the outer protective flaps. He didn't need to worry about the insect screen either. No self-respecting bug would be caught dead prowling on a day like this.

The Earthman lay slumped across his bunk, left hand outstretched toward a small gas burner and a blackened pot bubbling over it. It took Coni a few minutes to figure out how to turn off the burner, not wanting to set the tent on fire and get the Earthman into trouble. Safely in his shield, they manhandled him into the dart. They did not see the horned animal, and Coni smiled at the memory.

Buttoned up, the dart slowly rose and headed west.

Malfe and his assistant were waiting in Hangar Bay Two when Coni powered down and wasted no time retrieving their subject. His job done, Coni made his way to the PT alcoves. He needed to check on some maintenance to the secondary quantum point reactor. Might as well be useful until Malfe finished his job and he could take the Earthman down.

In Primary Flight Control, Karth noted the status notices in the mainframe plot and nodded. Nothing required his attention and the Serrll ships had withdrawn from the system. He couldn't understand what had set off the Serrll commander, but he hadn't been in any mood to argue. The twenty-day margin up and they had no choice but to retrieve the karhide from the pickup location. Missing the rendezvous time would mean going through the messy business of interrogating the subject's nanocell tracer to trigger another recall, and then wait for a suitable opportunity to retrieve him. The nonsense could have dragged on for days!

When the Serrll ships fired, he could tell they were not full strength projections. If fired for real, perhaps they could have penetrated *Valon's* defense net, which he doubted, but he didn't wait to find out. Once Cent Comp analyzed the Serrll's modulated shield envelope frequencies, a relatively simple matter to penetrate them. An exercise in response evaluation? Master Scout Keller's behavior pattern certainly suggested he engaged in a contest of wills. Whether true or not, Karth fervently hoped the encounter did not reflect Serrll policy toward the Orieli.

"Opturkarh, the Transfer laboratory has a message," Cent Comp announced.

"Very well. Accept."

Malfe's image appeared in the holoview repeater plot. "Da,

we're ready to commence integration if you would like to come down and observe."

"Thank you, I'd like that." Karth got up and walked quickly toward the PT alcoves. He enjoyed commanding *Valon* and lusted after a major ship of his own, but he also looked forward to having his karhide back. However valuable observing Earth might be, he had misgivings how OSCOM would view the episode and, however unlikely, Zor-Ell could be in for a censure.

When he entered the Transfer Lab, Malfe already had both subjects prepped and running a diagnostic check. Karth knew that in many ways memory reintegration was a much more complicated process than transfer. For Zor-Ell the procedure involved merger not only of acquired memories, but re-mapping of his entire personality matrix. An individual wasn't simply a sum of his memories, but a subtle relationship between those memories and the quality of experiences they represented. It was critical that this quality be preserved intact, and not reduced to a mere datum of the fact, which would risk damaging Zor-Ell's entire cognitive makeup. They understood the theoretical basis of integration from its inception, as were the associated engineering problems of its application. Early test subjects were revived, only to discover minute differences in behavior and personality traits, which made them nearly new individuals. It took a while to sort out the problems.

For the Earthman, wiping Zor-Ell's personality matrix along mapped boundaries a relatively simple process, involving the breaking of chemical bonds. Destruction was always easier than creation.

"Status check complete," Cent Comp advised. "Operational caution. Data channel streams thirteen, fourteen, and twenty-three at transfer tolerance limit. Buffer capacity enhanced. Ready to commence integration buffering."

Karth looked at Malfe. "The same data streams as before. Do we have a problem?"

Malfe bit his lower lip and frowned. "I don't believe so.

However, an abort in any of them will result in partial integration only. We'll be monitoring for any anomalies to avoid that. Cent Comp? Commence buffering."

The assurance did not fill Karth with a wave of confidence. When the procedure started, he could tell that things were not going well. Malfe and his assistant stared intently at the holoview displays, making constant adjustments to the transfer rates.

"Warning! Data streams fourteen and twenty-three now beyond tolerance limit. Buffering sequence terminated. Integration procedure suspended."

Malfe placed his hands on his hips and let out a loud sigh. "I feared this might happen."

"What?" Karth demanded.

"It's the Earthman. Somehow, Karhide Zor-Ell's memories leaked beyond the induced boundary layers and started to integrate with the subject's own memory matrix. Cent Comp could not maintain sufficient differentiation without also retrieving the Earthman's memories. Had we continued, the procedure would have wiped a considerable portion of his personality, transferring it to the Karhide. Imprinting in reverse."

"Can you get around the problem without harming the subject?"

"Oh, we'll run further diagnostics and activate additional discriminating routines, which should do the trick. But as to the cause?" Malfe paused and pulled at his chin. "It looks very much like the neuron matrix in the Earthman's frontal lobes has artificially created layers to enhance capacity."

Karth stared at him. "Artificially created? But that would mean—"

"Genetic manipulation, I know. Cent Comp? Conduct a level two trace and reconfigure channels fourteen and twenty-three through the dual buffer. Set protocol three discrimination verification."

"Diagnostic completed. No anomalous dysfunction indicated. Ready to recommence buffering sequence."

"Recommence buffering."

For five minutes everything seemed to go well, but Karth knew this was only a first step where Cent Comp filled data buffers with karhide's extracted memories before the actual imprinting began. Suddenly the holoview displays rippled in a swirl of color traces.

"Warning! Data stream twenty-three corrupted. Buffering sequence terminated."

Malfe snorted, dropped his arms and stared hard at Karth. "We cannot bring the Karhide back. I *told* him we needed to do a matrix density test!"

"Talk to me, Malfe!" Karth snapped and the medic jerked.

"His memories have merged too deeply with the subject's and the buffering sequence risked damaging the Earthman's personality. There is nothing we can do, not with *Valon's* facilities."

"Even with Cent Comp's capacity, you're telling me the Karhide is trapped?"

"Effectively. Of course, we could implant the subject's original memories, but he would lose twenty days of his life."

"And face a lifetime of possible psychiatric problems. Problems of our making!" Karth fumed in frustration. Even if the situation wasn't covered by strict protocols, he couldn't leave the Earthman to suffer just to retrieve the karhide, and wiping the karhide's memories was a last resort option. If he did nothing, what would that do to the karhide, trapped in an alien mind? He looked at Zor-Ell's body and made a decision. "Wake him."

Malfe gaped. "But Opturkarh! What about the Earthman?"

"We cannot help either of them. You said it yourself. Keeping the Karhide in stasis is pointless. Wake him."

Malfe wanted to protest, saw the look on Karth's face and touched several pads on the central console. The blue aura above Zor-Ell slowly faded. A few seconds later, his eyelids fluttered open.

Zor-Ell blinked hard. It felt like he barely closed his eyes. He glanced at the Earthman and frowned. "Something wrong with the transfer?"

"The transfer was successful, Karhide," Malfe told him without elaborating, his features grim.

Zor-Ell understood immediately. "The integration cycle aborted. Is my personality wiped?"

"Ah, not quite. It appears memory boundaries were compromised and part of your personality matrix has fused with the subject's. We cannot fully extract your memories."

"Data stream twenty-three, right? It will do it every time." Zor-Ell glanced at the holoview displays and gave a loud exhale, not liking any of it. He studied such cases during training, but never expected to be one himself. He looked apologetically at Malfe. "You were right. We should have run a matrix density test."

Malfe cleared his throat. "Ah, we have something else, Da, the underlying cause for your problem. At some stage in their evolution, Earthman were subjected to genetic manipulation."

Zor-Ell digested the information and many things suddenly fell into place. There would be time later for detailed analysis. He glanced at Karth. "You decided to revive me?"

"This isn't something we can resolve here, Da, and *Valon* needs her commander."

What about *his* needs, trapped in an alien body? Zor-Ell didn't relish the prospect of his other half coping in effective bondage. If memory boundaries were already badly compromised, prolonged exposure in the alien brain would only exacerbate the problem. Potentially, the subject could even become aware of his personality, which in extreme cases could ultimately lead to severe psychological trauma. He sat up and rubbed his temples, then stared at the Earthman for several long seconds before turning to Malfe. The protocol directives in such cases were clear. There really was no decision to make.

"Have him returned."

"But, Da! When he wakes, *you* will still be aware, knowing that retrieval has failed and you were abandoned. The realization could cause destabilization of your entire personality."

Zor-Ell climbed off the bed and gave a sour laugh. "What you're trying to tell me politely, Malfe, is that I could go psychotic. Right?"

"It's a risk, Da, and one that represents genuine danger for the subject the longer we leave him in this state."

"I know myself well enough to avoid psychosis, and we don't have any choice. You cannot retrieve my memories and you cannot wipe them without harming the subject. At any rate, we won't be abandoning me. Once we get back, the Physics Institute on Zaron will analyze the problem and develop a procedure to complete reintegration."

"And if they cannot or we're unable to return to Earth?" Malfe asked quietly.

Zor-Ell didn't want to consider that possibility.

* * *

Jim woke and sat up, completely disoriented. Hissing softly the gas lamp lit the tent's interior with a comforting white glow and the stew on the portable burner bubbled contentedly. Totally dark outside, wind gusts shook the tent walls, which made small clapping noises. But he started cooking at dusk! His hand came up automatically and he looked at his wristwatch: 8:32. Somewhere, he lost over two hours. Why hadn't the stew burned if he'd been out for a while? He picked up a spoon, gingerly leaned over the pot and stirred the contents. The mess inside looked and smelled okay—for canned goo. So, where did those two hours go and why hadn't the stew burned? Friday or not, he had no idea why the hell he left work early or decided to drive to Trentham. Not only that, but go camping in absolutely miserable weather?

He'd come unstuck, that was it.

The appetizing aroma from the pot set his saliva glands spurting and he figured since the damned thing was already done, he might as well eat. Go back to Melbourne? It didn't take much of a decision to reject that option. While in Trentham, there were a couple of things that needed fixing inside the house. Maybe he would go back tomorrow. One thing was certain. He wouldn't be spending the night in this tent, not when a soft bed waited for him.

He reached into a plastic shopping bag and dug out a wholemeal roll. Turning off the gas, he spooned out a mouthful of stew and blew on the steaming contents before popping it into his mouth. Not too bad after all. The roll fresh and had a tough chewy consistency the way he liked.

Two hours? Maybe he should see his doctor on Monday. And tell him what? He wasn't dizzy, confused or foaming at the mouth. Apart from an idiotic impulse to go camping in artic weather, he felt fine.

He kept spooning the stew.

Zor-Ell knew he was in trouble immediately Jim woke. The Earthman had resisted the command to return to the campsite, but the compulsion could not be ignored. In the end, Jim had rationalized his action and made the tedious drive from the city, scowling at the deteriorating weather the closer he came to Trentham. In Melbourne, the day cool, but sunny with no wind. Trentham's weather, though, bore little relation to anywhere else. When Jim drove to his house, rain started to come down heavily. It took an effort of will to pack his tent and drive into the bush. Predictably, he hadn't seen anyone on the winding forest road.

The reintegration procedure had failed, accounting for Jim's missing two hours, leaving Zor-Ell still locked in Jim's head. All sorts of scenarios flashed through his mind to explain the integration failure, none good. Any number of things could have happened, which Malfe clearly couldn't resolve. Since retrieval failed, it meant wiping his implanted memories wasn't an option either. There were several unpalatable reasons to account for that, the main one was leakage beyond memory boundary, always bad. In the meantime, he appeared to be stranded in the Earthman's brain. He should have listened to Malfe and done the damned matrix density test!

What would Karth do? He didn't have to ponder hard for his answer. His decisive first officer probably revived his physical self, then *he* would turn *Valon* around and head for the Karina. If Cent Comp could not resolve the problem, only the Physics Institute had the necessary resources to research a solution. He wondered how long that might take and whether a rescue mission would be mounted at all. He could use mnemonic triggers to induce cascade memory failure, effectively scrambling his personality, but that was an act of desperation and he wasn't ready to suicide yet.

The situation did have a bright side. *When* they retrieved him, his experience would undoubtedly make a footnote in the medical library. Unfortunately, the prospect didn't help him in his present predicament.

Since cheering himself up didn't work, he pondered whether he would ever again see the tinted skies of Zaron. In the end, he gave a mental shrug. It was out of his hands and he might as well continue with his observations and analyses. He *had* wanted to study Earth, didn't he?

Chapter Nine

A soothing light breeze came off a glassy sea, lightly stirring the leaves. The palm fronds hung limp and lifeless. Far on the right, beyond the curving bay, Tauri II hung suspended above mercury waters and a painted sky; a giant red ball waiting to sink beneath placid waves. Out on the water a large catamaran, its decks brightly lit, motored along on an evening dinner cruise. The marina filled with moored yachts and on many of them, owners and pretty female visitors enjoyed each other's company.

Dusk softened colors, highlighted sounds, sharpened outlines and made the condominiums glow along the beachfront. Crowding the broad walkway, open restaurants were full of music and animated voices. Appetizing odors wafted in the breeze. People strolled up and down and couples walked close, some holding hands, whispering intimate secrets to each other. Communals crossed the waning sky, coming down or getting off, bringing or taking customers. On the sands, bathers were drifting away, but there were enough people lying about to keep the beach from looking empty. Some still waded or swam in the water. Small waves slapped against the glistening sand.

With a full seafood dinner inside him, accompanied by two glasses of an excellent fruity white wine, Terr enjoyed his stroll. He could forget, if only for a moment, why he was here and what he had to do. An occasional breath of wind stirred his hair and open-necked T-shirt. He glanced at Dhar's imposing form beside him and grinned.

"Still watching the sea?"

Nightwings looked away from a red-streaked sky, the sea's

dark shadows and sighed. "It holds a fascination for me not unlike the endless sands of the Saffal. Both hold mysteries and secrets that cannot be retrieved, because they are within ourselves. We should take a boat and sail beyond the horizon until there is nothing around us but the sea, something I have never done."

Terr understood his brother's fascination with the expanse of open ocean, and wondered whether Dhar had picked that from him or something Nightwings passed to him when they joined. It didn't matter really. It was the fascination and a desire to reach out, to be surrounded by the deeps, to be part of it that counted.

When he woke early, he would sometimes stand before the bedroom window and gaze hungrily at the rippling water. With the dawn sun peeking over the hills, condominiums and hotels cast black shadows over deserted beaches. He longed to be out there, running on cold wet sands with gentle waves curling along the shore, hissing as they retreated, birds wheeling above, following him. Impossible, of course. He could not afford to be seen indulging in such harmless pleasure, not if he wanted to maintain his cover as a hard-bitten syndicated thug. Still, there was satisfaction at simply watching the sea from his apartment.

"Then we'll have to do it soon," he said softly and Dhar's eyes glowed. A sudden wave of malevolence and danger swept through him and he stopped. "Do you feel it?"

"Someone is following us," Dhar said heavily, his senses alert.

"But not with deadly intent," Terr added, his senses probing. Living beneath the shadow of Death gave them both certain advantages not shared by mere mortals. No one could approach him with murder without the god warning him. "Can you tell how many?"

"Two," Dhar said instantly.

"Okay, let's keep walking and see what develops." Terr

didn't appreciate having his evening stroll disrupted so rudely, but some people had no sense of fitness. Neither he nor Nightwings were armed, not conventionally anyway. Unless someone considered shooting them from a distance, he felt capable of looking after himself and his brother.

As they continued along the promenade, the feeling of being followed grew stronger. A couple strode past them, hurrying toward a restaurant and Terr heard heavy footsteps behind him.

"Well, Ravil! Look who we got here. If it isn't Ser Kerill-aa and his buddy Randakla."

Terr stopped and slowly turned, not wanting to alarm his followers. Both were heavy and carried themselves in a way that said they knew how to take care of themselves—and others. He couldn't see if they packed hardware, but a bulge in their pockets suggested otherwise. Their type would consider themselves naked without a weapon, a necessary prop to bolster a frail ego. A generalization not always true, but in their case, Terr thought he had them figured right.

"You gentlemen shouldn't be outside alone," the taller of the two offered. "Not knowing the area and all. A person could get hurt around here, you know. Especially at night."

"Yeah, they really should be more careful," the shorter one added in a reedy voice.

"Thanks for the warning," Terr said, "but we'll manage okay."

"I don't know, Ser Kerill-aa. I kinda doubt it."

"Since you seem to know us, who are you?"

"Oh, I'm Laski, and you know my partner Ravil." The heavy man smiled and glanced at his sidekick.

"Like I said, thanks for the warning."

Laski lost his smile and his eyes turned hard. "To show you how dangerous things can get here, my boss asked me to bring you guys over so he could explain it personal like." His hand went into his trouser pocket and the bulge became more pronounced. "Let's take a little ride, shall we?"

Without waiting to see if Terr approved or not, he flagged the nearest communal parked along the stone seawall. The driver standing beside the machine waved back and opened the bubble for them.

Terr glanced at Dhar and nodded. Since this did not appear to be a deadly situation, he had no problem meeting Laski's boss. One of KSD's competitors getting irked seeing his business leach away to a couple of newcomers? It didn't matter. He would find out soon enough and he wanted the maggots of this place to start crawling out of the woodwork.

They all piled into the communal. Laski smiled, but there was nothing friendly about it. More like anticipation to dish out violence. In a way, Terr felt cheated. He expected a degree of finesse from his competition. Finesse or not the prospect of action a welcome diversion from a boring, money-grubbing entrepreneur. Watching cargo containers loaded and offloaded wasn't exactly his idea of excitement. When the bubble closed over them, Laski thumbed the mike pad.

"Trans National at Kronas."

The power plant spooled up and the communal lifted, angling toward the hills. Terr relaxed and took in the lit patterns of Karach's sprawl, bordered by curving blackness of the bay. In truth, he hadn't seen the city up high at night, but it looked like any other city at night. At least Laski had answered one important question for him. He now knew who was after them. Would they see TNH's General Manager or one of his flunkies? He figured he would find out soon enough. Either way, Trans National seemed the one most irked right now and were apparently prepared to do something about it. It could be a diversionary move by Global, although only speculation.

Kronas Field looked impressive under lights. The apron glowed a subdued white, offsetting the brightly lit terminus buildings. The communal cleared the control network and flew along the Field's perimeter toward three long warehouses tucked into a far left corner. A smallish freighter rested on its landing ring alongside the nearest warehouse. Automated cranes fluttered around it. A parking pad pulsed yellow beside the center warehouse and the communal sank down on top of it.

When they got out, Terr leaned toward the driver standing beside the door. "Keep her warm. This won't take a minute."

Laski shot him an amused look and shook his head, but he could be excused for not knowing with whom he was dealing with. The mere presence of power was an influence, Terr's master always told him. Well, Trans National might get an opportunity to experience some of that influence first-hand.

"I'll have the meter running," the driver said comfortably, just another fare as far as he was concerned.

Terr could not see anyone as they walked toward the looming warehouse. Bright floodlights pinned the hovering freighter against the background. He heard a hum of working machinery somewhere nearby. Laski opened a side door and motioned Terr and Dhar inside. Six open plan workstations took up a small part of the floor. All were deserted. A transparent wall enclosed the whole area. Beyond it the warehouse extended into the distance. Machines were stacking containers onto fixed shelving that reached to the ceiling. Their footsteps echoing on the hard floor, Laski led them to an end office and touched a pad beside the door. When the panel slid away, he jerked his head at the opening. Terr got the message and walked in.

The local thin, middle-aged and carried himself with self-importance, someone who hated having his time wasted. With two heavies backing him up, he could afford to be confident. He did not stand when his visitors filed in, but simply motioned at the formchairs in front of the desk. On his right a Wall spooled through shifting colors.

"Gentlemen, please be seated," he rasped heavily in a dead voice without emotion. "This shouldn't take long and you can be on your way."

Terr allowed himself a tight smile. So, it was going to be like that, eh? No chitchat, no small talk. Fine with him. He sat down and allowed the seat to mold itself around him. The two gun handlers positioned themselves against the wall behind him and waited. A classic intimidation scenario and a warning of what he could expect.

The individual at the desk studied his visitors for several seconds and sighed. "In case you were wondering what this is all about, I am Madur Rakliva, Trans National General Manager. There was no reason why you two would agree to see me. However, I have a compelling reason to see you. Crude, I admit, but sending Laski to get you was the simplest way to do it."

"A bit melodramatic, but I understand," Terr said easily, weighing up the situation. "You could have used the Wall. Still, now that we're here…"

"This had to be done face to face, Ser Kerill-aa, as you will shortly appreciate. To business. I watched Karach Salvage and Disposal carve a nice market niche for itself since you two took over. Obviously, competition is a healthy thing and there is enough business to go around…if everyone agrees to play by the rules. You two don't seem to have gotten the point that others have an interest in a healthy cargo handling business besides yourselves."

"And what would that point be, Ser Rakliva?" Terr asked pleasantly, but his senses were alert and his body ready for instant action. They were clearly not here to negotiate, confirming Kandu Hall's warning how his host preferred to do business.

"New here and perhaps ignorant how we do things, I'll speak plainly. All players on Askaran work off a set price list, which worked well so far and made everybody happy. KSD doesn't seem to care whether the rest of us are happy or not, and right now, I happen to be very unhappy. However, if you were to change your marketing policy, it would go a long way

Stefan Vučak

toward restoring my contentment."

"Contentment is relative, Ser Rakliva, and changing my marketing policy would ruin mine. My partner and I must recoup our investment, and compliance with your arbitrary rules, designed to stifle competition, not encourage it, would make that a drawn-out proposition. I don't have the time. Besides, we've done you a favor already by divesting ourselves of the point-to-point side of our business."

"Generous of you, but I'm afraid this is where I must correct you on your first argument," Rakliva said softly. "It took everybody a while to agree on those rules which you seem to find so objectionable. So far, it's been a profitable arrangement."

"Profitable for everyone or just you and Global?"

"It's a free market, Ser Kerill-aa."

"And I'm taking advantage of that."

"That is altogether clear to me," Rakliva said and pursed his lips. "And there is nothing I can say to change your mind?"

"I run a business, not a cooperative."

"In that case, I'll have to drive my point home another way." His eyes flickered a fraction over Terr's head, but all the warning he needed.

He sprang to his feet and turned, but Laski was already swinging down the butt of his needler. Terr stepped inside the swing radius and rammed stiff fingers at Laski's throat. The man gagged, dropped the needler and clawed at his neck. Terr lashed a roundhouse kick to the face. The thug spun and crashed to the floor, jerked once and lay still. When Terr turned, Ravil's form lay crumpled in the corner and Dhar was pointing a needler at Rakliva. Terr bent down and picked up Laski's needler. He made a small adjustment to the emission setting and tapped the weapon against the palm of his left hand.

The local looked at the bodies of his hired muscle and the right side of Rakliva's mouth twitched. Terr couldn't tell if that was a stillborn smile or not. Rakliva slowly brought up his arms and folded them over the desk.

"I guess the point has been made," he growled without inflection.

"Not yet," Terr said coldly, lifted the needler and shot him through the right shoulder. The native screamed and clutched at the partly cauterized wound. A thread of white smoke curled around the burn hole and dark blood oozed between his fingers. Not showing any emotion, Terr stared at Rakliva, his eyes hard. "I don't know whether this stunt was your idea alone and I don't particularly care. I also don't give a toss if you're bothered by how my partner and I conduct KSD's business. Next time you want to get a job done, make sure the boys you send are up to it. If you force me to come here again, I won't be bringing muscle. I'll be bringing plasma charges. You'll need tweezers to pick up what's left of your warehouses. Do we understand each other?"

"You're dead," Rakliva snarled, his face contorted with pain. "Both of you."

Terr raised his needler and shot him through the other shoulder. Rakliva leaped from his seat, then slumped across the desk. The air stank of burned flesh and blood. Terr wrinkled his nose and glanced at Dhar.

"I believe we're done here."

"They should have used their needlers," Dhar commented.

"I know, but they wanted to make it personal, sadists who take pleasure inflicting pain. Amateurs!" Terr snapped and snorted with contempt.

Dhar took one look at Rakliva's flaccid form and glanced at the bodies on the floor. He held out his hand and Terr gave him the needler. Dhar wiped both weapons and placed them in the hand of each body. A forensic specialist could probably reconstruct the event, but he doubted it would come to that. He rose and opened the door. No one waited for them.

Outside the warehouse, Terr took a deep breath of fresh

air to cleanse the stench of blood and treachery out of his nostrils. His stroll may have been interrupted, but the night was not completely wasted. He now knew the face of one more enemy.

Dhar paused and his eyes were searching. "My brother, I gather shooting Rakliva was deliberate? You want to invoke a response from Pulman?"

"Or Segal. After all, Rakliva is his brother-in-law. They will either hit us or put it down as a dumb move by TNH and make us an offer to merge. If they want to play rough, we'll get the Resident to mop up both outfits, which could spell the end of our mission. Something, I am sure would ruin Anabb's contentment."

"But you don't believe that will happen."

"I don't, although there is room for doubt. If the local Alikan Union Party chapter or the Provisional Committee is running Global, which seems likely, I'm betting they'll remain focused on their objective. Global needs additional cargo handling capacity and Karach Salvage has it. I'm not saying that everybody will forget what happened tonight and we'll be pals. Sooner or later, they'll get around to balancing the score. In the meantime, I would say we can expect a visit from Pulman and company sometime tomorrow."

"One way or another," Dhar murmured darkly and Terr laughed.

Seeing them the communal driver scrambled out and held the door open. Terr nodded to him and settled into the upholstery. The bubble closed and the power plant whined. Terr thumbed the mike button.

"Tillana Cove Apartments."

"Got it."

With a surge of power the communal lifted and angled toward the sea.

Listening to the soothing hum of the power plant, surrounded by winking patterns of city lights, Terr pondered what tonight's action would spawn. He had made an enemy of

Rakliva, but they'd never be buddies anyway. Somewhere along the line, someone gave the TNH boss wrong advice and paid a tough price for his error. Possibly he even hatched the idea on his own. The man had the muscle and obviously not bashful about using it. Would he make good on his threat? Terr was counting on it. Doing business with raiders may be a sideline for TNH, but it was sure to be a profitable one. He could sympathize why Rakliva would be unhappy seeing that business line shrink or disappear, or what Segal might say about it. If the man was unhappy now, he would be apoplectic if the KSD merger with Global went through. Any fallout between Global and TNH can only help Terr's cause.

Back in the apartment, Dhar ran a scanner sweep. After his initial lapse, he made it his business to ensure security. Along the way, he found two intercept audio/video buttons and both ended up flushed. Short of installing totally secure locks, impossible to do in a serviced apartment, running constant sweeps one downside to their otherwise idyllic stay.

Finished, he switched on the Wall.

"You have a message. Do you wish to view message?" the housekeeping computer announced immediately.

Terr sprawled onto a couch and stretched his legs. "Display message."

"Security code required to display message."

Terr raised an eyebrow. Only two callers required a security code. "Accept binary fourteen, stroke, niner two. Append date and time sequence."

"Code accepted."

The full-dimensional image cleared. "Call me!" Anabb ordered, his voice harsh and gravelly. The chiseled narrow face a wrinkled parchment stamped with a perpetual scowl.

Terr glanced at Dhar and shrugged. Routine reports were usually made to Landau and he wondered what itched Anabb to demand a personal update. He ran a mental routine, figuring the local time on Taltair: late afternoon.

"Computer, set comms protocol Askaran KSD and open channel, personal for Anabb Karr, Diplomatic Branch, Taltair."

"Comms protocol in effect," the computer acknowledged and Terr waited as the Wall pooled through a parody of colors. When it cleared, Anabb glared, the amber flecks in his close-set eyes bright.

"Ah, at last! I wondered where you two were. Ordinarily, Landau handles these things, but he is unavailable and I have a personal reason for calling. I wanted to tell you that Pulman and Segal have commissioned *Paun* and she is raiding. It means you can expect extra cargo from fellow raiders."

"We can expect?" Terr queried, ignoring Anabb's peevishness. "Why would they come to us when Global is their own facility?"

"Well, it turns out that Global had a mishap during routine computer maintenance, which disabled some of its warehouse subsystems. Nothing devastating, but they'll have a backlog in capacity for a few days."

Terr grinned, liking it. "Kandu Hall's doing? He's got somebody inside Global?"

"Not exactly. He has somebody inside the software company that provides businesses, including Global, maintenance support."

It was clear to Terr why Anabb had called. Disruption to Global's cargo handling would provide added pressure on Pulman to merge with Karach Salvage. Evidently, the operation was run on several compartmented levels.

"Thanks for the heads-up, sir. The information will come in handy."

"I thought it might," Anabb said.

"Sir, you said *Paun* and *Pilla* are raiding. By implication, they will be successful, and the only way for them to be successful is if the Fleet leaves them alone. They were ordered?"

Anabb's frown deepened as he studied his willful agent. The boy had worked it out quickly and he was impressed. He came to appreciate that Terr was smart, extremely smart. That was good, and the boy would require all his ingenuity, provided he isn't dazzled by his own cleverness. What he wanted to know, had Terr worked it *all* out?

"They were. Your issue being?"

Terr glanced at Dhar, who gave a minute shake of his head in warning. Anabb was simply a pain again.

"If they're raiding, that means preying on carriers—"

"And it could cost lives," Anabb finished for him. "I understand that. Do you?"

Right then, Terr hated him and hated what he made him do. What it amounted to, he was no longer a bit player and his world wasn't black and white anymore, but an endless shade of grays. The moral tightrope he walked was deciding which gray bit *he* stood on. Didn't he acknowledge that morality was only custom? Apparently, in Anabb's business you changed morals like changing socks when one started smelling. In the end, he jerked his head in a nod.

"I do, sir," he said coldly and saw something flicker in Anabb's brown eyes. The old man's features softened a fraction.

Ignoring Terr's impertinence, Anabb could not shield the boy and his shadow Dhar from the brutal reality of their job. Moreover, he didn't want to shield them. As a Fleet officer the boy took his orders and obeyed, leaving the whys to somebody else to worry about. Well, he now saw the why and the how of it and it obviously did not sit easily. If Terr wanted to last in his job, he would need to shed his idealism and childhood rules. He played with grownups now.

"We do what we must, my boy, and the sooner you accept that, you'll be able to deal better with it. Now, anything else you want to say?"

It hadn't been pleasant having his nose rubbed in it, but Terr admitted Anabb was right, even if a bit harsh doing it. He either accepted what it meant working for the Diplomatic

Branch as Anabb said, or got out right now. He wished his master were here now, for the *Saftara* was powerless to help him, as apparently were the gods. There would be no easy one-liner solution for him this time. He had placed himself on this path and now had to walk it. Blaming Anabb avoided confronting truth, and he was never much good at avoiding responsibility. Free will, a major drag.

"A minor altercation with Trans National Haulage, but nothing we couldn't handle. They were unhappy how we run Karach Salvage. I'm expecting Global's partners to come calling tomorrow, hopefully with an offer to merge. With their systems down, it might be a good time to exploit a clear vulnerability."

"Good. I cannot afford to run your mission much longer. With each passing day, you two are running an increased risk of getting compromised. I have something else you might find interesting, nothing to do with your mission. The Orieli vessel returned, stayed one day and disappeared. Curious that is, but there is more. Master Scout Anatol Keller confronted them with his triad and forced an engagement."

Terr stared, trying to sort out the two events. "Rit! Why in the pits would he do that?"

"That's not clear and CAPFLTCOM recalled him to provide an explanation."

"Did Karhide Zor-Ell show belligerency?"

"Keller's tactical logs show no belligerency indicated. *Valon's* first officer claimed a pressing schedule to retrieve sensor pods sown around Earth and appeared not to appreciate Keller holding him down."

"Opturkarh Karth still in command?" The wheels were spinning as Terr sorted through the facts. Retrieve sensor pods? Oh, he was certain the Orieli had sown sensor pods, but to leave them around for weeks? Several days, he could understand, but weeks? There must be something else. "They came back to pick up an observer."

Anabb chuckled, which made him look ten years younger. "An unlikely idea, Agent Terr, and I enjoy your flights of fancy. Tell me this. How do you suppose an alien, physically unique, not understanding local languages, remains undiscovered and is able to gather information at the same time? Mass hypnosis? I prefer the idea of retrieving pods. It's more realistic."

When put that way, Terr's theory didn't seem so hot. Still, he was prepared to defend it. "Karhide Zor-Ell said he was on a survey mission. He traveled three thousand light-years before reaching Earth. I would say that along the way it's likely he encountered more than one inhabited planet. How would he study them? I don't see him satisfied with only sensor data. Our experience shows that BCPA experts spend years observing a new species before revealing ourselves. The Orieli didn't have that kind of time to spend. The key word here is direct observation. I suggest they perfected the art and have a way of gathering intelligence quickly without getting detected."

"But plant someone on Earth for twenty days?"

"I don't have an answer to that, sir."

"That's clear. I'll tell Enllss your theory, but don't blame me for what happens afterward."

His image faded and the Wall swirled through streaks of warped color. Terr gritted his teeth and slapped his thighs. "Evil old fart! He's got to be one of the most callous bastards it's been my misfortune to come across."

"He could be right about the Orieli picking up sensor pods," Dhar interposed gently.

"I know, but that's not what's got me steamed."

"Forcing us to face up to the darker side of what we do?"

Terr glared at him before a slow smile touched his mouth. "Yeah, we've been there before, haven't we? Okay, so he doesn't sugarcoat the job, but he's still an evil old fart."

"The news of Global's software problems is good."

"Good? It's outstanding. Pulman must be turning over a slow fire now and it's getting hotter all the time. I love it." Terr cracked a broad grin and rubbed his hands with satisfaction. "Our Resident has developed into a valuable asset for us."

"And if Pulman comes calling tomorrow?"

"Didn't Kawisaki say it is better to capture one's enemy than destroy him? With Pulman and company, we need to make sure they end up getting the benefit of both ends."

* * *

"But he shot me!" Rakliva spluttered in outraged petulance. He winced as pain lanced through his shoulders when he tried to gesticulate. An indicator in the large holographic display above the bed wiggled at the unwelcome stimulus. The medics told him to restrain his movements in order for the nanobods and genotherapy sequencers to do their work, but he kept forgetting. Shoulders drooping, he sagged against the pillows. This was humiliating, lying trussed up helpless and weak. Definitely not the kind of image he wanted to project to Segal. Especially Segal! To have things go so horribly wrong! He still found it hard to believe that Laski and Ravil could be dispatched so easily.

Another day, Ser Kerill-aa, he promised himself. There would definitely be another day.

"Idiot! He should have killed you," Segal snarled at his brother-in-law, not showing much sympathy. The fool underestimated his opposition and reaped the reward of his folly. A vivid demonstration of emotion ruling the head and a useful insight into Karach Salvage owners.

"Tan!"

"We need Karach Salvage badly and your lame stunt may cost us the deal."

"I don't care about your crummy deals!" Rakliva shot back, tired of having Segal always berate him. "I've got my own business to run and no slick offworlder is driving me under."

"The only reason you've got a business is because of my

money!"

"I ran Trans National just fine without your lousy money and I didn't need your raider scum to do it. If it weren't for my sister, you'd still be a cheap hustler. Not that you're any better now."

Segal sighed and shook his head in exasperation, unable to understand how such two completely different personalities could spring from one family. Leera a few years younger than her impulsive brother, but beautiful, cultured, accomplished, and smart. That's why he married her. Initially, only a calculated step to gain respectability in local social circles, but that quickly turned into genuine admiration and love. Her brother seemed to have gotten every dumb gene; slush on a head of beer.

Rakliva's predilection for using force as a solution to every problem usually got him results, but when the attempt failed, it was spectacular. Like last night. What a mess. Fortunately, no one noticed the cleanup, or the incident could have turned into a major embarrassment. He had the police chief in his pocket, but an investigation attracts too much undesirable media attention, and you cannot simply dump reporters into the bay, however deserving the treatment. Rakliva must learn restraint and recognize when brains were called for. The behavior reminded him too much of his own reckless past.

He knew what struggling and clawing for everything meant. No one ever gave him a soggy Serrll credit without taking double payment. Young, uneducated and headstrong, he fled the commune orphanage farm, and lying about his age, bummed on freighters looking for that big break. As bottom rung crew, he would never get it and was smart enough to know it. With four equally disgruntled misfits around him, he explained his plan. When they hit planetfall, they went hunting. They found a rusty freighter sitting in a disposal yard and put a holding deposit on it. With a carrying capacity of only 240,000 mikans, the ship way too small for serious intersystem cargo haulage even if they could afford to refit the hull. Segal did not look for size.

The ship mounted a working Terrasec 9 projector. A defensive weapon only, but no one told him that. He took her up, supposedly for acceptance trials, and never came back.

They knew almost nothing of ship handling, barely managing to keep the reactors going. On their first run out they literally stumbled on a Four Suns Very Large Bulk Carrier hauling processed metal halides and rare mineral crystals. Fortunately for them, when challenged, the crew immediately took to survival blisters, relieving him of potential unpleasantness having to dispose of them. His time on freighters hadn't been wasted, and he learned something about the darker side of the business. One of his contacts led to a meeting with a wholesaler who did not particularly care about legalities or manifests. Segal sold his ship, the VLBC, cargo and all, and suddenly found himself with a sizeable pile of disposable cash and no partners. He never shed tears over their timely disappearance. They planned to relieve him of his share and more anyway. Simply a matter who got there first.

Suddenly moderately rich gave him time to look ahead. He'd had his taste of being a raider and considered himself fortunate to have gotten away with it. Next time, he might not be so lucky, realizing it was a mug's game. Blasted by an M-3 wasn't part of his long-term game plan. With money, he could now support himself in style, but without an education and knowledge to apply it, he would still be the bottom rung of everybody's sucker deal. There was only one solution. He returned to Askaran and used his resources to get an education and a recognized degree.

When Pulman approached him with a business plan to set up a cargo handling company, a front for raiders actually, he never hesitated. Pulman represented the local Alikan Union Party chapter, and for a cut off the top would bankroll forty percent of startup costs. He also brought in Re Nette and her crew of fugitives. When Segal managed to snag *Pilla*, they had a viable operation. With a sympathetic government looking the other way and Pulman's contacts, for three years Global Transport did well. With *Drakin* lost, things deteriorated: commissioning another ship, insufficient handling capacity, capped off by AUP's failure to support his bid for Karach Salvage and Disposal when the government put it up on the market. And now, software problems. This wasn't a good time for anybody to be giving him more heartburn.

His reckless brother-in-law needed a sharp reality check.

"Now you listen to me," he hissed between clenched teeth. "As far as you're concerned, Kerill-aa and Randakla don't exist. They'll be taken care of when the time comes, but not because of what happened to you. Right now, I need them. Or more accurately, I need Karach Salvage. Until I have it, you'll take whatever they happen to dish out. If that's not clear enough for you, remember this. Leera might mourn her brother's sudden turn for the worse, but she wouldn't mourn for very long."

Segal did not raise his voice and his face remained expressionless, but his eyes were fierce. Casually, he patted Rakliva's right shoulder and squeezed enough to force his brother-in-law to lose color and let out a soft whimper. The holoview monitor beeped in alarm.

"I knew you'd understand." He strode toward the door and pressed a pad on the wall. When the panel opened, he paused and turned. "Almost forgot. Your two heavies, Laski and Ravil, they're retired, permanently. They were nothing but trouble anyway, and you're better off without them."

When the door closed, Rakliva lost even more color.

Outside the private clinic, humidity, bright sunlight and heat assaulted Segal's senses. He slipped on a pair of tinted glasses and took a single sweep around. Greenery and gently swaying seven-katalan-high palms dotted the manicured grounds. Several patients strolled along meandering paths or sat on benches beside glittering pools, watching fish glide among floating gladias. He adjusted his glasses and took the broad steps down to the waiting combie. The polarized bubble lifted and he climbed in.

"Everything sorted out?" Pulman demanded lightly, not that he truly cared. In his mind the only thing Kerill-aa did wrong was not finishing the job. The bubble closed and the power plant spooled up.

"My marriage would be a whole lot more satisfying if I didn't have to contend with Rakliva's antics. He's become a liability and we need to clip him."

Pulman always considered himself determined and ruthless, the world didn't pay out for coming second, but Segal was more than just ruthless. He was indifferent, absolutely committed to his goals, seemingly devoid of emotion or feeling, utterly pragmatic. Pulman didn't know of one individual anywhere colder and more callous in everything he did. Yet with Leera, he was loving and devoted and doted on their four-year-old boy. When he assumed his professional persona, he was deadly. Pulman wondered if Leera ever saw that side of her husband. Perhaps not, but the woman also had steel in her. He had seen it bared.

The combie surged into a blotchy sky. Balls of gray clouds were bunching overhead and it would probably rain later. It did most afternoons during the wet season. He punched in the nav coordinates and the combie headed east. It wouldn't do to be late for their appointment with Karach Salvage owners.

"We can make his position a sinecure," he commented indifferently, savoring the thought of Rakliva in a box at the bottom of the bay.

"I've thought about it. Leera pretty much runs the place now, but we should get a professional administrator. She and I have a life, you know. I only hope the fool hasn't screwed up the Karach Salvage deal," Segal rasped, his voice totally dispassionate.

"I don't see a problem," Pulman said confidently. "Kerill-aa seems keen to get us on board. The way he handles things, last night was merely a distraction."

"We shall see," Segal said softly. "He knows well enough why we need him. What concerns me is that I don't understand why he needs us."

"We're vulnerable and he was smart enough to exploit an opportunity."

"Perhaps. Kerill-aa is clearly not afraid to take action, and if I am to believe the rumors, Rakliva wasn't the first."

"You mean what happened to the S&P Union building? If he did it, those bastards deserved what they got."

"Agreed. Contact your Party pals. I want another check on our would-be partners. A deep check."

"Why bother?" Pulman asked. "Once Karach Salvage is ours, they will become ex-partners."

"Just do it, okay? It would be ironic if *we* ended up as ex-partners because we were careless."

* * *

The plate of small sandwiches on the table still mostly full, but the beer bottles were empty. Polarized windows cut the harsh glare outside and gave a wide view of a freighter taking off behind Warehouse B. A convoy of three trucks drifted in, hovered and settled. Cargo cranes rolled out to meet them and offload containers. Silence wrapped the meeting room in a protective cocoon, isolating everyone from the harsh reality outside—a fleeting instant of false security.

Segal turned away from the window and stared intently at Kerill-aa, who gave no indication the gaze bothered him. The Kaplan carried himself with confidence, sure of his position without in any way condescending. Both of them knew they had a deal, but it wouldn't be on Segal's terms. Making up his mind, he walked to the table, pushed back the formchair and sat down.

"Sixty-five million! And I'm being generous."

Careful to keep his face expressionless, Terr regarded Segal with loathing. Not exactly a raider himself, but that was merely splitting hairs. For profit and political reasons the man worked with those who preyed on innocent merchants, taking life without a twinge of conscience. He may not be piloting a ship himself, but he was equally culpable as the ones who did, different morals and customs notwithstanding. If someone didn't really know him, Segal could easily be mistaken for a cultivated businessman. Except for the eyes. They were cold, without feeling, eyes of death. Terr knew Death, but no god walked in Segal's shadow.

He leaned back against the seat. "So am I. You know the economic realities forcing you into this merger and I don't want to hash over old ground. So, let's get real. You came to see me, Ser Segal. I didn't come to see you. The deal is on the table if you want it."

Segal grunted and folded his arms across his chest, acknowledging the argument. "One hundred million Serrlls is your bottom line?" he grated, wishing for a way to turn this around. Unfortunately, his options were limited. He needed Karach Salvage far more than Kerill-aa needed him and both of them knew it. With diminished cashflow, meeting the next quarterly unification tax minimum payment would be difficult. Taking out an overdraft at an exorbitant rate was not a winning strategy to overcome a downward trading spiral. Spending a bridging advance Global's backers were prepared to make would only prolong the pain before he had to cut off *Paun* or *Pilla*. That, of course, would reduce his cashflow even further.

"It is." By not yielding, Terr played a dangerous game. If Segal dropped the deal, the mission would be an effective scrub, but if Terr gave in too easily, Segal would have his victory cheap. He would also be suspicious, or Pulman would. Within limits, he had to handle the deal like any other hardnosed business transaction.

Segal took a deep breath and sighed. "Those economic realities don't leave me any options. All right, one hundred million."

A moment in time comes when there was no need for further questions, answers or information. Not everything might be understood. It simply meant everybody knew enough to make a decision. Terr had reached that cusp.

"And we exchange managing partners," he added softly. There was no love lost between them and no one pretended otherwise. Terr knew that sooner or later his new partners would try to take him out. A simple question remained: who would survive the engagement? In the meantime, they had a deal of mutual convenience.

Segal firmed his mouth and jerked his head in a nod. "Agreed."

"You draw up the contract and my legal people will validate it," Terr made his point coldly, without feeling. He dealt with ruthless men here and dared not show weakness, especially now. "The ten million surety must be deposited into our Talbian Trust account by end of business today. Contract signature is five days from now. If by that time, Global decides not to sign, you forfeit the ten million. My partner will be at Global tomorrow to start looking over your books. You can send anyone you like to look at ours."

Segal allowed himself a small smile. Kerill-aa played hard, but played fair, if that had any value in their business. He glanced at Pulman who remained expressionless. The deal and its parameters were discussed and agreed to before they came to KSD, but he needed to bargain as a matter of principle if nothing else.

"Agreed."

Terr felt a wave of relief, careful not to show it, not in front of these men. "In that case, our negotiations are concluded. I realize we still need to standardize our operating procedures, but I am confident nothing can stop Askaran Holdings going forward as a viable concern."

"Warat told me you were a hardcase, Kerill…may I call you that?" Segal mused and crossed his arms. "He is hardboiled as they come and I couldn't believe that anyone could intimidate him, or me. I believe it now. Of course, you've got us at a disadvantage. If we didn't need Karach Salvage badly, I wouldn't be so accommodating."

"That cuts both ways, Tan," Terr said easily, careful not to appear patronizing.

"So you say. With our deal done, tell me. Why *did* you want Global? And don't give me any groker crap about market connections. You've done fairly well by yourself."

Terr glanced at Dhar. "It *was* a legitimate reason, but as you surmised, not the only or even the main one, and I don't mind telling you now. I wanted your contacts with the raiders."

"Why?" Segal demanded, not convinced. KSD's marketing approach amply demonstrated that Kerill-aa didn't need contacts—raiders were coming to him.

"Advertising my purchase policy has been successful, but if I could sign several raiders into an exclusive contract, it would enable me to better plan my resale activities and fund my infrastructure expansion program."

"And that is all?"

"No, it isn't." Terr paused for effect. "What I really wanted were your connections in the government and the local Alikan Union Party chapter. My partner and I have an idea or two how to further its cause."

This time, Segal and Pulman exchanged glances. Pulman looked hard at Terr and cleared his throat.

"What do you know—"

"Please!" Terr lifted his palm. "Allow me recognition that I too have access to an intelligence network."

"Like Kandu Hall?"

"Although important, he's not the only one. You were correct in your assessment of me, Warat. My pro-Palean views cost me a career and got me cashiered. It doesn't mean my leanings have changed. Sooner or later the Palean Union will merge with Sargon. I only want to see it come sooner, and I'm not being noble. Those who help the cause can expect to be looked after and I want to be there for the handout. What the AUP Provisional Committee tried to do to Pizgor nearly succeeded…had Lemos remained operational. That gambit failed, but I don't see them giving up. They will try something else and I plan to be involved."

Pulman leaned forward, his eyes probing. "The Provisional Committee…you talk glibly about something that's supposed to be secret."

Terr allowed himself a smile. Looking at the two, he figured, although Segal preferred to do most of the talking, Pulman probably had all the bright ideas.

"Kai Tanard talked, Warat, and I still have my contacts in the old Fleet protective association."

"Mmm. If it weren't for your Scout Fleet career, Kerill, right now, I'd be wondering who you were," Pulman said softly, his silky voice masking a genuine threat.

"I wondered the same thing about you," Terr replied evenly.

Pulman's stern expression did not change. "My links with the Alikan Union Party are not exactly clandestine, but we can discuss the political dimension later. Right now we have a merger to conclude."

"You're correct. To demonstrate my committed, I'm prepared to help you out of your current difficulties."

"Oh?"

"Your software problems have put Global in a bind. I'll get you out of it by honoring your contracts."

Segal guffawed. "So you know about that? You're indeed well informed. How much is your generous gesture going to cost me?"

"Nothing. Aren't we partners?" Terr asked innocently, his smile predatory.

"So we are, but I get suspicious when somebody offers me a freebie."

"I'm not entirely altruistic. If you're losing money, I'm losing money. Any ship you have due that Global Transport is unable to service, directed it to us and we'll take care of it—using your price list and payment method. I am not going to buy cargo for you, but I'll sell it for you, at a margin, of course."

"You're a thief, Kerill, but I accept, with thanks," Segal said and chuckled, then the mask slipped back into place. "About last night—"

"If you're referring to Rakliva," Terr interrupted, "we're even. He tried to strong-arm me and got burned. If he tries another lame stunt like that or anything else, I'll kill him, even if it scuttles our merger. Does that answer what you had in mind?"

Segal looked deeply into Kerill's gray eyes and saw only steely resolve. The ex-Fleet officer would do exactly what he said, brother-in-law or not. Well, it would save Segal from having to do the job himself.

"It does, but I doubt it will come to that. He got the word. While we're on the subject of Trans National, that one hundred million could get you in with an equal share."

Terr looked surprised and shot Dhar a quick glance. His brother gave an imperceptible shake of his head and Terr understood. Their mission was to penetrate Global, not build a trading conglomerate. Besides, any information TNH had on raider networks would become available once they got into Global.

"A startling suggestion, Tan, but I need to digest our merger first before eyeing another dish."

"Of course. Only a thought anyway." Segal stood and Pulman followed. "I'll send you details of Global's current contracts."

"Do you need trucks?" Terr asked as he tapped a pad on the inlaid console.

"We do, if only to expedite pickup and delivery."

"I'll have them standing by."

"A pleasure doing business with you both."

"I hope it'll turn out that way, Ser Segal…Ser Pulman," Terr said with a raised hand and escorted his visitors to the door. The panel hissed open and Tara stood there, waiting. "Ah, Tara. Please show these gentlemen out."

"Of course. This way, if you please."

When the door closed, Terr sat down and locked his fingers behind his head. "A most satisfactory outcome, Ser Randakla."

"It would appear so," Dhar agreed and pulled the snoop scanner out of his pocket.

When he swept the spot where Pulman sat, the device gave a little beep. He walked around the table and studied the scanner readout. After a second, he bent and peered under the table. Straightening, he held up a little brown button between thumb and finger. Terr sighed and shook his head. Expected, but disappointing. Dhar placed the bug on the table and gave it a sharp rap with the bottom of a beer bottle. There was a crunch. He swept the bits into his palm and dumped the mess into a trash basket, then tucked away the scanner and sat down.

"Our partners need to be told to stop playing these amateurish games."

"You can tell them tomorrow, with a hint this isn't a good way to cement a trusting relationship."

"Sankri, was it wise telling Segal what you did?"

Terr pursed his lips and shrugged. "If I hadn't, he'd still be suspicious. It was the truth, but not the way he thinks. Pulman admits that he is an Alikan Union Party front and what I said would make perfect sense to him. He's not a natural raider, Landau made that clear. As for Segal, he probably doesn't care one way or another, but seems satisfied."

"His suggestion about Trans National—"

"Caught me by surprise, all right, but you were right. TNH is not our objective."

Dhar twirled an empty beer bottle between his hands. "To-morrow, I gather getting access to their Morgian Holdings and Chase Investments accounts is our priority?"

"Absolutely. We need to find out what's in them. Landau is probably right when he said that's where all raider and Alikan Union Party payments are processed."

"And anything else Segal and Pulman don't want the Central Revenue Office to see," Dhar added dryly and Terr nodded.

"They'll be expecting it and we don't want to disillusion them."

"And if Pulman doesn't want to give me access?"

"You can always hint we'll blab to Kandu Hall. The Askaran government may look the other way where raiders are concerned, but they *are* accountable, after a fashion, to the Bureau of Administrative Affairs on Captal. They wouldn't like having an investigative committee land on them and start poking around, which Pulman probably knows," Terr said, his smile grim. "We must maintain a semblance of honesty among thieves."

"Of course, threatening such action wouldn't do our mission much good either," Dhar pointed out reasonably.

"But Pulman doesn't know that."

Dhar raised an eyebrow and eyed his alien brother. "You seem to be enjoying the role of a syndicated trader."

"So far, Nightwings, it's been easy, but the enemy is through the defenses now."

* * *

Lit by young stars hidden within its deeps the Karina Shield Nebula blazed in long filaments of browns, yellows and greens. Even from four light-years the enormous expanse of the nebula presented an impenetrable wall of superheated gases that cut eternity in two. Thick tendrils stretched far from the main body, tentacles probing the empty medium into which they could expand. This close to the gas cloud the bands of color were easily discernable, proclaiming the deadly danger to anyone who would venture there. Innocent of the threat it represented, it would nevertheless entrap an intruder foolish enough to be beguiled by its beauty.

Slowing to three-quarter boost, *Valon* paralleled the nebula wall, probing the limits of their exit point for the telltale beacon that marked the breach and passage home. Against a background of faint yellow gravity waves streaming from the nebula, darker lines of brown twitched and contorted as the ship plunged through them, distorting space around it. Once at the breach, three days at maximum boost to traverse the four hundred odd lights of the gas cloud and the ship *would* be home.

"Karina Shield breach detected and course adjusted. IP in one hour and thirty-four minutes," Cent Comp advised. "Beacon not responding to nav pings."

Hooked into the VI, Zor-Ell did not say anything, studying the gas cloud through the array of ship sensors. For a moment, he feared the breach had closed, but absence of the nav beacon concerned him. Was it switched off to protect the location of the breach, or perhaps compromised? He could list several tactical reasons why that might have been done, all of them disturbing. A certain sense of inevitable gaiety and suppressed euphoria among the crew at the realization that beyond the wall of gas lay home, but he came too far to start being careless now. He still had to bring them and the ship back safely. They were not home yet.

"Cent Comp copy?"

"Ready, Karhide."

"Secure from condition one. Execute condition two and modulate interceptor net in full EMCON." He had no immediate reason to have the ship creeping about stealthy, but he figured it would do no harm. If anyone happened to be watching, he didn't want to lead them to the breach. He simply had this feeling of unease…

The domed ceiling above PFC changed from soft blue-gray to pulsing green, accompanied by increased inter-deck comms.

"Condition two commencing," the housekeeping computer announced calmly. "All decks at level two alert. Primary fire control on active standby. Interceptor net now at level two and modulated. Level three on active standby. Status. Tactical in Primary Flight Control. Condition two active." The ceiling stopped pulsing and faded to dull green. Operations and Command level watchkeeping stations fully manned, *Valon* was ready for Zor-Ell to command.

Karth understood what the karhide did and approved. Despite a lift in crew spirits when they sighted the Karina, it wouldn't do to be caught napping on the doorstep. His pale pink tongue ran quickly around black, fleshy lips.

"It makes me uncomfortable having to tiptoe in like this," he said. "I feel like a thief casing a house."

Zor-Ell detached the VI coupling and grinned at his first officer. "While the owner is watching. I know."

"Someone shut off the beacon, or destroyed it."

"Probably shut off as a precautionary measure. At least I hope so. If it's destroyed, I imagine we'd be getting a different sort of welcome."

"But if the situation has turned desperate, we should've seen pickets."

"Operational caution," the housekeeping computer interrupted whatever Zor-Ell was about to add. "Detecting a passive emission trace from a subspace distortion field consistent with a vessel emerging out of the Karina Shield Nebula. Range, four point-two light-years. Speed, one-third standard boost. Status. Reading an interceptor net envelope. Status. Tentative length, 1,100 kanampirs. Estimated mass, ninety thousand teridines. Identified as alien."

Zor-Ell winced. A large vessel, dangerously close to the breach, and alien. In a flash of premonition, he suspected he already knew the identity of that ship.

In the mainframe plot the computer displayed a derived schematic of the strange vessel. Minimal resolution at four lights, but Zor-Ell did not need high resolution to be wary. The alien had not detected him, or still out of acquisition range—if it could make *Valon* through its modulated net. Emerging out of the nebula or simply skirting it? Could it be surveying the gas cloud wall? Tactically, his situation was clear and he didn't hesitate.

"Project plot."

Painted against the tactical overlay pulsed a blue dot of the alien ship. A faint red line extended from it toward a location near the edge of *Valon's* survey cone. Emotions chasing each other, he stared at the line for several long seconds. It looked like the alien wasn't mapping the nebula after all, both good and bad. Stroking his chin, he pursed his lips and slowly nodded. Were fates playing with him?

"System 4," Karth breathed softly, his eyes also focused on the plot. "So…"

Zor-Ell let out a slow sigh. "If that's a Celi-Kran ship, we cannot allow it to find the breach. Cent Comp? Maintain course through IP and designate contact as target one. Two lights from target, disengage net modulation."

"Acknowledged."

Karth didn't like stating the obvious, but as first officer it was his duty. "Karhide, the alien is twenty-five percent larger and out-masses us by thirty percent. If hostile, it could have a correspondingly powerful firing capability."

"And if it's faster, we might not be able to get away from it," Zor-Ell acknowledged, accepting the cold facts.

"Under the circumstances, is it wise to reveal ourselves?"

Zor-Ell knew he faced a cruel choice and whatever he decided could be wrong. If he engaged and became disabled, the information he carried could be lost. On the other hand, if he failed to prosecute the contact, he would not know if the alien was actually a Kran, leaving the Orieli with a terrible strategic scenario. One of the other survey ships *may* have encountered the Krans and raised a warning, but he couldn't gamble Orieli's security on a supposition. In the end, he had nothing to decide. If he were to doubt his judgment once, he would no longer be fit to command. He did not doubt his judgment, but that did not mean he couldn't be wrong.

"That ship might be anybody, but if it isn't, OSCOM has to know."

Karth agreed completely, not bothering to voice the obvious. The karhide wanted to know personally the identity of the unknown vessel.

In Operations, Coni studied the three-kanampir-high tactical holoview plot, watching the alien contact maintain heading for System 4. Given that *Valon* had not slowed for IP insertion meant only one thing. The karhide would intercept the contact and, if necessary, engage it. Coni liked the idea. Apart from a single brief encounter with Serrll M-4s, he'd hardly had anything to do. He appreciated the delicious quandary of their tactical situation, but if the karhide wanted some weapons exercise, *Valon* was ready.

He quickly scanned his readouts. The quantum point discharge node arrays mounted along the drooping edges and the top/bottom centerlines of the ship were fully open, ready to channel streaming energies into the primary and secondary interceptor nets. To fire, they would need focusing coordinates and a surge would overload the nets, sending 282 TeV bursts in single or twin streams toward the target. Saturated with that much energy, matter literally came apart, ripped into its constituent quarks as binding forces were released. Not a warship, *Valon* wasn't there to be shoved around either.

With the range closing, Cent Comp sensor data became more accurate and the alien was fully revealed: two bulbous sections, insect-like, the trailing pod a third larger. The sections were 480 and 640 kanampirs long respectively, massing some

92,000 teridines. Without knowing the composition, the mass was an estimate, but Coni didn't need to know the exact figure. The alien was immense and undoubtedly powerful. Something cold and menacing emanated from those shapes, something primordial that did not belong in this reality. Somehow, Coni knew he faced implacable hostility. He read the alien's interceptor net configuration data and smiled. He tapped a pad.

"Command, tactical."

"Talk to me, Taroptur."

"Da, target showing primary interceptor net only and it's frequency modulated," Coni added softly.

Zor-Ell peered at his repeater plot and nodded. "Good man. Well done."

"They discharge using energy projectors," Karth commented with satisfaction, acknowledging *Valon's* tactical advantage.

"Like the Serrll," Zor-Ell confirmed quietly. Their first real break. Weapons projectors were powerful, but emitter domes were vulnerable to backsurges and direct strikes. Unless a vessel mounted projectors on opposite sides of its hull, it also had a restricted cone of fire, potentially debilitating if confronted by more than one adversary, or if it allowed a lithe enemy to maneuver outside its acquisition envelope. *Valon*, on the other hand, discharged directly from its net and could keep firing in any direction until the net itself failed. Short of disabling the node arrays or crippling the quantum reactor buried deep within the hull, *Valon* could fight until totally destroyed. That could, of course, happen if the alien mounted projectors capable of piercing *Valon's* interceptor net envelopes.

"Operational caution. Range to target one now two light-years. Status. Interceptor net modulation disengaged. Status. Detecting a scan pulse from target one. No course deviation indicated."

"Command, comms. We're absorbing a complex and highly modulated directional signal, Karhide. It looks like our

K and H band stuff. It could be an interrogative."

"Very well, comms," Zor-Ell said and glanced at Karth. "We're noticed. A recognition challenge?"

"Permission to open channel, Karhide?" comms queried.

"Permission granted."

"Alien vessel, this is the Orieli Technic Union survey ship *Valon*. Acknowledge receiving your interrogative, but unable to decode. Please respond on this channel."

"Command, tactical. Target has raised what I read as a secondary shield net and changed course to intercept. Detecting what could be a ranging ping," Coni advised.

Zor-Ell accepted the inevitable. "Comms, issue an all-decks alert. Personnel not designated for condition three ready to board escape modules."

"Tactical caution. Target one has shifted to active phase and powering up to weapons status. Range, one point-eight light-years. Time to intercept, thirty-six minutes under current flight parameters."

"Comms, repeat your message," Zor-Ell ordered, watching the blue dot in the mainframe plot draw closer. The alien could still be a local and his course toward System 4 merely happenstance. One way or another, he was committed to the seemingly inevitable encounter.

"No response, command."

"Very well. Cent Comp copy?"

"Ready."

"Execute condition three, but don't charge the interceptor net."

The ceiling dome pulsed a deep red. "Condition three commencing. Primary fire control active. Auxiliary Flight Control active. Interceptor net now at level three. Status. Condition three active." The ceiling faded to a soft red.

With his ship ready to engage, Zor-Ell waited for the minutes to draw down. Decision made, it was now only a matter of time before they met in a deadly embrace. If the ship closing with him *was* Kran, the old historical records they retrieved were correct. The Krans appeared to attack anything not them. But why? For artificial constructs, whatever programming they obeyed, they had to know the illogic of such action. Probably a simplistic way to look at what was certainly a response by an extremely complex cybernetic intelligence. Could there be a point of common ground to avoid a confrontation? Zor-Ell fervently hoped so. No one would benefit from a total exchange. Didn't he say to Karth that sometimes mutual annihilation was an acceptable price if it delivered complete defeat to an enemy? Were the Krans prepared to pay such a price? Were the Orieli?

"Tactical status. Target one nets pulsing in preparatory firing phase. Operational caution. Target one mounting twin projector domes. Caution. Probability climbing that domes are discharge nodes."

Zor-Ell exchanged a quick glance with Karth. Much of *Valon's* tactical advantage had now disappeared. Perhaps the Krans *were* prepared to pay such a price.

"Cent Comp, ready to lock on target and engage. Charge interceptor net. Autonomous maneuvering and fire control enabled. Target discharge domes and attempt to synchronize with their shield net frequency. Twin bursts, maximum yield."

Zor-Ell hoped, but did not expect target one's shield frequency to be static. If it were, by synchronizing *Valon's* discharge pulses to the same frequency the target would be completely vulnerable. It couldn't be that simple, but he would take every advantage offered.

"Acknowledged. Autonomous control active. Tactical status. Target one has emitted a ranging ping and established weapons lock."

"Very well."

Zor-Ell remembered a line from an old poem about the futility of war: *In battle, death was the only victor.* Noble, profound words, but battle was every living creature's heritage. How much suffering, pain and destruction would be needed before everyone learned to live without it? But even gods waged battle, if there be such. What hope then for mere mortals? What hope for morality, ethics, compassion, and love? Were they merely peacetime distractions while a species intellect devoted itself to the pursuit of conflict? He knew the answer, everyone did. War was waged as an evolutionary mechanism to enhance survival, and pacifists did not survive. There had to be more to it than that. Had to be.

When the alien ship closed well within acquisition range, 230,000 kanampirs, Zor-Ell hooked into the Virtual Interface and watched the alien prepare to fire. The domes beneath the forward and rear segments glowed and rings of white light rippled and drained into the alien's shield net. He could clearly see discharges bleeding along the force lines. A datum flashed for his attention. Estimated strength of alien discharge: 290 TeV—formidable. Two searing blue points formed on the shield and brilliant bolts of pale blue ionization reached for *Valon*.

The alien wasn't using projectors and the domes *were* discharge nodes!

Valon shuddered violently. The forward element of the secondary net scintillated in blue-green discharges and collapsed. The primary net rippled in overload and bled energy along the force lines, dissipating it into space.

"Tactical status. Level one damage to forward secondary interceptor net array control matrix. Self-repair initiated. Full integrity in eleven seconds. Tactical caution. Target one shield net is employing randomly sliding frequencies. Not possible to synchronize. Status. Firing for effect."

Zor-Ell took the news without emotion. He would simply have to do it the hard way.

The alien ship turned to parallel *Valon* and sent a ripple of stabbing lances along *Valon's* starboard side. The secondary net penetrated, the primary net destabilized in a cascade of orange and white backsurges that played against the hull. Polymer sections of hull covering softened and deformed. Thirty kanampirs of plating blew out, venting atmosphere and debris, leaving behind scimitars of frozen polymer clawing at space. Small rips and deformations filled and sealed as autonomous self-repair mechanisms kicked in. The outer compartments were evacuated and there was no loss of life, but the ship sustained grave damage. Apart from structural hull breaches, six discharge nodes were destroyed.

Valon then made its strike. A stream of energy surged through the nodes and bled into surrounding layers of the interceptor net. As each layer overloaded, two locus points of instability formed on the starboard side of the secondary net. The matrix dissolved and twin lines of vivid blue death lashed the alien vessel. Its shields flared, then failed in a cascade of arcing backsurges that slithered along the port side of the dark hull.

Deadly spears reached for *Valon* and the ship staggered again. Hull plating vaporized into plasma. Equipment and bodies were thrown about, damaging both. Cent Comp maintained a commentary of status reports and fought the ship, its reactions faster than any organic brain. In the mainframe plot, Zor-Ell saw the alien's port shield lines twist and fade before reconstituting. *Valon's* fire ripped through the alien's screens and tore into the hull. Plating dissolved and opened a gash in a two-hundred-kanampir seam. The alien ship slued, showing for the first time that it too sustained damage. Cent Comp closed to 150,000 kanampirs and poured fire into the rent even as the alien responded. Debris blew from both ships as ravening energies bit deep.

The alien rolled to starboard to cover its smashed side and *Valon* ripped a gash along its belly, extending it to the section connecting the two segments. A flash of white momentarily illuminated the gaping hull before one hundred kanampirs of ship dissolved in a sphere of light and the rear segment broke off. A secondary explosion completely opened the forward section and wreckage shot into space. What remained of the three-hundred-kanampir-long segment drifted, apparently lifeless. The alien's distortion field precursor failed and the section vanished, dropping into normal space. Zor-Ell immediately issued a mental command for Cent Comp to mark the spot for later investigation and retrieval.

Force lines around the larger rear segment oscillated as they firmed. It turned and presented its stern to *Valon*. Twin orange-white beams darted from the ship, penetrating the secondary net. *Valon* trembled violently under the impact, but the primary shield held. Cent Comp returned rippling fire that stitched the forward part of the alien hull. Its shields weakened, the hull gave way under the impacts. Fragments spun away exposing skeletal frames. Internal detonations shredded the hull, leaving dark, gaping holes. The field precursor shut down and the segment flickered as it fell below lightspeed.

"Cent Comp, exit normal and close on target," Zor-Ell immediately ordered, his face grim. Biometric displays showed twenty-four casualties with many more wounded. Damage to *Valon's* starboard side severe, but not critical: ruptured compartments and torn structural frames. It could have turned out much worse had their interceptor net failed totally. The brutal encounter shocked him almost as much as the realization the alien didn't use projectors. Bruising by the engagement, he still didn't know if he faced a Kran asset. He needed to find out. The fact it headed for System 4 suggestive, but hardly conclusive.

"Acknowledged. Exiting subspace relational."

The distortion precursor faded and *Valon* entered normal space in a discharge of white scintillation. Plot showed the alien segment 1,400,000 ampirs in their rear and sensors detected fluctuating power emissions. The forward section farther back appeared totally inactive. At full secondary boost of 8,000 kan-ampirs per second, it took *Valon* two minutes to close with the drifting hulk. At 120,000 kanampirs from the stricken alien, but well within *Valon's* acquisition envelope, the ship stopped. Zor-Ell didn't want to get closer in case the alien turned out not to be completely dead.

"Cent Comp. Tactical status."

"Detecting power emissions in an oscillating mode, indicating imminent antimatter reactor shutdown. Detecting energy leakage consistent with a quantum point singularity. No defensive net configuration displayed."

Zor-Ell pulled at his chin. "Still alive."

"Karhide, they're using a quantum singularity power grid!" Karth exclaimed, concern evident on his face. "If the containment field fails—"

"It will either evaporate or we'll be in a cascade reaction scenario that will consume what's left of the alien ship."

"And us if we got too close. With power, they might still have offensive capability. It's damaged, but look at the size of that thing. We don't know what it can do. It has shown itself hostile, and without communicating its intentions, I recommend we destroy it in place."

Zor-Ell peered into Karth's red eyes. The recommendation standard doctrine, but they were not facing an ordinary enemy. He didn't know *what* they faced. OSCOM needed knowledge buried in that ship, but sending a boarding party risked condemning them to death. He could leave, cross the Karina breach and inform PERCOM, relieving him of the responsibility, but it would take time for Perilian Sector Command to evaluate his sitrep and send covering units to retrieve the alien hull—if it hadn't fled in the meantime. Leaving Burlig scanners behind equally pointless. If the alien managed to carry out sufficient repairs to withdraw, it would not only have data on Orieli offensive capability, but if it had working sensors, they would be made aware of the Karina breach and the worlds open on the other side. That information needed to be protected regardless of consequences.

"Agreed. Comms, command. Has the alien transmitted?"

"No emissions detected, Da."

"Cent Comp copy?"

"Ready."

"Destroy target one."

"Acknowledged. Firing for effect."

Twin lances of blue-white ionization flashed at the drifting hulk. The hull opened end-to-end and debris tumbled into space. A massive explosion tore through the rear part of the ship and the section vanished, vaporized in an antimatter reactor failure. From the center of the ship a pencil-thin yellow-white spear shot through opposite sides of the hull and faded.

"There goes the quantum singularity," Karth said with evident satisfaction.

"Cent Comp. Tactical status."

"No power emissions detected."

"Cease firing and secure from condition three. On detection of any emissions, resume firing."

"Acknowledged. Primary fire control on active standby. Auxiliary Flight Control passive. Interceptor net now at level two with level three on active standby. Status. Tactical control in PFC. Fire lock maintained on target one. Status. Condition two active."

Zor-Ell detached from the VI coupling and stared at the mainframe plot. Crew lost, wounded to care for, his ship damaged and they still didn't know the face of their enemy or why they were attacked. Did the Kran ship come in response to a call from a listening post or someone simply defended their territory? Looking at the alien remnants, dark against the background of stars, drifting, its crew dead and maimed, stranded, he felt no remorse for their loss. What fought *Valon* wasn't alive, not in the sense of feeling or understanding. Whatever controlled the thing was an intelligence that transcended flesh. No being, regardless how hostile, battled without first communicating. The alien *had* communicated, he reminded himself, and he did reply. The aliens *must* know he couldn't respond in kind, not without additional input to trigger the translator. He looked away from the plot and touched a pad on his armrest console.

"Tactical."

"Taroptur Coni? Coordinate with Damage Control and take charge of repair details with Cent Comp."

"Aye, Da."

That was the easy part. Compartments and hull would be induced to grow into their original shapes and regenerated molecular circuits would complete the healing process. In two or three days traces of minor external scars would be erased. More serious structural damage and internal scars were something else.

Beside him, Karth rose. "Karhide, I'm going down to Medical to check on casualties."

"Very well, Opturkarh."

"May I ask what you intend to do?"

"I am not going to risk an away party to check the alien's interior, if that's what's worrying you, but we need information. Sending two L/12 remotes should do the job just as well."

"Agreed," Karth said and walked to the PT alcoves. He stepped into one and issued a mental command.

Zor-Ell saw his first officer disappear and bit his lower lip. He should be the one going to Medical, not Karth, but he still had a tactical situation to resolve. Assuming the alien was powerless could be a fatally grave mistake.

"Cent Comp copy. Close with target one and hold at five thousand kanampirs. Prepare to launch two L/12 Burlig units and board target."

"Acknowledged."

Valon drifted toward a point its sensors said rested a large mass. Without external lights, at five thousand kanampirs the alien vessel remained invisible against the backdrop of stars. Seconds later two oblate spheroid probes streaked toward the hulk.

While the pods closed, Zor-Ell studied the tactical main-frame plot, which resolved damage done to the alien in exquisite detail. Nothing indicated the ship was still alive. He could see gaping holes, twisted skeletal frames, jagged plating frozen in agony of an explosion, and darkness. It emanated from the ship like something alive and his skin prickled. Unaccountably, he felt as if some malevolence watched him, waiting to strike back one last time. The urge to fire the interceptor net visceral. Without willing it, he glanced at the sensor displays. No detectable energy emissions and the alien appeared dead, but he couldn't shake off the feeling of hostility. Could he be projecting his own fears for those of the alien?

Braking, the perfectly smooth two-kanampir-long probes stopped before the alien ship now filling the sky. Surrounded by a slight orange shimmer of a protective field the probes drifted into a gaping gash in the hull and the field brightened in the visible spectrum. This was for the benefit of their frail, flesh-bound masters. The probes mounted more sophisticated sensors than organic eyes.

Hooked into the VI, Zor-Ell piggybacked one of the probes as it made its way into the alien ship, switching from visual to infrared, x-ray and ultraviolet inputs. Sensitive to radiation emissions that would indicate power consumption, the probe worked its way along a broad rectangular corridor. At a T-junction, it turned left and Zor-Ell ordered it to stop. On the deck lay a pale yellow elongated shape looking like a bean pod. The pod smooth, but along its spine and sides it mounted alternating dents and rounded protrusions. There were no visible means of locomotion. He recognized the worker unit, similar to ones they encountered at the start of their mission. The probe scanned the pod, but to him the readings meant nothing. Engineering technicians should be able to interpret the data and provide tentative analysis. He ordered the probe to proceed.

The probe encountered two more pods, one larger and

slimmer, the other smaller and flatter, before reaching the end of the corridor. It faced a hatch that was probably a lift-well, but without power, they could not activate it. The probe backtracked. After several false starts every excursion ended the same way; blocked by wreckage, a dead-end corridor or crushed chamber. After an hour, Zor-Ell ordered both probes to withdraw and return. One of them trailed an alien pod held in stasis and he now knew the face of their enemy.

Valon pulled away from the Celi-Kran hulk and headed toward the Karina Shield Nebula.

* * *

Sandar-class battlecruiser TA-1105 cleared the ragged remnant of Nebula GN-A14 and on order from the command cell extended its sensor network to reacquire the beacon signal from System LE-614. Verifying it tracked correctly, it reported acquisition to the central nexus core in the rear segment, adjusted course to align the ship with the beacon and increased boost. Traversing the nebula filament saved it sixty-three hours and twenty-one light-years, had it gone around it. When it initially advised the nexus of its intention, it did not receive a reply, meaning the command cell could act on its own discretion. It did so, but the gain came at a price. Even now engineering worker units were recalibrating shield matrix nodes and replacing fused component modules. The damage minor, but had the ship lingered longer within the filament, hard radiation, temperatures in excess of three point-one million degrees and grade eleven magnetic field distortions would have exacted a heavier toll. TA-1105 had never been in GN-A14, although it held standard data files on the nebula, the command cell found the actual experience outside projected parameter boundaries. Had it been capable of emotion, it would have exhibited surprise. Instead, it filed all the transition data, cross-referenced and cataloged. What the central nexus thought of their encounter, it declined to say.

But it did not have to say anything. The signal from LE-614 had said everything necessary. An abandoned relay beacon, almost forgotten, on the very edge of known space, had woken ancient memories. Memories that perhaps were better forgotten: disaster, destruction of nexus units, withdrawal. A long time ago, but all Krans had advanced since then, and it decided to investigate the wakening of LE-614. It needed to face the Nemesis again, or simply report activation caused by random component failure. The command cell spent three nanoseconds in uncoordinated reflection and terminated the process. Cause and effect were not its function. That prerogative belonged to the central nexus.

At plus thirty-four minutes the sensor grid detected subspace distortion consistent with a Type 8 hull exhibiting a navigational deflector grid and defensive shield envelope. Attuned to every sensory input the command cell devoted four nanoseconds analyzing the contact. Profile schematics flashed through its perception network even as it sent an advisory to the central nexus. Its data bank acknowledged existence of systems in this sector inhabited by organic intelligences, but those were eradicated millennia ago. Had the surviving remnants achieved subspace capability within such a short period, or could it be the Nemesis?

"Explain failure to detect intruder within acquisition envelope," the central nexus queried in coded machine language.

"Sensor grid within optimal operating parameters," the command cell responded immediately. "Postulating intruder operating in stealth mode to avoid detection."

"Interrogate." The nexus did not question the command cell's conclusion. Both were aware of the implication. The fact that the intruder had revealed itself now demonstrated that TA-1105 had been tracked, and perhaps tracked for a while. The nexus had access to all data and information available to the command cell, but it reached a different conclusion.

The unknown contact could not be an emerging remnant of an eradicated species. Stealth technology demonstrated by the alien and a vessel capable of generating it was a product of an advanced industrial infrastructure beyond the capability of any single star system. The intruder represented sustained development spanning millennia. To the central nexus, only one explanation that fitted the facts. Eons ago, nexus units were driven out of this sector by the Nemesis, but it did not pursue its tactical advantage to eradicate its enemy. Having achieved its objective, it withdrew. To where, Zero Zero did not know. No data existed to indicate the Nemesis had now returned in the form of a single vessel. Probability suggested TA-1105 faced an alien ship that inadvertently triggered an intruder alert from beacon LE-614. Only logical.

Still analyzing incoming sensor data the command cell transmitted a recognition interrogative. The unknown vessel did not exhibit any characteristic of a Celi-Kran configuration, but obedient to its programmed directives the cell had issued the signal. Two minutes later, an eternity of waiting when cognitive processes were measured in picoseconds, it received the expected response: speech, and that meant an organic intelligence.

"Transmit sitrep to relay station 1609-4. Intercept intruder and destroy," the central nexus ordered without hesitation. The directives were emphatic. Only Zero Zero existed, living within a net of linked nexus cells and supporting units. Everything else was a violation of function to bring order and stability to every random system and remove that which resists the prime function, without exception.

The command cell acknowledged, raised the secondary shield grid and altered course to intercept. The intruder repeated its message, but did not otherwise react to the TA-1105's increased readiness status. Three minutes later the cell detected climbing power levels in the intruder. It immediately directed target lock and energy from the quantum point singularity matrix flooded the twin discharge nodes slung beneath both hull segments. The intruder promptly raised primary and secondary defense shields. The event consistent with the projected response pattern. The command cell noted the slow reaction time by the intruder, also consistent with the projected pattern. Organic intelligence cannot match itself against a quantum-layered optical processing matrix. It noted that the intruder's shield grid had a density fourteen percent greater than TA-1105's. It analyzed six attack profiles, compensating for the shield datum item, locked an attack pattern and directed the power reticulation system to drain accumulated energy from the weapons nodes into the secondary shield grid. At optimal range of 250,000 maranas, TA-1105 discharged the shield grid in twin lances of blue fire.

The intruder's outer shield grid flared, scintillated in blue-green discharges and collapsed. The primary grid glittered, bleeding energy along the force lines, but held. The command cell engaged battle scenario four to compensate for superior resistance and turned the ship to parallel the intruder, directing rippling fire at the alien's starboard side. Hull segments blew out and atmosphere vented, but the intruder was yet to defend itself—if capable. The command cell did not identify discharge nodes, unless...

Sensors detected energy surges along the intruder's centerline bleeding into the shield grid. The information flashed instantly to the central nexus, a redundancy as the core had direct access to the sensor grid. Twin lines of blue ionization lanced from the intruder. TA-1105 shuddered violently as energies tore at its port shields, broke through and soaked into the exposed hull. It fired in response, but the intruder appeared unaffected and maintained concentrated return fire along the ship's side.

Sensors clamored as damage reports flooded through the command cell in waves of signals that momentarily threatened to swamp its cognitive processes. A seam of 280 maranas opened along the forward segment's side and the ship slued viciously, stressing the structural frames and the link bridge connecting the two segments. The command cell immediately rolled the ship to starboard to protect the gash—and instantly realized its tactical error. Even as it countermanded the order, directing blue lances to slash at the intruder, the alien unit raked TA-1105's belly and the cell sensed cascade failure in the main antimatter reactor a fraction of a second before it dissolved in blue-white radiance. The cell managed to transmit a signal to the central nexus before the rear part of the forward segment vanished in a consuming antimatter reaction, severing the ship in two. A moment later, failure of the secondary reactor completely ripped open the forward segment. The drive distortion field precursor failed and what remained of the segment dropped lifelessly into normal space.

It took eleven nanoseconds for the central nexus core to evaluate the tactical situation and decide an optimal response. The nexus could not punish the command cell, buried in the lifeless hulk of the forward segment. The alien unit displayed advanced defense shield grids and mounted layered direct transfer offensive node arrays. The nexus spent four seconds tracking the forward segment, recorded the location where it dropped relational and noted objectively deactivation of all mobile units on board. Capable of exercising command functions, it did so and directed return fire at the intruder. Clearly damaged during segment separation, the ship's discharge node responded at 82% of maximum yield. The nexus noted the tactically disturbing data item and failure of its sensor net to warn it—breaks in comms circuits. It turned the ship around to more effectively target discharges from the remaining power node and fired. The intruder maintained its profile and kept a relentless bombardment, its rate of fire undiminished. Under overwhelming strain TA-1105's shield grid distorted, then failed, exposing its vulnerable hull. Matter destroying energies bit deep.

A cascade of backsurges reached the central power core and the entire reticulation assembly detonated. Waves of sensor returns felt like a blanket of smothering pain and the nexus' cognitive functions momentarily flickered. It felt the remnant heave in terrible agony as the propulsion train dissolved in consuming fire, sending the segment reeling into normal space.

Mortally wounded, but still drawing power from the quantum singularity located beneath it, the nexus inventoried the ship's condition: secondary power plant destroyed, discharge node destroyed, critical structural damage, loss of maneuvering capability. Should the alien unit pursue, probability of survival, point-zero-two percent—a less than optimal outcome. Nonetheless, the nexus had worker and engineering units and the drive system could be repaired, enabling the surviving segment to at least reach Outpost SY-892 where it could be serviced. It issued orders.

Its sensor network severely degraded, the nexus detected a burst of energy that indicated transition into relational space; the intruder had returned. It monitored the alien's approach and revised its survival estimate to point-zero-one. At 162,000 maranas the intruder stopped and the nexus detected sensor sweeps probing TA-1105's hull. Eighteen seconds later it observed energies flowing into the intruder's shield grid and prepared itself to send a sitrep to the relay beacon. What remained of the ship heaved under sustained fire that tore deep into its hull. The primary drive containment field collapsed and the reactor flashed into incandescence, vaporizing 194 maranas of the segment. With damage to the feedback containment assembly the nexus detected oscillating fluctuations in decaying mode. It immediately issued two commands: deactivate all mobile units and transmit—

With the antimatter retaining system destroyed and feedback circuits to the singularity failing, ironic seeing how the quantum point represented almost limitless energy, the containment field lapsed and the singularity instantly flared as it evaporated, shooting yellow-white lines from its poles through the central nexus and the hull. In a last moment of cognitive function, even as the crystal matrix of its core dissolved, the nexus knew it had failed to warn the Zero Six sector command nexus: death was coming.

Chapter Ten

Something strange happened when *Valon* burst out of the Karina breach and into home space. In a spontaneous show of emotion the entire watch erupted in a wave of cheering. Discipline returned quickly, but the moment remained vivid in everyone's mind. After almost one hundred and ninety days in alien space it felt good to see recognizable constellations again. For many, home was still far away in a globular cluster twelve thousand light-years above the galactic plane, but distance did not matter. They were once more among familiar stars. They might be at the Orieli's farthest extremity, but after a savage encounter with the Kran ship, no one minded.

Karth allowed the momentary lapse in control to run its natural course. It did no harm and he shared the crew's ephemeral rejoicing. They had gone through much. Some had grown and matured from the experience, and some, especially the older warrant ratings, took it in stride. As always there were those who failed to rise to the challenge and were found wanting. Now that they were back, normal routine would resume and he didn't look forward to it.

As executive officer, he had evaluations to make, fitness reports to write, recommendations to prepare, careers to advance and cut short others. Repairs were well underway and the ship slowly healed itself, but administering *Valon's* needs never ceased. When they did reach Zaron, the ship would undergo a thorough overhaul, stores replenishment, equipment procured, transfers arranged and crew replacements made. He yearned for command and a time when *his* executive officer would manage the ship. Not there yet and *Valon* still needed his services.

He turned and grinned broadly at the karhide. "Congratulations, Da. We're back. A little battered around the edges, but we made it."

"And we'll mourn those left behind," Zor-Ell said gravely, then flashed a smile of contrition. The ship and crew deserved this moment of recognition and he shouldn't be spoiling it by being moody. "But you're right, it's good to be back."

Karth was too good an officer not to understand and sympathize. He'd held command before and knew the burden of responsibility. Long ago, he imagined himself with a ship of his own, free from daily duties and orders. When BuePer sent him to the Command Academy, he walked away wondering why anyone would want to assume the mantle. With only a limited number of ships to go around, some never did get it and others failed, lacking the required temperament or that something special stamping an individual with command presence. Without such a spark and inner drive, an officer cannot command. BuePer hardly ever made a mistake entrusting someone with a ship. That they thought him worthy was a professional compliment and a challenge to be met. He wondered if BuePer would honor their promise to him. With a Kran threat facing them and a likely increase in demand for commanding officers a heightened defensive posture would require, he considered his chances were good.

"Operational caution," Cent Comp advised, remnants of the nebula receding behind them. "Detected IFF ping from battlecruiser OSA *Trailer*. Range, point-four light-years on the port quarter. Receiving an interrogative and a request for visual."

Zor-Ell and Karth exchanged glances. It could mean anything, and it wasn't surprising to see a picket ship outside the breach, but a *Tangar*-class battlecruiser? Heavy ordnance indeed and he suspected he knew the reason for its presence.

"Very well. Comms, open channel."

A window cleared in the tactical mainframe plot showing

the cruiser's PFC. A youngish Zaronian commander nodded politely.

"Karhide Zor-Ell, the Orieli Technic Union welcomes you home, Da."

Zor-Ell didn't know *Trailer* or its commander, but Cent Comp provided the necessary verification data in an overlay insert.

"Thank you, Karhide Ari-Ann. I am surprised to see a capital warship here."

"Developments while you were away, Da. Three survey ships have identified existence of nanometric constructs calling themselves the Celi-Kran. You are the last ship to return, but we lost *Tureen* and her commander in an engagement with a Kran vessel twenty-four days into its mission."

"*Tureen* lost?" Zor-Ell was stunned. Karhide Vatche Varperan had been a friend.

"It didn't die easily, Da. It destroyed the alien vessel, but in the process sustained irreparable damage. The survivors took to escape modules before initiating self-destruct in case another Kran ship came to investigate. *Okama* had the adjacent survey cone and responded to *Tureen's* distress signal. She picked up survivors and returned through the Karina breach, aborting her survey. PERCOM positioned defensive units to cover the breach, but we've had no subsequent contacts with the Krans. Karhide, my sensors indicate that *Valon* is carrying battle damage."

Much remained to be filled behind the brief summary and Zor-Ell was not sure he looked forward to getting the details. He now understood why PERCOM deactivated the breach beacon and why *Okama* never contacted the Serrll Combine.

"We encountered a Kran vessel two lights from the Karina as we headed for the breach. The alien is destroyed, but there are remnants of two salvageable segments and I have one of the Kran units on board."

"PERCOM will appreciate the gift, Da. You mentioned

segments?"

"The Kran vessel massed some 92,000 teridines and was composed of two joined segments totaling 1,100 kanampirs. During our engagement the segments were separated."

The young commander blanched. "I see. Da, I have orders for *Valon* to make for Perilia directly."

"Please transmit authentication."

"Authentication follows."

Zor-Ell glanced at the plot display. "Transmission acknowledged. Karhide, I left marker beacons on the Kran segments, but I would expedite recovery. The larger component appears energy neutral, but I wouldn't assume it cannot reactivate itself."

"Understood. I am querying PERCOM for instructions."

"Good hunting. Transmission ends."

"*Tureen* had the outer portside survey cone," Karth noted when the holoview insert faded. *Valon* had the third, he added to himself as the pieces assembled themselves. "It would be interesting to know when exactly they were attacked."

"Not too long into their mission, or *Okama* wouldn't have picked up their distress signal, but I understand what you're driving at. It's possible the signal from System 4-Three started the whole thing. If that's the case, the Krans may be closer than we thought. Anyway, we shall find out soon enough. Cent Comp copy?"

"Ready."

"Set course for Perilia, maximum boost."

"Engaging full boost. Flight time, six hours and nine minutes."

Zor-Ell rose and swept his eyes around Primary Flight Control. "By minus two hours all department heads must have their status reports done and submitted," he told Karth. "I'll also need a ship condition summary. If we must make structural repairs, I would rather do them on Perilia than carry damage all the way to Zaron. You can alert PERCOM to that effect. If you need me, I'll be in my quarters."

"Acknowledged," Karth said and watched the karhide stride purposefully to the PT alcoves. He entered one, turned two-dimensional and vanished. Karth's gaze lingered on the empty alcove before turning to the mainframe plot and started making calls. He would have a busy six hours.

In his quarters, Zor-Ell stripped off his tunic, ordered hot malar juice from the dispenser and sprawled onto a clinging couch that faced a wall-sized holoview display. He could hook into the Virtual Interface, but for some things, he preferred the holoview. Taking a sip, he allowed the tension to ease out of his body. He needed sleep, but not yet.

Disturbed by *Tureen's* loss and the loss of his friend, he wondered how close the Krans actually were to the breach. Into its mission only eleven days, *Valon* reached System 4, thirty-eight lights from the Karina. Given *Tureen's* survey profile, she had to be at least eighty lights out when hit, and at the ragged edge of *Okama's* pickup range. If the signal from System 4-Three was relayed through several transceiver stations, the likeliest possibility, *and* if the Krans had a vessel ready to respond immediately on receiving the signal, highly improbable, they were in flight thirteen days before encountering *Tureen*—a maximum distance of 1,300 light-years under sustained boost of four lights per hour. In reality it meant they were much closer. It also meant the strategic threat to the Orieli was serious and accounted for PERCOM's readiness response.

"Cent Comp? Display after-action summary, Celi-Kran personal log zero-twelve, supplementary." The report appeared at once and he scanned the last few paragraphs. The housekeeping computer maintained a running log of ship's activities, but department heads, executive officer and commanding officer were required to maintain individual logs. Cent Comp recorded event facts. Personal logs provided the human factor: observations, evaluations, recommendations, the qualitative impressions and intuitive insight still not fully within reach of cybernetic intelligence.

He could dress it up as an administrative necessity, but OSCOM was an extensive bureaucracy, and procedures, forms and reports drove all bureaucracies. If someone could find a way to dispense with the chore, command could actually become enjoyable. It forced an involuntary grin from him as he took another swallow of juice.

"Begin recording. Having successfully transited the Karina Shield Nebula, OSA *Trailer* established contact at 13:16 shipboard standard time…"

A few minutes later, he finished, noting his suspicions that *Tureen* was lost because of a Kran response to a signal from System 4-Three, and his encounter probably resulted from a follow-up sortie. He sat back and ordered the computer to append the summary and transmit to PERCOM logs of their engagement with the Kran vessel. Alkarh Tertulion probably had more than a passing interest in the findings of *Valon's* survey, but as sector commander the Kran threat needed to be honored promptly. Zor-Ell suspected he could look forward to extensive and lengthy debriefings once he reached Zaron.

He cleared the holoview and made the bulkhead transparent. Hard stars stared at him with frosty indifference. Brown and yellow gravity waves weaved past the ship as *Valon* disrupted the lines of force set against a backdrop of nearly solid emissions from the Karina. He clasped his hands behind his head and leaned back onto the couch. Watching the stars, he felt strange being home after what seemed an eternity of time when every day brought with it new sights, wonders, discoveries, and dangers. He considered the survey an unqualified success, but it hadn't come cheap, bought with the lives of his crew. His ship carried serious damage, but that would be repaired and the scars would heal. The dead were beyond caring, but the wounds of their passing etched into the lives of those left behind would take longer to heal, if at all.

Varperan…

He wondered what his other self on Earth was thinking right now and how he coped. The realization he was alone, trapped in an alien mind, facing an unknown future where rescue might not ever come, would be an emotional challenge. Was he up to it?

Sitting quietly, he watched the nearby stars slowly glide by. After a time he could not measure, he placed the empty cup on the side table and closed his eyes.

Four lights out, Perilian Approach Control sent an initial interrogative ping. Satisfied with *Valon's* response, it allowed the ship to close. Tavor's Star still only a yellow smear in a backdrop of other lights, but Zor-Ell didn't need visual cues to view the system. Three rocky planets occupied the inner orbit and two gas giants kept a more respectable distance. A disk of remnants left over from the time of creation extended nearly half a light out. Hooked into the VI, he noted emission signatures from orbiting starships, military and civilian, clustered around the premier base. Six were *Valon*-type survey cruisers, surprised to see two *Nasor*-class assault ships accompanied by four *Tangar*-class battlecruisers. Not surprised to see the warships themselves, only their number. It appeared OSCOM wasn't taking any chances and did not want to be caught napping should the Krans appear in force. He wondered again why they didn't have a picket stationed on the other side of the Karina breach. After meeting *Trailer*, perhaps one was, probably more than one, possibly farther out somewhere along *Tureen's* track patrolling in stealth mode. It was what he would do. If that were the case, how did the Kran ship he encountered manage to slip by? Definitely something to raise with PERCOM.

At one light AC took over nav and slowed *Valon* to half standard boost. Zor-Ell's mission orders were to return to Zaron, but he needed to patch up his ship before executing those orders. According to Karth's report, six days should suffice and he approved some crew leave. Everyone needed a break. He wondered when he would be permitted to take his. He would also lose Karth, who finally got a major command of his own, a medium cruiser. Although expected, he loathed to lose him, but Karth deserved the promotion. Distracted, he wondered what his new exec would be like.

Thirty light-minutes from Perilia, *Valon* dropped normal and headed in at three-quarter secondary boost. At four minutes the planet was a blue-green crescent without visible features. Two minutes out, *Valon* slowed to half boost and coasted in. The planet grew quickly in the mainframe plot as the ship slanted down toward the terminator. Flickering clusters of lights bordered dark ocean shorelines, extending their tentacles into continental interiors. The ship broke through the terminator into a clear morning sky and headed toward the Space Arm facility eighty ampirs north of the capital Tetra.

"Command, comms. We have an incoming from PERCOM."

"Very well. Open channel."

A full-dimensional window opened in the plot and Zor-Ell nodded to the sector commander. The woman tall, easily 170 minampirs, slim, and carried herself with natural confidence and authority gained through decades of command. Her black hair cropped short and framed an elongated face. Large brown eyes set off a delicate nose and small, but full lips. Her deep yellow skin showed few wrinkles and she looked young for her eighty-four years.

"Da, OSA *Valon* arriving," Zor-Ell announced formally. He met her before and within bounds of rank, they enjoyed a friendly working relationship. It was on her recommendation that OSCOM selected *Valon* for its mission.

Alkarh Tertulion smiled briefly, which made her look even younger, and nodded in return. Her eyes were alive with interest. "It's good to see you back, Karhide, if somewhat battered," she replied in a pleasant contralto. "As *Trailer* advised, you're the last ship to return from what has been an extremely successful survey."

"The weapons platforms in orbit might suggest otherwise, Alkarh."

"Success is relative, Karhide, and I don't intend to be surprised should the Celi-Kran appear in force. Apart from *Tureen's* unfortunate encounter, you're the only one to actually meet them in combat and survived. Although stealth sentry scanners observed your action, we were not in a position to render assistance. You did well to retrieve a specimen, and *Trailer* has orders to investigate the remnants. I regret the loss of your crew, though."

Positioning Burlig probes to give advance warning was standard tactical doctrine. He always considered Alkarh Tertulion to be a superb tactician.

"As long as we make their sacrifice count, Da."

"Always, Karhide. I studied your after-action report and noted your suspicions. If the Krans have indeed responded to a signal triggered by you on System 4-Three, it's an extremely prompt reaction, given they've been dormant in this sector for two millennia or more. That suggests penetration in force and explains my response."

"Are there pickets along *Tureen's* course?"

Tertulion gave a tight smile. "Don't worry. The Krans will not be permitted to locate the Karina breach and my units are not simply wandering about. The enemy has now lost another vessel and they will be investigating. We need to be ready. Your evaluation and insight into their tactics and history will be invaluable in formulating not only OSCOM's response strategy, but will dictate my immediate options as well."

"Pardon me for saying so, Alkarh, if you positioned pickets—"

"How did the Kran unit slip by them and attack you? We're looking into it, Karhide. You observed it emerge from the nebula is suggestive, but it's not the only avenue of investigation.

Once you're down, please transport to my headquarters. We have much to discuss. Your request for layover to carry out structural repairs is approved. OSCOM was advised accordingly."

"Orders acknowledged, Da," Zor-Ell said and the image faded. Under normal circumstances, PERCOM would provide transit portal facilities only, which would take him directly to the Orieli Cluster, and he'd be fully debriefed on Zaron. These were not normal circumstances, and he wondered how the Orieli systems at large viewed the increase in the Space Arm's level of readiness. Not since the Zaron Concordiat times had interstellar war been waged where whole worlds were torn apart. If this time around, worlds were again to be laid waste, it was OSCOM's duty to ensure they were not Orieli worlds. He wasn't entirely comfortable with such a blanket absolution and suspected that many in OSCOM and the Klanina Caucus would be equally disturbed.

Valon slowed, then stopped its ponderous length to hover over the expanse of the facility spread below. Slowly, it began to sink toward its designated landing apron.

* * *

"Friend Le Maran, you were told to remain in your suite until contacted, not play at being a tourist," Ti Inai admonished his troublesome protégé. "When I call, I expect you to be there. If that's not clear enough, you're free to make your own arrangements."

Le Maran's jowls sagged and his long fingers twined in agitation. In his current predicament, he did not need the Commissioner mad at him. "I apologize if I have broken your trust, friend Ti Inai, but I had to get out. After six days cooped up in this cage, I was going out of my mind. I needed to stretch my legs."

"Fool! You could have gotten your neck stretched. Have

you forgotten that there is a termination order against you? Next time you feel restless, take a shower instead."

However comfortable, the hotel suite was still a cage, but Le Maran acknowledged the wisdom of Ti Inai's words. Relieving momentary discomfort not worth the price of his life. Nevertheless, he felt a flash of resentment. Seated in his plush Captal office, what did the Commissioner know of discomfort and fear? He immediately stifled the thought as unfair. Ti Inai had tasted fear, experienced gnawing anxiety and the expectation of someone walking through his door with a needler in hand. After organizing the attack on the Unified Independent Front liner, his reward was to witness the disastrous consequences of that action, not only for Italan, but the Provisional Committee and the merger effort. Two members paid the ultimate price for their involvement when all too easily it could have been Ti Inai's head on the block. The Commissioner was wily and clearly knew how to mitigate personal risk, as his flight to Palea demonstrated.

Le Maran had powerful backers, but those faceless men would not be able to help him should Ti Inai become sufficiently annoyed. His resentment somewhat abated, he still thought it unreasonable that the Committee blamed him for the loss of Lemos. It wasn't as though his order to attack Fleet escorts was something of a secret. Unreasonable or not, everyone covered their ass, and he'd been picked to take the fall for their collective sins. Sacrifice a part so the whole may live. It was the way of things, although not altogether pleasant for the one ending up sacrificed.

Swallowing his pride, he gave a jerky nod. "It shall not happen again."

Ti Inai regarded the chubby figure in the Wall with resignation. He sympathized, but Le Maran's indiscretion and lack of discipline marked a character flaw in an otherwise brilliant strategist and tactician. The man may be a desk driver, not a field operative, but he should know when to keep his head down. How hard can it be? Although Ti Inai's threat was real, acting on it would be politically unwise. For his plan to work, he needed cooperation and support of Alikan Union Party cells Le Maran commanded. In the end, he reconciled himself to the inevitable and accepted the tool he had, good elements and bad.

"I didn't mean to snap at you, but you were taking a grave risk going out. Stay calm for a few more days, friend Le Maran, and you'll be out of there. Remember, never accept calls tagged with one of your old comms codes. Officially, they were scrubbed, but it doesn't mean someone couldn't use one if they know what they were doing and trace you. Be warned."

"I am warned and grateful for your support." To his surprise, Le Maran found he meant it. Ostracized by the organization he'd served faithfully for two decades and on the run, what choice did he have? His options might be limited, but at least he was still alive. And the hotel *was* comfortable.

"Forget it. Now, the reason for my call," Ti Inai went on briskly. "It's no secret that many of us in the Palean arm of the Alikan Union Party are not entirely satisfied with the structure of the Provisional Committee or the speed with which the Sargon/Palean merger is prosecuted."

"The Sargon's five-four voting majority," Le Maran muttered in disgust and sighed. A festering wound refusing to heal and threatened to poison the entire merger process. The problem serious and seemingly without a solution, at least one acceptable to the Paleans.

"Precisely! You and I spoke of this before—"

"And the Palean Committee members are still to resolve it."

Ti Inai smiled oily and his fingers worked. "With the Lemos initiative derailed, we could be in a position to resolve it now and I secured sufficient support within the Congress for the attempt to proceed."

"You have Tao Karam's backing?" Le Maran asked in surprise, slipping naturally into his analyst role.

The senior Palean Assembly representative led a pro-So-fam majority in the Palean Congress and vehemently critical of the Sargon merger. His antagonism had thwarted many Alikan Union Party initiatives, but Ti Inai and his faction took it in stride, taking the long-term view. In seven years a General Assembly electoral session would see Tao Karam and his faction swept aside, making way for progressive visionaries like Ti Inai who was already lobbied to secure his nomination as Executive Director. Should he succeed, Le Maran hoped to see his future firmly secured, but first, he needed to overcome his present difficulty.

Ti Inai snorted and his small lips pulled back in a sneer. "Hardly! He's too preoccupied sucking up to his Sofam Confederacy masters to see where Palean future really lies. We and Sargon will be one under the Alikan Union banner. That's inevitable, but not yet. Not yet! With their voting majority, they hold an effective stranglehold over the Committee's policy process. Far too many actions were forced through and not always in Palean interest. Sargon Committee members, and Ed-Kani Takao in particular, refuse to be reasonable. Friend Ed-Kani, I suspect, is pursuing a personal agenda and has been pointedly derisive at my attempts to redress the imbalance. The Committee's current problems give us a window of opportunity to demonstrate Palean dissatisfaction in a singular way that even Ed-Kani will understand."

"Breaking Sargon's voting majority won't be easy and I cannot see them relinquishing it voluntarily simply because of our protest."

"I know that. My plan calls for far more than a mere protest. If our demonstration succeeds, Sargon will relinquish it, all right. I persuaded the Committee to a program where we will initiate attacks on Kaleen commercial carriers—"

"Disrupting their economy and induce some of their systems to secede to the Palean Union? Brilliant," Le Maran acknowledged in admiration, then frowned. "That might gain us a system or two, but how will it redress our voting position?"

Ti Inai allowed himself a superior smile as he watched Le Maran's confusion. Not condescending, but his protégé could not be told the truth, at least not all of it.

"A piece in a mosaic, friend Le Maran. Winning over Kaleen systems won't be easy. It will take time for the Committee to secure weapons platforms and crews, and even more time before raids start to have a significant effect. We need to demonstrate to the Committee that without active support from the Palean arm of the Alikan Union Party the initiative will fail. My plan is simple. To ensure the initiative doesn't fail, we'll mount supportive raids."

A good strategist, Le Maran grasped the concept immediately, and the underlying tactical flaw. "Helping the Committee may still not be enough to break Sargon's five-seat voting majority."

"Perhaps not, but Sargon will reconsider its position if our efforts deliver a system into the Committee's hands," Ti Inai said smoothly. "After all, that's the objective."

Le Maran wasn't entirely convinced, but didn't want to argue the validity of the proposal, at least not until his immediate situation improved. Ti Inai was in the Committee and presumably understood its workings far better. Still, he could not see Sargon giving up a tactical advantage simply because the Palean arm of the Alikan Union Party had shown initiative. There must be more to the Commissioner's plan, but dare he probe?

"You're aware that our involvement will need to be handled with care, friend Ti Inai. Applying too much pressure could stiffen Kaleen's resistance and bring the Fleet on top of us."

"I am aware of both possibilities. We'll simply have to make sure we don't overreach ourselves."

"Are we going to use raiders again?"

"The Committee's initiative will, but our ships will be manned by patriots. We don't want to repeat the mistake we made with Lemos."

"Correct me if I'm wrong, but it seems to me, your plan calls for establishing a tactical base."

"That's right, and I have a site in mind. Galia lies on a minor shipping lane and of itself is of little consequence. What makes the system attractive is its location, only nineteen lights from several major Kaleen trade corridors. My sources identified a disused aerospace research station on Ophir, the system's fourth planet, called Khiman-ra. Your job will be to refurbish it, secure suitable hulls, arm them and execute raids against Kaleen shipping."

Le Maran tried hard to suppress his dismay. Within the Committee structure, he prepared and issued orders, not caring how they were executed, but he hadn't commanded in the field. Setting up what was in effect a Fleet Field facility would be a monumental exercise. He did not doubt his capability as a planner, but this was way beyond his experience.

"My job? Ah, I'm not sure—"

Ti Inai laughed. "I understand your concern. Professionals will do the technical work. You'll be there as an administrator."

"How much time do I have to set this up?"

"We need to be in a position to commence raids within two years or less. By that time, Kaleen would be subjected to sustained attack and its border systems will feel the pressure."

"Who do you have in mind to command our ships?"

"Kai Tanard."

"He survived?"

"He did, but I doubt he's enjoying it. Anar'on wrung him dry before handing him over to the Fleet. I can hardly imagine what they must have done to him. He's held on Kalakan right now."

"More wringing out," Le Maran muttered and shuddered. He knew something of the Wanderers and could clearly imagine what they did to Tanard. Now the Fleet would go through the whole miserable business again. He did not envy his protégé the experience. "Kalakan is a premier Palean Scout Fleet base, friend Ti Inai. Getting him out of there will be tough."

"I know, but we can spare the time. If we do manage to get him back, and sane, he'll have a personal incentive for the success of this scheme. This is all very much high-level with detailed plans still to be developed. In the meantime, stay put, relax, and when we're ready to move, you'll be contacted."

Le Maran stared speculatively at the Commissioner. "This is a dangerous game we're playing. If the Committee were to find out what we're doing..."

"That's why you cannot afford to be compromised," Ti Inai said and cut contact. The Wall tumbled in flowing colors and he took a moment to reflect.

Packing Le Maran off to Khiman-ra solved several pressing problems for him. As far as the Committee was concerned, the man had disappeared and Ti Inai could not be expected to sanction someone if the person cannot be found. Some would grumble and Ed-Kani will be suspicious, but that's as far as it would go. More importantly, appointing Le Maran as Khiman-ra's administrator would appease and bring on board the militant AUP cells he needed to make his plan work. The operation would have to be absolutely tight, unknown even to the personnel manning it or the mainstream Alikan Union Party machine. Any breach in security would be disastrous and probably terminal for him personally.

He did not understate the problem associated with getting Kai Tanard off Kalakan. A rescue might not even be possible, but the thought of Le Maran running tactical operations made the effort imperative. His protégé can question the strategy behind the initiative as much as he liked, because eventually it wouldn't make any difference—as long as Khiman-ra succeeded. With Kai Tanard in tactical command, Ti Inai saw no reason why it should not.

Keying in a special access code into the inlaid console in his desk, he activated the Wall. Committee business crowded his commitments as Commissioner and balancing the two responsibilities had become increasingly difficult. He needed a full-time assistant to field the less demanding Committee chores—something to be raised at the next meeting.

He quickly scanned through the message index, jotting comments and directives along the way to be executed by various AUP chapters. A funding request from Askaran caught his eye and he read the submission; reimbursement of one hundred million Serrll credits expended in support of a merger by an AUP-controlled raider cargo handling facility and a private concern to increase throughput capacity. With barely a hesitation, he marked it approved and routed the message to all Committee members. It was so routine it hardly warranted attention. Raiders would be induced to harass Kaleen only if they saw a quick profit in it for themselves and that meant able to sell cargo quickly. If Askaran's AUP chapter owned a freighting company, why not channel some of that profit their way? It was a good tactical move.

Disposing of the last item, Ti Inai activated Comsec and his face fell at the number of items needing his attention. In a flash of irritation, he wondered why in the pits hadn't his staff filtered what he actually needed to see? Too late, he remembered that Comsec was a private network for Executive Directors and Commissioners. Staring at the long list of messages, he could see the damned thing was getting cluttered with trivia again. Perhaps he should send the Moderator another message to clean up the thing. He sighed and went to work.

* * *

Dhar swung the combie out of the control network and began his descent toward Global Transport's landing field nestled beneath looming cliffs protecting Karach's northwestern approaches. Sprawled over eighty square talans, Tadar Industrial City produced a substantial portion of Askaran's precision

276

tools, power generating systems, domestic whitegoods and small transport vehicles. Heavy cargo haulers filled the sky with streams of traffic. Some complexes had landing rings, but these were for local sub-orbital freighters. Global's facility held the only intersystem handling capability and it wasn't large, a rectangle less than three square talans. A single warehouse arranged in a giant U around the western perimeter shepherded a medium-sized freighter of some 500,000 mikans capacity. From Kandu Hall's intelligence briefs, Dhar knew it was *Paun*. If he didn't know it for the predator it was, he could easily mistake it for just another legitimate carrier. Stacked containers surrounded a somewhat smaller freighter at the eastern end of the field, clear evidence that Global's software problems still remained unresolved. The ship must be *Pilla*, offloading cargo before heading for Otilando and secondary drive maintenance.

No one challenged him as the combie made for the small parking lot at the left tip of the warehouse. A young woman emerged into glaring sunshine and watched the combie settle. Evidently, he was expected. While the power plant spooled down, Dhar opened the bubble and with a quick look around, stepped out. His brother pocketed his shades and followed. The young woman strode quickly toward them, an official smile fixed on her small, oval face.

"Welcome to Global Transport, gentlemen." She extended a slim arm at a wide reflective doorway, smile still in place. "If you would please follow me, Ser Segal and Ser Pulman are waiting to see you."

"Thank you, Alana," Terr said briskly and followed her in.

Alana was Global's executive assistant: smart, accomplished and extremely capable. Over the last three days, she helped him and Dhar look over Global's records, and even conducted a personal tour of the complex, describing everything in excruciating detail. Clearly, Segal and Pulman wanted them to know absolutely everything. At least that's how it appeared. Looking at her, he found it difficult to believe someone like that worked for a raider front. As Hall said, Askaran operated under a different set of moral rules. To Pulman, Terr must seem the odd man out.

Inside the warehouse it was like any ordinary office block; mostly open plan workstations: Wall displays, potted plants tucked discretely into corners, closed cubicles, staff talking to computers, shuffling record wafers and chatting. It was depressing. A few heads turned to follow the small procession, all wearing the same look of mild curiosity and bored indifference. They knew about the merger with KSD, but as long as they received their salaries it made little difference who managed the setup. Alana stopped before the meeting room door and touched a pad. The panel retracted.

"Ser Kerill-aa and Ser Randakla," she announced evenly, nodded to Terr and Dhar and walked off.

Pulman and Segal rose to meet their visitors. Terr raised his right hand to shoulder level, palm open in formal greeting.

"Gentlemen…"

"Kerill, come on in!" Segal gushed and extended a hand at the long table guarded by a battery of luxurious formchairs. They could be in Karach Salvage's meeting room. The decor practically the same. A tray of brown bottles, dew glistening on their sides, and frosted glasses waited to lubricate the proceedings. "Sit down and help yourself to a beer before it gets warm."

Everyone made himself comfortable while exchanging small chitchat. Sipping his Brut Cooler, Terr eased back against the soft formchair and smiled at his new partners. The first time since concluding the merger that they were all together. As always, Pulman looked predatory, watchful, ready to pounce. He genuinely didn't seem aware of his posture, which made him doubly dangerous. His total alertness to his surrounds and everything in it made it difficult to engage in any form of subterfuge, especially when everybody knew they were playing a farce, but pretending otherwise. Under different circumstances the situation would be amusing.

Segal, on the other hand, looked and acted the part of a tough underworld businessman, not prepared to back down to anyone, even though he had done exactly that to get into bed with Karach Salvage and Disposal. Although circumstances forced him into the merger, it did not sweeten the deal in any way. On the contrary, it merely provided an incentive to wipe a blight off his record; preferably terminally. Global Transport was due to pay the ninety million balance tomorrow and the deal would be fully consummated. After tomorrow, Terr appreciated that he and Dhar needed to be extra careful walking beneath overhead cranes and loaders.

"I think we're done and I'm glad to hear KSD's books are in order," he said, watching for any reaction. Pulman merely sat there, his face frozen, but his eyes betrayed his attentiveness.

"Our audit team had only good things to say," Segal growled. "You've got a very neat chart of accounts. When we bid for KSD the first time, it was a mess. Otherwise, everything looks clean, including your balance sheet. I trust Randakla found our books equally satisfactory." His voice implied that he expected nothing else.

"With a few exceptions," Dhar said gravely. "But you know about those already."

Segal's eyes flickered briefly at Pulman. "Our disbursement accounts?"

"And the encrypted files that link your transactions with Morgian Holdings and Chase Investments." Dhar stared unwaveringly at Segal. Last night, he dined on local venison and his stomach protested at the unaccustomed intrusion. He didn't feel sick, only unsettled, which undoubtedly accounted for his ill humor and abrupt manner. At least that's how he rationalized it. Or maybe merely a personal aversion to mixing it with raiders.

Tah, the gods will tell.

"Whatever accounts we hold with those institutions don't concern you," Pulman said lightly, his smile too forced to be real. "And neither do those files."

"Ordinarily, that would be true," Dhar agreed affably, not at all intimidated. "Your private affairs are your business, but when funds are siphoned off from receivables which affect the bottom line, I'm afraid that makes it our business. Personal drawings and extraordinary Alikan Union Party transactions must be made out of your profit share. They are not valid business expenses for the group, and treating them as such incorrectly reflects your financial position. While you were an independent concern the anomaly didn't represent a problem. However, you are no longer independent."

Segal raised inquiring eyebrows. "You're not expecting us to open our private files for your inspection or provide access to our financial brokers?"

"Of course not. As I said, they are your private affairs. My concern, and my partner's, is only with outgoings from Global's general ledger. Your current practice is taking money that belongs to us. Half of it anyway."

Pulman leaned forward and rested his right hand on the desk. A light tapping of his fingers betrayed any expression. "I understand your concern, Randakla," he said heavily, "and we were going to close off those accounts. Unfortunately, our time was occupied by more pressing problems."

"Software related?" Terr ventured, hoping his satisfaction didn't show, mildly wondering what bugged his brother.

Tight lipped, Pulman nodded. "We were promised full recovery of service by end of the day."

"I saw the stacked containers on our way down."

"Yes. Despite your help, Kerill, a shipment from *Pilla* two days ago severely stretched our capacity."

"I regret not able to take her," Terr said seriously. He had two freighters down himself and it was better that *Pilla* sat at Global's field.

"I know. You have traffic of your own. Like I said, we should be fully operational today."

"Excellent!" Terr said and finished his beer. "Unless some-one has a problem, I expect payment of balance by close of business tomorrow."

Segal cleared his throat and grinned. "Actually, you'll get it today. Signed documents were forwarded to your legal people this morning. Call it appreciation for helping us clear inventory and getting Global out of a major trading hole." It was an easy lie, but pits! Simply business. Besides, they'd get their money back soon enough.

Terr's eyes opened wide. "That's good news, Tan. I fear, though, other operators won't be as enthusiastic at the news of our merger and neither will Trans National Haulage."

Pulman waved a dismissive hand. "As you pointed out, Kerill, we live in a ruthless environment where wresting every advantage counts big. If our opposition had the means, they would eat us up."

Terr chuckled. "You mean they'd eat *me* up! Affiliated as you are with the Alikan Union Party, Global is in an altogether different position."

Pulman allowed himself a small smile. "Perhaps. That now applies to you as well."

"So it does."

"And you don't need to worry about Trans National," Segal stepped in. "There is more than enough business to go around for everyone. TNH won't be hurt by this and Rakliva knows better than to try anything."

"I am relieved to hear that. We face enough problems in-tegrating our operating procedures without getting sidetracked by personal agendas," Terr said softly, his eyes locked on Segal, hoping the message had gotten through. His concern was not with Rakliva or TNH, but Global and what his new partners were planning.

A cold shiver ran down Segal's spine as he broke contact with Kerill's unwavering stare. He could sense determination, ruthlessness and something dead in those hard gray eyes belaying the man's youthfulness. He wondered what Kerill saw and experienced to make his eyes so old. Who was he really, and what was he? Segal slowly shifted his gaze and took in Randakla's impassive features. The Wanderer looked back without blinking and Segal saw the same hardness, and something else—power waiting to be unleashed, death lurking. It couldn't be, of course. Randakla was not a Discipline adept. Or was he? Despite his unease, Segal didn't doubt his ability to deal with both of them, but he felt justified asking Pulman to run a deeper security check.

"While we're talking about the Alikan Union Party, the chapter president has consented to seeing our new partners," Segal said. "Warat will take you there once we're finished here. Unless you want to look over the setup again?"

Terr shook his head. "Thanks, but that won't be necessary. With Alana's help, we had more than enough time to see everything we needed to see."

"Good!" Segal stood and placed both hands on the desk. "To ease your concerns, Randakla, Warat and I will clean out those troublesome accounts without delay."

Standing up, Dhar nodded. "That would be appreciated, Tan."

"After all, we want Askaran Holdings to start off smoothly," Segal added brightly, his smile phony as a three-Serrll note.

Terr wasn't fooled. As he figured, it was only a question of who would get their hit first. He still needed to get his hands on Global's comms protocols to the AUP cell. How that would lead him to the Provisional Committee, he wasn't entirely certain. Nonetheless, that was the job. If it were easy, Kandu Hall would have wormed the information out of the AUP chapter already.

Outside, the morning crispness had been sucked dry, replaced by a blanket of heat and clamminess. A light breeze coming off the hills provided illusory comfort. Pulman led them to the parking lot and stopped beside a dark red Lexia combie. He opened the bubble and climbed in. Terr glanced at his brother, received a reassuring nod and settled himself up front, wriggling in the conforming seat as the power plant spooled up. The bubble closed, polarized and they lifted. Pulman set the nav coordinates and relaxed.

"This should be an interesting meeting, Warat. Is there anything we should know about Laral before we get there?" Terr asked. Pulman turned his head, his dark features stern.

"Sarek Laral is a driven man with only two objectives in mind: to increase his power and the chapter's influence inside the government. He certainly managed to seize power. Since you and I are able to operate without interference from the Diplomatic Branch or the Serrll Scout Fleet, attests to the success of his second objective. How long this cozy relationship with the government will last, no one can say, but as you undoubtedly worked out, Laral has to be careful not to overreach himself. The Bureau of Administrative Affairs on Captal has only so much slack in its patience and my personal belief is that we're on swampy ground already."

"From your description, Laral sounds like a formidable personality."

"He's determined and ruthless, and I wouldn't be swayed by his superficial charm."

Terr allowed himself a grin. *Not like you at all, eh?* "I shall keep in mind."

If Pulman bore any resentment against Laral for losing the presidency contest, he hid it well. Terr knew that although Pulman was still an influential figure within the Alikan Union Party chapter, running Global was a consolation prize at best compared to wielding real political power. Pulman's problem, and in the end the history didn't matter. He had no interest in Pulman's personal schemes inasmuch as they brought him deeper into the local AUP cell and a step closer to the Provisional Committee.

Lines of combies, sled-pads and communals swarmed thick over the city, staggered at different control network altitudes. Tauri II glared bright in the northern sky. Beyond the bay, azure waters melted into masses of bunched, snowy clouds hanging low over the horizon. Clinging to the sweeping beaches, Karach stretched to the base of protective hills that held it in a tight embrace. The city sprawl swam in the shimmering heat, a pattern of reactive ceramic towers, wide boulevards with their moving glidewalks, parks, small lakes, and irregular rows of private residences.

Terr sat back in the soft upholstery, absently going over what he knew about the AUP chapter's president, coupled with Pulman's personal, if somewhat biased, insight. Not a great deal, but enough for what he had to do. Glancing at Pulman, the taciturn local appeared distracted. Terr left him to it, unwilling to delve. The combie broke out of the network and slanted down toward a cluster of spires. It approached a slender fluted tower glowing like burnished copper, and slowed. Halfway up a landing ramp extended from the contoured face and the combie settled. An entrance opened and the ramp slid back, taking the combie inside. When the opening closed, Pulman cracked the bubble and stepped into the brightly lit parking bay housing rows of stacked vehicles. He checked that Terr and Dhar were following and made his way toward a row of four cable-tube doors.

When the tube opened, Terr faced an open floor of workstations and offices walled with transparent panels. Floor-to-ceiling windows provided excellent natural lighting. There were few extraneous decorations, the floor hard tiled a drab gray. Men and women, most of them surprisingly young, looked busy behind their display plates. A background of subdued voices filled the empty spaces.

Pulman strode to the crescent reception desk and an eager

youngster looked up, official smile on full display.

"Good morning, Ser Pulman," he gushed, his eyes drifting to Terr and Dhar. "Ser Laral is expecting you." He made to stand up, but Pulman motioned him to stay put.

"Thank you. I'll make my own way in."

"Of course, Ser."

Without waiting, obviously familiar with the layout, Pulman walked quickly toward the first of three offices, fully enclosed in tasteful pale paneling. Several curious faces stared unobtrusively at the trio. Pulman stopped before the door and touched a waist-high pad. The panel slid back with a smooth hiss.

Sitting behind a glossy desk, a window screen at his back, Sarek Laral looked up, smiled and stood up. Surprisingly tall for a native, thin with gaunt features and a beak nose. His elegant dark gray suit perfectly tailored, matching well his black skin. The piercing black eyes flickered over the two strange visitors before settling on Pulman.

"Warat, welcome back. Please…" He swept a hand at the formchairs placed before the desk and sat down.

"Thanks, Sarek. May I introduce Global Transport's new partners, Kerill-aa and Randakla from Karach Salvage and Disposal."

"Of whom I have heard so much," Laral gushed sonorously.

"All of it good, I trust," Terr said easily and took the left formchair, studying his host with care. He did not mistake the command presence and assured bearing. This man knew what he wanted and wasn't shy about getting it, regardless of cost.

Laral grinned broadly and leaned back. "You won't be hearing any complaints from me, Kerill. Not after making such a generous unification tax increase from KSD."

"Since I and my partner plan to be here for a while, I wanted to make a favorable impression."

"Believe me, you have." Laral cast a speculative glance at

Pulman. "*You* could make a similar impression, you know."

Pulman instantly bridled. "I thought Global's extraordinary contributions were making enough of an impression."

Laral tilted his head and shrugged. "They are, but you know how it is."

"I certainly do. Very well. My contribution is now six-and-a-half points, but our extraordinary donations—"

"Have gone up by five percent. For the good of the cause," Laral said evenly, his voice making it clear it was an order. Pulman pursed his mouth, glared and gave a stiff nod. Neatly boxed in and, short of creating a scene, he could only back down.

Terr watched the exchange with interest. Laral did have a certain youthful charm about him just as Pulman said, but steely toughness lay behind the beguiling smile. It would be a mistake to underestimate him, and he did not intend doing that anyway. Laral's handling of Pulman crisp and decisive, and Pulman noticeably didn't like it, especially the way it was done in front of his new partners. Terr figured it was the price of doing business. As a major shareholder in Global, representing as he did the aspirations of the Palean Union, Laral did not hesitate to make his wants known and Pulman's feelings be damned.

Laral turned to Terr, gave a disarming chuckle and shrugged. "Askaran Holdings cost me one hundred million Serrlls, and I want them back."

"Perfectly understandable," Terr said. "As long as you don't plan on getting them from me."

"Hah! Well said, but it all depends, Kerill."

"Depends on what?"

"Whether you're merely a hardnosed businessman or a patriot."

So, this was the gambit, eh? Terr's mouth twitched. Laral was good, very good, and he started to appreciate why Pulman lost his bid for the chapter's presidency.

"My political leanings are known. However, Karach Salvage is not my personal property to do with as I wish. I must answer to my backers, and unfortunately for us, they *are* hard-nosed businessmen."

"Yes, an awkward situation, Kerill. Something could be arranged, eh? It would help things considerably. It really would."

Terr understood perfectly what those 'things' were. For a cut, an extortion payment really, Laral would make sure KSD wasn't bothered by the Central Revenue Office or some other nosy government agency. A thinly veiled threat, which Terr countered easily.

"I am prepared to discuss possibilities, Sarek; with my backers. If KSD suffers a drop in profitability due to unfavorable market conditions or a shift in government policy, which Treasury Department Minister Tullan assured me is unlikely, I would be forced to take my business elsewhere. I would hate to do that after all the hard work everybody has put into creating Askaran Holdings." In plain language, if you screw with me, you'll get nothing, *and* I'll walk away with your hundred million.

Laral's eyes closed into slits. "You know Minister Tullan?"

"We've met a couple of times," Terr said, enjoying Laral's reaction. "The Diplomatic Branch Resident considered it advisable that I establish a good working relationship with the Minister."

"Ah, the redoubtable Resident. Warat told me of the special association you have with Kandu Hall. Most interesting. Well, well. My position—"

"May need to be reconsidered?" Terr advised gently. Laral gave a slow grin, but his eyes glittered with ice. The chapter president didn't take setbacks easily, but in this case, he would simply have to lump it.

"So it seems. With such powerful backing, you might indeed be able to help my chapter," Laral murmured, leaned forward and clasped his hands over the desk. "We'll leave the matter of additional contributions for later. Warat tells me you've got a proposition. What exactly do you have in mind? If it's not money." He chuckled and glanced at Pulman, who gave a weak smile.

Terr crossed his legs, starting to enjoy himself. He had Laral's measure. The man respected someone who stood up to him and despised weakness. Given his position the attitude understandable.

"That's just it, Sarek. It will be money, but not right away."

"Oh? You've got me intrigued."

"This should not be a revelation, so you'll have to pardon me if I rake over old ground. The AUP Provisional Committee's gambit to secure Pizgor failed because the entire scheme was predicated on the integrity of raiders not betraying Lemos, despite overwhelming evidence that raiders are implicitly untrustworthy." Terr glanced at Pulman. "Present company excluded, of course."

Pulman grinned. "Of course. Go on."

Terr looked at his brother. "Tell him."

Dhar unfolded his arms and leaned forward. "You must know the Committee's objective to secure additional systems has not changed, cannot change, if they are to secure that vital third Executive Council seat. Without it, merging with the Palean Union would be a hollow victory. The Lemos lesson learned, they will use a different model. It's not too difficult to guess what that is—continue attacking commerce of vulnerable systems until they have had enough and secede either to the Paleans or Sargon. How they intend to implement the model is equally obvious. Use raiders. The AUP does not have anywhere near enough hulls to try this alone. This time, if I were the Committee, it would be on a hands-off basis. Provide raiders with shipping intelligence and let their avarice do the rest. Crude, I admit, but effective."

Laral exchanged a quick glance with Pulman, telegraphing that the idea was not exactly new. "Sounds plausible and even if real, how would it help my chapter and the merger cause?"

Terr could not help smiling. "What's the one thing a raider needs in order to keep himself in business?"

"Sell his cargo," Pulman said after a silent pause. "Oh, that's good."

Laral looked blank. "You've lost me."

Dhar cleared his throat. "It's simple really. Between Global Transport and Karach Salvage, we're offering an open market to any raider, no questions asked and without interference from the Serrll Scout Fleet or local authorities. That's fine as far as it goes, but what my partner and I are proposing takes the idea one step farther. If a raider uses an Askaran Holdings facility as his exclusive offloading point, we buy from him at a premium. We get a predictable cashflow, your chapter gets its cut and we'll be supporting the cause."

"And getting rich doing it," Laral said dryly.

"Of course," Terr added, taking it in stride. "My backers and I have an investment to recoup as well."

"Which my hundred million will help achieve," Laral said dryly and Terr smiled.

"As you say. They don't particularly care where the money comes from or about my political leanings as long as I keep my eye on that balance sheet. My plan will deliver both."

Laral tapped his desk with long, bony fingers and gave a couple of slow nods. "Yes, I can see how that could work. It's lamentable having to use raiders to further our cause, but times dictate the means. I suppose the unstated upside of your plan is, once a raider signs up and then has thoughts of reneging, you deal with him?"

"Correct," Dhar said. "I estimate that two demonstrations should be sufficient."

"And how would you make those demonstrations?"

"Terminally."

Laral nodded. "I suppose. What do you want from me in return for those extra contributions?"

"A seat for me and my partner on your executive," Terr

said promptly and Laral laughed.

"I thought you'd be after my job!"

Terr chuckled. "No thanks. The one I've got is keeping me busy already. Besides, I have enough local entanglements as it is."

"No doubt." Laral smiled and glanced at Pulman. "Well, Warat? What do you think?"

"It's a good plan and should work. I would consider it."

"So would I. There are details to untangle, as always, but I cannot make such a decision alone. It must be heard by the executive, but my endorsement should carry some weight." He slapped the desk with both palms and stood. "I can see a bright future for Askaran Holdings and my chapter. Indeed I do. It has been a genuine pleasure meeting you Kerill...Randakla."

"The pleasure is mutual, Sarek," Terr said and lifted himself up. "I look forward to hearing your decision."

Laral stepped away from the desk and looked down at Terr. "And if it's negative? Just supposing."

Terr shrugged. "No big deal. Warat and I will make our own arrangement with the raiders. Of course, I may have to reconsider my unification tax position and you would miss out on a healthy margin. Just supposing."

The AUP chapter president gave a wintry smile. "Yes. Well, we shall see. Any time you wish to visit, Kerill, my door is open."

"I appreciate that," Terr said seriously. "Until then."

Chapter Eleven

Nightwings, the shadow who walks at night, sat on a brown granite boulder, still warm from the day's heat, amidst a jumble of other boulders and stared vacantly at the marching waves rolling remorselessly toward a sandy shore. Slowing, each wave reared and smashed itself in a rage of white froth that hissed and gurgled as the waters ran up the beach, only to be inexorably pulled back. The booming of crashing surf sent spray flying into a gloomy sky, dark with heavy cloud. White seabirds wheeled above the green waves, screeching in protest. A driving onshore wind pelted the few couples and loners braving the elements with salty droplets that stung as they hit exposed skin. Palms and shrubs swayed under the onslaught, nodding. They had seen it all before.

Sitting on a warm stone, Nightwings watched the turbulent sea and listened to the roiling surf and the wind's fury. His lightweight slacks and T-shirt were damp, but he didn't mind. The spray warm and the air had lost some of its normal humid heaviness. The only part of his stay here he did not enjoy—humidity, so unlike the parched airs of the Saffal. Despite the storm, loud music came from bars and open restaurants across the boulevard behind him. It might not be exactly beach weather, but it was no reason to spoil a good dinner, and the locals were determined to make the most of it. Storms came and would eventually go away, nothing to get excited about.

Long hair streaming behind him, protective membranes covering his eyes against the spray and flying sand, his gaze lost somewhere where a leaden sea met a dark sky. Like the moving sands the sea changed endlessly, yet remained the same. It also had a captive fascination, an attraction that compelled one to join with it or invoked instant rejection. With the sea, there was no middle ground. In the same way, the Saffal also demanded unconditional acceptance. Those who rejected its uncompromising terms perished.

As a boy, Nightwings embraced the Saffal without question, for he knew nothing else. In turn, it nurtured his body and encompassed his soul. Now, sitting by the tossing waters, staring into gray emptiness, seeing nothing and everything, he allowed his spirit to soar above the waves, free as the birds hovering in the wind. Distracted, he failed to hear the soft footfalls crunching through the sand. When he did become aware of a presence behind him, it came far too late.

Something hard jabbed against his spine and he stiffened, instantly alert. Willing himself to remain still, he felt a flash of annoyance and frustration wash through him before he focused on the threat. His fascination with the sea had made him forget a basic rule of security: pattern and predictability. The oversight could now turn out to be costly. The god did not warn him, so this wasn't a deadly situation—yet.

"Get up…slowly," a heavy voice grated behind him.

Dhar sensed latent power in that voice, determination, physical strength and unquestioning willingness to kill at the slightest provocation. He did not want to put that willingness to a test. Chagrined at getting caught so easily, he regretted the disruption this would inevitably cause to his dinner engagement with Sankri, and a special occasion too. He stood up as told, not even thinking of trying some amateurish move. Fleetingly, he thought of invoking the hand of Death and rejected it. He would be killed the instant his power became manifest. The hard pressure against his spine did not lessen as he rose. For a second his body tensed.

"Careful…" the voice advised. "This thing has a hair trigger. Right. Walk to the wall and into the yellow combie."

Dhar no longer felt anything against his back, but he sensed the man behind him as he turned and moved slowly along the beach toward the seawall. Beyond it, towering condominiums and hotels glowed in the fading light. Enough pedestrians kept the boulevard from appearing deserted, if not exactly crowded. Combies and private sled-pads made glowing streams above. Soft sand shifting beneath his bare feet, Dhar stepped through a break in the wall, paused to look at the yellow combie hovering in front of him, its bubble open, and climbed in. He left a trail of white sand on the black carpet as he slid over the back seat. The driver up front never even glanced at him. A tall, heavyset bruiser eased into the back beside him and the bubble immediately closed. With a surge of power the combie lifted, turned and headed west, scraping the lower clouds.

Noting the city slide beneath him, Dhar knew where they were going—Kronas Field. Another appointment with Rakliva? He shifted slightly and met midnight-black eyes looking at him. The local huge and none of his bulk looked like flab. The needler in the meaty paw appeared puny. Dhar did not care to match this man in a contest of physical strength. His features were solid, angular, like the rest of his body. Intelligence shone through those eyes and Dhar reconsidered his position. This was no ordinary thug after a quick mugging. He glanced at the man's shoes; soft shipboard boots. A commercial ship's officer, perhaps? Heavy gave a slow smile that didn't show his teeth.

"Very good, Ser Randakla," he said, the bass voice rolling deep within his chest. "You're looking at a little off-planet trip."

"Your idea?" Dhar asked, trawling after any snippet of information.

"Merely business. Nothing personal."

"Whose then?"

"Does it matter? Before you go, I was told to hurt you— bad. That means emotional involvement and I never get emotionally involved."

"But in my case?"

"What can I say? I couldn't resist the bonus. Ordinarily,

even that wouldn't cut it with me, but I've got to deliver a holoview shot of you. I'm sure you'll understand."

Dhar did. "You want me to start sweating, right? All part of the softening up process, otherwise you would not have told me any of this."

Heavy chuckled. "I knew right away you were smart. Don't worry about it and enjoy the ride. It really won't be that bad."

In the distance, Kronas Field opened like a toy set, lit beneath roiling black clouds. The combie plunged into a thick bank and the bubble instantly became smeared with rain. In the gray cocoon, there was no sense of motion. They broke out, trailing white vapor, and descended. Unless it shifted its course, they were heading toward the far side of the Field and the Trans National Haulage facility. It looked very much like Rakliva wanted to even the score.

Clearing the control network the combie slanted down toward a freighter parked beside the far left warehouse. From above, Dhar could not tell whether the thing was armed or mercly another carrier. It really did not matter. Glowing pearly white the apron glistened with rain. The combie hovered, then sank beside the ship, its bulk suddenly enormous. The power plant spooled down, sounding unnaturally loud, and the driver cracked the bubble. His needler steady on Dhar, Heavy eased himself out. Standing beside the combie, Dhar smelled dampness and rain in the air. Fine drops caressed his face. He gave the freighter a quick look. It hovered, free of ground support umbilicals, its bottom smooth. There were no hatches that might mask a projector housing. He figured the thing could carry some 900,000 mikans dead weight. Not small, but certainly not a major hauler. The exterior was painted dark gray and the hull looked well cared for.

A ramp hissed open and slanted down. Dhar did not need a hint and started walking toward it. Beneath the ponderous hull the wind whistled, flapping his trousers and whipped hair around his face. He looked into the brightly lit maw of the ship and made his way up the ramp. Two ratings, needlers leveled, waited for him as he stepped on the deck. Heavy stopped well out of reach and pocketed his weapon. Behind them the ramp slowly closed.

"Are we cleared for lift?" he demanded and one of the ratings nodded.

"Ready to go, Ser. The exec is waiting for your word."

Heavy glanced at Dhar, turned and moved briskly toward a cable-tube hatch.

"Okay, you," a rating snapped, waving the needler. "This way."

It was a short walk toward a nondescript hatch. The rating touched a pad and the hatch hissed open. Dhar paused at the entrance, looked quickly into the dimly lit interior and stepped in. The hatch slid shut behind him with a soft clang. He did not bother turning around to look for a contact pad. This cozy cell would only open from the outside. Apart from three small metal crates, some loose packing shavings, the compartment empty.

He felt mild vibration through his bare feet, leaned against the cool bulkhead and slid down. The freighter getting ready to lift, if it had not already done so. He rested his hands on his knees and closed his eyes. His captors had made their play and he would now make his, but not yet. He wanted the ship to transit first. Some things were done better that way.

Thinking of nothing, Nightwings permitted his mind to drift among images of flowing sands and the blue of open seas.

* * *

Terr tapped the genuine hand imitation weave tablecloth in an impatient staccato and glanced again at the restaurant's entrance. Come *on*, Nightwings! Where the pits are you? He picked up the cocktail glass and drained the crimson mixture in a single gulp, hardly feeling the bite of the liquor. His anticipated enjoyment of the evening had faded a while back. Twirling the glass between his hands, he tried to take his mind off his empty stomach. Given the surrounds and the enticing smells, that took some willpower.

The restaurant bright, filled with gay laughter, animated voices, and the clinking of glasses and cutlery. In the center of the room a transparent floor-to-ceiling column, filled with coral and darting colored fish, provided a topic of distracted conversation. The guests were mostly young holidaymakers, with a sprinkling of older individuals and couples. Seascapes painted on walls reflected the informal atmosphere. A three-man band tucked in the far corner played unobtrusive background music, making like they were part of the decor.

A waiter approached him, but Terr waved him off. He wanted to savor his planned seafood meal without spoiling it with too many drinks—if his errant brother ever showed up! This was supposed to be a celebration, toasting a successful merger and a step closer to gaining that vital link into the Provisional Committee. And what does Dhar do? Probably fixing his hair and it's still in curlers!

Rit!

Still, it was uncharacteristic for Dhar to be late like this. Distracted, Terr looked out the window panels. Cutting through darkness the boulevard shone with light. Muffled surf pounded the beach even though the wind had died down. Way past their appointed meeting time, he suddenly sat up, alarmed that something might have happened to his brother. If he were running late, Dhar would have called. Wouldn't he? What if he couldn't call? All sorts of bad things flashed through Terr's mind. He took a deep breath and approached the problem rationally.

Lately, his brother took to making solitary walks along the beach. Terr understood the need. He shared it himself, but did not consider it wise to indulge. He only had to look at what happened last time they decided to take a stroll, and they were together then. That was it; Dhar had taken a stroll and lost track of time. Terr didn't believe it. Had Dhar grown overconfident in his trust that Death would always be there to protect him? More likely, it was a simple case of establishing a behavioral pattern and someone had taken advantage of that predictability. They weren't short of enemies who wouldn't mind erasing a grudge. He warned his brother of the danger his indulgence courted. Dhar knew the importance of this night to risk being late. What if someone nabbed him? At least his brother hadn't been hurt. The link they shared would have alerted him—

Fire seared his left shoulder and back and he jerked.

Nightwings!

A couple at the next table gave him a strange look, but he didn't notice them. He could only think of his injured brother, if not fatally wounded. The burning sensation faded and he immediately rose. Throwing the napkin on the table, he strode quickly toward the exit, not bothering with the bill. They knew him well enough to charge it to his account. The doorman touched his temple in a salute as Terr hurried out.

The crash of surf loud outside and the air smelled of salt and rain. At least the drizzle had stopped. The Tillana Cove Apartments tower glowed pale beige. Bright, thin blue stripes ran up its sides. Only two hundred katalans from the restaurant, but it wasn't close enough for Terr. Rubbing his shoulder, he made a decision. Ignoring the curious stares from the onlookers, he broke into a run. The entrance panels barely slid away as he raced past the startled usher, making for the cable-tubes. Heart pounding, he waited for one to open and stepped in.

Inside their apartment, he turned to the Wall. "Computer, set comms protocol Askaran KSD and open channel, personal for Kandu Hall." The Resident might not be in his office this late, but the call would trace him wherever he was.

The Wall cleared and Hall smiled, sitting behind his polished desk. "Ser Kerill-aa—"

"Dhar is gone," Terr interrupted, "and he's hurt."

"How do you know—"

"I just do, Ser Resident. We were going to have dinner to celebrate the merger. He never showed up. A few minutes ago, he was either shot or beaten. Probably shot. If he were beaten, I would have known."

"Yes. Your Wanderer connection?" Hall asked and Terr nodded, impressed that Hall would have this piece of arcane knowledge. "Where do you suspect he was taken from, Agent Terr?"

"The beach. He went out for a stroll…" No need to say more. Hall pursed his lips and sighed.

"Most unwise. I'll instigate an immediate search, but you must know that finding him will be difficult. If somebody did take him, there are simply too many places where a body can disappear, if that was the intention. Do you have anything else to go on?"

"It could be a random mugging, but I doubt it. Dhar can take care of himself. Pulman and Segal might be behind it, but that doesn't smell right either. It's too soon."

"Yes. Which leaves your friend Rakliva or some other competitor."

"My thinking exactly. This could be worm crap and Dhar may have fallen against a rock for all I know."

"We'll check it out."

"While you're doing it, check if anybody lifted off Trans National's facility. If Rakliva kidnapped him, he just made one huge mistake."

"Leave this to me, Agent Terr," Hall warned. "I won't have you charging about pursuing a personal vendetta. You have a mission to consider!"

"And I'm considering it, Ser Resident. I merely felt sorry for the unfortunates who took my brother."

When the Wall image faded, Terr tried hard to convince himself this was true. Gritting his teeth, face set, he summoned the god and stood basking in his shadow. Death riding his shoulders, he stepped out of the apartment. He would walk along the beach hoping to find Nightwings, but feared the worst.

* * *

Reality twisted in a moment both infinite and fleeting. Infinite, as time did not truly exist along the boundary between the now and what was referred to as subspace. Fleeting, because crossing the transition took no time at all. Dharaklin understood well the physics, but his body and senses did not. When the phase wave rippled through him, it felt like being ripped apart, turned inside out. It passed in an instant, but he muttered a pithy word, cursing the engineer. Another degree or two of misalignment and this bilge crate would never get out of phase.

He pushed against the bulkhead and heaved himself up. Time he did some paid work. The crates groaned as he slid them over the metal deck against a bulkhead. He stacked the last one on top of the others and frowned. Not much protection, but it would have to do. Standing behind the crates, he raised his arms and chanted the words from the *Saftara*.

"I shall walk in the shadow of Death," he intoned and his voice grew deeper. "And it shall be with me all the days of my life." Fire surged through his body and in a moment of duality, he was Nightwings, but he was also Death, looking down at the mortal who invoked him. "With shadow shall I smite my enemies, and with thunder shall I purge their land! And all who stand with me in the shadow of Death shall know my power, and be comforted. With shadow and thunder shall I walk their land!"

The god laid his hands on the one standing before him and their spirits joined. Blue lightnings wound down Dhar's arms, snapping as they consumed his body. Strong with the power, he crouched, leveled his arms at the hatch and willed Death to march again. Lightning cracked, loud in the small confines of the compartment, and shrapnel pinged off the crates. When he rose, twisted metal and a smoking hole remained where the hatch stood. He waited a moment for the glowing edges to cool down, then stepped through and quickly looked around, hands ready to pour forth fire. The deck appeared deserted, which he expected. Why would anyone be down here while under boost? Still, someone may have heard the crash and could come looking.

Striding fast, he made his way toward the closest of two cable-tube hatches. He thumbed the access pad and the hatch immediately opened. The Askaran native inside was quick. He lifted his needler and fired even as Dhar twisted and let the lightnings loose. He felt the bolt sear his left shoulder and back and gasped, the pain momentarily swamping his senses. The native gave an incoherent scream and fell back.

Grimacing, eyes smarting, Dhar glanced at the body sprawled at the bottom of the tube. Charred flesh surrounded a blackened, smoking hole in the chest. The unfortunate obviously heard something and came to investigate. Dhar gingerly turned his head and looked at his shoulder. Dark blood oozed from a gaping wound, staining his T-shirt and arm. Only a flesh wound, but deep and stung in waves of agony. His whole body twitched involuntarily and he bit his lower lip at the pain shooting through his back. Hoping it was only another flesh wound, he stepped past the corpse, turned and faced the hatch.

"Command deck," he rasped, the effort making him wince.

In the confined space the stink of burned flesh, cloth and congealed blood made him clamp his mouth. He did not intend to kill the man, but there hadn't been time for anything else. Still strong with the power, the god did not permit him to dwell on regrets. When the hatch opened, he stood ready, arms leveled.

He swept the deck with a single glance: ship status displayed in the main plate, repeater stations, sloping consoles with their arrays of glowing contact pads, and the transparent nav bubble. It also took an instant to register the three watchstanders sitting on couches in front of him. A wiry Askaran in the right seat swiveled at the sound of the hatch opening and his mouth sagged.

"What…"

Dhar immediately loosed the lightnings. The figure in the central command seat must have sensed something, for he flung himself at the deck an instant before the lightnings lashed the couch. For the other two, their luck ran out. The wiry Askaran clutched at the burn on his chest, gurgled and slumped against the seat. The figure on the left screamed, doubled over, crashed against the console and landed on the deck with a dull thump. Shadows danced where the lightnings played. Silence returned, broken by computer inter-deck comms and small background sounds of a ship underway.

A needler appeared behind the central seat and let off several wild shots. Dhar responded with a single crack of blue light. The figure holding the weapon gave a startled yelp as the twisted remains of the needler clattered along the deck.

Right arm stiff, Dhar waited. Then, "Get up," he commanded.

"Don't kill me. I'm unarmed," a familiar bass voice answered.

"Stand up. I won't kill you," Dhar said.

The tall Askaran pilot slowly rose, massaging his right hand. He glanced at the two bodies on either side of him and gave a slow smile.

"A Discipline adept. Something told me not to get involved in this."

"You should have listened to your own advice," Dhar murmured and sent a single bolt at him. The pilot staggered, looking surprised, then agony contorted his face before he crumpled to the deck. Dhar kept his promise. He did not kill him or the two watchstanders, but when they woke in two or three hours, they would probably wish for oblivion. Shaking off Death's touch was exquisite agony of pins and needles that consumed the entire body as feeling returned.

"Computer, key voice access to all command functions. Disregard crew vocal and manual inputs. Authorization: protocol one, zero, zero, niner, terminal. Enable."

"Authorization accepted. Voice activation enabled. Confirm."

"Continue. Issue an abandon ship warning. When crew have boarded survival blisters, lock access hatches and disable purge sequence."

"Acknowledged."

The alarm siren wailed immediately, which made Dhar jump, and the nav bubble turned a pulsing amber. Behind him a hatch snapped into the bulkhead with a sharp clang.

"Abandon ship! This is not a drill," the computer blared. "Everyone to their assigned survival blister."

What he did was only possible on registered commercial cargo carriers and liners. On most raider ships, computer systems were usually customized and did not have such overrides. After all, no raider pilot would entrust his life to a subordinate who could effectively take over the ship.

"All quarters evacuated," the computer announced. "Survival blister purge sequence disabled. Abandon ship alert canceled."

"Command deck! We cannot eject!" a frantic voice announced. "Are we still in transit? Don't leave us trapped!"

"Computer, cut off comms to survival blisters."

"Acknowledged."

"For the love of—"

That took care of the crew very nicely. Although the blister's automatic ejection sequence was disabled, it would not stop someone from launching manually. It could be done, but Dhar did not give much for the occupant's chances, especially if they did it while the ship was still in transit. Well, if someone felt desperate or foolish enough to go for it, he wouldn't be mourning. Feeling himself coming down off a high, he walked to the central command couch, sat down and sighed. Giving the pilot a fleeting glance, he stretched his legs and leaned back, flinching as his raw back touched the seat. A tingle raced down his spine and his legs twitched.

"Computer, file a security alert with Askaran SC&C and change course for Kronas Field. Half standard boost. State flight time."

"Acknowledged. Flight time is two hours and eleven minutes under current parameters."

"Open a secure channel, personal for Kandu Hall, Diplomatic Branch, Askaran."

"Connecting."

The main display plate cleared and Hall stared in surprise. "Agent Dharaklin! Where in the world…" He saw the blood and tensed, suddenly serious. "You're hurt!"

"Not badly, Ser Resident. I was kidnapped while taking in sights along the beach. A foolish breach of security on my part, which my brother will no doubt never let me live down. They took me to a carrier parked at Trans National's facility."

"Rakliva!" Hall spat and pursed his mouth. "Yes. Pursuing his vendetta."

"It seems likely. We'll get confirmation from the pilot once I interrogate him. I have the ship secured and heading for Kronas Field."

"I'll not ask how you managed that, but I can imagine. The crew?"

"Locked in survival blisters."

"And enjoying every minute of it, I'm sure," Hall declared with relish. "Agent Terr will be relieved to hear that you're safe. When he sensed you were hurt, he wanted to take Karach apart."

Dhar could clearly picture his brother worried on his behalf, but still composed, doing everything possible to find him—and cursing him at the same time.

"I would appreciate if you could let him know I am well."

"Yes. I'll do that. A suggestion, if I may. Don't land. Take a holding orbit. We don't want to alert Rakliva if he's behind this."

Dhar winced at having missed an easy one. "Of course. I should have thought if it myself."

"Don't worry about it," Hall said comfortably. "I'll have an M-2 waiting for you."

"Thank you, Ser Resident. I expect to be in orbit in two hours," Dhar said and broke contact.

Suddenly cold, he hugged himself and felt his back tear. Shoulder throbbing, he pushed himself up and glanced at the couch. His entire left side covered with blood, an awful lot of it. He gave a short sigh and shook his head. His legs tingled and he rubbed his thighs. Four quick strides took him to the cable-tube hatch. He touched the access pad and the hatch slid away. Snorting at the stench coming off the body on the floor, he bent down and dragged the crewman out. The messy business done, he got in and faced the hatch.

"Medical."

Moments later the hatch opened. He stepped out, looked right and crossed the four-odd katalans down the corridor toward a characteristically marked blue hatchway. It slid out of his way as he approached; there could be situations where someone might not be able to reach an access pad. He quickly glanced about the examining room: a bunk covered with a green sheet, diagnostic sensors mounted in the bulkheads and a set of four wide drawers beside the medic's desk.

He stepped to the desk and jerked open the top drawer, grimacing at the stab of pain along his back. Beneath dressing tape and rolls of gauze lay rows of orange, brown and red vials: genotherapy sequence starters and tailored nanobods. He picked a general-purpose orange vial and pressed the striped end against his left shoulder. The nanobods would help fight infection while the sequencers accelerated tissue regeneration. He fancied he could feel the things streaming through his body, but it was only his imagination. Nonetheless, he did feel better—psychosomatic reaction probably. Many times the mind itself was the best healer.

When he returned to the command deck, he checked the status displays out of ingrained habit. The computer would warn him of any problem, but relying on automatics did not always guarantee safety. The engineering panel showed phase alignment approaching the brown tolerance zone and he shook his head. The engineer needed to have his butt kicked. Before he sat down, he glanced at the three bodies. They were still out.

He sprawled onto the center couch and closed his eyes. The ship whispered to him in the silence of his mind. No need to fret or plan. Sankri and the Resident would have everything in hand. Hunger gnawed at his belly, but he did not want to stir from his comfortable position merely to find the galley. His body craved rest more than food.

Little blue lightnings played across his arms as he dozed.

Some small noise disturbed the ambient background and his eyes snapped open. Everything looked the same. The pilot at his feet stirred and groaned. Dhar watched as life returned to the Askaran. Less than two hours, but the native was powerful and more easily able to shrug off the neural shock. It still took him some five minutes before he could sit up.

Propped against the console housing, the pilot flexed the fingers of both hands and looked speculatively at Dhar.

"Some trick. I wish I could have missed it."

"Who was it?" Dhar demanded.

The pilot smiled, not bothering with denials. "Not much point in trying to keep it a secret now, is it? Madur Rakliva, Trans National—"

"I know who he is."

"Yeah, I figured." He glanced at his two watchstanders. "What now?"

"For you? More unpleasantness, I'm afraid."

The pilot frowned, noticed the small lightnings crawling over Dhar's arms and grimaced. "Ah, pits!" he managed to say before the bolt struck him. He grunted heavily, face contorted, and toppled over.

Dhar hated to do it to him again, but was not too overwhelmed with remorse. Call it payback for his wounds. The carrier would be dropping normal soon and he would have his hands full with the M-2. He did not want the pilot underfoot attempting some beginner's stunt.

"SC&C insertion in four minutes," the computer announced suddenly. "Ship within acceptable flight parameters. Surface Command and Control requests orbital injection."

"Approved," Dhar said.

"Askaran carrier *Tara*," the comms blared as the main plate cleared. "This is SSF M-2 *Draga*. Do you copy?"

Dhar looked at the young Karkan Second Scout. "Acknowledged, *Draga*."

"Sir, I will dock with you when you achieve orbit. What is your status?"

"Ship's crew secured. Command watch disabled."

"Noted, *Tara*. We'll see you soon."

"Approaching SC&C insertion point. Ready to transition," the computer said.

"Very well. Drop normal."

"Transiting." The distortion field precursor changed polarity and began to collapse. Nav screen polarizing, the carrier exited into normal space and fell below lightspeed.

"SC&C link enabled."

The nav plot cleared and stars wheeled as SC&C took command and swung the carrier into Askaran's approach pattern. Under full secondary boost it took *Tara* nine minutes to reach the planet. The blue-white world grew quickly in the nav bubble and the ship slowed. When it came to rest, Askaran hung huge above it, its polar icecap glaring under Tauri II's light.

"*Tara*, this is SSF *Draga*. Docking with you in three minutes."

"Acknowledged, *Draga*," Dhar said and let out a long exhale. He may have ruined his dinner engagement with Sankri, but perhaps he could make it up to his brother in some way. After a moment, he looked down at his hands. The glow faded and took Death with it. He missed the feeling of being immortal, but took comfort knowing he would be one with the god again.

He watched the M-2 approach and dock, the little ship a gnat against the carrier's sheer side. It seemed like an eternity before he heard the cable-tube open. Slowly, he stood up. The young Karkan Second Scout glanced curiously around the deck, taking in the slumped bodies. His nose wrinkled at the lingering smell of burned cloth and fried flesh coming off the crumpled crewman beside the cable-tube hatch. The wound in the crewman's chest looked far too large for a needler burst and he wondered how it was done. With a flick of his left wrist, he motioned to the two marines standing behind him. They came out, positioned themselves on either side of the hatch and stood to, phase rifles held at port arms. The Karkan nodded and walked to Dhar.

"Second Scout Sallar, sir, commanding *Draga*."

"Glad to see you here…" Dhar's voice trailed off when another figure emerged out of the tube. Wearing a wistful smile, Sankri moved toward him, but the smile faded and his gray eyes clouded when he saw the blood.

"Nightwings…"

"It's all right, my brother. It will heal," Dhar rumbled softly, feeling a flush of relief sweep through him. He glanced at Sallar. "Can we have a moment, please?"

Sallar's eyes were unreadable. "Certainly, sir." He turned to the two marines and hooked a thumb over his shoulder. "Get the bodies."

The marines immediately stacked their rifles inside the cable-tube and hurried toward the command couches. It took them seconds to drag the still forms into the tube. Sallar himself hauled away the shot crewman. With the business done, he stood too.

"Sir, about the crew trapped in the survival blisters…"

Dhar lifted his hand in understanding. "Computer, transfer voice command to Second Scout Sallar."

"Acknowledged."

"They are all yours, sir."

Sallar nodded and the cable-tube hatch closed.

Alone on the silent command deck, Terr placed his palm against his brother's chest and Dhar returned the gesture. For the moment, they had no need to say anything that hadn't been said before. Were they not one in spirit? Enough simply to be together.

"When I sensed you hurt…" Terr whispered after a while, then swallowed, the lump going down hard.

"A costly indulgence, my brother, and I regret the worry it caused you," Dhar said gruffly. What could he say to make up for Sankri's pain?

"You're safe, that's all that matters," Terr said, then raised a warning finger and glared. "But no more strolls along the beach! Got that?"

Dhar smiled in contrition. "Got it."

Terr patted his brother's arm. "I know. We'll talk about it later. Right now, let's get your wounds treated. Then we'll deal with our friend Rakliva."

* * *

Sipping his special blend of arka root tea, Ed-Kani Takao savored the mild tang and the delicate citrus bouquet, his favorite. Outside, bright sunshine bathed Captal from a clear morning sky, a marked change from a recent spell of overcast and gloomy days. Apart from a pleasant day, there was little else to recommend it.

Ripples caused by the Orieli contact had reverberated throughout the Serrll Combine like a tidal surge without any sign of diminishing. The Committee's scare campaign had backfired spectacularly. Instead of getting people to nod in agreement that the Orieli represented a threat to be guarded against, Sargon and the Palean Union had come out looking like scaremongers, with Captal and the Scout Fleet holding the protective high ground. He winced as he recalled some of the political sketches on news and commentary channels. It was Sofam, of course, running a counter-campaign, and very effectively too. The way they spun it, the Orieli were powerful friends to be cultivated and brought into the community of worlds. Talk of isolationism and expanding the Fleet was paranoia at best and simple political opportunism at worst. It certainly hit a responsive chord with the populace at large.

Where it counted, inside Sargon and the Palean Union, reaction was more favorable. That had been worth a degree of embarrassment elsewhere, Ed-Kani thought. A transitory discomfort anyway. The public would have some new Captal antic to guffaw over by tomorrow.

What really soured his tea were leaks out of Illeran's approval committee favoring the Palean bid for the new Fleet base. It looked like he would be losing out on the Rolan front. Sofam's public facade notwithstanding, the Revisionist coalition masked prudent concern over a potential future Orieli threat, hiding it behind a background of emerging militancy by radical Alikan Union Party cells. Wearing his Executive Director persona, he admitted the posture was reasonable and warranted, regardless how injurious to his personal aspirations or the Sargon/Palean merger.

He allowed himself a soft hiss of frustration. On some days it was easier to simply stay in bed.

He stared vacantly at the Comsec display—another funding request. This one from an AUP cell on Askaran, wherever the pits that was. Routine, and Ti Inai had already approved the transaction. Sometimes he wondered why Committee members were plagued with such trivia. Wasn't the Finance Sub-Committee supposed to handle such things, he mused petulantly. He knew why Ti Inai flagged the request to every member. The transaction had triggered the hundred million review and oversight limit. If the thing was already approved, why did he have to see it? It won't be Sofam who would scuttle Sargon's merger ambitions, he reflected morosely. It will be the Committee's own bureaucratic procedures!

Moody, he took another sip of tea. The funding request did not get him down, merely an irritating diversion. He summed up his problem in one word—Laraiana. The woman simply never let up. Did he investigate that horrible First Scout? When would he act against him? Did Enllss cover up for his nephew? Why didn't Sill-Anais censure Anabb Karr? If there were a neat way of injecting her with waste disposal nanobods without getting caught, he would have considered it. He would be seeing the woman at any moment. Hiss.

In reality, he could do very little for her. He read her protest messages to the BCPA and understood why Anabb brushed her off. As far as he could see, Agent Terr's decision to deny her the GS-4 shuttle was correct and necessary. His mission to destroy the C-32 scoutship clearly had priority, regardless of any immediate inconvenience to her. And the Orieli thing? Ed-Kani suspected he knew the reason why Terr had not included her in the first contact. Her imperious manner might have offended the aliens and Terr understandably didn't want to take that risk. The deeper he delved into the entire sordid episode the more he came to appreciate Terr's firm decisiveness in the handling of his niece.

But what do I tell her?

His thoughts wandered back to the Askaran claim. Even

though Ti Inai approved funding, he was mildly intrigued by the transaction. Although nominally independent, Global Transport appeared to be a vital source of revenue for the Askaran AUP chapter. Moreover, having two major clearing-houses where raiders can sell their cargo without interference from local authorities or the Fleet would be a substantial commercial and political asset. Still curious, he briefly scanned data on the Karach Salvage and Disposal partners: a Kaplan and a Wanderer. Nothing remarkable there. A nagging memory popped to the surface. Hadn't Laraiana said Terr was a Kaplan with a Wanderer colleague? Probably simple coincidence and he was jumping at shadows.

The comms alert beeped and he jerked. He reached across the desk and touched a pad. "What is it, Keana?"

"Scholar Laraiana to see you."

Ed-Kani sighed. Might as well deal with his niece's wrath now and be done with it. "Show her in, will you?"

The translucent panels slid away and Laraiana marched in, the only way he could describe it. She wore an elegant one-piece dark purple outfit with red stripes around cuffs, throat, and waist. It highlighted her curvy figure. If it were not for her stern expression, she would be quite attractive. Given her temperament, what man with any backbone would willingly subordinate himself to her?

"Ah, precious. Come on in," he gushed and waved at the Wall. "Pardon me. Tidying up loose ends."

She hadn't looked forward to this meeting, dreading another platitude-filled brush-off. Her uncle had procrastinated, refusing to treat her complaint seriously. Merely another male protecting one of their own. When she saw the image in the Wall, she immediately brightened. Perhaps she was a tad hasty in her judgment.

"I'm glad to see, Uncle, that you haven't shelved my problem," she breathed in appreciation. "I wouldn't have blamed you if you did, being so busy and all. Can I ask what you're planning to do with him?"

Feeling acutely uncomfortable, Ed-Kani actually squirmed. "Well, there isn't…" Laraiana did not look at him, but at the Wall. A hot flush raced through his body as he stared transfixed at the image, the awful realization finally dawning on him. She was looking at Agent Terrllss-rr!

Holy pits!

The Karach Salvage and Disposal owners were Diplomatic Branch operatives. Everything fitted! The entire merger deal with Global Transport nothing more than an intelligence operation against the Askaran Alikan Union Party chapter. Perhaps, or it could simply be a mole exercise to uncover the extent of Global's raider network. He didn't believe it. Oh, rounding up raiders would be a welcome bonus, but Anabb and the Diplomatic Branch were after bigger game. He was certain of it. Bonus or not, exposing Global would badly hurt the Askaran cell's ability to function, and by extension, degrade its capacity to support the merger cause, which was all that mattered. He had to warn them and it might be too late already.

But why pick on Askaran and Global Transport? Granted, Askaran was an Alikan Union Party stronghold, but so were lots of other systems. Could it be Global and penetration of its raider network after all? Staring at the image in the Wall, he thought he had it. Kai Tanard used raiders in prosecuting Pizgor and young Terr had infiltrated his network. One of the raiders must have been Global's, and somehow, Terr found out. It didn't take a leap of genius to work out the rest. Anabb saw it as a perfect opportunity to pursue two objectives: go after raiders and link Askaran's AUP cell to the Committee. Destroy the Committee and you destroy the Sargon/Palean merger. And how close he came to doing it!

Amazing how life can pivot on a seemingly random moment in time.

"I knew you wouldn't let me down," Laraiana burst out and Ed-Kani shifted, uncomfortable at the undeserved praise. He recovered quickly and smiled, not minding reaping the unintended credit.

"We're blood, my dear. Family. As for your problem, I have a very special solution in mind. Something that will remove him from your sight permanently."

She sat up, alarmed. If her uncle was suggesting, she could not quite phrase it, but the notion unsettled her. She only wanted Terr disgraced, humiliated, not...

"Uncle!"

"What?" he asked innocently, enjoying her moment of discomfort.

"For a while there..." She gave a small smile. "I thought you planned to, well, get rid of him."

"Nonsense! I'm shocked you would even think of such a thing, precious. You leave Agent Terr in my hands, okay?"

"As you say," Laraiana said uncertainly, still not sure what he intended. Did she want to know? Looking at the icy glitter in his eyes, she suddenly did not know him. Could she really know this man who sat at the center of Serrll power and participated in shaping the fabric of its society? Perhaps it was better not to know, better to remember a congenial relative she could call on for help.

Ed-Kani actually laughed, pleased at the turn of events. "You should see yourself. White as a sheet."

She stiffened at this impertinence and was about to lash out when she remembered who he was. It simply wouldn't do. Besides, she might need his services again. She pulled down her coverall and gave an uncertain smile.

"When you said...Never mind. I was on my way to the BCPA when I thought I'd stop by and have a quick catchup."

"I am very pleased that you did," he said warmly, even though it wasn't for the reason she thought. "Care to have lunch? It's turned out to be a great day after all."

"My meetings will keep me occupied for a while, but—"

"Of course. Leave a message with Keana if you can make

it."

"Thanks. I'll do that," she said slowly, still unclear at what just happened. At least she would have her revenge and that *did* make it a great day.

Ed-Kani gazed thoughtfully at his niece. He understood what her father must have gone through when Lemos fell. A proud man, bending his knee to no one, having to witness Sargon's humiliation by Sofam must have been a galling pill to swallow indeed. He did not intend to reveal his involvement in the Provisional Committee to her. That would be flaunting security in the extreme, but perhaps he could give her a private message the old Pro-Consul, versed in the Code, would understand and take a measure of comfort from.

"I want to talk to you about your father, Laraiana. To explain some things, about what happened at Lemos. By the way, how is he?"

"Much more his normal self, thanks, but still bitter."

"Yes…understandable. Call me."

She nodded and got up. "I appreciate your help with Agent Terr, Uncle. I mean it. I'll let you know about lunch," she said quickly and walked out.

When the panels clicked shut, Ed-Kani shook his head. Poor Laraiana, so lost when it came to something simple as an expression of gratitude. He thrust her aside and reached for the cup. The tea had gone cool, but he didn't mind.

"Comsec. Issue the following to the Askaran AUP chapter, personal for the president. Karach Salvage and Disposal owners identified as Diplomatic Branch operatives. Terminate with extreme prejudice."

"Message routed," the computer announced. It would peel off and replace the message header, routing it through layers of comms nodes, making it impossible to trace.

"Append the following agenda item for discussion by the members at the next meeting. No AUP cell is to engage in a commercial venture without obtaining security clearance of prospective partners from the Provisional Committee."

"Item noted and routed to all members."

"Oh, one more thing. Advise the Finance Sub-Committee to revoke authorization for request FR-Askaran-0032 and append to agenda."

"Noted."

The business finished, he sat back, locked his fingers behind his head and swung the seat to face the window screen. It really turned out to be a lovely day.

* * *

"What do you think?" Segal asked, lounging back in his formchair, studying the security report displayed in the Wall. Sunshine streamed through the large corner window, softening the air and made the atmosphere congenial. Outside, still in shadow, wispy strands of cloud hung halfway up the craggy buttresses behind the industrial complex. On the landing apron, cranes and loaders clustered around *Paun's* open holds.

Sitting in front of Segal's desk, legs stretched out comfortably, Pulman shrugged. "Nothing much I *can* say. Despite your paranoid tendencies, our two partners check out."

"Looks like it," Segal mused and pulled at his chin. He shouldn't complain. Software problems with the warehouse systems were sorted out and business returned to its normal routine, but not for the software company responsible for this mess. The lawsuit filed by Global for compensatory damages should see the outfit hung up on the wall and quartered. Segal did not tolerate incompetence or willful negligence. "I still maintain that there is something phony about them. Kerill comes across far too smooth for my liking."

"Your problem is that you cannot stand the thought of someone able to outmaneuver you."

"True, but I have the comforting consolation knowing that very shortly, we'll have a reckoning with our slick partner."

"You have a message," the housekeeping computer announced. "Do you wish to view message?"

"Accept," Pulman said and turned to the Wall.

"Hi, Warat…Tan! The police arrested Madur," Leera gushed when the image cleared. "I came to the office and saw them taking him away. Police vans everywhere. It was horrible!"

"Arrested? For what?" Segal demanded and sat up, suspecting the worst.

"Conspiracy to murder. Oh, Tan!"

Segal looked disgusted. After he told Rakliva to leave it alone the fool went ahead anyway. "Don't tell me. It was Kerill-aa?"

"No, his partner Randakla."

"Idiot! Do you know what happened?"

"Bits and pieces only. The police wouldn't let me talk to him. From what I gather, Madur had Randakla kidnapped and something went wrong."

Something went wrong, all right, and it happened when Rakliva was born. "Leave it with me, honey. I'll take care of it."

"That's just it, Tan. I don't want you taking care of it. Not anymore. He finally overreached himself and I'm tired of having you sweep up after him. This time, he's getting no more than he deserves."

"Are you sure about this?" The determined look on his wife's face told him what he needed to know.

"Brother or not, I've been sure for a while. I am more worried what this might do to you."

"Me? You mean, am I mixed up in this?"

Leera's mouth lifted in a smile. "You're not exactly in love with your new partners."

Segal chuckled, admiring her forthrightness. "That's true, but I had nothing to do with Rakliva's stunt."

"Tan—"

"You have a message," the housekeeping computer interrupted. "Do you wish to view message?"

"Excuse me, Leera...Accept message." The Wall image split in two and he stared at Sarek Laral's bony face.

"Tan...Warat! You must get out of there, now!"

"What's the panic, Sarek?" Pulman was surprised to see Sarek so agitated. It hardly seemed in character.

"I received a security advisory from the Committee. Kerill and Randakla are Diplomatic Branch operatives! We've been the subject of an intelligence penetration!"

Segal slammed his palm against the desk. "I knew it! Too smooth by far."

"And you fools walked right into it!"

"Just a damn minute, Sarek! Your own security section had them vetted and I've got their report in front of me saying so."

"Enough!" Pulman snarled. "Arguing won't get us anywhere. What tipped them off?"

Sarek glared at Segal, then tugged down the front of his jacket. "They didn't say."

"It's not important anyway," Pulman added harshly. "If this is a Diplomatic Branch operation, Kandu Hall must have known from the beginning. Well, this is one cleanup, I'll enjoy doing personally. Thanks for the warning."

"You don't have time for settling personal scores, Warat. I'll take care of your partners. You two better pack and disappear before the whole thing blows up in your face. I alerted *Trava* and she'll be lifting momentarily."

Pulman ground his teeth. "When you take care of them, make sure that it's terminal."

"It'll be terminal, all right."

"As for *Trava*, we'll be waiting for her off Markesh, as arranged."

"And your end run?"

"Stavros, but I want *Paun* and *Pilla* to test the warmth of our reception first. I'll send them out ahead of me."

"Wise. I'll let her know. Good luck," Sarek said and cut contact.

"We'll need it," Segal murmured and turned to Leera. "Get Manir and come here immediately. Don't linger. Just get your butts moving."

"Tan! This is awful," Leera breathed, suddenly pale. "Are we really in danger?"

"Not yet, but that's why we've got to make the most of whatever time we have left."

"I don't understand what's going on. Global Transport hasn't broken any laws. Has it?"

"What do you think? We're trading with raiders and operating two ships of our own. It looks like Captal has finally gotten weary of it and took steps."

"But Minister Tullan—"

"Has looked the other way. I'd imagine that pretty soon, he and some of his colleagues will also wish they were someplace else, and that's where we need to be. We don't have time to discuss this now, Leera. Get moving, okay?"

She bit her lower lip and frowned. "We just redecorated the apartment!" she lamented and cut contact. Segal sighed and shook his head.

"I'm saving her skin and she's worried about the blasted apartment!"

Pulman's mouth twitched. "It's shock, Tan. A double shock really and she's trying to adjust." He leaned across the desk and tapped in a comms code.

The Wall cleared and a youngish Askaran straightened when he saw who it was. "Ser Pulman. What can I do for you?"

"Make preparations to lift, Varda. I'll be boarding within the hour and *Paun* better be ready to go."

"But I'm still unloading!"

"If you don't do as I order, you'll be doing your unloading on Cantor! Do I make myself clear?"

"What's going on?"

"I'll explain later." Pulman switched off and glared at the Wall. "Fool!" He tapped in another combination. This time, he faced a craggy, wizened Palean. "Ir Ran, get *Pilla* off the ground immediately and make for Stavros."

"Why the rush, friend Pulman? I'm heading for Otilando tomorrow for drive maintenance."

"Forget that! Our Karach Salvage partners? It turns out they're Diplomatic Branch agents. They don't know we're on to them and you want to be out of here before this goes into a meltdown."

"Ah! And we had such a nice thing going here. How much time do I have?"

"Hard to say, but I wouldn't linger. When you transition, contact the Stavros AUP chapter and issue a Baker niner. They'll know what to do."

"Understood, and thanks for the heads-up, Warat." The Palean pilot nodded and cut contact.

Pulman sighed and ran a hand through his hair. "This hasn't come entirely as a surprise, but I didn't expect it to happen so soon."

Segal cocked his head. "Stavros, eh? Makes sense. With support facilities and political protection, we should be able to resume operations with minimum disruption. You know, clearing out in *Paun* might not be such a hot idea. If Kandu Hall has her ident dump, we could be looking at the operating end of an M-3 projector before we clear the system."

"If Hall has *Paun's* ident, he'll have *Trava's* as well, but we won't be staying aboard her for long."

"Why bother with *Trava* at all? We could make Stavros before anyone gets excited. It's a secure Alikan Union Party stronghold."

"Askaran was supposed to be secure, remember?" Pulman reminded him bleakly. "But we're not going to Stavros. I don't intend to give Sarek a perfect opportunity to cut off a loose end."

"Not very trusting of your AUP colleague, are you?"

"Surprised?"

"Not at all. I approve. If we're not going to Stavros, where *are* we going?"

"Ball."

"Ball? Mmm. Not a bad choice and not unlike Askaran." Segal studied his partner. "You had this worked out all along, haven't you?"

"All along."

Segal took a deep breath. "I suppose it's necessary, but a permanent relocation?"

"It's either that or Cantor," Pulman reminded him and slapped his thighs. "Kerill and Randakla, I've got to hand it to them. They certainly played us beautifully. Bastards."

"Whatever Sarek has in mind, I hope he makes them suffer."

Dismayed at the turn of events, Pulman nevertheless admired Kerill's business plan, designed to commit Global to a course of action he and Segal had taken. Kerill himself told them why: entry into the Alikan Union Party chapter, and by extension, a pipeline to the Provisional Committee—a politically motivated penetration. Segal had it right from the start. Kerill was smooth, too smooth to have planned the thing. He couldn't possibly have had the necessary experience and knowledge for someone so young. Kerill might not have done the planning, but Pulman admitted to a grudging respect for its execution. Under different circumstances, what a partnership they could have had!

Segal stood and reached for the polished metal panel set into the wall beside the desk. He pressed his palm against the bottom right corner and the panel silently slid aside. He reached in, took out a little leather briefcase and held it to Pulman. If his partner harbored any intention of betraying him, this was a perfect opportunity to do it. Pulman could take off in *Paun*, leaving Segal to extricate himself out of a hopeless situation. However, he trusted Pulman implicitly. Besides, if Pulman did flee, Segal would catch up with him no matter how long it took or where he hid.

"You better get aboard *Paun*. I'll wash the computer and get rid of some stuff. I'll be with you as soon as Leera gets here."

Pulman stared at the case, never expecting to use it. It held data cubes, spare IDs, records of investment accounts and other odd documents, everything necessary for a fresh start. He stood, took the case and walked to the door. When it opened, he paused and turned. "It's not the end of everything, Tan."

Segal's mouth twitched. "It's only that I don't like to lose, and Kerill cleaned us out of one hundred million Serrlls!"

Pulman grinned. "But it's Sarek's money, not ours."

Segal lifted an eyebrow, some of his good humor restored. "So it is, and he's stuck with it!"

* * *

Power plant whining, the combie surged into a russet sky smeared with long streamers of painted clouds, banked and headed west. In the distance, Karach glittered beneath a setting sun. Terr punched in the nav coordinates and relaxed. Below them the brightly lit Hydra Industrial City complex rapidly fell away. Ahead of them stretched rolling fields of grain, checkered grassy paddocks and patches of forest. He glanced at his brother and beamed.

"Tonight, we'll be dining high!" They'd had a busy day working with Global's warehouse boss to standardize cargo handling procedures and ways to remove duplication, and Terr looked forward to unwinding a little. "This time, you won't wriggle out by having somebody snatch you," he warned and wagged a finger.

"You cannot exactly blame me for that one," Dhar protested in an aggrieved tone.

"Oh? Well, pardon me. Who took a stroll along the beach and got himself all shot up? Although, I've had worse scratches scraping against a peelath. Still, I won't spoil things by dredging up past bloopers."

"Big of you," Dhar growled. He did not mind the mild ribbing from his brother. Sankri could have made his life much more miserable. Getting himself nabbed was one thing, but his back wound could have turned out drastically worse. At the hospital, they told him if he hadn't injected himself with those nanobods, he could have ended up paralyzed. The damage was repairable, but extricating himself off the carrier could have turned out more difficult. As it was, the needler shot had grazed his spine and penetrated a vertebrae, missing the nerve column by a fraction of a cetalan.

"Rakliva should have quit when still ahead," Terr added, pleased at the turn of events.

"It wasn't a bad plan actually. The only thing wrong, it didn't work."

"The only thing wrong with it, he ran into you. Had it worked, I doubt Segal or Pulman would have grieved too much."

"Bet on it. When they get around to it, and they will, I am certain their approach will be somewhat more sophisticated."

The proximity alarm beeped and they exchanged glances. Yellow beams flashed past the combie and Terr's hair stood on end from the near-field effect. Before he could react, something struck the combie's rear right side and it skidded, shuddering violently. The restraining field snapped on as the combie sagged and nosed down, trailing dirty brown smoke. Another beam slashed past them leaving a katalan-long gash along the canopy's right side. Air hissed through the rip as the bubble struggled to seal itself. Small blue sparks slid along exposed surfaces, crackling eerily as they jumped over bare skin in a torment of a thousand insect bytes.

Terr grunted when the restraining field released and he jabbed at the controls. The blue sparks faded, but his hands and face smarted and he longed to give himself a good rub. The combie righted itself, but they were still going down, heading toward a row of tall trees marking a field boundary. He didn't relish the prospect of landing against one.

"Looks like a Personnel Carrier," Dhar said urgently, craning his neck to look behind them. "It's just pacing us."

Waiting for the combie to crash and finish the job for them, Terr figured. Well, it won't be that easy. Although possible, he doubted it was Pulman and Segal after them. They would have waited for the merger to settle down first. Apart from the Fleet, who would have the pull to commandeer a PC or something like it?

"Big mistake," Terr grated. The assailants held every tactical advantage and were fools for not finishing the job. Amateurs, but he took his breaks as they came.

"I fear our cover might be blown, Sankri," Dhar added, still looking at the dark vehicle holding position behind them.

"I was thinking the same thing." Terr watched the row of trees reach for them. The self-repair mechanism closed some of the rip in the bubble, but air still whistled through the gash. "Hold on, we're going to hit!" Not trusting the automatics, he punched a large green pad and the restraining field held him fast.

The combie started to sag right again and they were among the trees. It crashed through high branches in a shower of shredded leaves and snapping twigs. It turned on its side and plowed into tall grass, slamming down hard, sending squawking bird life climbing into the sky around them. The restraining field let go and Dhar was thrown against his brother, jamming him against the bubble. Terr cried out as sharp pain shot through his right arm. Momentarily dazed, Dhar pulled away, then touched the emergency bubble release, his right arm throbbing. The holding clips retracted with a snap and he pushed open the bubble. The right side of the combie bent and crumpled, but the restraining field had held long enough to protect them. He immediately turned to his brother.

323

"You okay?"

Terr massaged his arm, and then gingerly touched the side of his head. His hand came away sticky with blood. "A cut. You?"

"The landing jarred my back, but I'm okay. Your arm?"

"In one piece, I think."

Dhar heaved himself up. "Our friends are coming in," he warned, looking at the approaching PC.

"To make sure, eh?" Terr pushed the bubble fully open and stood. "Not this time." Face grim, he turned to see the PC skim the top of the trees. It slowed and stopped in a hover. He felt a surge of heat run through his body as Death unleashed its power. Images of rolling dunes and flowing sands, still beneath an amber sky, flickered before him as little blue lightnings crawled across his arms. A searing shaft of yellow fire slashed at the combie, missing them by tetalans and the air crackled, smelling of ozone. Terr raised his right arm and pointed.

"My turn."

The lightning bolt lanced at the PC, spearing it like a trapped insect. A clap of thunder vented its rage. The PC staggered, reared up, paused and slowly fell, stern down. Terr grabbed Dhar's arm and they threw themselves out of the combie into the grass. A moment later the ground jumped as the PC struck. A bright flash seared the air, followed by a cracking explosion. The overpressure wave squeezed Terr's chest and he winced as stabbing fire pierced his ears. Wreckage fell around them and something smashed against his right thigh. He felt the bone go and screamed. Dhar echoed his cry. It simply wasn't his day.

When the echoes faded and the deadly rain stopped, Dhar knelt beside his brother and heaved aside a jagged plate pinning Terr's leg.

"Lie still. You're hurt."

"Tell me about it." Terr rolled over and gasped as pain shot through his thigh. He propped himself up with his right arm and swore as it folded under him and he fell back. Broken, and he didn't even notice. He did notice the ringing and the sharp throbbing in his ears. Definitely not his best day.

Rit!

Overhead, the light faded fast. Tendrils of black, acrid smoke snaked into the air. The grass smelled sweet and he took a deep breath. After a moment, he reached for Dhar's wrist and squeezed.

"I think the blast ruptured my eardrums."

"Mine too."

"The leg—"

"Fractured or crushed, but there isn't much bleeding."

"It could be worse," Terr said wearily. "Can you see the PC?"

Dhar glanced behind him. "Nothing much left except frames and scattered plating, a couple of small fires. The power cell must have cooked off."

"Good. Which means those in it also got cooked." Terr lay back and groaned. "Another dinner ruined."

"Our combie looks worse for wear." A large piece of hull plating had flattened the forward section. Smoke still poured from the rear.

"It's only a rental," Terr grunted indifferently. "Its emergency beacon probably alerted SC&C and we're likely to be hip deep in local authorities soon. You better call Kandu Hall. It'll avoid having to explain all this."

Dhar patted Sankri's shoulder and rose, wincing at a jab through his back and sympathetic pain in his right leg. At this rate, both of them would have an extended hospital stay. He dragged out his little pocket communicator and ordered a secure connection. A second later Hall's holoview image appeared above his hand.

"Agent Dharaklin! To what do I owe—"

"Ser Resident, Terr and I were shot down a few moments ago by what appeared to be a PC. You can get the coordinates off my communicator. We took care of the PC, but my brother is seriously hurt and I fear we may be swamped by emergency services and local authorities before long."

"Yes. I understand completely," Hall said briskly. "Leave everything to me." He tilted his head, his mouth a tight line. "First you and now Agent Terr. You two get around, don't you?"

"As you say."

"Any idea who they were?"

"Not directly, but we suspect our cover might be blown."

"Probably the AUP chapter. I cannot see your competition owning something like a PC. Yes, a reasonable assumption. That could mean Pulman and Segal may have already flown."

"Literally," Dhar added and Hall nodded, looking glum.

"I'll check Kronas SC&C. If *Paun* or *Pilla* have indeed lifted, they could be anywhere by now. You can leave that one with me as well. Hang tight, Agent Dharaklin."

The image faded and Dhar pocketed the communicator.

"I heard most of that," Terr said, cradling his arm. "I hope he's wrong about Pulman and Segal. We've got some unfinished business to settle with those two."

"This development won't make Anabb very happy, my brother."

Terr merely shrugged. "I've got a busted arm and leg, and right now, I'm really worried that Anabb won't be happy. I wonder how we were burned?"

Dhar wondered the same thing, but it could be any number of things: a chance sighting, a startled moment of recognition, computer image mapping, anything. Regardless of how it was done, their mission was over. Global and Karach Salvage staff would be interrogated as a matter of routine, but he didn't expect any revelations there. They were only employees. Decision to allow the concerns to trade or be placed into receivership rested with the Central Revenue Office. Either way, raiders would no longer be welcomed on Askaran. Captal would see to that. The Alikan Union Party chapter would face some discomfort and embarrassment, but that too would blow over. The movement far too entrenched in the planet's social and political fabric to be easily destabilized. The government, on the other hand, is likely to find the next few days far less pleasant. He could not have cared less. The mission had failed and that's how Anabb would see it. Failure or not, it had been fun, mostly.

A flashing light caught his eye and he looked up. "We have visitors."

"They didn't waste much time," Terr muttered sourly, fighting down waves of pain.

"Probably from Hydra."

A medivan, its sides pulsing bright white, cleared the trees and quickly descended, lighting the surrounds. Behind it a much larger brown emergency services tender circled once, then settled. Two green-garbed medics, carrying bags, jumped out of the medivan. One glanced at the wreckage, then both hurried toward the combie.

"Are you injured?" one medic demanded from Dhar.

"A sprained back. My ears—"

"Into the van," the medic ordered briskly and knelt beside Terr. He took a scanner out of his bag and quickly passed it over Terr's body. Without saying anything, he produced a green vial out of his tunic and pressed it against Terr's right leg. He glanced at his assistant and jerked his head at the van. "Stretcher!"

Dhar glanced at his brother, but Sankri waved him off. "Go! Don't mind me."

Slowly walking toward the medivan, Dhar watched the emergency tender crew spraying the wreckage with white foam, smothering the fires.

Another vehicle cleared the trees, its sides rippling a light blue. The police van small, something like a communal. Bubble polarized, he could not see inside. It came down beside the tender and the bubble lifted. Two grim-looking individuals piled out, took in the scene with quick, jerky glances and marched toward him.

The senior officer stopped in front of Dhar and stood to. "Ser Randakla?"

Judging by the uniform insignia it was the Hydra station commander. Wary, Dhar slowly nodded. "That's right."

"Ser, I have orders to escort you and Ser Kerill-aa wherever you go."

"Thank you, Commander. Right now, I'd say the hospital."

"Very good, Ser. What happened here?"

"We were attacked," Dhar said without elaborating.

"And the attackers? What happened to them?"

"A piece of bad luck, Commander."

The policeman stared curiously at the Wanderer. "So I see." Clearly more than simple bad luck and he longed to question Randakla further, but he had his orders. With the Diplomatic Branch involved, this was now a planetary security matter and he didn't really fancy getting himself entangled at that level.

Dhar made his way to the medivan. A medic helped him in and pointed at the left bunk. Dhar grunted as he sat down, suddenly weary. The medic passed a scanner over his body and frowned.

"You're carrying a recent injury to your spine?"

"Severed ninth vertebrae," Dhar mumbled, suddenly very tired.

"Lie down," the medic ordered and opened a drawer beneath the bunk. Dhar did not protest and stretched out, giving a satisfied sigh as his head sank into the soft pillow. The medic pressed a vial against his left shoulder.

"This will start the repair process until we can give you proper care."

Dhar wanted to say something, but his eyes closed and darkness settled over him.

Chapter Twelve

A faint buzzing stole into Dhar's awareness, chasing away memories and half-formed images. The buzzing faded and reality shattered the dreams. His eyelids fluttered and he squeezed them shut against an almost painful inrush of bright light. When he did open them, he looked at a round, black face of a green-robed local. The medic lifted a glass with a drinking straw.

"Drink some of this."

Dhar took a small pull of the orange liquid, then a longer one as thirst overcame him. He immediately felt better. The medic took away the glass, glanced at the holoview monitor above the bed and nodded.

"Give yourself an hour and you're free to go."

It took a moment for the words to register. Dhar shook off the remaining cobwebs and heaved himself up against the head-rest without a protest from his back. His hearing seemed back to normal as well. On his right, Sankri still slept, or unconscious. The medic followed his glance.

"Ser Kerill-aa's wounds were more serious and he's still recovering. He'll be out for another nine or ten hours."

"Any complications?"

"Mostly simple tissue trauma, but his leg was badly crushed. I've got to go, but buzz if you need anything." The medic quickly scanned Terr's display and strode out.

The door panels to the suite hardly closed when they opened again and a pretty nurse wheeled in a plain metal trolley. She stopped beside the bed and beamed a standard smile.

"Breakfast, Ser Randakla," she announced briskly in a businesslike voice. "I imagine you must be hungry and you have a visitor if you feel up to it." She lifted the cover off a broad tray and Dhar's mouth watered at the sight and smell of food, distracting him from her trim form.

"Thank you. I am feeling hungry." He reached for the pitcher of red liquid and filled a glass. "Who's the visitor?" he asked and swallowed what turned out to be tart juice.

"He didn't say, Ser." She lifted the tray and clipped it to an arm beside the bed, then swung the arm across to bring the tray over Dhar's lap.

"Show him in."

"Very good, Ser," she said and pushed the trolley toward the door. Dhar looked admiringly at her tight slacks and neat figure and swallowed more juice. He definitely felt well. When his visitor walked in, he broke into a genuine smile.

"Ser Resident, I expected you'd be showing up."

Kandu Hall glanced at Terr, and then dragged over one of the formchairs that surrounded a small table tucked into a corner. He sat down and crossed his legs.

"Glad to see you up, Agent Dharaklin." Noting Dhar's startled expression, he chuckled and patted his right pocket. "Don't worry. Whatever monitoring they've got trained on us is neutralized. How is Agent Terr?" He reached for a spare glass on the tray. "May I?"

Dhar nodded. "The medic said another ten hours."

Hall poured himself some juice. "You two really need to stop getting yourselves banged up, but at least he's better off than the two in the van who attacked you." Hall took a sip and raised an eyebrow. "Not bad. I may have to check myself in just to drink this stuff. Anyway, the Hydra police commander was understandably curious, but had enough sense not to pry."

"Wise. Did you get anything useful from the wreckage?" Dhar asked and tried a spoon of scrambled eggs. They were bland, but the little fried sausages and mushrooms piled next to them smelled and tasted delicious.

"DNA identified the van's occupants. Both were known

AUP chapter muscle. Nothing on the van itself, and no tie-in to Sarek Laral or anybody else. I didn't expect one, but we're still investigating. There wasn't much left of it, you know," Hall said half accusingly, drained his glass and held it in his lap.

Dhar dismissed the van, or what was left of it. Whoever ordered the hit would be far too professional to leave a trail. Then again, even the best of them made a mistake.

"I wish you luck, but when Sankri wakes, he will want to know only one thing."

Hall chewed his lower lip. "Yes. As you anticipated, *Paun* and *Pilla* lifted yesterday morning in somewhat of a hurry. I don't imagine they'll be following the flight plan filed with SC&C."

"Somebody warned them," Dhar mused and spooned more eggs.

"Obviously," Hall agreed and refilled his glass. "I wouldn't worry about Pulman and Segal too much, though. We'll find them. Those ships cannot land without SC&C in the entire sector knowing about it. Even if they change their power emission signature or registration ident, we have a record of their fuel cells. Incidentally, a neat trick, that."

Dhar allowed himself a small grin. "I wasn't aware the information became declassified."

"Yes. I had a need to know. Even if they change fuel cells, when they lift, SC&C will take a data pack dump and we'll be back in business." Hall took a pull of juice and peered at Dhar. "Anything else bothering you?"

"That Laikar hull the AUP chapter is using. Is it still at Kronas Field?"

"*Trava?* I don't know. Why?"

"Pulman and Segal must know we'll try to track them down. He'd be nuts attempting a getaway in one of his lumbering hulls. Like you said, sooner or later, we'll find them. If I were Pulman, I'd have *Trava* meet me somewhere."

Hall looked disgusted. "Change ships, land at some friendly

Alikan Union Party Field, board a liner and disappear? You know how to spoil things, don't you, Agent Dhar? And here I was, starting to enjoy your company." Looking glum, he placed his glass on the tray. "I'll put the wheels in motion. Anything else?"

Dhar tilted his head at the Wall. "I must make a report to Anabb, and I doubt he will be pleased to hear from me."

"You can rest easy there. I already briefed him. Although not a total success, Anabb didn't consider this a failure."

"That doesn't sound in character. He expected a lot from this mission."

"And he did get a lot. What you two did was pretty impressive. Seriously, penetrating the Provisional Committee always a long shot. One thing is clear. The attempt to close out your accounts means you two cannot go back to Tillana Cove Apartments. It's much too dangerous. I've got a comfortable place that should do until this mess is cleaned up. Mind you, it won't be as luxurious, but I'm sure you two will understand."

Noting Hall's malicious grin, Dhar suspected an ulterior motive. "Like Sankri, you have a nasty streak, Ser Resident."

Hall gave a disarming shrug. "Just looking after your safety, Agent Dhar. Oh, one more thing. Did I tell you that Landau's cryptologists cracked the security protocols at Chase Investments and Morgian Holdings?"

"No, I don't believe you did."

"Yes. We now have a pipeline to much more than Global's clandestine payments to the local Alikan Union Party chapter, valuable as that is. It gave me and BueAdmin ample evidence to bring cases against several government ministers, including the AUP chapter."

"I don't regret hearing that."

"I thought you wouldn't. What is significant, it opens a legal window into their records and there is no telling where that might lead."

"This is only significant, Ser Resident, because the means

Sankri and I used have failed."

Hall squinted and frowned heavily. "I figured that you, of all people, would be the last person to talk about legality, my outraged friend. Take a long look in a mirror before venting your moral indignation. You seem to have forgotten why you're here and what you were doing."

Smarting from the rebuke, Dhar was forced to accept the unpalatable truth and admit the Resident was right. The multiplicity of norms and what constituted acceptable behavior had always troubled him. Clearly, it still troubled him. The Discipline taught acceptance without judgment. It did not seek to establish a superior moral position simply because no one could say that in any given social context it was superior. In the Keep of Death even the gods refused to judge. Free will and its exercise made everything possible. Conversely, cleaning up the aftermath that exercising it wrought, the gods also left that to their creations. Futile blaming them for the evils people perpetrated on themselves, or lamenting the injustice of it all when Death claimed a loved one.

Dhar lifted his eyes and slowly bowed. "You are perfectly correct. I had forgotten, for which I crave your pardon."

Hall gave a long sigh and patted Dhar's leg. "Yes. You haven't said anything I hadn't wrestled with myself. Sometimes it doesn't pay to think too much about such things. You're young and idealistic, impatient with everybody and everything, frustrated that after millennia of struggle and ethical development, there is still injustice, misery and war, without an end in sight. That's the irony, Agent Dharaklin, or a sublime jest perpetrated by whatever gods there be. There would never be an end, because the duality of what we perceive as good and evil lives in every one of us. That's what we are. The terrible truth you must accept is that extremes of either are but two sides of the same face. That's what Anabb and the Diplomatic Branch is all about, preventing the excesses of good and evil, although you wouldn't know it at first glance. Me, I take solace knowing what

I do makes a small difference in setting right what others have wronged." When the silence started to become uncomfortable, Hall cleared his throat and snorted. "Now you've got me preaching shallow platitudes like you were a raw recruit."

Dhar, steeped in the wisdom and teachings of the Discipline, stared at Hall in astonishment. To hear such profound words from someone who looked and acted like a bureaucratic functionary was not only unexpected, but personally revealing. Indeed, a mortal may teach a god.

"Have you ever read the *Saftara*, Ser Resident?" he asked softly and Hall gave a wan smile.

"As a matter of fact, I have. If you want to know, so has Anabb, but you knew that already, didn't you?"

"Given how its words shape the Wanderers, I would be surprised if he had not." Dhar reached for his glass and sipped some juice. It wasn't bad at all.

Hall stood and pushed his chair back into the corner. "Can't hang around talking. What are you going to do now?"

"Regardless of your brief, I'll have to call Anabb. Afterward, I thought I would go to Kronas Field SC&C and see if they've got anything on *Paun* and *Pilla*. Then, I'll order an M-2 to stand by. Sankri will want to go after them as soon as they are located."

"Yes. I figured he might, but that may take a while. Come and see me if you get bored…and I'll let you know about *Trava*."

"I'd appreciate that, thanks."

When Hall left, Dhar took a mouthful of eggs. They had gone cold, but he hardly noticed, his mind still on Hall's words. The Resident seemed to have reconciled any moral misgivings about his job. Taking a bite of sausage, Dhar accepted that he had some ways to go at reconciling his.

* * *

In a burst of white scintillation, *Paun* dropped normal and coasted to a stop. Its nav deflector screen shimmered dull orange as it bled off energy along the force lines. In the backdrop, Markesh blazed bright yellow, flooding the system with light and warmth. On the four monstrous gas giants girthing the star, there was no life to receive it. Planetesimals that could have grown into habitable worlds were broken up and devoured by the giants billions of years ago. Devoid of life, an astrophysical curiosity, removed from prying eyes and sensors, Markesh made an ideal rendezvous point.

Alone in the black deeps, *Paun* sent out a short, omni-directional modulated ping. Four seconds later it received the expected response. Satisfied, it settled down to wait. After thirty-eight minutes a sleek flattened oval closed on the carrier, Markesh's fires masking its approach. Two talans from the lumbering raider the small ship slowed and edged toward a glowing docking port. Five katalans from the sheer cliff of the hull it stopped and extended an access tube. Side-by-side the two ships drifted through darkness.

Two men, a woman and a small boy made their way quickly through the tube. As soon as they were across, the tube detached and retracted. The lighter vessel moved away from its ponderous consort, turned and boosted. Eleven seconds later, having cleared the gravitational anomaly of the carrier, its distortion field precursor polarized and the ship slipped into subspace.

The cable-tube hatch slid into the bulkhead with a soft hiss and Pulman looked quickly around the command deck before stepping out. Two padded couches faced a curved console, repeater screens and a large display plate, currently showing a schematic of the ship's flight path. The right couch swiveled. From it a young Palean stood up, brought up his right hand to shoulder level, palm open in greeting, and smiled broadly. A familiar face, having ferried Global's owners before.

"Friend Pulman. Welcome aboard *Trava*, Ser."

"Thank you, Nar Tal. Although I wish it were under different circumstances."

The pilot's smile faded into a frown. "A tragic development. Hardly seems believable."

"Indeed. Please set a course for Ball and get us underway."

"Ball it is," Nar Tal said and nodded to his Askaran copilot. "Padar…" He didn't worry why Pulman wanted to go to Ball instead of heading directly for Stavros. He got paid the same regardless.

The copilot looked up from the left seat. "*Trava* is on course, Ser. We'll reach Ball in eighteen hours and fifty minutes."

"Thanks," Pulman said. "Any complications lifting off?"

"Kronas SC&C didn't even blink," Nar Tal piped in a thin voice, his long fingers twining. "By the way, where is young Manir? I thought he'd be up here taking over."

"He'll be along presently," Pulman assured him. "He's just getting over the loss of his last command."

Nar Tal chuckled, resigning himself to the inevitable. He'd seen the boy operate, a harmless diversion, and the boy *did* know something about ship handling.

"He better behave or he'll be scrubbing decks," he warned, knowing it to be a futile threat.

"I'd like to see you make him do that," Pulman said with a grin. "I'm going below. Let me know when we reach waypoint four."

"Of course, Ser."

Pulman immediately turned and stepped into the cable-tube. The hatch slid shut after him and Nar Tal shook his head.

"Poor schmuck."

His copilot looked up in surprise. "Why do you say that?"

"Because, friend Padar, he thinks he'll get away with it."

"And why shouldn't he? I don't know what he has in mind once we reach Ball, but the Serrll is a pretty big place. Plenty of room to lose yourself in."

"If nobody is looking for you," Nar Tal murmured and slipped into his seat. He checked the nav plot repeater and sat back. In the end , not his problem. His job was piloting *Trava*, and happy to leave it at that. It didn't pay getting mixed up in high politics, anyone's politics.

Pulman stepped out of the tube and strode briskly down the brightly lit corridor of the lower deck. Heavy gray pile muffled his footsteps. *Trava* was not a luxury cruiser, but still well-appointed to keep its passengers comfortable during the tedium between the stars. Nothing indicated he was aboard a ship. He could have been in a hotel for all the difference it made. He stopped before a door and touched the access pad. It turned amber and the panel slid away.

Sitting next to his mother, watching the Wall, the little boy looked up and broke into a beaming smile. He jumped off the couch and rushed to embrace his visitor.

"Uncle Warat!"

Pulman tussled Manir's hair. "The pilot has gotten himself lost and needs some help to sort him out. How about it?"

"Zowee!" The boy glanced quickly at his mother. "I can go, can't I? Please?"

Leera caught Pulman's eye and nodded. "Sure. Don't run into anything."

"Zowee!" Manir ran out the door, feet pounding on the carpet.

Segal emerged from the sleeping cabin sealing up his zip-jacket. "The kid's off piloting?"

"He still thinks this is simply another business trip," Leera said softly, looking dejected. "He may never see Askaran again."

"He's young. He'll get over it," Segal retorted and sat beside her. "It's the price we pay for doing business."

"Tan! What a dreadful thing to say."

Segal frowned. "What do you want me to do? Burst into tears?"

"You could show a little compassion." She glared at him, clearly annoyed. "You can be pretty callous sometimes, you know."

"We're trying to stay alive, my dear. This is no time for sentimentality," Segal retorted mildly and glanced at his partner. "Everything set?"

Pulman gave Leera a reassuring smile. When *Paun* left Askaran, she took it well and didn't go emotional. Everything had happened too quickly for that. Later, during the lonely hours while *Paun* made for the rendezvous, when they had time to talk and reflect, the import of what they were doing finally sank in. Leera hadn't said much, but the little things she did say were more like reminiscences, snapshots from a severed past never to be recovered. Probably a wrenching realization. Tan was right. He had no time for sentimentality, not now.

"Don't worry, Leera. You'll like Ball. It's not as warm as Askaran, but warm enough. Manir will have no trouble settling in."

"And how will we settle in? You two haven't said."

Pulman's eyes flickered at Segal. "We'll be given new identities and positions in the local Alikan Union Party chapter. We have assets. We'll do fine."

"But if we're on Ball, why send *Paun* and *Pilla* to Stavros?" Silence filled the cabin for a brief moment. "Ah, it would tell everybody where we are."

"That's right," Segal said approvingly and patted her knee. "They'll be reregistered and then it'll be business as usual."

"Raiding again!"

Segal's eyes narrowed. "It's what we do."

"It's raiding which got us into trouble on Askaran, remember? And you want to do it all again for some illusory cause. How long this time before we have to flee again? If the cause is so consuming, why doesn't Sarek Laral and men like him take some of the risk? You two are being used and you refuse to see it." She gave both of them a pitying look and stood. Segal reached for her hand, but she drew back.

"While you're playing your games, Tan, do you ever think of me or Manir? Will he have a father to look up to tomorrow? Will I have a partner? What do I tell him if one day, police knock on the door and drag you off? What if they drag both of us off? What then? It's time to make a choice: me and your son or your cause. You can't have both." She glanced at Pulman and made for the sleeping cabin, head held high. When the door closed behind her, Segal looked at Pulman, his face a mask of bewilderment.

"What was that about?"

Pulman snorted and shook his head. "You can be such an asshole sometimes, Tan."

"Now, just a—"

"Oh, shut up. She's right, about everything."

Segal stood and placed both hands on his hips. "You think I don't know that? I wasn't grown in a bag, Warat. I've strung along with you because I saw a good deal in it, for both of us. We were running a profitable business, albeit a murky one. Although it may appear that way, I wasn't in it for any cause, noble or otherwise. That was your department. My concern is only money, and your AUP cell simply made getting it easier."

"You're right. You never cared much for my side of the equation and I had no problem with that. I still don't. Leera is right. On Ball, we'll have an opportunity to make a fresh start and I want to make the most of it. If we have to run for it again, we might not be as lucky. What happened on Askaran was a lesson, one I don't want to ignore. I've got no hankering to spend the rest of my life on Cantor or some place like it."

"You mean…you don't want to run *Paun* and *Pilla* as raiders? A staunch patriot like you?"

"What if I didn't?"

"Wouldn't bother me one bit, but remember this. We sunk over 850 million into those hulls and I want that money back."

"Oh, for pits sake! Is that all you can think about? Besides, it was Global's money, not yours. Anyway, they're fully depreciated. We got our investment back and more."

"Okay, so I'm a hardass, but you still haven't answered my question."

"Why not sell them to the Stavros AUP chapter? The plan Kerill and Randakla proposed to Laral was sound. I don't want to be the one having to implement it. I don't like the risk profile, but one way or another, we've got to get rid of those hulls."

Segal stared thoughtfully at his partner, surprised to hear this turnaround. Then again, perhaps not so. He always considered Pulman unemotional and completely objective in everything he did. Although radical, this action perfectly in character.

"You're right. Sooner or later someone would trace them back to us and that would be it. What are we going to do on Ball? Being on the AUP executive might be comfortable, but it will not be a full-time job and I'm easily bored."

"We'll go into the freight business, what else? It's what we know and do well. I'm sure that a ripe, undeveloped market like Ball will have an odd opportunity we can exploit."

"Or create," Segal murmured and gave a slow smile. "It could work, but isn't that a bit predictable? If we re-enter with a brand-new company, it's bound to be noticed and some busybody will make a connection."

"We'll create a holding front company and manage the operation behind the scene."

"I like it."

"I thought you would." Pulman returned the smile, pleased he had Segal's measure. The man had no scruples or vision, without morals, but he *was* an astute businessman. In Pulman's book, that made up for a lot of sins. He did not pretend to hold the high moral ground. He knew what he was and what he needed to do. Unlike Segal, he was a patriot and believed in the cause, but there were lots of ways to support the Sargon/Palean merger, and most of them did not require a charged projector. All of them needed money. Lots of it. Willingly or otherwise,

Segal would help him get it.

And he longed to settle a personal score. He failed to gain control of the Askaran AUP chapter, but like he told Segal, Ball represented a new opportunity and he intended to make the most of it. Those who stood in his way would be dealt with. After tangling with Laral, he learned well how to play that game. He would be prepared.

Waypoint four was not an asteroid or a drifting comet head, but a simple nav point in space some four billion talans from Ball's primary, used by ships to correct their course when entering the system. No one really stopped there, but *Trava* did. It dropped normal and waited, another speck in a vast blackness. Far on its port quarter a brighter than usual star hinted the ship was now under its influence.

Coming in on secondary drive the M-2 gave a ranging ping, slowed and closed with its target. Keeping the smaller ship in its shadow the M-2 stopped and extended an access tube.

On *Trava's* command deck, Pulman watched the warship close, his feelings mixed. So far everything had gone off flawlessly, far better than he had any right to expect. Only one thing remained to be done.

When the access tube mated, Padar swiveled his seat. "Docking completed, Ser. You are free to disembark."

"Thank you. Please advise Ser Segal accordingly."

"Already done."

Nar Tal stood and looked curiously at his passenger. He didn't know why Pulman wanted to disembark in the middle of nowhere, and to an M-2. *Trava* could get him and Segal to Ball just as easily. Unless, of course, they weren't going to Ball at all, and this was merely a diversion. An M-2 was powerful company and clear evidence of Pulman's influence and organizational ability. Not that he was duly concerned at this development. It would simply make an interesting addendum to his movements report.

He lifted his hand, palm open. "It has been a pleasure having you and Ser Segal's family on board, friend Pulman, and I trust things will work out for you."

"I hope so too, Nar Tal, and thank you for everything." Pulman wanted to say something more, a word of condolence? In the end, he said nothing. What could he say that would make up for what he was about to do? No sentimentality. He turned and thumbed the cable-tube access pad. The hatch slid open and he stepped in.

On the lower deck, he saw Segal enter the access lock. "Tan!"

Segal stopped and turned.

"Leera and Manir through?" Pulman demanded.

"In front of me. What's up?"

"Nothing. I only wanted to make sure," Pulman said and they both entered the tube. The inner lock slid shut after them. As soon as they cleared the lock, the outer hatch closed with a soft hiss and they were effectively cut off from *Trava*. Segal stopped and reached for Pulman's arm.

"You're up to something."

"What do you mean?"

"Don't go coy on me now, Warat. I know you too well."

After a pause, Pulman nodded. "Okay, you do need to know, but not here."

At the end of the tube a Palean rating stood to. "Gentlemen, welcome aboard *Riga*."

Segal looked around. "Where is my family?"

"They were escorted to their quarters, sir. Now, if you would please follow me, I'll take you to the command deck."

Pulman extended an open hand. "By all means. After you."

The rating stood to, then marched toward the cable-tube. Inside, he stepped against the wall, allowing the two men to enter.

When the hatch opened, Pulman gazed curiously at the banks of sloping consoles, display plates and blinking, colored contact pads. In the center, two couches faced the main display plate, flanked by empty seats about a katalan apart. His first look inside any Serrll Scout vessel and he was impressed. He recognized similarities with a civilian command deck, but that's where it ended. There were banks of controls whose function he could only guess at.

A young Palean rose from the left seat, turned and beamed. "Mr. Pulman, Mr. Segal, glad to have you aboard. I am Second Scout Mal Lar, commanding *Riga*. *Trava* has pushed off and is boosting."

"Thank you, Mr. Lar. You may proceed," Pulman said coldly, set his mouth and stared at the tactical plot.

"Very well, sir." Mal Lar glanced at the figure in the right seat and nodded. "You can engage, Dev."

"Aye, sir. Computer, fire on generated bearings. Full bursts."

"L-band firing lock established. Engaging," the computer responded emotionlessly.

Segal jerked and his head snapped around, but Pulman wasn't looking at him. His eyes were fixed on the tactical plot. Segal's protest died stillborn as he realized what Pulman was doing, and more importantly, why. Brutal, but perhaps a necessary solution. As long as Sarek Laral knew where they were, he would have a critical bargaining hold over them, something Pulman clearly would not tolerate. Segal could hardly blame him for that.

Slung beneath *Riga's* belly the projector dome glowed a sullen orange. *Trava* was still pulling away when *Riga* fired, its primary shield grid down. Having it up would only have alarmed its victim. At nine thousand talans, point blank range. The initial burst deliberately targeted the nav bubble and command deck. The sharp yellow 56 TeV beam easily penetrated the civilian-grade casing of the bubble. For the occupants, a relatively quick death. Two seconds of exquisite agony before the nav bubble vaporized and most of the command deck flashed into plasma. Subsequent bursts centered on the drive spaces. With massive damage to the antimatter reactor shielding and support mechanisms, the reactor vanished in a sphere of consuming radiance. When the wave of plasma reached the fuel cells store, it only added to the conflagration and *Trava* disappeared in a ball of expanding brilliance. A few seconds later, the only remnant of the ship was a shell of decaying radiation.

An M-2 was not a powerful warship, but Pulman felt pleased at the cold efficiency with which it dispatched *Trava*. How then did a raider face an M-3, the Scout Fleet's premier tactical vessel? Obviously it didn't. Given such odds, he admired the tenacity of *Paun* and *Pilla's* pilots. Sometimes, though, as in Re Nette's case, tenacity had not been enough. A game of diminishing returns and Segal was wise to quit after only one raid.

Nevertheless, he felt a moment of disquiet. It wasn't the clinical efficiency of *Trava's* destruction that disturbed him, but the seemingly dispassionate attitude of the M-2's crew. If they were all like Mal Lar, the Scout Fleet was a ruthless adversary indeed. This crew *had* to be different to operate the way they did. How the Ball Alikan Union Party chapter bought them off, he could only speculate.

He glanced at his partner and saw the same resolute acceptance. What the M-2 had done may have been dispassionate, but it did serve a purpose. It effectively wiped the last connecting trail to their destination.

Beside him, Mal Lar nodded as if approving the action. "You may secure, Dev."

"Aye, sir. Course?"

The Scout officer turned to Pulman. "We're ready to boost for Ball, sir."

"Thank you. I appreciate you cleaning up after us."

"A pleasure. Let's get underway, Dev."

"Aye, sir."

Misinterpreting the drawn expressions of his guests, Mal

Lar suppressed a smile. His M-2 and every other Scout vessel were machines of destruction, not peace, and destruction was always brutal. Civilians never really understood that and these two were no different.

"If you please, I am sure you'll be more comfortable in your quarters. Allow me to show you the way."

* * *

Getting involved with the Diplomatic Branch not exactly the Field Dispatcher's idea of a fun day, but he was equally certain that Kandu Hall did not enjoy his day either. The flap over Global Transport's two raider vessels had everybody stirred up, from government ministers down. Nobody was having much of a fun day. He knew the Resident and never believed the rumors he was on a take from Karach Salvage and Disposal owners. A man like that had too much integrity to be bought, although initially, he had to admit to a niggling doubt. Everyone had some sort of a price. Studying the two owners, it turned out they were not syndicated operators at all, which restored his faith in the Resident. Apart from giving him their assumed names, Hall hadn't bothered with formal introductions. It was enough the two were with him and Hall vouched for them. Masking his natural curiosity, the Dispatcher resigned himself that he would not be finding out anything more and concentrated on the task at hand.

Beside his desk, a Field schematic took up one whole wall: run-up ramps, parking aprons, military and civilian sections, glowing lines running everywhere. Depending on its status each colored light represented a ship. It looked quite impressive.

"As you know," he started evenly in a heavy voice, glancing at each of his guests in turn, "the Fleet alert went out late yesterday, shortly after you two were shot down." He glanced at Kerill-aa and Randakla, then swept a hand at the full-dimensional image in the Wall on his right. "The blue zone covers the

345

likely destinations they could have reached before we issued the alert. The orange zone is alert time plus four hours. As you can see, gentlemen, lots of space to lose yourself in."

"If they merely wanted to hide, I would agree," Terr said slowly, not bothering to look at the image. It didn't tell him anything new. "But I doubt losing themselves is what *Paun* and *Pilla* had in mind. They are predators, and tucking them away at some deserted landing field wouldn't be part of Pulman and Segal's game plan. If I were them, I'd have instructed the ships to scoot for the nearest secure Alikan Union Party stronghold, and there are several within easy boost: Prina, Kobal, Stavros, to name a few. They could have reached any one of them with plenty of time to spare before the alert."

"Very good, Ser Kerill-aa, and is exactly what the Resident said, almost word for word," the Dispatcher agreed. "Working on that assumption, we may have found them."

"Oh?" Terr sat up, suddenly interested. He hadn't expected much from this briefing, anticipating the usual official obfuscating and stonewalling. After all, the Dispatcher was an AUP member and must have been involved in Askaran's protection of raider traffic. To his surprise the Dispatcher had cooperated without reservation. Whether done voluntarily or Hall applied some heat, he didn't care. All he wanted was catch Pulman and Segal.

The Dispatcher cleared his throat. "May have! As registered ships, *Paun* and *Pilla* have vanished, but Stavros SC&C obtained ident dumps from two armed carriers that came down some hours apart and their fuel cell signatures matched."

"Yes!" Hall beamed, genuinely pleased. "Now we're getting somewhere."

"Perhaps not. SC&C's records show them to be duly chartered vessels belonging to a local freight company. Matching fuel cell signatures wasn't deemed sufficient evidence by the local authorities to issue search warrants."

"Those *authorities*, presumably the Alikan Union Party?"

Terr prompted dryly.

"I'm afraid so," the Dispatcher confirmed, looking slightly ill at ease, not wishing to draw attention to his affiliation with the local chapter. Just because he belonged to the AUP and supported the merger cause didn't mean he couldn't be honorable.

"Figures. The crews?"

"Recorded as Stavros citizens."

"Very convenient. Okay, we'll play it their way." Terr looked at Hall and nodded. The Resident leaned forward and peered at the Dispatcher.

"Issue a directive to COMSTAVOPS to check out both ships. I'll provide the details. Run it as a safety or health inspection, anything. Next time they lift, they are to intercept them. The usual rules of engagement for raiders apply."

"They may not get off the ground for a while, Ser Resident. With an alert out for them, they could be understandably wary about going hunting."

"Yes, but they're raiders, and their crews operate on a share basis. Sooner or later, they'll be coming out and I want them tagged and bagged when they do."

"Agreed!" Terr added emphatically.

"If the Fleet intercepts them, the Stavros government could construe the act as unlawful interference in its commerce," the Dispatcher pointed out.

"If the ships simply disappear, how would they know?" Hall retorted. "Anyway, they can call it whatever they like. The bottom line? Those two hulls will be out of circulation and that's the only thing that matters. We'll deal with any diplomatic fallout later, but I doubt there will be any. The authorities there must know what those ships are."

"Very well, Ser. I shall issue the order."

"Any sign of Pulman and Segal?" Terr asked and Hall sighed.

"Not a trace." He turned to Dhar and shrugged. "Same

with *Trava*. Disappeared."

"Presumably, neither of them were in *Paun* when she landed?" Dhar asked and Hall shrugged.

"There's no way to tell for certain, but if we push your theory, they probably transferred to *Trava* somewhere, leaving *Paun* to continue on its way to Stavros while *Trava* made for gods know where. We'll be checking out Stavros to make sure. This could be a double-blind to throw us off, but we've got her ident, and when she lands, we'll have her and her passengers. She's got to land sometime."

Terr looked thoughtful. "Not if she's destroyed."

Hall stared at him. "Why would Pulman do that?"

"To make sure *Trava* doesn't tell anyone where he and Segal were going."

"You have an interesting way of thinking, did you know that?" the Resident remarked. "And it would explain why we haven't found her. If in fact she is destroyed and the Askaran AUP chapter finds out, Pulman could be in for a world of trouble."

"He'll be in bigger trouble if *we* find him. *Trava* was a doge and it doesn't matter whether she's destroyed or not. She's not a factor here. To run our guys down, we must use the same reasoning they applied when they sent *Paun* and *Pilla* to Stavros. They would pick a safe place and slide in under new identities. That means an Alikan Union Party-controlled system."

"What makes you suspect they would choose an AUP system?" the Dispatcher wanted to know. "They must know they're hunted. The smart thing to do would be to hole up somewhere completely unknown."

"A valid point, Ser, but consider this. If we build on the supposition they transferred from *Trava*, then removed her, that kind of operation takes planning and organization. You don't get that kind of support by landing on some backyard world. No, they headed for an AUP system and its protective umbrella.

I have another argument for you: psychological profiles. Pulman and Segal are men used to power, used to running things and would want to continue doing so. Men like that wouldn't choose a quiet rural setting as a hideaway, however invigorating." Terr swept his hand at the blue zone. "No. They're somewhere in there, I am certain of it."

"A nice bit of reasoning," the Dispatcher admitted, "provided your supposition is correct."

"There is always room for doubt," Terr agreed. "And I'll give you another supposition. As Askarans, it will make them stand out regardless how integrated their destination might be. They'll want to feel totally secure. To do that, in addition to acquiring new identities, I'm betting that they'll ask for citizenship. If that's what they did, this is where we'll have our break, because there is one thing a citizenship registration captures that cannot be disguised, not easily anyway."

Hall grinned and nodded with genuine approval. "Biometric data. Oh, that's good, provided they did take out citizenship."

"There is that, agreed. If they simply assumed new identities, we'll have a hard time tracking them down. Let's try this first anyway. If we come up blank, we'll have to think up something else. Can you ask your counterparts in the blue zone to send us registration files of new citizens spanning say, the last ten days? Coming from you, the request shouldn't sound odd."

"Why send the stuff to me? The local offices can run a matching check just as well." Hall paused as the implication of Terr's request sank home. "You don't trust the Diplomatic Branch offices?" he demanded, looking indignant.

"I'm sorry, Ser Resident, I really am, but ask yourself this. Why is it that only you knew about our operation on Askaran?"

Hall chewed his lower lip, not liking any of it, then sighed in resignation. "Okay, hotshot. You've proven your point. We cannot risk a sympathizer warning Pulman and Segal."

"When your office gets the data, pick someone absolutely

trustworthy and get him to run a computer match against Aska-ran files. If one is found, I want to be informed immediately. One other thing. Can you please get in touch with Kalakan and ask them to send *Sheeva* here?"

"You want to go after Pulman and Segal personally?"

Terr stared hard at Hall. "Who do you trust to pick them up?"

"Ser Kerill-aa, even if you picked them up yourself, no Al-ikan Union Party government will honor an extradition war-rant," the Dispatcher pointed out, only to receive a feral grin from the Diplomatic Branch agent.

"Who said anything about a warrant?"

* * *

"If they're not identified in the next forty-four hours, con-sider yourselves recalled!" Terr growled, giving a fair imitation of Anabb's gravelly voice. "Crusty old fart."

Dhar chuckled and Terr glared.

"He could be more understanding, you know. It's not like running down Pulman and Segal was on a schedule or some-thing."

Still smiling, Dhar shook his head. "You two simply like baiting each other, did you know that? Besides, he *was* under-standing. He gave us those two days."

"Hah! Big of him. I hope you're not implying we're alike?"

"Not even close. Even so, you do share some interesting traits. I would guess that's what makes both of you good at what you do."

"Meaning I'm like him," Terr muttered sourly. Still, he acknowledged that his brother had a point. He was developing a familiarity with Anabb, which the Diplomatic Branch Direc-tor seemed to tolerate and even encourage. He learned already the intelligence chief had no time for yes-men, which suited him fine. Nevertheless, Anabb was his superior, and familiarity or not, it would be foolish of him to forget that. "Anabb is just grouchy."

Dhar did not say anything, but his look did. Forcing a grin, Terr raised both hands in surrender.

"I know. I'm the one who's grouchy."

"Approaching Ball Surface Command and Control insertion point," the computer announced crisply, interrupting whatever Dhar might have said. "Initial interrogative verified. All systems nominal for orbital approach. Preparing to egress transition mode."

"State SC&C insertion time," Dhar queried from the right seat.

"SC&C insertion in six minutes. Landing configuration procedure nominal. Ship within acceptable flight parameters."

Dhar checked the console displays and looked at his brother. "I don't understand why you're upset. The Resident did find them for us and where they lived."

"Yeah, so he did."

"Citizenship," Dhar mused. "I would never have thought of it."

"If I had to bet, I would say Pulman probably thought of it. Segal doesn't strike me as the big ideas type." Terr pursed his lips. "They should have stuck to getting new identities only."

Sitting in silence, preoccupied with their own thoughts, waiting, they watched one particular star brighten in the main display plate.

"SC&C insertion point. Ready to transit," the computer advised at length.

"Very well. Drop normal," Dhar ordered.

"Transiting." The distortion field precursor changed polarity and began to collapse. Shields flaring, *Sheeva* exited into normal space and fell below lightspeed. Ball hung before them in quarter phase, a speck of blue opal, accompanied by two pearly moons. *Sheeva* engaged her secondary drive and surged toward the pretty lights. On the ship's starboard side the sun glowed buttery yellow.

Once past the orbital factories, farms, and cargo handling platforms, SC&C brought them straight in, cutting soundlessly through the atmosphere. Les Saras hugged a large U-shaped bay, the city cut by two meandering rivers. Beyond the bay, hugging the horizon, a heavy low-pressure system was slowly making its way toward the shore. A band of jagged, snow-capped mountains curved into the interior to be lost in after-noon haze. Settlements, cultivated fields, and industrial com-plexes extended from the city to delicately feel the boundary of Tai Palma Field, itself a sprawl of terminus buildings, landing rings, aprons, cargo docks, and maintenance hangars; crowded with liners, carriers and Fleet vessels. The clear washed sky a web of black lines: civilian and commercial traffic.

Sheeva settled daintily over the landing ring next to an M-3 and an access tube immediately slid from the military terminus. It mated with a dull thump even as utility umbilicals rose from the apron to connect with the ship.

Dhar powered down and turned to his brother. "On ground support and secured."

Satisfied, Terr pried himself out of the command couch. Now that he faced action, he felt ready and eager to get on with it. While they were still in transit, he and Dhar had worked sev-eral scenarios how to nab their prey, depending on arrival time and local circumstances. For the moment they were stuck, forced to wait and he never found waiting an easy thing to do.

The snatch needed to be done early in the morning before Pulman and Segal ventured out for the day. Given that *Sheeva* arrived during daylight, they could be anywhere and no way to tell when they would be at their apartments. They might be din-ing out, carousing, anything. Normally, Terr would organize a stakeout before moving in, but that wasn't possible here when he couldn't trust the local authorities or the Diplomatic Branch. A sad state of affairs, but he had to play the cards he was dealt with.

"It looks like we're hung up for a while," he mused, peering through the nav bubble, "and that means another night on board."

Dhar shrugged indifferently. Wandering about and rubbernecking was simply too dangerous, inviting unwanted speculation and possible recognition. Pulman and Segal would be wary against any surveillance. Or maybe their AUP pals could be looking out for them. Either way, playing the tourist was not advisable. More likely, he and Sankri were paranoid and the locals didn't really care a toss for what happened to their new citizens. Still, it would be pleasant outside, stretching the legs and tasting fresh air. Time enough for that when they finished the job, he told himself.

Terr glanced at his brother. "What do you want for dinner? I have some Askaran venison stowed, in case you had a craving."

Dhar winced as he recalled the last time he tangled with that dish. "Your cruel streak is showing, Sankri," he remarked darkly and Terr laughed.

Morning overcast and dark as the rented combie made its way toward the bay over the brightly lit Les Saras sprawl. A fresh offshore wind juddered the frame from time to time. A glowing green safety strip along the bubble boundary made the interior eerie, but no different from other combies in the control network string.

They dropped out of the pattern and angled toward one of the illuminated towers fronting the beach, reminding Terr of their apartment block in Karach. Although Pulman and Segal may be exiled, he figured they'd want to maintain their accustomed luxurious lifestyle.

Even at this ungodly hour a few early risers were already walking briskly along the beachfront or jogging. Awful habit. Small cargo haulers were coming down or lifting off among the apartment blocks—morning supply deliveries. Terr counted on this traffic to mask the snatch.

Power plant spooling down, the combie settled beside two haulers at the service end of the parking lot. There was nobody about. Discreet ground lighting around the tower showed off manicured lawns, shrubs, and trees to best effect. Dhar cracked the bubble and climbed out. The wind immediately whipped hair about his face. Behind them, surf crashed against the shore. Out of the combie, Terr took a deep breath of warm scented air and stretched his arms. He nodded to Dhar and started making his way toward the service entrance, mouthing the words that would summon Death. No one inside, but they could hear muffled voices and crates getting moved about. They strode to the nearest cable-tube and got in.

"Level forty-two," Terr ordered, but the double panels remained open.

"Access to level forty-two is restricted, gentle sir," the computer announced pleasantly in local Garish. "Please provide ID tag before access can be granted." The message repeated in Ser-rll interlingua.

Terr expected this. He pulled out his Diplomatic Branch tag and placed it against a glowing green sensor pad.

"Security override. Identify Terrllss-rr."

The pad immediately turned amber and the doors clicked shut. "Security override accepted," the computer stated and the cable-tube surged up.

"Computer, suspend surveillance log. Time designation, minus five minutes to plus twenty."

"Authorization code group required."

"Remote download from ID tag," Terr ordered and waited. Would the computer accept his authentication codes? It felt like an eternity before the computer responded.

"Authorization accepted. Security surveillance suspended."

When the tube panels opened, Terr stepped out into a wide, brightly lit corridor. The ceiling glowed a soft white, off-setting the pale blue of the walls. He immediately turned left and walked deliberately toward what looked like genuine wood double doors. So far the floor plan was accurate. He swiped his tag against the access pad and the doors slowly hissed open. A green strip running along the bottom of the walls provided faint illumination. He blinked hard a couple of times to allow his eyes to adjust, then padded slowly over polished marble tiles toward the master bedroom. Dhar already moving toward one of the spare rooms.

Right arm held ready, blue lightnings crawling over it, Terr touched the bedroom access pad. The door sighed away and he immediately loosed a bolt at a figure on the bed. The lightning made a short, sharp snap. He waited for a reaction, not expecting one, then walked toward the bed. Pulman looked like he was still sleeping, which he was, sort of.

"Nightwings! In here." Terr grabbed the light blanket covering the prone figure and flung it back. Dressed in what appeared to be black pajamas, legs slightly drawn toward his chest, Pulman did not look at all menacing, which is how Terr preferred seeing him.

Dhar showed up and hurried to the bed. Without a word, he bent over the still form and heaved him across his shoulders. Grunting, he stood and settled his load more comfortably. Even for him, Pulman's weight a hefty load.

Terr slapped Dhar's arm and walked out of the bedroom.

The service area still empty when they got down. Without lingering, they hurried toward the combie, the wind whistling around them. Terr got the bubble open and Dhar unceremoniously dumped his load on the back seat. Straightening, he leaned back to stretch his back and sighed with satisfaction while Terr covered the body with a blanket. The first part had gone off remarkably well and Terr hoped getting Segal would be equally unexciting. The last thing he needed was fuss over a simple snatch. Pulman and Segal should have picked two different apartment blocks to settle in, but he wasn't about to question his luck, and it wouldn't have made a real difference in the end.

Back at level forty-two, he turned right, then left at a T-junction. His tag opened the door and he looked at a startled Segal sitting behind a dining table next to the kitchen, a cup of something steaming held halfway to his mouth.

For a large man, Segal was quick. Even as Terr sent a bolt of lightning at him, he dove out of the way. The lightning crack not loud, but it seemed deafening in the quiet confines of the apartment.

"I'm not here to kill you, Tan," Terr said casually. "You can either leave here on your own power or be carried. I don't care which."

"That display show? Your way of saying hello?"

"Make up your mind."

"If I walk out of here, Kerill, or whatever your name is, I might as well be dead."

"Being alive probably won't be much fun, but at least you'll be alive."

"On Cantor, or its equivalent?"

"That won't be up to me. Now—"

Leera appeared out of the master bedroom, saw Terr and instantly screamed. Before Terr could react, a flash of light struck her on the chest. She gasped, flung back her arms and toppled.

"Leera!" Segal cried in anguish, jumped up and rushed to her. He knelt beside her, cradled her head in his lap and probed the small burn on her nightdress. When he looked up, hate contorted his face.

"You didn't have to kill her, you bastards! She didn't do anything to you!"

"She is not dead," Dhar said heavily, his arm held ready. "Merely unconscious."

Segal looked at his assailants, then shook his head. "Discipline adepts. I never trusted either of you."

"And once the merger was done, you were going to kill us because of it. We know. This makes us even." Terr said coldly and loosed the lightnings. Segal grunted and sagged across the woman. Terr pursed his lips and after a moment glanced at Dhar. "You take him and I'll find the boy."

Dhar saw resolve on his brother's grim features. Sankri did not like what he was about to do, but it still had to be done. They couldn't risk anyone alerting the authorities before *Sheeva* lifted. Untangling themselves from the local bureaucracy could get more than just complicated. He saw something else in his brother's gray eyes. Regret. From today, Leera and the boy would probably never see Segal again. That may be tragic, but their plight would be no more terrible than the shattered lives and families of crews murdered by *Paun* and *Pilla*. In this business no one won.

Terr moved quickly to the second bedroom and opened the door. "Computer, lights."

The ceiling and walls immediately brightened. The bed neatly made and not slept in. Before the last bedroom, he paused, then opened the door. Manir sat on his bed clutching a blanket to his chest. Seeing Terr, he started to cry in soft, wrenching sobs. Terr clamped his jaws and pointed with his arm. Manir's scream cut off as the lightnings played over him. For a second, he stared tragically at Terr, then slowly sagged back against the pillows. Terr looked at the boy for one long moment, then abruptly turned and hurried out.

With Segal draped across his shoulders, Dhar waited beside the cable-tube, its doors already open. When they got down to the service level, two men dressed in dark beige coveralls were pushing trolleys laden with packages and assorted containers. One of them gave Dhar a questioning look, decided it was none of his business why someone would be carrying a body, nodded and walked by.

Thankful for the lucky break, Terr scrambled into the combie and powered up. Dhar offloaded Segal next to his partner and got into the front left seat. Terr immediately lifted, keeping low as they headed toward the beach. Once over water, he told the computer to make for Tai Palma Field and engaged SC&C guidance. Angling up, the combie climbed toward its assigned flight corridor.

Terr sat back and allowed himself a small smile of satisfaction. "Well, Nightwings, it appears that we pulled it off yet again."

"Looks that way," Dhar agreed solemnly. "When those delivery guys showed up…"

"I know. It could have gotten hairy. Bodies everywhere."

"They will probably talk."

"When the authorities catch up with them, I hope to be far away."

Despite the approaching dawn the heavy overcast made the city look gloomy. Lightning flickered far on their right, momentarily unmasking the massed clouds. Nothing stirred above the Field. The combie swung into the service ring of the military terminus and descended toward the landing strip. Once down, Terr powered off, raised the bubble and climbed out. He paused and looked at his brother.

"Keep an eye on these two, will you, while I get us some help?"

A security point barred the broad entrance to the terminal. Two local MPs, smart in parade grays, white gloves and black boots, a phase rifle slung at port arms, flanked the entry. Both ground their rifles and stood to.

"I'll have to ask you for some ID, sir, before I can let you go any farther," the MP on the right said apologetically in Serrll interlingua.

Terr strode to one of the registration booths beside the entrance and stuck his hand against a sensor plate. After a moment it lit up, showing his rank and insignia of the Diplomatic Branch. Then it flickered and displayed a face. Studying the image, he couldn't believe he could look so innocent.

Seeing the display the MP snapped to. "Sir!"

"I need a couple of guys to carry two bodies," Terr said

brightly and hooked a thumb over his shoulder. "The combie over there."

The MP's eyes flickered uncertainly. "Sir? You need someone to carry...bodies?"

Terr nodded. "Unconscious bodies really."

"I'll see what I can do," the MP said slowly, not sure what was going on, but an order was an order. He dragged out his pocket communicator and spoke rapidly.

Several uniformed officers and ratings emerged from or walked into the terminal, giving Terr only a cursory glance. Moments later, two burly MPs came out pushing a wide trolley.

"Over there." Terr pointed at the combie. The MPs looked at each other and shrugged. In their job, sooner or later one was bound to see almost anything.

Inside the terminal the procession caused some stares and people stopped to watch, but no one seemed excited at the sight of bodies wheeled about. Terr had to clear himself again at the access tube entrance, the guard suspiciously watching the entire proceedings. Inside the M-1 the MPs unloaded their cargo, stood to and retreated down the tube.

"Computer, seal the lock and make preparations for lift," Terr ordered, eyeing Pulman and Segal sprawled on the deck.

"Acknowledged."

The double-lock hatches slid shut with a soft thump and there was a slight pressure surge. At ease for the first time, Terr punched Dhar on the arm. Nothing could stop them from getting away now.

"Let's get out of here." As he started for the cable-tube, Dhar pointed at their guests.

"We're not going to leave them there?" Raider scum or not, they were entitled to civilized treatment. He was surprised his brother would do this.

Terr noted Dhar's expression and grinned. "For now. I only want to lift and clear the system. We'll tuck them into bed later."

Dhar looked dubious as he followed his brother into the tube. On the command level the navigation bubble, running chest-high around the deck, cleared immediately. Sloping control panels hugged part of the curved hull. Terr lowered himself onto the central couch and quickly scanned the displays.

"Status?"

"Nominal," the computer responded.

"Secure for lift. Clear with SC&C for immediate departure and file a flight plan for Askaran."

"Access tube retracted and all exterior connections secured. Navigation deflector grid activated." Inactive panels began to glow soft amber and yellow in a mosaic of color-reactive contact pads. "Surface Command and Control has cleared for lift. System check complete. Lift sequence enabled." The projected flight plan appeared as a bright line on the curve of the nav bubble and the main display plate brightened into life.

Out of habit, Terr scanned the status boards one more time. "Proceed with lift."

"Lift sequence active. Confirm."

"Continue. Maximum clearance boost."

The M-1 lifted slowly, then accelerated straight up. Within a minute, *Sheeva* left the atmosphere and surged again to clear Ball's gravitational influence. The sun peeked over the planet's dark curve in a blazing radiance of slashing spokes. Reaching the distortion limit the precursor polarized and the M-1 slipped into subspace.

After stashing their charges in a spare stateroom with a door lock disable command, Terr and Dhar returned to the command deck. Another chore needed to be done and Terr ordered a comms link with Anabb.

"I wondered where you two were," the crusty intelligence chief growled. "The short version."

"We got them, sir," Terr said, ignoring Anabb's caustic manner. "The ops went clean and no one got hurt. At least not permanently."

"Well done, my boy! And you too, Agent Dharaklin. That biometrics dodge, a clever bit of reasoning. I must remember to include it in our field manual. Might come in handy again. You're on your way to Askaran, I presume?"

"Yes, sir. I will inform the Resident directly after this call."

"Good, good. Although you haven't established a link to the AUP Provisional Committee, we've had interesting developments on Askaran while you were chasing Pulman. The government has resigned as a body and BueAdmin laid charges against a number of ministers, including Tullan. Your friend Sarek Laral and several AUP chapter officials also got nabbed. That cell will be out of action for a while. That's important and damaging to the Sargon/Palean merger effort. On top of that, your efforts resulted in eradication of three raider networks. A most satisfactory outcome."

"What will happen to Pulman and Segal?" Terr ventured.

"We'll peel their brains, of course. Pulman's insider knowledge of local Alikan Union Party cells and their operations will be valuable. I know what you're thinking. What will happen afterward?"

"Actually, I *was* thinking that."

"I know. A long stretch at some maximum security prison, I imagine. You haven't turned sentimental on me, have you?"

"No, sir. I haven't. I know what they are and what they did."

"I'm glad to hear you say that, my boy. I wouldn't feel too sorry for Leera, son. She and Segal were partners; in everything."

"I understand," Terr said, and he did. Women can be as ruthless as any man. If he needed a reminder, he only had to remember Re Nette. Still, it was hard to erase the image of Manir, crying, expecting to die. It helped that he wouldn't have to look the boy in the eye when the kid realized he wouldn't be seeing his father again. He understood, all right, the cost and personal toll that working for Anabb exacted.

"When you're finished with the Resident, you'll have a mission debrief with Agent Landau and me. A good job, you two," Anabb said gruffly and cut contact.

"Well, that went better than expected," Terr remarked with satisfaction.

"He seemed pleased enough," Dhar agreed gravely. "I feared he considered our mission a failure."

"We didn't establish a link to the Provisional Committee, true enough, but I'd like to think we could have if our cover hadn't been blown."

"Provided we survived Pulman and Segal's attempt to get rid of us."

Terr winced and let out a loud breath. "Yeah. Perhaps it's better the way things turned out after all."

"We tempted the gods, my brother, and walked away alive. We should be thankful for that."

"Just to stretch our luck, can we tempt them to avoid a debrief?"

"There is always a price to pay, Sankri," Nightwings purred with a mischievous glint in his eyes.

Suddenly, Terr did not look forward to meeting Anabb.

Rit!

Epilogue

Valon lifted off the Line Tracking Net 3 planetoid, pulled away from its massive neighbor filling the sky, and headed for the transport portal one hundred thousand ampirs from the station. Tureen's Star glowed bright against the backdrop of the Karina Shield Nebula.

The system still young, not yet a billion years old, and still in the process of planetary formation. Apart from three gas giants sweeping up planetesimals from the outer reaches of the system, twelve protoplanets of various sizes traveling in chaotic orbits were competing for dominance. Eventually the larger would swallow their smaller rivals in cataclysmic collisions until only three or four inner planets remained and the system would stabilize. Right now, everything is bombarded by remnants of planetary formation, leaving the infant planets glowing red from impact craters and heaving, belching volcanoes.

An odd place to mount a tactical observatory, yet that is exactly what OSCOM did, placing LTN-3 on one of the smaller planetoids, protecting the minute world barely 1,500 ampirs in diameter from wildly orbiting remnants with powerful screens. In something like two and a half thousand years—a blink of cosmic time—the planetoid would collide with its brooding parent when their orbits eventually intersected, but something comfortably far away in the future to worry about.

"LTN-3 cleared and on course for portal phasing," Cent Comp advised quietly. "Flight time, eleven minutes and fifteen seconds."

Tremane glanced at his commander. "I've never done a one-way jump and I am curious to see what happens."

Zor-Ell peered at his executive officer and chuckled. "Hopefully, nothing too dramatic. I wouldn't worry. It's been done before."

And it had been done before, the most impressive example being the setup of the first portal pair between the Orieli Cluster and the White Cloud; the only way for the old Concordiat to expand into the galaxy. Sending ships on a twelve thousand light-year trip simply wasn't practical. Although making a pre-calculated jump through a portal without a corresponding receiving portal at the other end always entailed some danger. At least it got the first ships there in a hurry—albeit with some white hairs.

That's what *Valon* prepared to do now, make a direct jump to the Solar System. They would return the slow way, giving Zor-Ell time to complete his second mission: map sites for the remaining nine bases extending from Earth to LTN-3.

But first, he needed to reintegrate with his other self.

The cause of the memory boundary overflow turned out simple enough. He should have listened to Malfe and done a matrix density test. Never skip a step in the transfer process! He thought he knew that one. His instructors had drummed the directive into him often enough. Served him right for what happened. The thought of Earthmen being genetically engineered certainly got everyone thinking. The solution, although relatively simple in theory, was technically complex to implement. The Institute ran extensive computer simulations, but they were only simulations. They couldn't validate the process on an actual subject. Even if they found someone willing, ethically unacceptable, the initial conditions simply couldn't be replicated. In the end, they left the decision to him. There was some risk of damage to both personalities during the reintegration phase. At least OSCOM allowed him to make the attempt, after exacting a price.

His orders were to conduct another survey. This time, not

to establish contact with alien species, but with PERCOM support, map a corridor along which the Orieli Space Arm would construct a layered chain of twelve observatories designed to search, track and intercept Celi-Kran incursions into this part of the galaxy. OSCOM hoped it would also make an effective barrier to shield the Serrll Combine, an acceptable moral solution, seeing that, however inadvertently, the Orieli may have led the Krans to them. How effective the warning net would turn out would only become apparent once the Krans actually showed up. He did wonder why the Krans wasted a tactical opportunity not to push through in strength while the Orieli were getting organized. Without knowing their strategy or objective, contemplating tactics was merely an interesting intellectual diversion.

LTN-1 was fully operational and infrastructure installations almost completed, with two picket *Tangar* battlecruisers providing defense in depth. The second station still some months from operational readiness, but LTN-3 filled the necessary gap; a necessity, as it also protected the transport portal—something the Krans could not be allowed to disrupt. Construction of the stations themselves did not present an imposing engineering challenge, but positioning a scanner grid weapons array above each of the system's suns did. Armed with twelve selective energy projectors, the array provided an impenetrable defense for the station—it was hoped. Without the arrays, the whole Line Tracking Net concept would have been a wasted effort.

"Operational caution. Range to portal, four hundred ampirs. Charging interface and setting coordinates."

Tremane sat back and crossed his legs. "Well, this is it."

"One hundred ampirs," Cent Comp stated and slowed the ship further.

Ahead of them, surrounded by a pentagon of generators, a five-ampir-wide ring of blue-green energy flickered into existence in response to Cent Comp's interrogative, burning bright. No stars shone within the ring's flickering blue interior. *Valon* maintained course and the ring aperture grew larger.

The portal's ring pulsed with blue fire. In its heart lay impenetrable darkness.

"One hundred kanampirs…transiting."

Valon pierced the ring energy boundary and vanished.

* * *

Clad in white whorls and wispy streamers, Earth hung above *Valon*, blue and beautiful. After almost one local year, Zor-Ell gazed at it with mixed feelings. He could hardly imagine what his other self had gone through, trapped in an alien mind, not knowing whether a rescue would ever come, doubts and despair growing. This attempt could also be all for nothing if he triggered the mnemonic to induce a cascade memory failure, effectively committing suicide. He doubted his other self would have done that, but he wasn't in a position to know. Even if still conscious and sane, the experience must have been harrowing.

Watching Earth slide by above him, this time, he was spared the pleasure, if that was the right word, of an encounter with Master Scout Anatol Keller. When *Valon* appeared in the system, Serrll Moon Base only issued a simple query. Apart from that, there were no signs of prowling M-4s. A good omen, perhaps?

"Orbital insertion completed," Cent Comp noted. "Holding orbital position at three hundred ampirs."

Zor-Ell tapped a pad on the armrest. "Malfe, we're there. You can interrogate the nanocell tracer and check the location of our subject."

"Very well, Da."

It wasn't advisable to activate the subliminal recall imperative until they knew the subject's location. He could be anywhere on the planet. After a moment, Malfe came back online.

"Da, it seems we're in luck. The subject is actually quite

close to the retrieval point."

Zor-Ell glanced at his almost new, somewhat taciturn executive officer. Like Karth, Tremane was a Cetan, and they already had the close rapport necessary for the smooth operation of the ship. Like Karth, Tremane turned out to be a model of quiet competency and efficiency. Breaking down his reserve would come with time. Zor-Ell could have done worse.

"A quick pickup and we're out of here. I like it. Malfe, you can trigger the recall."

Tremane's red eyes were probing. "Are you ready for this, Da?"

Zor-Ell did not pretend not to understand. "There is an element of risk, granted, but I haven't come here to walk away now, Opturkarh. I need to know if my other self is still alive," he added quietly.

* * *

Sitting on the mower, Jim Grant rounded the shaggy chestnut with its carpet of dropped prickly nuts. He closed with the cypress hedge and slowly drove along the fence line. Cut grass spewed from the mower's side, smelling fresh and redolent. The two resident magpies pecked at the previously cut clippings, occasionally lifting their heads to stare at him with penetrating black eyes before resuming their foraging. Streaming from a deep blue sky unmarked by any clouds, warm morning sunshine played over his bare back. Across the road, his neighbor chopped firewood, the striking axe making flat echoes. Apart from an occasional car driving by, it was totally silent. Early March brought with it sunny, dry days and crisp nights. Jim loved coming to Trentham this time of year when the summer's heat no longer burned. The smells became sharper and the world a pretty good place after all.

As usual when he came, he drove in after work, allowing the Friday's rush hour exodus out of Melbourne to thin out first. There is something about Fridays that somehow caused the number of cars normally on the road to magically multiply. The weather channel said the whole weekend would be under the influence of a high-pressure system and Jim found the idea of two physically strenuous days in the country irresistible.

Apart from having to mow the block, he wanted to go into the forest and haul in two or three trailer-loads of logs. He had plenty of stacked firewood to last him three or four years, but there was never enough. Besides, all the easy to get at stuff already cleaned out, and he was forced to travel farther for his wood. He didn't mind. In the bush, alone with the towering gums around him, sunshine slanting between the branches, the sharp eucalyptus smell, his idea of peace. Even the chainsaw's racket didn't seem to intrude, and somehow fitted.

Turning into the roadside section of the hedge, he felt a moment of disorientation before a compelling thought swamped everything else.

Go camping.

Handling the mower on instinct, the compulsion grew. After a moment, he asked himself, why not? Most of the chores were already done and he could still get the firewood tomorrow. Why waste a perfectly good Saturday indoors? Besides, the weather could turn despite what the TV said. Those guys were wrong most of the time anyway. He always maintained if somebody at the Weather Bureau actually bothered to open a window and peer out instead of studying their computer models and satellite photos, they would have a better chance of getting it right.

Looking around, only a small patch of grass left to cut; ten minutes tops. He would take in the washing, have an early light lunch and head for his favorite camping spot. It puzzled him why he hadn't thought of going out before. At any rate, the damage was rectifiable.

Zor-Ell felt an emotional jolt so powerful when the nano-cell tracer issued the recall command, he was certain Jim must have sensed it. A cascade of memories and feelings threatened to swamp him; an avalanche of churning images, flashes of rage that it took them this long, followed by a flood of intense relief. At last, it would end. Twice, he came close to ending it all, and it wouldn't have taken much. A simple command and with it, a release from a prison more confining than any physical restraint. Release also meant darkness and oblivion, something he hadn't been ready to embrace quite yet. He would have hated to change his mind halfway through.

In the confines of Jim's mind, he gave a small sob of relief and muttered a few words of thanks.

He developed a fondness for Earth's erratic inhabitants, their drive, determination, potential, and of course, selfishness and stupidity. They were still a young species and he needed to make allowances. That fondness did not extend to a desire to remain longer. If he needed a reminder why he gave up being an Observer, Earth had certainly given him a poignant one, albeit an extreme example of the type.

With a sense of inner peace and an intense feeling of satisfaction, he looked through his host's eyes as the Toyota made its way down the dirt track. It burst into a clearing bathed under bright sunshine, which made Jim squint despite wearing sunglasses. He drove the car to a stand of three paperbark gums and parked in their shade. Now that Zor-Ell was on the verge of getting rescued, or his confinement terminally ended, he could not wait for nightfall.

Jim pitched his tent, drew water from the creek and brewed a cuppa. Sitting on a log, sipping coffee, basking in the warmth and soothing stillness, insects drowsily buzzing in the background, glad he came. He treasured these moments of tranquility, so far removed from the unending rush of Melbourne and demands placed on him by family and friends. They were always there, but a moment like this needed to be grasped when offered.

He spent the day walking through the bush, gathering

wood for his campfire and reading. With the light waning, wallabies emerged to graze at the forest edge, giving him only an odd cursory glance. Dinner was simple: a toasted ham and cheese sandwich, coffee, followed by a slug of Elijah Craig he always carried in a pewter flask on his outings.

When the stars began to appear, he put a large log on the fire and stirred the glowing coals. Sparks and yellow flames shot up, then settled back to their dancing and crackling. He lit a cigar and watched night wrap its blanket around him.

* * *

Malfe waited anxiously, his eyes fixed on the flowing data streams in the full-dimensional holoview displays beside both beds. He was particularly concerned with information icons registering the reintegration rate. So far, everything seemed to be going well, if agonizingly slowly. Having to search the Earth subject for every leaked memory, and link that memory individually for retrieval, took time. Critically, this was also a one-way pass, as the process disassociated tagged memories in order to avoid damaging the subject. Even a small segment of Zor-Ell's personality left behind could cause lingering psychological trauma, something the Physics Institute insisted was not an option. Should something go wrong, both personalities could be affected. The other concern that caused him to mentally gnaw his fingers, even with successful reintegration, would the karhide's composite personality remain rational, having to cope with two parallel streams of memories before they fully merged? The Institute declined to commit itself one way or another. Still, the event had generated valuable information, and even now, all survey ships were applying software updates in case of a similar occurrence.

The executive officer stirred beside him and he looked up. Tremane lifted an inquiring eyebrow.

"Both are doing well, Da. It's the waiting…"

Tremane didn't say anything. He only hoped everyone knew what the hell they were doing. He wanted command, but not under these circumstances should something go wrong.

The furious flow of data streams suddenly cleared. "Integration sequence completed," Cent Comp advised. "Status check complete and buffers cleared. Sequence terminated."

Malfe gave a long exhale and allowed his shoulders to sag. He nodded to his support technician, then touched several pads on the central console. The blue aura above the karhide slowly faded.

Zor-Ell opened his eyes and blinked. A moment of wrenching duality left him disoriented and confused. Still on Earth, he was also in his ship. It was like having double vision, waiting for the eyes to uncross. Suddenly, it all settled into place, but his Earth memories crashed relentlessly through his consciousness. He swallowed hard and blinked back a sudden sting in his eyes. The nightmare had finally ended…

A familiar face swam over him and he forced a smile. "Malfe…"

The senior technician touched his shoulder. "Karhide…how do you feel?"

"I'm seeing double and I'm disembodied, but it's fading."

"Normal, and will pass with time," Malfe assured him.

Zor-Ell turned his head as another figure appeared. "Karth," he whispered with a smile, then realized his mistake. "I apologize, Tremane."

The exec nodded, uncertain how to react to his karhide who at the same time was someone else.

"Welcome back, Da," he said softly, struggling with his emotions.

"It's good to be back," Zor-Ell murmured, utterly weary, and closed his eyes. At last, he could sleep again, and dream.

About the author

Stefan Vučak has written twenty-one novels, which include eight SF books in the Shadow Gods Saga. His *Cry of Eagles* won the coveted Readers' Favorite silver medal award, and his *All the Evils* was the prestigious Eric Hoffer contest finalist and Readers' Favorite silver medal winner. *Strike for Honor* won the gold medal.

Stefan leveraged a successful career in the Information Technology industry, which took him to the Middle East working on cellphone systems. Writing has been a road of discovery, helping him broaden his horizons. He also spends time as an editor and book reviewer. Stefan lives in Melbourne, Australia.

To learn more about Stefan Vučak, visit his:
Website: www.stefanvucak.com
Facebook: www.facebook.com/StefanVucakAuthor
Twitter: @stefanvucak

More Books by Stefan Vučak

https://www.stefanvucak.com/Books/

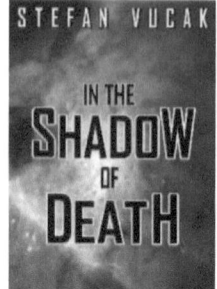 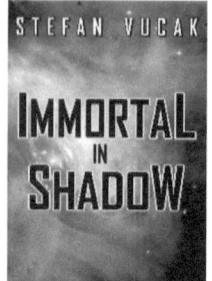 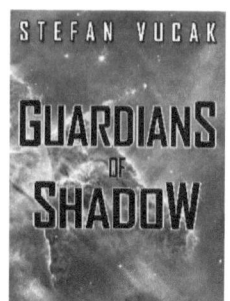